'Fanny has made this little corner of womankind, with all its humour and trials and tribulations, her own'
Penny Vincenzi

'I love that she writes about women our age, and the painful and wise truths we know'   Marian Keyes

'A true celebration of love and life in all its forms; full of joy, hope and triumph'   Cathy Bramley

'No one does family and friendship better than Fanny: the crises, the dilemmas, the divided loyalties, the betrayals... A perfect summer read'   Veronica Henry

'Warm, wise, witty... Fanny Blake's gift is for making her characters so real they leap off the page'   Julia Gregson

'Fanny Blake writes brilliantly about women of a certain age, and this latest is her best yet. It's richly emotional, sharply perceptive and full of fabulous lifestyle detail'
Daily Mail

'So engaging, insightful and honest about marriage, motherhood and second chances'   Kate Eberlen

'With her trademark warmth and insight, Blake offers a deliciously irresistible peek into one family's enthralling drama'   *Sunday Express*

'A heart-warming tale of secrets slowly revealed and family tensions... A compelling and delightful read'
Santa Montefiore

'The perfect, intelligent, moreish, uplifting read, with characters who are completely believable and real... poignant and uplifting'   Lucy Atkins

Fanny Blake was a publisher for many years, editing both fiction and non-fiction before becoming a freelance journalist and writer. She has written various non-fiction titles, acted as a ghost writer for a number of celebrities, and is also Books Editor of *Woman & Home* magazine. To find out more visit www.fannyblake.co.uk, follow her on Twitter @FannyBlake1 or on Facebook @FannyBlakeBooks

Also by Fanny Blake

What Women Want
Women of a Dangerous Age
The Secrets Women Keep
With a Friend Like You
Red for Revenge (Quick Read)
House of Dreams
Our Summer Together

An Italian Summer

Fanny Blake

ORION

First published in Great Britain in 2018 by Orion Books,
an imprint of The Orion Publishing Group Ltd
Carmelite House, 50 Victoria Embankment
London EC4Y 0DZ

An Hachette UK Company

1 3 5 7 9 10 8 6 4 2

A CIP catalogue record for this book is
available from the British Library.

ISBN 978 1 4091 7712 8

Typeset at The Spartan Press Ltd,
Lymington, Hants

Printed and bound by CPI Group (UK) Ltd,
Croydon, CRO 4YY

www.orionbooks.co.uk

For Tessa Hilton
with love and thanks

January, 2017

Sandy had been rifling through her mother's desk for stamps when she found the letter tucked into a cubbyhole between a small red address book and some left-over Christmas cards. Her mother could only have written it weeks earlier when she was still able to come downstairs. The writing was familiar but shaky and the envelope not properly addressed. Thinking perhaps she should finish the job and post it for her, Sandy leafed through the little book, noting how many names were crossed out and initialled with a big D. Death had claimed so many of her mother's friends before her. But there was no Anna Viglieri among them, alive or dead, and no one who lived in Naples.

When the nurse had finished washing her mother and giving her fresh sheets, Sandy returned upstairs, taking the letter with her. Miriam was lying propped up on a mountain of pillows, her face pale and gaunt, eyes half open. She managed the slightest of smiles. Sandy sat close where she could be sure to be heard.

'Mum, I found this. Shall I post it?' She held up the envelope where her mother could see it. It seemed important to keep up a pretence of some kind of normality, although it hardly mattered now. 'Who do you know in Naples?' She took the bottle of Chanel No. 5 from the side and dabbed a little on her mother's wrists: the perfume her mother always wore and that Sandy associated with her all her life.

A flicker of recognition, a movement of Miriam's head. Her mouth moved but the words were so faint Sandy had to guess at them.

'Find her?' she said, leaning forward to catch a sound as her mother's lips moved slightly. 'Who is she?'

But the drug being pumped into her mother's thigh to ease the pain had reclaimed her. Death wasn't far away.

Sandy looked at the envelope again. *Sra Anna Viglieri. Naples.* While her mother slept, she went downstairs to make a cup of tea. The nurse was in the kitchen, putting the sheets in the machine.

'How long, do you think?' asked Sandy, a tremor in her voice.

The young woman looked up, kindness in her eyes. 'You can never tell. Maybe a couple of days, but I couldn't say definitely.' She slammed shut the door of the washing machine.

'Tea?'

Having made them both a cup, Sandy left the nurse alone while she went back upstairs. She paused by the front door to open the face of the grandfather clock, take the crank from the plate on the hall table and put it into the winding holes one after the other. This was a ritual her father then her mother had performed for as long as she could remember. It felt good to continue the tradition; steadying. That's all she had to hang on to now the last link to her past was about to be broken. Her relationship with her mother had never been easy. How she had envied her schoolfriends with their warm kitchens and mothers who were always there for them, cooking and caring. But that was long ago, before she was sent away to school, and now she was the only family member left to see Miriam out of this world. She went back upstairs, her limbs heavy, walking on the sage-green carpet that was faded with age, past the pictures that had always hung in the shadows of the dark stairway. Back

2

in the bedroom, she took up her knitting, and began to talk softly. This might be her last chance to say anything important.

'Why did you push me away, Mum? Perhaps, if you hadn't, we might been closer instead of having this strange sense of duty towards one another.' She paused. 'You must have felt it too or you wouldn't have been there for me when Matthew died.' She thought of her husband with the habitual longing that still haunted her. When she had been blindsided by his unexpected death, her mother had come good for her at last: cooking, doing her laundry, tending her garden, tidying the house, caring for her – all those things that she had no energy for herself. And now, only two and a half years after his death, she was losing her mother. 'But we did love each other, despite everything. I know we did.'

Her mother didn't respond. Just the rattle of her laboured breathing filled the room.

'They say a person's hearing is the last thing to go, but how does anyone know that? Am I really just talking to myself?' Sandy felt the tears stinging as they had so often over the last week as her mother drifted in and out of consciousness. The two of them would never make up for lost time now. Everything between them was over. 'There's no point in having regrets,' she went on. 'They say that too. But I do have them – in spades. Why wouldn't you talk to me about your family instead of clamming up or changing the subject? In the end I gave up asking. Just accepted.' She reached over to pull the pot of deep-red tulips, the ones her mother loved, to a position where she might see them. 'I should have insisted.'

Four hours later, she was still sitting there, having made another cup of tea and moved from her knitting to the cross-word, although her brain wouldn't compute any of the answers. Her mother's favourite music flowed softly from the ancient CD player: Ella Fitzgerald, Nat King Cole, Frank Sinatra and Billie Holiday. Staring out of the window at the flat grey sky,

Sandy hummed along to 'Cry Me a River' under her breath, wishing Matthew had been able to die at home. This end to a life was so tranquil compared to the incessant hubbub of a hospital ward. He hadn't known where he was, of course, but all the same she would have liked him to die in peace. It was starting to drizzle when she heard a movement behind her. She spun round. Miriam's eyes were open, her fingertips touching the envelope Sandy had left on the bed. 'Anna,' she whispered.

Sandy leaned over her again.

'Who's Anna, Mum?'

But her mother's eyes had started to close.

'Mum! Who's Anna?' She was overwhelmed by frustration and sadness.

The thin white lips moved again. 'Find ...' Then nothing. Just breath. Perhaps that was not even what she had said. There was no way of intuiting what might be going round her mind so close to the end, especially when she was under such heavy sedation. But more than anything Sandy wanted to believe that her mother knew she was there and wanted to tell her something.

'Find her,' she said, taking the envelope. 'Is that what you meant? Well, I'll try. God knows how but I will try.' She slid her hand into her mother's and gently squeezed it. In return, she felt her mother's fingers tighten round hers. She had heard her.

Twenty-four hours later, her mother was dead.

I

Rome – August, 2017

Rome's Termini station was loud, crowded and confusing. Sandy gripped the handle of her case, staring at the unfamiliar signs, until she saw one that would take her out to the side of the station. A man approached her and took her case, flinging it into the boot of his car.

'*Dove si va?*'

'Hotel Cecilia in Trastevere.' The unfamiliar words felt like cotton wool in her mouth. She held out the piece of paper with the full printed address.

The taxi driver smiled, adjusting his back-to-front baseball cap. Thick black hairs covered his arms. He held the door open for her then slammed it shut.

In the back of the cab, Sandy tried to point out that he had forgotten to turn on the meter. She had been warned always to check. 'Fleecing dim unquestioning tourists is a national sport.' Steven's words rang in her ears. She thought of him with a pang and tried to dismiss it. She couldn't be missing him already. These two weeks away were meant to be time during which, among other things, she could work out how serious her feelings were for him. Was she ready to commit herself to another man?

The driver turned to look at her, his eyes dark, threatening. 'Thirty euro. Same for everyone.'

'The meter,' she insisted, gripping the door handle, aware she was risking losing her luggage.

He banged his fist on the steering wheel, letting loose a volley of incomprehensible Italian before getting out. He opened the boot, took out her case and dropped it on the pavement, shouting at the other drivers, gesturing towards her, arms waving.

Sandy took her case, and walked back into the station, heart pounding. Confrontation was not something she enjoyed. If Matthew were with her, he would have sorted everything out. But he had been dead almost three years and besides, she reminded herself, if he were alive she probably wouldn't be here. He had admitted himself that he had been irrational in his refusal to travel abroad. He felt there were plenty of underrated and unexplored places to go in Britain. Because she loved him, and because she was frightened of flying, Sandy went along with it and he was grateful that she understood. In return, she insisted that he made all their travel arrangements, which were often complicated. It was only after his death that she'd found the emails to the travel agent on his computer, enquiring about travelling by train to Italy the following summer. Had he been thinking of going back on everything he'd said and surprising her? She'd never know. But what a surprise it would have been.

Matthew's death had nearly broken her. But, with time, she had learned to live with her loss. She was on her own now, although she suspected grief had weakened her, made worse by the subsequent death of her mother. Since then she had felt bereft, untethered, unsure of where she was going. Nevertheless she had no choice but to deal with those feelings. She looked around her. People dashed by, whistles blew, the fancy shops were crowded. *For heaven's sake*, she reprimanded herself. As a woman of a certain age who could run a classroom of thirty pupils, she ought to be able to find her way to a hotel in an unfamiliar city. How hard could it be?

She took a deep breath, squared her shoulders and walked out of the front of the station, past a homeless man sleeping by the plate-glass window and into a vast open space busy with traffic. She saw a Taxi sign where an official was directing people into the crowd of white vehicles. She joined the queue and, when it came to her turn, she took the one she was shown to.

She was relieved to see the driver put the meter on straight away. He was pleasant and spoke enough English to ask her where she came from. What was the weather like in St Albans? 'You will like Rome,' he said. 'Good food, lots of sunshine.'

As they drove down the hill from the station, she stared out at the grandiose shuttered buildings, the plethora of tourists, the signs she couldn't understand. Through the window, she could hear a cacophony of traffic noise and car horns that seemed to beep for no reason. The sun was shining and she felt light-headed, excited. They swept past an enormous white monument with tourists swarming up and down its steps, a bronze chariot crowning each end of its imposing pillared facade. 'Vittorio Emanuele,' said the driver, as if she'd understand. He turned off the road running by the wide-flowing river and over a bridge into a very different neighbourhood of narrow cobbled streets, ochre- and terracotta-coloured buildings, busy outdoor restaurants and streets teeming with more people. When they pulled up at the Hotel Cecilia, the fare was eighteen euros. A frisson of satisfaction ran through her as she over-tipped him.

She pressed the button at the side of the large iron gate and a small gate within it clicked open. She walked down the passageway as the gate swung shut behind her. She had arrived.

Her room was painted a soft yellow with a stencil of branches laden with oranges running round the top of the walls. There was a bare minimum of furniture but everything was clean. The sheets looked inviting and the loo paper folded into a triangle made her smile.

Matthew would have joked about it. For a second or two, she imagined the conversation she might have had with him.

Looks bloody uncomfortable. Are we meant to refold it, every time we go?

Don't be such an old fossil.

We-ell. He'd rub the end of his nose and give his endearing squint smile. *You know.*

And she usually did.

She turned her mind to her fellow travellers. 'A Taste of Italy: small group tours', the advertisement in the local paper had said. 'No more than ten,' the man at the end of the phone who took her booking assured her. But suppose she didn't like them? Suppose they didn't like her? She wasn't sure which would be worse. For some reason that hadn't been a consideration at the time. It had sounded perfect. Her grief for her mother had subsided to a manageable level and she wanted to do something new, something that would test her. She couldn't feel sorry for herself forever. By the end of the summer term, she had desperately wanted to get away. By then she felt strong enough to think about looking for Signora Anna Viglieri, her mother's friend.

While clearing out her mother's house, dismantling her life bit by bit, she had found various things that surprised and touched her. There were mementoes of her own childhood that her mother had stashed away – school reports, childhood games, postcards and letters she'd written home. They made Sandy realise that she must have meant more to her mother than she sometimes believed. But more puzzling was the travel journal found in a box at the back of a drawer in the spare room, long forgotten. Her mother was twenty-one and writing about a journey she'd made to Italy, at first as a companion to a Mrs Robson and then joining an Anna in Naples.

Was this the Anna Sandy was looking for?

She took the journal out of her bag, opening it at the first page, now able to picture the scene her mother wrote about much more clearly.

THIS JOURNAL BELONGS TO MIRIAM MACKENZIE

Italy 1952

Rome station was hellish. Mrs Robson in a panic that no one would come to meet us. Flapping and shouting. Nightmare. And so embarrassing. Luckily someone from the hotel eventually found us and mounted a rescue. Mrs R calmed down in the car... The hotel is as smart as I'd hoped it might be. Mrs R likes her comforts, thank the Lord. We're very central, near an enormous square called the Piazza Navona... more later.

Miriam Mackenzie, May 3rd 1952 – Rome

Sandy recognized the chaos of the station – nothing ever really changes, she thought wryly. A couple of days later:

Mrs Robson is rather too demanding. She wants me at her beck and call all day long but I'm determined to get out of the hotel on my own. I'm going to try to sneak out when she's having her siesta. Ignazio, the barman, has said he'll take me to Trastevere... I've got to see a side of the city that Mrs R might not appreciate.

The entries began enthusiastically then became shorter until they petered out all together. The young woman writing was so unlike the mother she knew – flirtatious and fun-loving – Sandy found it hard to believe they were the same person. And now here she was, following in her footsteps, staying in the city her mother had visited so long ago.

A Taste of Italy offered guided tours round the main sights of Rome and Naples. 'At least you won't have to do all that queuing for tickets,' Steven had pointed out. 'And plenty of leisure time to explore the rest for yourself. Look, you've even got an optional cookery course thrown in.' It had looked ideal, thrilling even, and just what she needed after so many months as principal carer to her mother as well as getting her Year 12s through their A-levels. But now, with the prospect of spending two weeks with a group of strangers very much a reality, who they were seemed of paramount importance. Well, she reminded herself, if nothing else, she'd have something interesting to write in her diary – just like her mother.

She tapped her fingers on the guidebook to Rome that Steven had given her and that she had yet to read. He had been so kind and supportive during her mother's illness. A rock. Since they'd met in the choir, he had become the most steadfast of friends and latterly her lover. The first time they went to bed together, she had to exercise all her will power not to call him Matthew. He was the first man she'd made love with since her husband and it had felt strange and unfamiliar although things had improved with practice. Recently he had occasionally made the odd suggestive remark such as 'When we can be together' or 'How we might go away at Christmas' or, 'There's a wonderful pub with rooms that I've found in Oxfordshire.'

But, but... she still missed Matthew. He still influenced her mind and memories.

Her mother, too.

The last time she had seen Steven, a few days before she left, he had pressed the book on her, insisting how much she would love Italy. All she had to do was ask, and he would have jumped at the opportunity to come with her. But that would have been a mistake. She needed time away. Time for herself. Time to think and regroup. And she was grateful he hadn't pushed. Committing herself to him seemed like a huge leap and, even after all this time, such an act of disloyalty to Matthew, despite Sandy knowing he would want what made her happy. But would it? That's what she had to work out.

Besides, there was her mother's letter, tucked safe inside Sandy's suitcase, a stranger's name on the envelope. She had promised she would try to deliver it and this holiday gave her the chance . Anna Viglieri lived somewhere in Naples. Was she wondering why she hadn't heard from Miriam? Sandy realised she would be delivering the news of her mother's death as well.

She checked the time. Almost six-thirty. That was when the 'small group' had been asked to meet in the hotel bar where they would be introduced over drinks and have the timetable for the next few days explained to them. Seven days in Rome and then on to Naples. At the thought, her heart lifted. Nothing would stop her enjoying herself – on holiday for the first time in ages.

Before joining them, she had to choose what to wear. She stared at her clothes, hanging limp and uninteresting in the wardrobe. Clothes spoke volumes about a person but what would these say about her to the others? Surrounded by the business and clatter of Rome, the sunshine, she wished she had chosen differently. What would give the right first impression? Definitely not the yellow dress she had bought on a whim: too much of a statement. Her walking trousers were too utilitarian; her tan capri pants just too tight; her olive-green skirt and white blouse too reminiscent of school. In the end she chose her black linen dress with blue swirls, a scoop neck and cap sleeves: sophisticated but summery. She pulled her sandals from the case and put them on, curling up her toes, glad she'd decided on that pedicure. She reached for her lipstick and drew it across her lips, rubbing them together, enjoying the easy slide of them.

A quick squirt of something Jo Malone (Steven again) to give her that extra confidence, and she was ready.

Standing at the corner of the cloister surrounding the hotel courtyard, she spotted the group immediately. They were sitting outside around three circular tables that had been roughly pulled together, most of them holding a virulent orange drink rattling with ice. They were sheltered from the sun by huge cream parasols and several orange trees, burdened with fruit. A slim woman, elegant in grey linen, her hair in an elfin cut, sat by a grey-haired man who was equally trim, wearing chinos, a navy-blue shirt and deck shoes – her perfect match. They were having what looked an awkward conversation with a small plump middle-aged man, hair on end, a neat goatee, his face flushed. To one side, a much younger woman wearing a short figure-hugging dress, blonde hair scraped back into a scrappy little ponytail, was poring over a set of papers, separating them into piles. A diamond flashed on her ring finger. Was she their guide? She didn't look authoritative enough. Was this all of them?

For a minute, Sandy froze. Fright battled with curiosity. Should she turn tail now? Run back upstairs to her room? But curiosity won. As she was about to take a step towards them, someone came up behind her.

'Are you part of the Taste of Italy trip too?'

She turned to find a pleasant-looking, generously proportioned woman of about her own age flanked by a man who was glancing around him, distracted. She couldn't help the passing thought that he must have been very good-looking once. 'I am. I'm a bit nervous though,' she confessed.

'Don't be. We've done this sort of thing before. It usually works out, doesn't it, darling? I'm Alice by the way, and this is my husband, Mark.'

He looked at her. 'What? Yes, usually.' As he straightened his glasses, Sandy noticed his right pinkie was awkwardly bent at the first knuckle. He looked straight at her with sharp blue eyes. 'And there's always plenty of free time so you can escape if you want to.'

That was another thing she was going to have to deal with. In her present state of mind, the idea of being let loose in a foreign city filled her with panic. This was one of the reasons for joining a group in the first place. 'I'm Sandy and I haven't been abroad for years,' she confided in a rush despite having promised herself she wouldn't admit that to anyone.

'There's nothing to worry about.' Alice's voice was reassuring. 'We'll make sure you're OK, won't we?' The question was asked as if accompanied by a gentle nudge.

Sandy could see Mark's attention had drifted from them again although he did manage a distant, 'Of course.' Making sure anyone was 'OK' didn't look as if it was his sort of thing at all. And why should it be, Sandy reminded herself. After all, they were all on holiday. Then, she remembered her mother's white envelope upstairs: the one aspect of this trip that was not holiday at all.

'Come with us.' Alice smiled at Sandy as they crunched over the pebbles to meet the others.

'Welcome!' said the young woman sorting out the papers. She stood up, her face shiny in the heat. 'I'm Gilly. I'm going to be travelling with you for the next two weeks. And you are? In fact, stop! Let me get you a drink and then we can all introduce ourselves. Aperol spritz?'

Sandy nodded, with no idea what it was, but when in Rome . . .

'Actually . . .' Mark waved a hand to get Gilly's attention. 'I'd prefer a whisky.'

'Are you sure, darling?' Alice sounded concerned.

'Quite. Thanks.' He gave her a tight little smile.

Gilly raised her hand to summon the waiter and gave the order. 'Now. Are we all here? We've got two more joining us later who are on a late flight from Germany.' She tallied the group up, pointing at each one of them with the end of her Biro.

God, thought Sandy, *this is like being back in the school playground*. She consoled herself with the thought that at least she wouldn't be back at school for another four weeks. Here, she could be herself or indeed, anyone she wanted. She could shake off all the constraints that made her Mrs Johnson, Head of History. Seconds later, the waiter was back and putting one of the orange drinks in front of her. She picked it up, curious.

'*Grazie*.' Steven and she had gone through the basics in his old phrasebook together, laughing as they wondered when she would ever have to ask the way to a watchmaker's. She poked at the ice in the drink with the black plastic straw.

'We're still missing someone,' said Gilly. She bent to consult her notes as another woman emerged from one of the rooms in the cloister, smiling, her hand up in a wave, 'Hi everyone. *Buona sera!* Sorry I'm late.' She let the door slam behind her.

Sandy heard the voice and looked up from the bitter but not wholly unpleasant Aperol spritz. It couldn't be. But she recognised the slight southernised Brummy twang with an uplift at the end of a sentence that took her straight back to her last school assembly. It couldn't possibly be. But there was no mistaking the cropped red hair, the smile that Sandy knew from experience was not as genuine as it was wide, and the same irritating way in which she stood on the balls of her feet as if she was about to bounce off. All Sandy's effort was focused on keeping her face in neutral as she gazed at the newcomer in disbelief.

Lia French. Head of Computer Science at Ecclesworth School. Her school.

As Sandy tried to recover her composure, Lia turned and noticed her for the first time. Her smile slipped for a second before it reasserted itself. Shock. Her eyes hardened. The hands stilled for a second. Then, 'Sandy! What on earth are you doing here?' Her eyes darted from Sandy to the rest of the group and back again with that intent-on-mischief look with which Sandy was only too familiar.

2

The others in the group looked from Lia to Sandy, waiting to see what she was going to say.

'I . . .' But the words stuck in Sandy's throat. Of all the things she had worried might happen, this was not one of them.

'I thought you weren't going to take a holiday. I heard you talking in the staffroom.' Lia pressed her hands down the skirt of her bright floral dress, then clasped them tightly together. 'You said you had too much to sort out.'

'I wasn't, I did have but I changed my mind.' None of them needed to know how debilitating dismantling her mother's life as she waited for probate had been, and how much better she felt now.

'Obviously.' That trill of a laugh again. Lia's lips then pursed in what Sandy recognised as displeasure.

The heat rushed from Sandy's chest to her face as she struggled for breath. She *had* said that in a conversation she thought no one else had overheard. But later that same day, in the wine bar after choir, Steven had persuaded her that going away was exactly what she should do. 'A break will do you good. See the world. Recharge the batteries. You can finish sorting out the last of your mother's stuff when you get back. I could even come with you.'

She didn't think he was serious. 'Don't be daft. I wouldn't dream of asking you to.' That's when it had crossed her mind that travelling to Italy might give her the chance to solve the mystery of her mother's letter. 'Besides, this is something I need to do on my own.'

Of course Steven knew just the person to help her conquer her fear of flying. Why hadn't she ever tried hypnotherapy, for heaven's sake? A half bottle of wine had been all that was needed to persuade her.

'Come on, ladies! Put us out of our misery.' Gilly was on her feet. 'You two obviously know each other. How come?'

'We teach at the same school.' Aware that everyone was still looking at them, Sandy tried to make it sound as insignificant a detail as she could.

'And you didn't know you were both booked on the same trip?' Gilly was incredulous. 'Wow! That's amazing. I've never had this happen before.'

How Sandy was wishing it wasn't happening now. She took a fat green olive and bit into it.

'Well, what a wonderful surprise!' Gilly took charge, sitting down and smoothing over the awkwardness. 'In a moment I'll give you these updated schedules, but first, I'm Gilly, your tour leader and guide. As you know, the tour's arranged with one main visit a day, with the rest of the time your own, if you have the energy for more in this heat.' She picked up a wooden slatted fan painted with flowers, flicked it open and fanned herself, her diamond ring winking in the light. 'We'll meet together for supper and lunch when specified in your schedule but we want you to be able to explore on your own too. I'll be travelling with you and if you need anything, anything at all . . . well, within reason . . .' Obviously a joke she had used before. They all laughed on cue. '. . . Or have any questions, all you have to do is ask. I'm very happy to be joined for supper on the other nights, so if you'd like to, do let me know in the morning so I don't go off without you. After all, a woman's got to eat!' More polite laughter, nobody catching anyone else's eye. 'After we've introduced ourselves I'm going to give you these updated schedules so you can see the expeditions we've planned. There's no obligation to come on them, but you have paid for them. There's no getting your money back.' She smiled round them all but in a way that suggested a streak of steel within. Gilly was not someone to mess with.

Her relentless cheerfulness was beginning to grate on Sandy. She took a breath. *It's the shock of Lia turning up*, she told herself. *Give the woman a chance. And the others.* She watched Lia lift her drink to her lips then, aware that she was being observed, turn to Sandy and raise her glass in her direction. 'Cheers.' Sandy couldn't read her expression. She raised hers in return.

But Gilly hadn't finished. 'I've booked us a table at the Albergo San Paulo for tonight. It doesn't look much, but in Rome you can find the best food in the most surprising places. And trust me, I know.' She rested a hand on her non-existent stomach and laughed. She was enviably slim, as if eating came very low on her list of priorities. 'So. I guess we should start with you, Lia. Last in and a story to tell . . .' She let the sentence drift, waiting for Lia to pick it up.

Lia put down her glass, looking round at the others, her gaze lingering on Mark for a moment longer than necessary. 'Well, like Sandy here, I teach at Ecclesworth School in St Albans. She's in the History department while I . . .'

Sandy stopped her glass halfway to her mouth. Surely Lia wasn't going to bring their work differences into the open here? Competing against one another for the deputy headship was bad enough and something she'd hoped to forget over the holiday.

' . . . teach Computer Science.'

That said it all really. *Dusty and old-fashioned compared with contemporary and up to the minute*, Sandy thought. *That's how they'll see us now.*

Lia continued. 'I'm here because I'm learning Italian. I can't speak it very well but being here should help me. My holidays are limited because of my work and my cat so I wanted a way of seeing as much as I could in as short a time as possible...'

Ho hum, thought Sandy. *What a talker she is* – something she had envied till now. Yet, with a start, she realised how little of what Lia was saying seemed to matter. She curbed herself as Lia's voice droned on, a background noise to her own thoughts. She couldn't help comparing her own experience to her mother's. Funny to think of her being so independent and outgoing (not traits Sandy knew in her) when all Sandy wanted to do was keep herself to herself. She must try harder.

One by one, they went through the introductions. The elegant couple were Peter and Brit Taylor from Oxford, a GP and a medical researcher. 'We've been to Rome before but want to revisit, don't we darling?' He nodded but didn't add anything. Alice and Mark Bennett she had already met, but discovered he was 'an academic' without specifying which discipline and Alice was his 'stay-at-home wife'. He spoke for both of them. Alan Taylor was in his fifties, divorced and didn't need to say he was looking for someone else. That much was obvious from the way he looked at Sandy and Lia, the two single women. More an appraisal than a leer, but even so ... At last, it was Sandy's turn. She spoke quickly. 'I'm Sandy Johnson. As you know, I teach History at the same school as Lia. I can't speak Italian but I do love exploring the past, learning how other people lived. My subject's English History so this is all new to me and I'm looking forward to it.' She stopped. They didn't need to know about the deaths of Matthew and her mother or the letter burning a hole in her case. They only needed to know what she chose to tell them about herself.

'Great.' Gilly stepped in. 'Thanks, everybody. If you've all finished your drinks, then why don't you leave the bumph in your rooms and I'll meet you here in ten minutes to go for dinner.

As they filed out of the room, Sandy waited for Lia. 'Truce?'

Lia stared at her. 'Of course,' she said stiffly. 'We shouldn't bring school on holiday.'

Sandy tried again. 'Why don't we—'

'But...' Lia didn't let her finish. 'May the best person win.' She managed to make it plain that she didn't consider Sandy to be that person.

Sandy regarded her thoughtfully. 'As you wish.'

'Stuffed courgette flowers! Ridiculous waste of cheese and anchovies if you ask me.' Mark switched on his electric toothbrush and shut the bathroom door behind him

'No one did.' But Alice knew he couldn't hear her. She, on the other hand, could still taste the dish that Gilly had told them was a speciality of Rome – the delicate orange-yellow flowers stuffed and fried to melt in the mouth – except that it had been followed by the pasta that had been light as a feather, just three ravioli filled with artichokes, pecorino and thyme. Crowning it all had been the saltimbocca. 'Jump in the mouth' Gilly translated for them and all was explained as Alice bit into the tender veal wrapped with prosciutto. As for the sauce... She laid her hands on the mound of her stomach and gazed at the mass-produced oil painting of the Colosseum by night. What was better than a well-earned food coma? Even in this heat. If tonight was anything to go by, this was going to be a wonderful couple of weeks. Gastronomically, at least. She could hear Mark swooshing water through his teeth, then the flush of the toilet a moment later.

Her thoughts moved on to their travelling companions. Did she and Mark have anything in common with any of them? Not at first glance. She ran through everyone she had met that night. Gilly was too young, too brash, too jolly, but that was her job, Alice supposed. It must be difficult trying to ensure nine people had a good time. Peter and Brit, his wife, had seemed pleasant although her Scandinavian elegance was intimidating and the way she tended to speak for her husband, answering questions directed at him, irritating. Alan, he of the goatee, who was divorced and here to enjoy himself, might be more fun. Sandy had seemed approachable – perhaps a little older than Alice, but quiet, as if holding something back. Even-featured, with straight bobbed hair and a warm smile when she gave it, she seemed to prefer being in the background. For a teacher, she was surprisingly unsure of herself. Alice made a mental note to find out more. Her colleague Lia was another kettle of fish. She had flirted with all the men throughout dinner, turning her attention from one to the next with skill, drawing them out, getting them chatting. She and Gilly had kept the conversation lively between them.

Mark emerged, smelling of peppermint and his antiseptic mouthwash, to sit on the end of the bed. He rested a hand on her thigh. 'What are you thinking?'

She turned her head to look at him and, remembering the man she had fallen in love with, put her hand on his. 'About the others. Sandy and Lia. What an extraordinary coincidence. Do you really think they didn't know they were going to be on the same trip?'

'Sandy looked stunned, though she tried to cover it up. Lia was more laid back. I thought she was quite fun.' He lifted her hand and kissed the back of it before walking round to his side of the bed where he picked up his book. 'Anyway, it's none of our business.'

Why were striped pyjamas so unsexy? But Alice was only briefly distracted. 'Of course it is. If we're going to be spending two weeks with them, it's definitely our business. I can't think of anything worse than a colleague turning up on the same holiday, even if I liked them.'

'You haven't got any colleagues.' He lifted the turned-down corner of a page that marked his place.

Alice gripped the duvet. 'I haven't forgotten what having them was like, though.' She wished he wouldn't dismiss her like that. 'And they obviously don't like each other much.'

'They were fine after a drink.'

'Your answer to everything.' She swung her legs off the bed and reached under the pillow for her nightie: long white cotton, bought from one of the vintage shops in town. She fingered the lace at the neckline, liking the idea that it had a history of its own. And not much more sexy than his pyjamas.

'Not true.'

Alice didn't miss that fleeting note of exasperation. She breathed deeply. 'I'm only teasing.' But she suspected drink had its part to play in their recent troubles. However, they had been through the worst and didn't dwell on the past. They were celebrating their nineteenth wedding anniversary and moving on together after everything that had happened.

Rome and Naples had been Mark's suggestion. They knew Italy a little, having honeymooned in Venice, and travelled round Tuscany staying at a couple of *agriturismos* when Pip was a toddler and Mark's boys nearly teenagers, but they had never been this far south. They holidayed in groups now, with friends or strangers. In those first heady days of falling in love, they would never have shared their lives with other people, but love changed with children and age. What was it they said? *The past is another country.* What Lia had said about seeing as much of a country as she could in a short time had chimed with Alice, too. Sometimes it was better following someone else's timetable than falling out over your own. She would never forget the time she and Mark had driven to the south of France together. What was meant to be a calm relaxing getaway had become endless bickering over the route, disagreements over where they'd stay or eat, what to see and do. And all of it punctuated by Pip's whining from the back seat and anxious phone calls checking the boys were all right at camp. They had never risked it again. This tour had seemed to offer the best of both worlds.

She went into the bathroom to undress. There had been a time when she didn't think twice about stripping off in front of Mark. In fact they had both enjoyed the way she slipped things off, slow and seductive. It had become part of their ritual foreplay. So long ago now. She remembered how they were in Venice, young, uninhibited and voracious. But years later, after his couple of affairs and after her body had changed with the weight she'd put on, she didn't have the same confidence or desire any longer. But perhaps if she made a concentrated effort over the next two weeks, that would help. She squirted some scent on to her neck.

She returned to find Mark deep in his book. He always brought some heavyweight history or philosophy with him to read. This time on the Italian Renaissance. She climbed in beside him and reached for her Kindle. 'Do you think it's going to be OK?'

He made the sound that meant he didn't want to be interrupted. 'What's going to be OK?'

'This holiday?'

'If we don't like it, we can always go off on our own.' He looked over the top of his specs at her then bent the sides of his book back until the spine cracked. 'Isn't that the point? A bit of both worlds.'

Her mobile stopped her replying, making them both jump.

'Who's that?' The book was put down with a sigh. 'If it's one of the boys . . . it'll cost them the earth to call us here.'

Her heart did a little skip when she saw the ID of the person FaceTiming her. 'It's Pip.'

He groaned. 'Now what?'

Pip generally only called when she wanted something or something had gone wrong. Between them, they had managed to bring up a young woman who got on with her life without relying on them every step of the way. Sometimes Alice regretted that she didn't have the sort of relationship with Pip where they chatted on the phone almost every day as one or two of her friends did with their daughters. But more often she was proud of Pip's independence and spirit. They had encouraged her to make her own decisions, so that's mostly what she did. All the same, Alice always got a frisson of pleasure when her daughter got in touch.

She ignored him as Pip appeared on the screen. Her long straight hair hung curtain-like on either side of her determined but pale face. She looked as if she was drowning in one of Mark's discarded jumpers, only the tips of her fingers visible as she raised her hand to push her hair back. The kitchen behind her was a mess. She obviously hadn't cleared up once since they'd left. Alice took a deep breath as she resolved not to comment. 'Hi, darling. What's up?'

'Sorry to call so late.'

Mark, grumbled something and rolled onto his side.

'We're an hour ahead here,' Alice said brightly.

'Oh are you? Sorry.' She wasn't. 'But this job is doing my head in.'

'I thought you were going to spend the evening at Flora's?' Alice didn't want to get into the ins and outs of her holiday job in Gap. That's all it was, after all.

'She's gone out with Em. They didn't invite me.' Her eyes flashed with anger. So that was it. Home alone on a Friday night with nothing but Saturday morning on the shop floor to look forward to. 'I wish I'd come with you now.'

'But you said you wanted to stay at home,' Alice reminded her gently while remembering Pip's furious insistence that she was old enough to be left alone. 'Where's Patrick?'

'Out too.' The youngest of her half-brothers had been tasked with keeping an eye on his younger sister. Four months ago, when this trip was being planned, he had agreed to move home for the fortnight but then he had met Jessie, whose siren call overrode any familial obligation. 'And, by the way, I don't like Jessie,' she added.

Alice had her own doubts about the girl who had snared her son's heart, but wasn't going to admit them out loud. She suspected that Jessie had her own agenda, based on the fact that Patrick had been modelling successfully for a year now and might provide a way for her into that world. 'She's lovely really,' she said. 'You'll get used to her. And have you walked Buffy?'

'Of course.' Pip adopted that exasperated look that signified how annoying she found her parents. 'Honestly, Mum, I don't think I can stand it! I spent the whole afternoon folding up jumpers. As soon as I'd done one, like, some retard' – Alice winced – 'would come and unfold it again. You've no idea how boring it is. I think I'm going to pack it in. Holly and Tess are going to Australia next month.' Alarm bells chimed. Alice knew exactly what that meant. Mark did too.

'If you give up the job, you won't have enough money to travel,' he said, rolling over and taking the phone from Alice. His face softened when he saw his youngest daughter.

'They're working their way round Australia. I'd do the same. Why not? Holly's uncle has a winery near Adelaide and he's going to get them started.'

'This isn't the time, Pip. Mum and I are about to go to sleep. We can talk about it when we're back and you've got your results.'

'It'll be too late then.' They could hear her frustration but she knew better than to express it. Then she'd lose the battle before it had begun. 'Give me back to Mum.'

Mark passed the phone back.

'OK, darling?' Alice's heart constricted.

'Yeah. I suppose so.'

Just two weeks and we'll be back. Stick at it. Love you.'

25

They said their goodbyes, and Alice leaned back against the pillows. 'I hope she won't do anything stupid.'

'She'd better not. I'm not paying for anything if she hasn't earned at least half of what she needs.' Mark was always so matter-of-fact when it came to his children. Perhaps they should have stayed at home until Pip's A-level results came through. But they badly needed this break. The important thing was to put their own troubles to rest. She put down her Kindle and took her guidebook from her bedside table, opening it at a spread of bright photos of the key sights, and her excitement began to mount again. 'Look at this. We're going to the Villa Borghese, aren't we?'

But her only reply was a low rumbling snore and a thud, as his book slipped on to the floor.

3

Lots of sightseeing today. Churches mostly! The police wear white uniforms. Lots of traffic. In the evening we met friends of Mrs R – the Flemings. They have a son Tony and daughter Fleur travelling with them. My age. They've been here before. Things are looking up. I really liked Tony and I think he liked me. They're staying at the same hotel. We shall see.

Miriam Mackenzie, May 6th 1952 – Rome

In her room, Sandy put down her mother's journal. Where her mother had been up for fun, Sandy had to try to come to terms with the fact that she was on holiday with Lia. Their last brush with each other had not been encouraging. She had been passing a group of the younger teachers in the corridor after school had ended for the day and had overheard Lia saying. 'We need to do something. There's no point having a deputy whose head's stuck in the dark ages. You know I could do so much better. I need you to help me.'

This was the first Sandy had heard about Lia mounting some sort of coup against her own claim to the position. She hated the idea of any kind of political confrontation but she was due this promotion – it had been as good as promised to her by Rosemary, the head. Surely, she and the governors would regard Sandy's impeccable record of service favourably. She had been head of department for the last nine years, and everyone expected that her next step would be to take on the deputy headship and withdraw a little from the front line. Though it was the front line that she loved, she reminded herself, however exhausting.

Throughout her mother's illness, Sandy had not missed a class till the last couple of weeks of her mother's life. It had been a difficult juggling act but with the help of the Macmillan nurses, she had managed. She was part of an old guard but she was still popular with her pupils, still able to bring the past alive for them. She was expecting the usual high success rate in the upcoming exams. That must count for something.

She stopped herself. To enjoy the next two weeks, she was going to have to forget all this. She would be wary but not un-friendly towards Lia. She would give nothing away and would not embarrass herself or the others in the group by being openly hostile. However Lia chose to play it, she would play better.

The evening had been overwhelming but everyone in the group had seemed pleasant enough. She sighed and opened the hotel mini-bar. And why not? She was on holiday. Matthew would frown on her drinking alone. Not Steven though. He would laugh. She'd restricted herself to a single glass of the fruity Montepulciano that was being liberally passed around that evening. Having Lia there meant she was cautious. Sandy had watched as her colleague took control of the table with Gilly. Lia was entertaining, funny, showed a flirtatious side that Sandy had never seen before. Of course she hadn't: they had only ever been colleagues and rivals, not friends. But having someone there who knew her made it much harder, if not impossible, for Sandy to shed her skin and become someone else, someone more intrepid, more outgoing, the woman she wanted to be.

The whisky blazed down her throat. She flicked the remote at the TV but as she surfed through the channels, glimpsing familiar black-and-white movies dubbed into Italian, finding nothing but the CNN and BBC news channels in English, she pressed the off-button. She didn't want to be reminded of how alarming the world was while she was on holiday. She took another sip. The last three years had been the toughest of her life and the emotion that still hijacked her at unexpected moments tugged at her, the tears welling in her eyes. She had no choice but to go forward. There was nothing to hold her back. She would not let Lia spoil her first holiday on her own, or get in the way of her discharging her last responsibility to her mother.

What she would do with the letter when she got to Naples, she had no idea. She had been tempted to open it, to see what was so important to her mother, yet not important enough to have written the letter sooner. But that would be disrespectful – 'only postcards are meant to be read by other people', her mother used to say – and she wouldn't be that, even though she had no qualms about reading the travel journal. No, Anna Viglieri was one of the reasons taking Sandy to Naples, whoever she was. But first, Rome.

The next morning, the sky was a bright cloudless blue. Somehow the concerns of the previous night diminished in the face of what the day might hold. Sandy dithered over her choice of footwear, in the end plumping for the sensible walking shoes over the sandals, teaming them with cream walking shorts and a shirt. *Put comfort before glamour*, she said to herself. *Walking round sights is bloody hard on the feet. Never mind what you look like.*

Downstairs, in the courtyard, the other couples sat at separate tables almost as if they hadn't met the night before. She looked around. No sign of Lia. Murmuring 'Good morning' here and there, Sandy chose her breakfast from the extensive buffet and took a table in the far corner.

'Sandy! Good morning.' Lia made a beeline for her.

Remembering her resolve, Sandy smiled. 'Morning. Isn't it glorious? So hot already.'

'Can I join you?'

'Of course.' Sandy sat down and watched as Lia went in to get her breakfast.

She returned with her plate loaded. 'I won't get through the morning without this.' She smiled up at the waiter. '*Un doppio espresso, per favore.*' She waited as the waiter brought her coffee, took a tiny sip, then looked straight at Sandy. 'I've been thinking about what you said. Neither of us want to be on holiday together, but we are. So we're going to have to make the best of it. Let's forget all the school stuff, especially the deputy headship, for this fortnight?'

Sandy returned the gaze. 'I'd like that,' she said, cautious all the same.

Lia relaxed, leaning back in her chair. 'I know we're not the best of friends but I'm sure we can get along fine. Let's face it, as the only single women on the trip, we need each other.' Lia paused. 'What did make you change your mind about coming?'

'After my mother died I was exhausted. I needed a break, to recharge my batteries.'

'You're not married, then?'

'No.' Surely she must have heard about Matthew's death. The staff had tiptoed round her for months as word went round. Nor did she want to talk about Steven. 'What about you?'

Lia screwed up her nose and tipped her head to one side. 'Not at the moment. I haven't given up though.' Her eyes glinted.

'I find that so hard to believe. Someone like you.'

'Nice of you to say.' Lia beamed. 'Too high maintenance, I guess.'

'So why did *you* decide to come?'

'Well, like I said yesterday. I'm learning Italian and, like you, don't have a lot of spare time on my hands.' That laugh again as her gaze drifted to Peter and Brit who were breakfasting over their iPads, then on to Mark and Alice. 'Actually,' she leaned forward again. 'I'm crazy about Elizabeth Gilbert too. She said learning Italian made her happy, mended her soul.'

Sandy was mystified. Was that one of the new younger teachers she hadn't yet got to know at school? Wasn't one of them called Liz? Was this some sort of a coming out? Was this why she hadn't had much luck in the husband department? 'Couldn't she have come with you?'

Lia threw her head back and laughed so loudly heads turned. 'I wish,' she said finally. 'No. She's an American writer. I read her book *Eat, Pray, Love* when I was in India – you've heard of that?'

Sandy shook her head. 'Vaguely.' She'd been put off by the title.

'Believe me, she talks so much sense. Her book really spoke to me. So much so, that I went to Indonesia last year – in her footsteps, if you like. But the point is, she started her journey in Rome so when I saw this trip advertised, I couldn't resist. She was more adventurous, of course. She came to live here on her own for four months. I couldn't do that.'

'Because . . . ?' How much easier Sandy's life would be if Lia did.

'Because I've got my cat, a job that I love and, if I play my cards right . . .' she stopped, as if aware she might be about to breach their recent truce. 'Anyway, I couldn't afford it.'

'I'd like to have done something like that – live somewhere abroad, somewhere different.' But Matthew would never have considered such a move. He'd spent his spare time wallowing in British history. Churches, stately homes, architectural ruins, library stacks packed with recondite snippets of information: Sandy had visited them all with him. Not that she had ever objected, because she shared his passion. She had made a career out of English history, after all. But sometimes she had wondered whether they should be a little more adventurous, seen more of the world. He had always countered by suggesting something surprising, somewhere she had never heard of that he thought they would enjoy together: the eerie ghost town of Tyneham in Dorset, the Hellfire Caves in the Chiltern Hills, Gunwalloe in Cornwall. And they always had. The furthest afield they had ever travelled together was the Outer Hebrides, to see the remains of the roundhouses at Cladh Hallan. That had marked the beginning of their love affair with Scotland, where they'd returned once a year until Matthew's death.

She would not go back.

'It's a wonderful dream but it's a pipe dream for most of us,' said Lia. 'Most of us are tied up with mortgages, jobs, friends, family – all that stuff or some of it. But it's having the balls to give it all up. That's the big ask. Something needs to tip you over the edge. In her . . . Elizabeth Gilbert's,' she explained to Sandy's frown. 'In her case, divorce and an unhappy love affair. But she was a journalist so she got a commission to come here. Think of that.'

Sandy couldn't. She was as far from being familiar with the world of media as anyone could be.

'Anyway, here we all are. What do you think of the others?' Lia lowered her voice almost to a whisper. 'I've been chatting to Alan, he's a hoot. Peter not so much. And I haven't decided what I think of Mark.'

'They all seem very nice.' Sandy was not going to get drawn into any backstabbing before they'd barely begun the holiday.

Lia nodded towards two men breakfasting together. 'Do you think they're the ones joining us?' Both were turned out in ironed shorts and walking shoes; both in pink short-sleeved shirts. One was a little shorter and fatter than the other. The taller and balder of the two wore specs. They ate in companionable silence.

'Maybe. We'll find out on our way to the Forum.' When

Sandy had woken at six that morning – old habits – she had devoted the next hour or so to reading about it, pleased that Steven had given her the book.

'Mmm.' Lia pulled a face. 'Not sure it's really going to be my thing. I prefer something a bit more recent.'

'You've come on the wrong holiday then.' Sandy laughed, thinking of the other buildings in Rome she couldn't wait to visit – *Churches mostly!* Her mother's note of desperation had amused her – never mind Pompeii and Herculaneum when the time came. The truth was she was nosy. What did people in the past *think?* What did they look like? Smell like? Was happiness something they thought about? She thought it unlikely that Lia would ever understand.

Alice watched as Sandy stood up and passed by their table. She smiled. 'Morning.'

'Good morning. Isn't it glorious? I'm just going to get ready. I'll see you in a minute.' Sandy disappeared round a corner of the building.

Looking back at the table, Alice saw Lia watching Sandy too, an expression on her face that she couldn't interpret. But she stared for a second too long. Lia caught her eye and came over, holding what looked like a sandwich and her cup of coffee.

'Can I join you?'

Mark grunted and turned to the side so he could continue reading the *Guardian* online. Despite her husband's unavailability at breakfast, Alice wasn't sure she wanted them to be joined by anyone else. 'We're just about finished.'

'Oh well.' Lia drained her coffee and put her cup on their table. 'Looking forward to this morning?'

'I am,' Alice said. 'You?'

'Absolutely. Mark?'

He looked up at her, irritated at being interrupted. 'Yes?'

'Are you looking forward to this morning?'

Alice was surprised by Lia's obviously unwelcome insistence, and even more surprised when Mark replied.

'I am. I visited it when I was much younger.' He put down his iPad. 'I wandered round without a clue what much of it was, so I hope having a guide will make more sense of it this time.' That was the longest sentence he'd spoken that morning.

Alice wondered what it would be like spending every moment of every day with Mark over the next couple of weeks. Usually they only connected over breakfast and supper. Even during the holidays, he took himself to the library or his study. 'Research,' he'd say, breezy but dismissive. 'Has to be done.'

He had hurt her so badly. However, things were better between them since seeing Jane, their marriage guidance counsellor. Mark had only agreed to the sessions because Alice had insisted, but despite apparently co-operating, he had always emerged analysing the process itself, confident that he was one jump ahead of Jane and determined to be selective in the information he gave her. When Alice pointed out that was negating the point of the whole process, he had apologised. 'But I'm really only going for you.' He continued to treat it like a game that he was in to win instead of the help it was intended to be.

He listened while she had talked about her family, her difficult mother for whom nothing was good enough, her separation from Jeff, the man she had lived with before he had left her and she had met Mark, her difficulties when she married Mark and became stepmother to Patrick and Henry. But he would never talk about Sally, his first wife and mother to his two boys, and why she left him and her children to disappear to Australia with a new man. How Alice had sometimes envied her since. The three of them had been hard work. Sometimes but not always.

And here they were in Rome. New beginnings. She sized her husband up as he and Lia carried on talking about the day ahead. His hair had thinned and he'd put on a little weight but he was still an attractive man. She looked at Lia, who had already found a way to make him loosen up. She was a bundle of energy. Not Mark's type at all. Alice didn't have anything to worry about there. She sipped her cappuccino and began to relax.

4

The Forum today – just a load of old stones. You can make out some of the buildings but... dullsville. Anyway the Flemings have convinced Mrs R that it's a good idea to let Tony, Fleur and me have supper without them this evening while they take her to a concert. We're going to a trattoria near the hotel and then Tony's said we'll go to Piazza Navona for coffee. Excited to see how things will progress.

Miriam Mackenzie, May 7th 1952 – Rome

Gilly was a talker. She barely drew breath as the minibus weaved through Trastevere – the neighbourhood that so enchanted Sandy – and as they swept along beside the Tiber. To her shame Sandy only heard part of what she said. The two German men from breakfast had been introduced as Benno and Alex and had taken the seats at the back of the bus. When they finally exchanged the chill of the aircon for the stifling heat of the day, Gilly gave them each a bottle of water and led them up a hill and past a palatial building she identified as the Capitoline Museum, then down some steps. Sandy took in the classical architecture, the other people, the statue of someone on a horse, a stray dog, a busker – everything was so new and exciting to her. She didn't want to miss a thing.

Gilly stopped every now and then to wait for the stragglers in the group. 'I don't want to hurry you but...' she'd say, the note of encouragement firmer than Sandy felt strictly necessary.

After all this was not a route march. '. . . We should get to the Forum before it gets too crowded. And then we'll go on to the Colosseum and, after lunch, a favourite church of mine.'

Sandy thrilled at the thought of the discoveries ahead of her. Avoiding Lia, she had attached herself to the newcomers, Alex and Benno. 'Have you been here before?' she asked, breaking the ice as they walked round a group of tourists, each with a set of green earphones, listening to their guide, who muttered into his microphone.

'We've been to most of the big Italian cities: Venice, Bologna, Florence, Padua, Mantua, Verona. You call it, we have been there,' said Alex with pride as he reeled off the names.

'We start at the north and work our way south,' added Benno. 'We love Italy but now we have children . . .' they exchanged a proud smile. 'We have less time.' They both nodded simultaneously as if they had spoken together. 'You?'

'My first time.'

Their faces lit up. 'You have so many treats in store.' Benno said. 'The paintings.'

'The architecture.' Alex chipped in.

'The food.' Benno finished off.

'I hope so.' But Sandy wanted to find out more about them. 'You're from Germany?'

Alex laughed. 'No, no. We took the children there to stay with my sister and their cousins. In fact we have a B & B near Arundel. I run the business . . .'

'When I was transferred by the bank to the London HQ, we move,' Benno explained.

Alex smiled at her. 'So I look after the house and the guests, and Ben looks after our finances.'

This curious experience of speaking to two people as if they were one continued until they were standing under the umbrella pines at the start of a large wide road given up to hundreds of

37

people. By that time, Sandy was feeling quite comfortable with her two companions.

Here, Gilly came into her own. 'Now that,' she announced with a flourish, interrupting them all, 'is Trajan's column. 'Built to celebrate the Emperor Trajan's victory in the Dacian wars and completed in 113 AD. Look at the bas-relief spiralling up the column.' As she went on, any fears about Gilly being a lightweight were quickly disproved. She knew her stuff all right. Sandy experienced a familiar glow of pleasure as she was drawn back into the past. She checked that Steven's guidebook was in her bag.

They walked up the busy Via de Fori Imperiali – Lia pronounced the words with an exaggerated accent. Around her neck was an impressive-looking camera, a camera bag slung over her shoulder.

Sandy couldn't catch what Gilly was saying over the sound of a street band which had just started up a few yards from them. But it didn't matter. She could and would read about it later. For the moment she was absorbing her surroundings, so different from anywhere she and Matthew had travelled to. Would he have enjoyed it if he had surprised her with the train trip? She suspected he might. If only she had pushed him harder.

'There's the Colosseum.' Benno pointed ahead at the familiar landmark.

Sandy looked up the road and thought back to her mother's journal.

A massive ruin on a roundabout with cars and Vespas whizzing round it. You couldn't miss it. Mrs R in raptures. What went on in there sounds pretty bloodthirsty. I'd love a ride on a Vespa. I wonder if I can persuade Ignazio (barman)...

Nothing much seemed to have changed.

'Can we go there first?' Lia asked.

'Well, I . . .' Gilly clearly wasn't happy about having her planned schedule questioned; then she rallied. 'We're meeting Massimo, our guide, at the gate to the Forum. You'll have to ask him, but we usually do it this way.'

'I really want to go there first,' Lia insisted. 'Does anyone else mind?'

'Let's stick to the plan,' said Brit, echoing Sandy's thoughts. 'Don't you think, darling?' She looked at Peter for his agreement. He nodded as she adjusted her panama to exactly the right angle.

'But I just thought . . .' Lia looked crestfallen. 'What does anyone else think?' She appealed to the rest of the group. Sandy watched, pretending indifference. She knew something that the group did not: Lia did not take dissent well.

'Let's have a show of hands.' Mark spoke up from the back. 'To do the Colosseum first.' He raised his and Lia shot him a look of gratitude.

Sandy, who was standing in front of Alice, heard her give a resigned sigh. When she turned to her, Alice shrugged. 'Sorry. But there's always one.'

Did she mean Lia? Or was she talking about her husband?

'And for the Forum.' Mark sounded as if he'd lost interest in the outcome now.

The others all showed their hands, just raising them to shoulder level as if embarrassed to commit themselves, glancing in Gilly's direction.

'Good. That's settled.' Gilly was back in control. They walked up the road, stopping occasionally to watch the men knocking out vivid spray-painted pictures of the sights, living statues apparently floating in the air, a team of breakdancers busting apparently impossible moves. They moved through tour groups, stepping aside for the odd horse-drawn carriage, tourists on

Segways, a police car. They stood staring over the wall at the Forum itself, already crawling with people. Sandy was quite unfamiliar with heat like this.

'And there's Massimo at the gate.' Gilly sounded relieved. 'He knows everything you need to know about ancient Rome and will be your guide here.'

'What are *you* going to do?' asked Lia, clearly still smarting from defeat.

'Sit in the shade.' Gilly did not extend an invitation. 'There's usually someone I know here.' With that, she walked over to a man standing by the gate and embraced him. He looked to be in his forties, tanned, with wild curly salt-and-pepper hair and beard, jeans and a T-shirt that showed off a lean body. She led him over to the group.

'Massimo, I presume' said Lia, sounding more enthusiastic.

Sandy thought she felt Alice give her a nudge. She turned to the other woman, but her face was impassive until a quick wink.

The man nodded and unleashed a dazzling white smile. Lia took a step towards him.

'This is Massimo.' Gilly stepped between the two of them. 'If any of you get separated, we'll meet back here at twelve.' She threw Lia a pointed look. 'Then, after the Colosseum, we'll have lunch. Some of you may want to head off on your own at that point – just let me know. In the afternoon, we'll go to one of my favourite churches, the Basilica di San Clemente.'

Sandy was wondering how she'd remember everything until she came to write her diary. On all her holidays with Matthew, she had been the diary keeper while he took the photos. She had always preferred to rely on her memory but this time had brought his old pocket camera with her, just in case. She touched its shape in her pocket – her talisman. But everything here was so unfamiliar, such an assault on her senses. She felt as if she was being buffeted into life again.

Massimo was every bit as authoritative and fascinating as Gilly had suggested he would be. Sandy was riveted by his explanations as he brought the ruins to life, rebuilding them in her mind and repeopling them so it became a busy city centre once again. She listened entranced as he told them the legend of Romulus and Remus, the mythical founders of Rome, and peered down towards the huts where the twins were said to have lived. Far from being the *'load of old stones'* that her mother had dismissed, this was a place that once seethed with life. If only they could have come here together, Sandy might have persuaded her to look at it in a different light.

As they stood looking down from the Palatine Hill, Massimo pointed out the various ruins again. Below them, the place was crowded; one group all wore yellow baseball caps, another identical jackets, others followed guides with penants held high. Among them wandered individuals travelling on their own, stopping to consult guidebooks, taking selfies or photographs of friends against the backdrop of the ruins. Above them all, a perfect summer sky.

Her appetite whetted by what she had already seen, Sandy made a mental note to put the Capitoline Museum that they'd passed earlier high on her to-do list. Mooching around cases of ancient relics and statuary was exactly the sort of thing she would enjoy doing on her own.

As they walked towards the Colosseum, past more street entertainers and artists, their backs to the bright yellow hoarding that hid the earthworks for a new Metro line, Alice caught up with her. 'My feet are killing me. I wish I'd been as sensible as you.'

'Sensible'. A word that had attached itself to Sandy throughout her life. Somehow it had become her default mode. She glanced down at her walking shoes. 'Mmm. Not glamorous but they are comfortable.'

'I should have taken Mark's advice.' Alice raised an eyebrow. 'He said sandals were a mistake. I've got a blister under the strap.' She bent over and tried to ease it.

'You could go back and change them when we stop for lunch.'

'Lunch!' Alice visibly perked up. 'I can't wait. The food here...' She didn't need to complete the sentence.

They dodged one of the men on wheelies advertising the hop-on, hop-off bus rides that seemed to go all over the city. He waved a pamphlet at them before moving on.

While they'd been in the Forum, the temperature had soared. Alice flapped her hat in front of her face.

'You have tickets?' A man stood in front of them. 'You want to jump the line?'

'We're fine, thanks,' said Alice, turning back to Sandy, who was rummaging in her bag.

She produced a small green box with a flourish. 'Here they are. Blister plasters. Would you like them?'

'You're a saint. Thank you.' Alice took them.

'I've got plenty.' Sandy had learned the wisdom of carrying blister remedies wherever she and Matthew went. They turned away from the dark mouth of the Metro station and focused on the Colosseum itself.

'Bloody good restoration job.' Mark had made his way over to them.

'Cynic,' said Alice with a smile, tucking her arm into his.

'This way.' Gilly and Massimo led them across the road, past the queues and inside. Looking at the remains of what lay under the stage, Sandy's mind filled with images of gladiators preparing themselves mentally for what lay ahead. She could almost smell the sweat, manure, wild animals and fear. Massimo and Gilly left them to wander round on their own. 'We'll be right here if you want to ask any questions.'

Sandy was amused to see Lia ask Massimo if he could help her set up her tripod. So far, the morning had been accompanied by constant intrusive clicking as she took photo after photo. Sandy wrapped her hand round Matthew's camera. She didn't need it after all. She would always be able to remember this. She walked round the arena towards the area where a stage had been set up over the groundworks, wanting to soak up the atmosphere with its memories of combat and death. Imagining the roars of the crowd, the shouts of the gladiators, unarmed men pitted against wild animals and even the flooding of the arena to re-enact a mighty sea battle, she took a deep breath, closed her eyes and let herself be transported back through time. When she next opened them, it was almost a shock to see the milling tourists in front of her.

She got out her bottle of water as she looked for the others. Lia was standing by her tripod, chatting to Massimo, her sunglasses in her hand. Alex and Benno were walking towards one of the archways leading to the outer ring. Alan had struck up a conversation with a couple of women tourists. When he offered them his bottle of water, they shook their heads and walked away. She couldn't see Peter and Brit but turning to her left, she spotted Mark and Alice. They were in earnest conversation. Then Mark raised his hand and Alice moved back from him. They were obviously disagreeing over something. What more apt place for a fight? They were too far away from her to hear what they were saying but something was obviously wrong. Alice was shaking her head. Mark shrugged with his hands outspread, and remained there as he watched his wife leave the arena.

Sandy kept looking as he removed his battered panama and scratched his head. He didn't try to call Alice back or to follow her. She turned to see if any of the others had seen what had happened. None of them was looking in their direction, except one. Lia. Her camera was trained on Mark and on the spot where Alice had been. She would have seen the whole thing. Sandy could almost hear the shutter clicking. As Lia began to dismantle her tripod, Mark got up and followed his wife outside.

5

After leaving the Colosseum, Alice hesitated, unsure where to go next. Her pride wouldn't let her go back. For all their good intentions, she and Mark had crossed swords again. All she had done was say how much she regretted her choice of shoes as she bent over to stick on one of Sandy's plasters.

'There's always something, isn't there?' Mark said, tetchy.

'What's that supposed to mean?" she asked, genuinely puzzled.

'Nothing's ever quite right for my darling wife.' He tipped the brim of his hat so it shaded his eyes.

She was tempted to flick it off his head altogether. 'That's not true. I'm just saying I've got a blister. What's wrong with that?' The tension between them sharpened. 'You just can't resist, can you? Despite everything we've agreed about trying harder.' She could almost see the figure of their counsellor rear up behind him, grey eyes intent, middle fingers tapping together, listening to where this was going, preparing to ask why Alice was overreacting.

'I'm sorry. I didn't mean it like that.' Backtracking now, denying anything he said might rock the boat. This was what he always did: back away from any blame. 'I meant for us. There's always something wrong for one of us.'

'That's not what you meant. I know you better than that.'

He gave a long sigh. 'Alice, please. Can't we try and enjoy this holiday just like we promised we would?'

They had promised, but it was hard. How could their

marriage be in as good shape as it once had been ... she'd lost count how many years ago now. 'I want to. I really do. But when you say things like that, it makes me so mad.'

His lips tightened in a thin straight line. That did too.

She paused, before she said more than she meant to, before she said something she couldn't retract. Then: 'Actually what it really does is hurt me.'

He held out his arms, palm up. 'That's what I mean. I'm not trying to hurt you. I just want us to enjoy ourselves, away from ...'

'Don't remind me.' Alice got to her feet. 'I think it would be better if I went back to the hotel and met up with you later. Let's put it down to the heat. We'll start over then, resolutions renewed.'

He looked at her, his eyes intent. 'What about lunch?'

'You go without me. Really. I'll be fine.'

At least he had the grace to look very slightly shamefaced. 'OK. I'm sorry.'

As she walked towards the exit, Alice felt a sense of relief mixed with guilt at her own childishness. Having walked away, going back would mean a loss of face and one of those told-you-so smiles from Mark. She should be bigger than that but her stupid pride stopped her from turning round. She would make up for it later. On her own, she immediately felt more relaxed even though she didn't have a clue where she was going to go. She quickened her step so there'd be no danger of him catching up with her. Right now, she wanted to be alone.

She set off back the way they had come, all the way to the commanding Palazzo Venezia, adorned with banners advertising Art City 17 and Laberinto del Cuore, whatever that was. The blister plaster made walking possible again. Turning left, she kept in the shadow of the palace, each step releasing the tension she'd felt all morning with Mark. This was silly, she told herself. But the irritation triggers were too embedded to ignore. She barely noticed where she was going, just heading down the most shady streets, guessing she must be going in the general direction of Trastevere. *How stupid to walk off like a sulky child*, she told herself. How hard was it to make more of an effort – after all, she wanted to save her marriage. That was what the counselling sessions had confirmed to her.

Suddenly hungry, she made a snap decision and walked into the small restaurant she was passing. The outside area was shaded by large parasols and surrounded by potted laurel bushes. Shown to a table, she scanned the menu, ordered herself an Aperol – everyone else was drinking them – and a plate of *pasta dei cornuti* just because she was amused by the story on the menu that this was a dish of pasta, garlic, oil and chilli that could be whipped up swiftly for their unsuspecting husbands by unfaithful wives who had spent the day otherwise engaged. She slipped off her sandals, glancing down to see their straps marked out in dust on her feet that were puffy with the heat. The blister plaster had stuck well.

Though fascinated by the couple at the table in the far corner, both of them busy on their phones as if the other wasn't there, her mind drifted back to Mark. Married for nineteen years. When they met, Sally had just left him. Not just him, but their two bewildered sons as well: Henry, then eight, and Patrick, five. They were in the same wine bar when Alice's brother had texted her to say he was running late. Mark was alone on the next table, staring morosely into his pint. When she'd looked at her watch for the nth time, he had looked up and caught her eye. 'I'd never stand up someone as beautiful as you,' he'd said. He gave her a sad but winning smile.

Thinking about it now, he couldn't have said anything cornier. At the time, she had been ridiculously flattered, intrigued by the smile, the sadness in his eyes, and had accepted his offer of another glass of wine. And, of course, she had fancied him. By then she had given up hoping that she would ever meet 'the one' – how she hated that expression. As if there was such a person for everybody. She was newly out of a ten-year relationship that had come to an end when Jeff had confessed that he did want children after all, and was leaving her to have them with a member of his team who was in her twenties. For ten years, they had agreed that they were happy without and had concentrated on their careers – his at the sharp end of government finance, hers as a development chef who had even made the final of a well-known TV cookery show – and living a full life with good friends, fine dining and luxury holidays. Then, when she had hit her thirty-fifth birthday, he made his announcement. So there she was, her child-bearing years almost behind her and wondering whether she had made a terrible mistake.

By the time her brother phoned to say he wasn't going to make it at all, she and Mark were so deep in conversation, she didn't have time to be angry. They agreed to meet the following day for lunch, Mark's availability otherwise circumscribed by his boys and babysitters. She had gone home, her head whirling with inappropriate thoughts. Their affair blazed with the speed of a forest fire, taken at stolen opportunities when she could escape work and he could get away. And then the introduction to the children.

'Shall we go to Whipsnade?' she suggested. 'That way they'll have lots to take their minds off me.'

She remembered how, the evening before, she put all her clothes out on her bed. What to wear for a day with two boys? She needn't have worried. They were so excited to be out with their father, she could have worn a tiara and they wouldn't have noticed.

Henry, a skinny serious-looking kid, had looked her up and down and offered his hand. 'How do you do?'

Patrick took his lead from his older brother, but bent his

middle finger and tickled the palm of her hand. Alice screamed and he collapsed in giggles.

'Patrick . . .' There was a warning note in Mark's voice.

'I thought it was a spider,' said Alice, winking at him to show she was pretending. Patrick jumped with delight while Henry ventured a grudging smile. 'High five,' she ventured. This she knew from her nephew.

Patrick jumped up to slap her hand.

'Down low.' She snatched her hand away as he tried to slap it again. 'Too slow.'

'Again.'

And so the ice was broken. Nothing gave her more pleasure than stepping into their mother's shoes, and after some resistance they had accepted her. Not as a new mother but as someone who was going to devote her life to making them a priority. To all her friends' and most of all her own astonishment, she swiftly became a regular part of the boys' lives. She had been there when they wailed for their mother, separated them when they fought, defused the situation when they blamed Mark or themselves for Sally's disappearance. Always and without fail, she had put herself last.

And then they had Pip. She came as a surprise to both of them, but nothing and nobody had given Alice more pleasure than this loving, defiant, wilful addition to their family who had made her character felt very early on, as she wound the three men in the family round her finger and soon had them dancing to her tune.

The scrape of a chair alerted her to someone taking the table next but one to hers. Before she had time to look round, the sound of a newspaper being unfolded and shaken made it clear it was someone else on their own. The elderly man was smart in a white short-sleeved shirt and dark trousers, distinguished by a grey beard and circular plastic spectacles. She liked the idea of having stumbled on a place where locals ate – must be a good sign.

She decided at that moment to take her time. The heat was so debilitating and the sandal on her other foot was beginning to rub so that there was no point rushing back to find the others. Instead she would relax, let her thoughts take her where they would. Then when she had eventually ordered them, she would find her way back to the hotel and Mark, and they would start over.

She had given herself so wholeheartedly to his family that perhaps she had let their relationship take a back seat. Perhaps, if she had been more careful, he wouldn't have felt the need for the attention of other women; although they had established with Jane that he loved the thrill of the chase. That was what gave him such pleasure. That, and the reassurance of being desired. Something she had definitely let slip as she focused on rebuilding a happy family for him.

'She wasn't feeling well.' Mark chose the chair next to Sandy and sat down. 'The heat's too much. Takes a bit of getting used to, after all.' He balanced his panama on the back of his chair.

'I hope she's all right,' said Sandy, thinking that the woman she'd seen leaving the arena didn't look remotely overcome by the heat. And, if she had been, wouldn't he have accompanied her back to the hotel?

'Oh yes. She's tough as old boots. It's just hotter than we expected.' He took the menu and began studying it. 'Gilly!' He raised his voice to be heard at the other end of the table. 'How many courses?'

Sandy gazed down the list of different plates of pasta, wishing she were hungrier.

'We've got to try the artichokes. They're a speciality.' On the other side of the table, Lia looked as cool as Sandy felt wrecked in the heat. '*Alla romana* or *alla giudea*? What do you think?'

Mark and Sandy dutifully listened while she explained the difference – deep fried or stuffed – and dutifully plumped for the *romana*.

'She seems to know what she's talking about,' Alan said, giving Lia the swiftest of winks.

'And artichokes is the least of it.' She gave a brief suggestive smile.

Sandy looked away.

'I'd steer clear of the artichokes, guys.' Gilly's voice carried down the table. 'It's not the season for the wonderful Italian ones yet. These won't be the same. From France, I think.'

'I'm going to have them anyway.' Lia was defiant.

'She always like this?' Mark asked Sandy.

She raised her eyebrows.

'So you teach at the same school?' He leaned forward, inclining his head as if he didn't want to miss a word.

'We do.' Sandy was aware that while the rest of the table were discussing the menu, Lia had homed in on their conversation. 'Ecclesworth – it's a girls' school, for our sins.'

'Sounds interesting.'

'Not really.' She was keen to head the conversation off, didn't want Lia getting involved.

'But you teach History.' He wasn't to be put off so easily. 'I was watching you this morning in the Forum and could see how you related to being there.'

Had her pleasure been so obvious? 'I've always loved grubbing around in the past, looking back at our roots and learning from what happened then. Not that I know anything about Italian history beyond the obvious. I'm more at home with English – that's what I teach.'

'And very well too,' Lia butted in, to Sandy's surprise. 'She's so popular with the pupils. You wouldn't believe it.'

Sandy waited for the bite that wasn't forthcoming.

Lia's face was nothing but friendly. 'And you, Mark. What do you do?'

He dabbed his forehead with a hanky he pulled from his shirt pocket. 'I'm an academic.'

'Still teaching?'

'Er . . . I've just taken early retirement.' He rushed over the words, glancing down as he twisted his wedding ring round his finger. 'But I'm working on a book.'

'Oh?'

'Something on the philosophy of mind. It's complicated.' He couldn't have been more patronising.

Something in Sandy's brain went dead. 'And Alice?'

'She looks after us all.' He spoke with affection.

'But before that?'

'She was a professional cook and since then she's had her hands full with us.' He gave an indulgent laugh. 'We're a full-time job.'

Sandy wasn't sure she liked the way he dismissed Alice as if she was some sort of domestic appliance, but decided it was better to let Lia take the reins of the conversation. Mark didn't seem to mind answering her questions.

After lunch, Sandy decided to go with Gilly to the church. To hell with her diary. Still to get her bearings, she was pleased to spend the first day completely in someone else's hands. Alex and Benno were the only ones to claim the afternoon for themselves and left to see the Caravaggios in the Capitoline Museum.

'Would it be an idea to go back to check on Alice?' Gilly asked Mark.

'If there was a problem, she would have texted me.' He looked at his phone. 'No. nothing. She'll be better off undisturbed.'

'Well, if you're sure . . .' She sounded doubtful.

'Quite sure.' He rolled up the shirt sleeve that had slipped down his left arm. 'Now which way?'

Up a straight street, Gilly led them to an inconspicuous doorway shaded by trees and flanked by a couple of potted palms. As they walked in, five white-robed nuns in the chapel to their left knelt in the pews like ghosts.

Gilly whispered to Sandy. 'I come here whenever I'm in Rome. There's something about it.' She drew in a breath. 'Oh no! I wanted you to see the mosaics.'

Sandy followed her gaze to the altar, which was obscured by scaffolding and dustsheets.

'Always happens.' Peter shuffled his feet behind them. 'Everything's always *in restauro* just when you want to see it.'

'When we went to Mantua, the same thing happened,' explained Brit. 'Didn't it, darling? But look at this.' She gestured towards a fresco of the crucifixion in another side chapel. 'This is magnificent.'

'And the floor,' said Sandy, admiring the intricacy of the tiling. This was nothing like any church Sandy had visited with Matthew. There was the same reverent hush of course, but the faintest whiff of incense, the lavish decoration, the space, gave it a very different feel. She couldn't help wondering what he would have made of it. Once they'd been taken to Westminster Cathedral for midnight mass by friends and it had been all she could do to persuade him to stay. 'Bigoted, outdated claptrap,' he hissed at her while agreeing to sit down out of politeness to their hosts. He'd refused to go to a Catholic service again. He hadn't always been the easiest of men.

'This way.' Gilly led them through a door to a ticket office, then down stairs that took them below the church. 'There are remains down here that date back to the first century. Pagans used to worship here.'

As Sandy started down behind her, she lost her footing for a second. As she swiftly righted herself, she felt Mark's hand on her arm. In the background the click of a camera.

'All right?'

She had to pull herself from his grasp. 'Yes, fine thanks. I slipped.'

'Well, I'm here if you need a hand.'

'Thanks.' He was being far too solicitous so she took a step away from him. Taking extra care in the dim light, she followed Gilly, aware of Mark being only a couple of steps behind her. Underground, the lighting was so subdued they could see very little although they could hear the constant sound of running water.

By the time they had finished looking at the church, Sandy quite understood Gilly's love of it. Without being remotely religious herself, she felt a peace here. She stood in front of the fresco, trying to fix its composition, the colours in her memory.

'Beautiful, isn't it?' Mark's voice was lowered to a whisper. 'But Gilly's going back to the hotel so Lia and I thought we'd go for an ice cream. Fancy joining us?'

Lia was hovering behind him. 'There's a place that's meant to have the best ice creams in the world.'

'Well . . .' Sandy hesitated. What about the Capitoline Museum? Shouldn't she soak up every experience Rome offered while she could? Her heavy legs said, 'Nope.'

'Oh, come on.' Mark encouraged her. 'It's good not to OD on sights. Otherwise they all muddle up.'

'Enough history for one day,' said Lia.

'Couldn't agree more. Can I join you?' Alan had wandered up to them. 'You can't keep these gorgeous women to yourself, Mark.'

'I've no intention of doing that.' Mark sounded put out. 'Of course you can.' Though it was obvious he'd rather Alan didn't. 'Sandy?'

'I don't know . . .' Sandy stopped. But wasn't having an ice cream as much of a Roman adventure as anything else?

The ice creams here are pure heaven. I've never tasted anything like them. Tony and Fleur took me to a gelateria – yes, I'm learning the lingo! – today. Bliss.

'Don't worry. We can leave you here.' Lia had linked arms with Alan, who was grinning. Her impatience decided Sandy.

'It's a great idea. I'd love to come. How do you know about it?' She caught Lia's look of despair before she replied.

'Elizabeth Gilbert.'

'Of course.' They were obviously going to become very familiar with Ms Gilbert's exploits while they were there.

One last look at the fresco fixed it in her memory just as Lia sidled in front of her, not stopping long enough to look at what was before her in any detail, and *click!* Another photograph.

6

*The food in this place is to die for. We had pasta again
today with eggs and bacon but better than that –
carbonara. I'm trying to learn what Italian I can so I'm
ready for Naples. In the meantime I'm making the most of
adult company before I start looking after the little girls!
Tony and I are getting on VERY well. Wish Fleur wasn't
hanging around us all the time. I've got to find a way to get
him on my own...*

Miriam Mackenzie, May 8th 1952 – Rome

They walked until they found a taxi rank. Lia immediately ran
up to the first in line, telling the driver where to go. 'Why not?'
she said to Mark who was looking surprised. 'It's boiling hot,
we're exhausted and it's a long way to the Pantheon.'

'I thought you'd had enough of ancient Rome for the day.'

'I have, but we're going to Il Gelato di San Crispino.' Out
came that accent again. 'They have the best ice cream in Italy,
if not the world. One or the other.'

'Who is Saint Crispin anyway?' Sandy got in the cab, going
along with whatever the others decided.

'The patron saint of ice cream?' Lia joked as she bounced her
way across the back seat to the far side, her hand on her camera.

'Hardly.' Mark got in the front and slammed the door.
'Wasn't it cobblers... or shoemakers,' he added to make sure

there was no misunderstanding. Lia and Sandy exchanged a smile as Mark bent over his iPhone to check. 'Yes, that's right.'

'How on earth did you know that?' Sandy was very aware of Alan's thigh pressed too close to hers.

Mark shrugged. 'My memory's a ragbag of useless facts.' He checked his screen. 'He and his twin were martyred together on St Crispin's Day. There. Nothing at all to do with ice cream.'

'We don't need a memory any more,' Alan said, adjusting his position. Sandy tried to edge away from him. 'Google is every old person's memory these days.' He laughed at his very old joke.

'I hope you're not including me in that!' Lia tapped his thigh. He grinned while the other two smiled gamely.

The taxi's aircon was a welcome respite from the heat of the street. Sandy turned her face to the window, resting her forehead on the cool of the glass, while Lia attempted to chat with the driver. She read the address of the shop from her phone, repeated it louder when he didn't understand, then had to pass the phone to him so he could see for himself. 'Aaaah!' Light dawned. '*La Piazza della Maddalena.*'

'Exactly! Didn't I say that?' Affronted, Lia took the phone back.

Yet when he said them, the words conjured up something extraordinary, something dark and exotic – quite different from Lia's version. Sandy allowed herself a moment of pleasure. 'Why this one in particular?' she asked, though suspected she knew the answer.

'This is in the Rome bit of the book,' Lia explained.

Mark looked puzzled.

'*Eat, Pray, Love,*' she explained.

He looked none the wiser. 'Is that some sort of treatment plan?'

She threw back her head and laughed. 'It's a wonderful book. I can't believe none of you have heard of it. And Elizabeth

57

Gilbert went to the Pantheon whenever she could, so we should do that too.'

'Have you got everywhere this woman went off by heart?' asked Sandy, incredulous.

'I did go through before I came and made a list of everywhere she went in Rome and Naples. I thought I'd try to go to all of them.'

'Seriously?'

'Totally. Why not? It's as good a way as any of getting to know a place. I'm not going to have a breakdown if I don't get to all of them . . .'

'That's a relief.' Alan spoke for them all.

Lia was not put off. 'Don't tease.'

He visibly glowed as she nudged him.

'But they sounded fun. Why wouldn't we want to try the best Italian ice cream while we're here? Or the best pizza in Naples?'

The car slowed down and turned off the busy main road into a warren of narrow, shady streets. Finally they pulled up in a small square dominated by the heavily ornamented concave facade of a church. Opposite it were a couple of restaurants with outside tables shaded by awnings or huge white parasols.

While Lia insisted on paying – 'No, no, my idea, my treat' – fumbling in her purse to sort out the right change, Sandy got out and stared up at the church. Behind the black railing, the door flanked by two statues was ajar, inviting her into its gloomy interior. 'Shall we go in?'

'Oh, please no,' said Lia, standing beside her. 'One church is enough for one day. We've come for ice creams. Look. This is the other Italy' She pointed towards two modest doorways in a large building occupying the whole of one side of the square. 'There it is!'

'It'll only take a minute,' said Mark, ignoring her. 'Come

'on.' He walked towards the church, beckoning for the others to follow him.

Sandy decided to ignore the imperiousness of the gesture, given that he'd supported her, and followed him. And indeed, they were only there a short time. The interior was breath-taking. She walked alone down the central aisle, her eye drawn to the painted cupola above her head.

'Over here,' Alan said in a loud whisper from a chapel to the right of the altar.

She went over.

He pointed in front of him. 'Have you seen the organ gallery?' He pointed upwards to above the door they'd entered by. 'Extraordinary, isn't it?'

'Too overdone for me,' said Lia, who had caught them up. But she photographed it all the same. 'Seen enough?' She turned back up the aisle.

'OK. We give in.' Mark raised an eyebrow towards Sandy and Alan as if to say 'lost cause'.

Not wanting to collude with him, however irritating Lia could be, Sandy went ahead, making sure her face gave nothing away.

In the ice-cream shop they were confronted by a semi-circular stainless steel counter, clinically clean, covered with stainless steel lids, the names of the different ice creams in Italian and English. Without waiting for the others, Lia ordered immediately, her eyes lit up like a child's on their birthday. '*Una coppetta di tre gusti.*' She held up three fingers to make sure she was understood before pointing at each one. '*Stracciatella, Meringa al Caramello* and *Crema al Cacao con Rum.*'

'Translation, please.' Alan was staring at the counter where all the ice cream was hidden.

'Chocolate, caramel meringue and rum and coconut,' said the Indian shop assistant.

Mark and Sandy ordered, as Alan dithered, finally settling on a tub of pistachio and apricot. '*Gelato d'Amore*,' he read from a poster. 'Even I can translate that. Let's hope.' He winked at Lia.

'In your dreams.' She dipped her plastic spoon into her ice cream, but smiled.

'Now what?' Sandy asked, as they left the shop, the taste of pink grapefruit sharp on her tongue. 'This is fantastic.' She took another scoop. This time of plum. The ice creams were already beginning to melt.

'Down here to the Pantheon and then back to the hotel.' Mark took charge as Alan struggled to find where they were on the map, gave up and followed him.

Sandy couldn't remember when she'd last felt this relaxed. Hot, yes. Tired, yes. But happy. She had no one to dash home to, no one chasing her up, wondering where she was. At last she had no one to answer to except herself. She felt a heavy weight of responsibility lifting from her and a delight in her new liberty taking its place. The smell of Rome pricked in her nostrils, the heat stroked her skin and warmed her feet. She had no cares. She was free for the first time in ages.

When they reached the Pantheon, the black-cobbled square was crowded, the sound of people's voices rising over the splash of water from the fountain. Over everything, the sound of an electric cello being played vigorously in a corner of the piazza. A group of Japanese tourists each carrying an umbrella walked in front of her, eager to get past the security men.

Twenty minutes later they had seen inside the Pantheon and were back in the street.

'I don't know why Elizabeth Gilbert thought it was that special,' groused Lia.

Sandy looked at her, astonished that anyone would not be overcome by such an extraordinary feat of architecture.

'I'm bushed.' Alan removed his hat. 'I need more than an ice cream.'

'A beer? Or a coffee?' Lia looked at him. 'Come on. You don't mind, do you, Sandy? We can work out the best way back to the hotel at the same time.' She headed in the direction of one of the bars at the edge of the square, dodging tourists and two parked police cars. 'This'll do.' She stepped in front of someone to put a hand on the back of a just-vacated chair. 'Mark, can you grab that one over there?'

Sandy held back, watching her take control.

'If you want to go back to the hotel, Sandy, that's fine.'

Something in Lia's voice told Sandy she was being dismissed. She was tempted to walk away but at the same time wasn't quite brave enough to attempt the streets of Rome on her own. Besides, her instinct was to rebel against Lia. 'No, I'd love a coffee.'

After they'd ordered, Lia disappeared inside to find the loo.

'I bet she's quite a handful at work, isn't she?' Alan invited Sandy to confide in him.

'She's fine really.'

'I don't really understand why she's here if she's not interested in the history.' Mark sounded puzzled. 'The language, I suppose. And this Gilbert woman.'

But Sandy wouldn't be drawn. 'What about Alice?' she asked instead. Why was he wandering round Rome with them while his wife was laid up at the hotel?

'She'll be fine after a rest.' He nodded. 'This isn't the first time. Honest. Sometimes she just prefers being on her own.'

'Tell us about you.' Alan took up the reins of the conversation. 'What brings you here on your own?'

Having the attention of them both made Sandy uncomfortable. 'There's not much to say. My mother died recently and it's time for me to get myself back together.'

Alan made a sympathetic noise. 'I know how hard it is.'

'I was Mum's main carer until she died in February,' she explained, shying away from his sympathy. 'I haven't had much time for anything else since then.'

'But she's back on track now, aren't you?' Lia pulled out her chair, scraping it over the black cobbles.

Sandy came to. 'Heavens, yes. I was just explaining why I was here on my own. That's all.' Why was she justifying herself to Lia? 'Has anyone looked at the map?'

'Have you noticed how many people are standing around with maps, trying to work out where they are?' Alan unfolded his. 'Where the hell are we?'

'They're so bloody hard to decipher.' Mark's reading glasses were in danger of slipping off his nose. 'The type's tiny and the buildings all face the wrong way – it's completely disorienting.'

'We're here, look.' Sandy leaned over and pointed. Between them and Trastevere was a maze of streets. 'If we head roughly in this direction we should end up at the pedestrian bridge we saw this morning. And then we're almost home.' She was good with maps, always navigator to Matthew's driver. They got where they wanted to go with never a cross word. He had completely trusted her.

Lia called for the bill. 'You sure?' She still had her map out.

'Looks good to me,' said Alan.

Mark fumbled in his pocket to get the right change, and before anything more was said, they were out in the street again.

'This way then.' Lia set off down a side street.

'Hang on,' Sandy called. 'Isn't it down here?' But Lia was already lost from sight as a tour group separated them.

'I'll go after her,' said Alan, and went in the same direction.

'Let's have another look.' Mark took the map from Sandy. 'There's no need for us all to be lost.' They pored over it together, his head just a touch too close to hers, although she was confident in her reading. 'Perhaps we should look for them,' she suggested.

'No, no.' Mark was quick to disagree. 'They'll find their way. At least Lia can speak the lingo.'

Sandy glanced at him, wondering whether he was joking. But there wasn't a flicker of humour there until he grinned, and she couldn't help smiling back. Walking through the streets was a pleasure for Sandy, despite her tired legs and aching feet. Away from the main tourist spots, the Roman people went about their daily life. The shops were open again. Women carried shopping home in plastic bags. In shady doorways, people stopped to chat. The smell of leather wafted out of the shoe and handbag shops, mixing with cooking smells from the restaurants and the occasional whiff of urine at a dark street corner. They found the bridge quite easily and walked across it to the sound of a busking guitar player. Sandy stopped to look at what Mark dismissed as 'rather generic' watercolours of Rome being sold on the bridge alongside African fabrics and wood carvings. Just to rile him, she bought a small painting of the Pantheon that she liked. Under them flowed the dark green Tiber, its watery smell in their noses.

'Ah, look – there's the Vatican.' Mark pointed to the other side of the river where she could see the dome of a church rising above the other buildings.

After a couple of wrong turns in Trastevere, they eventually found the gate to the hotel and saw Lia and Alan just ahead of them. Lia turned with a triumphant look. 'What kept you?'

Back in her room, Sandy kicked off her walking shoes and socks and lay on the bed, her feet tingling. Her legs ached from the unaccustomed exercise but her head spun with the excitement of it all. What a day.

She looked to see what her mother had written about the Pantheon.

What a miraculous, soaring thing. A beam of sunlight shone through the hole in the dome and hit the floor. You could see the dust dancing in it. Quite beautiful. Mrs R, the Flemings and I had the place to ourselves. Perhaps I'm coming round to what those ancient Romans could do, after all. Tony put his arm round me when he thought no one was looking. I pretended not to notice. But I did. So glad I came.

Sandy too had relished every moment of the heat, the crowds, the graffiti, the sense of chaos. What Matthew had missed. He would have been fascinated by the history, the churches, the vibrancy of the city. She had surprised herself by warming to something so different so quickly. It was as if she had been woken from a deep sleep and stood blinking in the daylight. She took a swig from her bottle of water. Marriage was an odd business. Whatever she and Matthew had done together, they had done his way. The last holiday they'd had, they had gone on the sleeper to Scotland. Neither of them had slept a wink. She had loved him and compromise had seemed the best way to deal with their differences. Looking back, perhaps she should have been a bit more forceful, said what she wanted. Perhaps she should have been more independent. But that wouldn't have done. She and Matthew had been a unit. Everyone said so – and many envied them. Since his death, she had continued their habits where she could, comfortable and reassured by them. Until now.

She wriggled her toes.

Perhaps she should call Steven, let him know she was all right. She owed him that. Taking her phone from the bedside table where she'd left it, she saw she had a couple of texts from Eve and one from Steven.

Mum. Call me. xx

Call me. Can we talk? Xx

What could be so urgent that it couldn't wait until Sandy got home? When she left England, she had been glad to escape her daughter's opinions, which were never less than forceful. Both of them argued for what they believed and neither was good at climbing down. Sandy was hoping a break would be enough to make peace between them between them. But there was to be no break. She dialled Eve's number, but there was no reply. A quick text would let her know she'd tried.

Steven's text read:

Miss you. Can we talk? Steven x

They had seen each other more often since her mother had died. During her illness they had danced around each other, he careful not to be too pushy, she not knowing which way she wanted the relationship to go. Since then they had got closer, despite something still holding her back. That something was Matthew, of course. She preferred staying at Steven's place because, however much she liked him, sex with anyone else felt all wrong in the bed she had shared with Matthew. More than that, she was scared of him disrupting the little routines she had established for herself since Matthew's death. He would want to help by putting out the bins, replacing light bulbs, doing the small garden – all those 'boys' jobs. But she was used to doing them herself, and doing them her way, Matthew's way. When Steven had suggested once or twice that he come over to help with the garden – 'Isn't it too much for you at the moment?' – she felt pushed into a corner, as though she was about to lose the autonomy she was only just beginning to value.

Perhaps she wouldn't phone him. A text would be enough.

Rome completely unexpected. Having a great time exploring.

She had neatly avoided both the question of his missing her, and his need to talk. Was that unfair? She deleted her text.

> Rome completely unexpected. Thrilling. Just about to go down for supper. Talk soon.

That was better. She added Sx. There. It was good to know he was missing her, but how much did she miss him? He would enjoy Rome in all the ways Matthew wouldn't. He and his wife had been well-travelled by all accounts and he thought nothing of going away on his own now. Perhaps she should have asked him to come with her after all. They did get on well. He made her laugh with his silly jokes; and with him, she could talk easily about anything. She sometimes felt he was like a breath of fresh air blowing through her life. At other times, she felt scared. What if committing herself to him was a mistake?

She got off the bed and went over to the wardrobe. She pulled out the case and got out the letter. She could have just thrown it away. Her mother would never know. But she couldn't deny her that dying wish and besides, she was intrigued . . . By the time they reached Naples, she would have found her Italian feet and be more confident about finding Anna Viglieri. That was her hope. And, if she didn't succeed, at least she would have tried.

She turned the envelope over in her hand. The corner of the flap wasn't completely stuck down. She pushed her little finger underneath it and tugged until the paper tore a millimetre or two. Then she stopped herself. This was unfinished business of her mother's. However curious she was, she couldn't read a letter that was not addressed to her. This was the sort of good behaviour she tried to drill into her pupil's heads. 'That's a note for your parents, not for you. Can't you read the name on the label?'

Ashamed, she popped the letter back in the case and returned to her bed. If she was lucky, she could grab a half-hour nap before they were all due to meet for supper. The day had taken it out of her, but her brain had too much going round in it to allow her to sleep. Instead, she lay there, listening to the sounds of the city, wondering what the next day would bring.

7

Alice was lying on her bed, very much at ease. Lunch had put her in a much better mood, making her feel more loving towards Mark. Watching the man on the next table, she had followed his example and ordered a glass of the lightest white wine to go with her pasta. If it weren't for her foot, the idea of an afternoon in Rome on her own would be appealing. Mark wouldn't worry about her. She knew from experience that he would be getting to know the group, making sure they were all his friends by the end of the day. He knew she could look after herself; after all, that was what she often did while he was away at academic conferences or working late. Within a long marriage, independence was a thing to be treasured: the gift of being allowed to be yourself.

But before she could do anything she had to go back to the hotel to change her shoes. When she eventually got back to her room, the bed looked so inviting, her feet were so sore that she couldn't resist. She had made herself a cup of tea – she never travelled anywhere without a stash of Yorkshire teabags – and lay down. Mark would be back soon enough and she would make things better between them.

She was woken from her nap by an impatient rap at the door. She got up to answer it, catching the faint smell of beer on his breath as Mark came into the room.

He chucked his panama and satchel onto the space where Alice had been lying then threw himself after them. 'God, it's hot!' He lay there, like a pinned insect, legs and arms splayed.

'Nice afternoon?' Alice moved her book from the bed to the table.

'I suppose so.' He shut his eyes. 'We went to a quite remarkable church together then Lia dragged Sandy, Alan and me off for ice cream near the Pantheon. I can't make out those two women. As for Alan . . . I'd have been better off on my own really. Or with you,' he added as an afterthought.

'I rather like Sandy,' Alice sat in the chair. 'I'm not so sure about Lia.'

'All that bloody photography. Never stops snapping. Why can't she just look and remember?' Mark said as he took off his shoes, then his socks, which he waved around as if drying them.

'Darling. Do you have to?' Alice put her hand to her nose.

'Sorry.' The socks fell to the floor and he lay back again with his eyes shut and fell asleep. Alice sighed. She would make this work. Remembering the children always made her focus. The boys had already been left by one mother, she couldn't do that to them again. *But they are in their twenties*, a voice inside her protested. *It's hardly the same.* By the end of her first afternoon with the boys, they'd been warming towards her, Henry even leaving his father's side to go with her to see the tigers while Mark and Patrick went to the birds of prey. That small trusting hand in hers had given Alice a new and completely unexpected sense of purpose. When, only weeks later, Mark proposed to her, she'd had no hesitation in accepting, despite all her friends' misgivings.

Within weeks, she had given in her notice to devote her time to these three needy individuals. None of her friends could believe what she was doing. 'All those years building your career and now you're going to throw it all away for a man you've only just met.' Katie had been incensed. 'Can't you take it slowly? There must be a reason why his wife left him. Aren't you suspicious?'

'Nobody's more surprised than me,' said Alice. 'But I know it's the right thing to do.'

Katie's face showed she was not convinced.

Alice continued. 'He's been devastated. And they need me.' She felt this as strongly as a religious calling. She was needed and she had no alternative but to respond to that need. The snort was enough to show what Katie thought of that. But for the first time, Alice believed she could make a worthwhile difference to someone else's life. She had never really believed in love at first sight until she met Mark. From the moment they met, she had wanted to wrap up her life with his. What she'd failed to take into account was the effect Sally's abandoning her family would have on Mark himself. She had left him with an unquenchable need to prove to himself that he was an attractive and desirable man who didn't deserve to be left.

How naive she had been. Alice could see that now. But that didn't mean it was too late to put their relationship on a new footing.

'Did you have a good lunch?' she asked when he finally woke up, showered and emerged from the bathroom, towel wrapped round his waist, hair flattened against his head.

'Not bad. Gilly talked too much but then redeemed herself when she took us to the church. You really did miss something there. You should have stayed with us.'

'I'm sorry I lost it. The heat got the better of me. And my feet.'

'That's OK.' He pulled her to him.

'Actually,' she confessed. 'I had an excellent lunch . . .'

'Where?'

'No idea. I just found a restaurant that looked nice, and it was. On my way back here, there was a busking oboist and I stopped to dabble my hands in a fountain . . .'

'Good.' He kissed her as he pulled her down on the bed, his towel coming unhitched at the same time.

'Have we got time?' She was so aware of how much weight she had put on since they first met. He used to tease her about her love of food and cooking, now not so much.

'Of course.' He nuzzled her breast.

She felt a quiver of desire and gave herself up to its pull as they fell into the familiar pattern of their lovemaking.

Afterwards they lay back, equanimity restored. 'I'm sorry you missed out on the afternoon. There was a beautiful fresco, and the Pantheon was magnificent, if packed.' He pushed his hair back off his face. 'What did you have for lunch?'

'Pasta with garlic and chilli. Very delicious it was too.'

He looked at her, weighing her up. 'Pasta again?'

'I'm not sticking to my diet when we're on holiday. I can't resist Italian food.' Trying to lose weight at home was hard enough but here it was impossible.

His raised eyebrow said it all.

She dug her nails into the palm of her hand so hard it hurt. 'I'll be back on it as soon as we get back.' Though why she had to justify herself to him . . . Once, she'd had prominent hip bones; now they were hidden under a menopausal layer of fat.

He made a tiny noise as if to say he didn't really believe it. 'What are we doing this evening?'

'Gilly has organised tables somewhere.'

'Tables? Good. At least we won't have to all sit together again. It's impossible to talk to Peter without Brit butting in and those two guys almost finish each other's sentences. And Lia won't stop talking but at least she's quite entertaining.'

'I thought you didn't like her,' Alice reminded him.

'A chap can change his mind.' He sat up and swung his legs off the bed. 'I'm going to get dressed.'

'You judged too soon. The same might go for the others.'

'I don't think so. My instinct's usually pretty good.'

*

When the time came for supper, to Sandy's relief Alice invited her to join them. Gilly had already corralled Lia and Alan to sit with her at an outside table in a restaurant on the edge of a small piazza, and the last thing she wanted was to have to sit with them. The night was warm. The restaurant was busy but the tables were far enough apart to give them some privacy. Once they'd ordered and Mark had a glass of wine in front of him, he began to relax.

'No word from Pip today. That's got to be a good thing.'

'Our daughter who's about to have a gap year,' explained Alice. 'But she can't make up her mind what she wants to do.'

'Mine's past that stage, thank goodness. She lives in London now. She's in brand management.' There was a pause as she waited for them to say something. 'Whatever that is. I've no idea.'

They all laughed.

'These twenty-first-century jobs,' said Mark, raising his glass. 'They all talk a completely different language now.'

'That's the ivory tower of academia for you,' Alice said. 'Keeps you sheltered. But it's hard when they go. I couldn't stop crying when Henry left. He's the eldest. And then when Patrick went, I bought a puppy to keep us company. Buffy the French bulldog.'

'I warned her.' Mark shook his head. 'But would she listen? That animal rules the roost now.'

'Matthew didn't like pets. However much we pleaded, he stood his ground. Once a cat belonging to one of Eve's friends had kittens. She brought one home without asking and he insisted she took it back.' He had been quite resistant to the sweetness of the kitten, to Eve's sobs and to her reasoning. They hadn't spoken for days after that. 'He said it was cruel to keep animals inside.'

'I don't think Buffy would agree with him. She's one of the most spoilt creatures on the planet.'

'That was the only thing we disagreed on.' Sandy leaped to his defence, having painted such a dark portrait of him. 'He had the kindest heart.'

'What happened?' Alice looked sympathetic.

'A stroke. He collapsed at St Pancras while he was waiting for a train home. It sounds so mundane now.'

'How awful.' Alice's face showed how shocked and sympathetic she was.

Mark went to pour them all another glass of wine.

'It was. But at least it was quick.' Sandy had frequently consoled herself with this thought ever since. Matthew would have hated to linger on in the way her mother had. He had always been in a rush to get through life, to get things done. He had approached death in the same way.

'Hard though.' Alice touched Mark's arm, stopping him filling his glass to the top. 'You've had a rough time.'

They waited as the waiter put their food in front of them. Two plates of lamb chops, and grilled veal for Sandy.

'But things are looking better now.' Were they? Really? She moved her knife and fork so they were neatly aligned on either side of her plate. 'I'm enjoying it here, and looking forward to Naples.'

'It'll be our first time there,' said Alice.

'Speak for yourself.' Mark sounded put out.

'But that was years ago. I bet you don't remember anything about it.'

'True.' The corners of his eyes crinkled as he smiled in agreement.

'Actually . . .' Sandy spoke before she had even thought what she was going to say. 'I need to try to track someone down there. An old friend of my mother's. I found a letter before she died and I promised I'd try to deliver it, but I've no idea where to start. If you wanted to find someone who lived in Naples – what would you do?' She hadn't expected to be asking

73

for their help. Including other people in such a personal search hadn't been part of her plan but Rome had got to her, reached into her heart and warmed it.

'What have you got?' Mark was looking interested.

'Just a letter addressed to a woman I've never heard of with her name and "Naples" written on the envelope. But I've no idea who she is. At least, she's mentioned in a travel journal I found from almost sixty years ago but it doesn't give me any clues. I've brought the letter with me so I can look for her when we get there.'

Mark looked doubtful. 'Didn't you ask who she is?'

Sandy felt a rush of grief as those last days with her mother, while she lost her fight for life, came back to her. 'Of course I did. But Mum was so stoked up on morphine by then. All she said was "Find her" – at least I think that's what she said. It probably sounds daft to you, but I promised I would, so I've got to try.'

'Of course you have,' said Alice. 'I completely understand. But if you can't trace her, couldn't you just post it, and hope for the best?'

'Without an address?' Scorn and despair registered in Mark's voice. 'That's not going to work.'

'What would you suggest then?'

Mark pushed his specs back up his nose. 'Isn't there an online phone book for every city. Did you try that?'

'I didn't even think of that.' Sandy made a face that acknowledged her failure.

'Well, I could check that for you,' offered Mark. 'I've brought my iPad.'

'That's kind but I'd rather try myself. If I get stuck, perhaps...' Sandy let the sentence trail away. All she really wanted at this stage was suggestions that she could follow up on her own.

Mark nodded once, as if he understood, and leaned back in his chair.

'What does the letter say?' Alice asked. 'Is it important?'

'Oh, I haven't opened it.' Sandy looked shocked. 'If Mum wanted me to read it, I'm sure she would have shown me.'

'But she'll never know.' Mark raised his glass, his red wine glinting in the light.

Affronted, Sandy sat straight. 'That's not the point.'

'Aren't you tempted? Alice took a mouthful of her lamb, shutting her eyes in pleasure.

'Of course. But it would be such a betrayal.' Sandy looked down at her hands, her fingers twisted together. 'You probably think that's ridiculous.' She stole a glance at Mark to see if he agreed.

'No it's not. Not at all.' Alice jumped in first. 'Except that there might be something in it that would give you a clue how to find her. After all, you haven't much time. We're only there for a week.'

'I know. I should have done something before I came but I had so much on my plate. But I'll start with the phone book. I don't know why I didn't think of that.'

'You've had a lot on your mind. There's always a lot to do after a death, so you have to put off what you can,' said Alice, laying her knife and fork on the plate. 'I remember that from when Dad died. Sorting out his estate was a nightmare.'

'Perhaps.' Sandy was grateful to be given the excuse.

'Now, are we going to have pudding?' Alice took the menu from the waiter.

'I think I'll have another glass of wine.' Mark drained his glass.

'Is that a good idea?' Alice passed him the menu, which he put on the table without looking at it.

'It's an excellent idea,' he said firmly.

Alice's look of disapproval evaporated as she turned her attention back to the menu. 'Sandy?'

'Yes, I am.' She was keen to get over this hiccup between them. 'The tiramisu sounds amazing.'

'I like her.' Alice said later, as she and Mark strolled down one of the narrow streets. Everyone was out enjoying the evening. If they weren't walking, they were standing outside bars, clogging the street, or relaxing at the many outdoor tables of restaurants. Lights shone in high-up windows, the soft glow of the street lamps falling on the dark cobbles, the street sellers out in force with their paintings, scarves, sunglasses and hats. From somewhere the sounds of a jazz trumpet floated up into the night. 'I wonder who this woman is and if she'll find her.'

'I shouldn't think so.' Mark draped his arm across her shoulders the way he always used to when they went walking.

Alice hesitated then put her arm around his waist.

'I'll offer to help her again tomorrow though.' He stopped to look at a shop selling leather jackets. 'I like a good mystery.'

'I felt sorry for her. She seems a lonely soul.'

'Mmm. I wonder how she really gets on with Lia. The afternoon I spent with them both was odd.'

A faint alarm bell rang somewhere in Alice's brain. 'How do you mean?'

'There was definitely tension there. I got the impression that there's little love lost between them.'

They came to the central square where a crowd had formed round a fire-dancer who swung fireballs round him as he whirled about to wild music blasting from a nearby speaker. They stopped to watch.

'How do you mean?' She clapped as the dance came to an end, before the music started up again.

'Nothing I could put my finger on. Just a feeling. Perhaps

it's just that they're very different.' He took a couple of steps forward to get a better view.

Meeting new travelling companions was always fascinating, Alice thought, craning her neck to see the finale. As the crowd dispersed, most of them rushing away to avoid putting money in the entertainer's hat, Alice and Mark began to walk back the way they came.

'I was thinking about Pip.' Alice had been wondering about encouraging the Australia idea. 'If this job's so awful, I wonder whether we shouldn't help her. I could say something next time we speak.'

'What? Give her more cash?' Mark stopped dead. 'No. Absolutely not. She can't expect us to bail her out whenever she doesn't like something. Support, yes. Cash, no. That goes against everything we've encouraged her to be.'

'I just thought...'

'She's got to learn to tough it out and take the rough with the smooth. Just like we did.'

Every cell in her body rebelled against Mark. He had such firm principals when it came to their children, he could be intransigent. But... but, she knew better than to argue when he'd had one drink too many. That's when he'd dig his heels in. As they came to the gate to the hotel, she realised how much she was looking forward to getting to bed.

8

Nobody goes to bed early here – apart from Mrs R. But the streets are full of life and excitement after dark when it's cooler. It feels quite risqué. Someone pinched my bottom yesterday! I screamed and after that Tony walked behind me and Fleur. Italian men are very good-looking but very naughty! I think Fleur might be getting a little bit annoyed with me always going out with them... I don't think Tony agrees!

Miriam Mackenzie, May 12th 1952 – Rome

'I thought you were avoiding me.'

Sandy closed her eyes and lay back against her pillow, the phone pressed to her ear, listening to Steven laugh. She pictured his wide face, the nose broken during a school rugby match, brown eyes, lined forehead, full head of grey hair swept back like an elderly lion's mane. 'Of course I wasn't. It's been busy.'

'So what's it like? Do you like them?' The slight burr in his voice gave away his Bristol origins.

'Everybody's still a bit wary of each other. But you'll never guess who's here.' She paused to add dramatic effect. 'Lia French. From school.'

There was another rumble of laughter in her ear. 'I'm sorry, I shouldn't laugh.'

'Don't be. You were right and I'm glad I'm here. We're both on best behaviour but all the same... well, it's difficult. She makes me feel awkward and, however friendly she pretends to be, I don't really trust her.'

'Such bad luck. Is there anyone else you can chum up with?'

'There's a couple I like. About our age. He's an academic. Philosophy, I think. I'm not sure about him but she and I get on. As for the others... well, it's early days but there are two gay men who seem fun. And there's Alan who's a bit of a creep.'

'Not giving you any trouble, is he?' An edge of something had crept into his voice.

'Don't be daft. I think I'm just about old enough to look after myself.' Now it was her turn to laugh.

'So tell me what you've been doing.' He knew her well enough now to pick up on her reluctance to elaborate and not press her on it, always respecting her wish to keep herself to herself. He understood that this was her adventure.

As she began to go through what she'd seen so far, she followed the pattern on her skirt with a finger. Having someone interested in what she was doing felt good. He knew Rome even better than she realised and had something to say about everywhere she mentioned. Then, 'Have you been to the Villa Borghese yet?'

'I think that's tomorrow.' She picked up the schedule on her bedside table and began flipping through. 'No, day after.'

'The Bernini statues are second to none. I can't wait to hear what you think.'

She remembered how he'd circled his favourite places in the guidebook, eager to share them with her.

'Have you been in touch with Eve?' His attempt to toss this in casually was like a warning flare going up.

Immediately she was on the defensive. 'Why? She's called a couple of times but didn't answer when I called back. I'm going to try again in a minute.'

'Good.' He was a man who preferred calm waters. 'Never go away on a row.'

'We'll be fine.' She sounded firmer than she felt. Eve was her daughter and they could sort out passing difficulties without his interference. They always had before, brought together as they had been by Matthew's death.

'Don't be angry.'

'I'm not.' She tried to explain. 'Only I'd rather you left us to it. I wouldn't tell you how to treat your children.' Steven's son had been killed in Afghanistan but he had two difficult daughters who had caused him upset ever since he and his wife had divorced some years earlier. The youngest, Tammy, barely spoke to or saw him, while the oldest, Tara, had no compunction about telling him how great the guy that their mother had subsequently met and married was. For 'great' read 'rich', thought Sandy. How easy it was to choose to spend Christmas in the Caribbean with your mother and her new husband and how hurtful to reject Christmas with your father in the small English cottage that was his home now he'd retired from his architectural practice.

'I know. I'm sorry. It's none of my business. But I know you'd be happier with it sorted out.' He was absolutely right.

'Don't worry.' She lifted her left hand and studied it. There was a dent around the base of her ring finger where her wedding ring had sat until the day before she left for Rome. Her hand looked naked without it. She had removed it on a whim, left it by the kitchen sink and forgotten to put it back. Her idea that coming away for two weeks would liberate her from all the concerns she had left behind had been pure fantasy. They had just come with her. Lia being here had wrecked her plans for a reinvention of herself, and calls from home just reminded her of the things she had yet to sort out. 'I love hearing from you.'

'I'll call tomorrow, then.'

They said their goodbyes, perhaps fonder than usual. His call had made her realise how much she missed his easy company. While she had never wanted to be totally reliant on anyone

– not even Matthew, close as they were – knowing she had someone looking out for her was reassuring. She saw that now. Without Steven, she had no one to laugh with. She missed that too. Since her mother's death, she had felt as if she had reached some sort of a turning point in her life but had yet to identify the paths open to her. Her continuing sense of loyalty to both Matthew and her mother weighed heavily, yet she hesitated before an independent, liberated future.

As she flicked aimlessly through the raft of Italian TV channels, she thought back to supper. Surprising how easy she had found it to unburden herself to Mark and Alice. She had been so much more forthcoming than usual but there was something about they way they listened, Mark especially, that had invited her confidence. He had seemed genuinely concerned. And Alice felt like a kindred spirit already. She was sure they were going to be friends. She hadn't meant to mention the letter to anyone, didn't want the entire group hanging on to her mystery, but surely Alice and Mark would keep her confidence. She would say something to them in the morning.

Propped up against the pillows, she took her iPad and googled 'Naples Italy phonebook'. Up came various ways of exploring the Neapolitan white pages. She linked to a page where she could insert a name. She typed in Anna Viglieri. The little wheel spun at the top of her screen while nothing happened. She held her breath as the screen changed. Up came the message – *Spiacenti. Nessun risultato trovato per Viglieri a Napoli (NA).* She didn't need anyone to translate to understand no results had been found. Her disappointment took her by surprise.

She switched off and picked up her phone, turning it over in her hand. Would Eve still be up? Her daughter's job meant long hours and demanding clients so she was always exhausted by the time she got home. Eve picked up immediately.

'Mum. At last! I've been trying to get hold of you.'

'I know. I've tried to ring you. This isn't too late?'

'Not at all. Are you having a good time?'

'Yes, wonderful. I never dreamed Rome would be so exciting. So different and so exhilarating – much more than I expected. But why did you call? Is something the matter?'

'No, not the matter exactly. Remember what we were talking about when I saw you last week?'

'Of course.' Why did she feel suddenly nervous?

'There's something I've got to tell you that can't wait till you're back. I'm too excited.'

'Go on then.' Sandy pushed herself up on her pillows and waited out the next short silence.

'Jen's pregnant!'

Pregnant! In her wildest dreams, Sandy had not prepared herself for this. 'Really! That's fantastic.' She sipped her whisky. Why was Eve so impulsive? Far better to have waited to break the news when Sandy got home.

Eve's voice broke into her thoughts. 'I know what you're thinking. You said as much when we last talked. Children need a father. But it'll be OK, you'll see. We're so happy and I want you to be too. You're going to be a granny!'

A granny! This was not at all how she'd thought it would be. 'Gosh. That's wonderful. When's it due?' She did her best to sound thrilled but she was struggling to get her head round the idea. She should have known that Eve would take no notice of her reservations. Children needed a mother and father. Sandy could never have brought up Eve without Matthew. He had provided the right balance to her mothering in a way she believed only a man could do. This might be old-fashioned of her but she had learned through experience. When she was flapping over something, he'd weigh in, always calm and considered. 'Pick your battles, Sandy. Whether she wears her school uniform to the concert is unimportant beside the fact that she's taking part in it at all. Leave her to make the decision about what she wears.'

It had been hard when Eve had told her she was gay – just ten minutes before they were due to meet her 'friend' Jen. Not that she was entirely surprised by the fact, just by the impetuous way in which it was announced. She liked Jen a lot. She was older than Eve by about ten years, with a steady head, and clearly adored her daughter. She didn't have to pretend her pleasure that Eve had found happiness – that's all she and Matthew had wanted for her – but secretly she had worried that Eve was too young to settle into a long-term relationship. She had been disappointed, however selfish she realised she was being, that she would never see her daughter married in the conventional way or have children of her own. But of course she had been wrong. Jen and Eve had married three years ago, even though Eve, aged twenty-eight, still seemed so young to Sandy. And now they were having a baby.

'Is that all you can say? Aren't you pleased for us?'

Sandy could hear Eve's disappointment.

'I am, of course I am,' she said hurriedly but it was too late.

'After what we said the other night, I thought you'd change your mind about children needing fathers. After all, plenty don't have them and end up far happier than being in some bloodless hetero marriage.' Sandy froze. She couldn't mean her and Matthew, could she? But Eve was still talking. 'I really thought you'd update your views. I thought I'd explained where we were coming from so that you'd get it. I knew Jen was pregnant then but it was too early to say. I was just testing the water. Now I wish I hadn't called.'

She sounded so let down that Sandy felt awful for not being the mother Eve wanted her to be. But how she had tried. 'I'm glad you did. I'm thrilled for you, of course I am. I just wasn't expecting it. How . . . I mean . . . Who . . .'

An exasperated sigh blew down the phone. 'Who's the father, you mean?'

'Well, yes.' This was awful.

'It's not an anonymous donor, if that's what you mean.'

Sandy shrank at the hostility in her daughter's voice. 'So, who . . .'

'Ian. He and Daniel are old friends of Jen's. We're going to share the parenting. So, even better than your traditional hetero scenario, this baby's going to be loved and looked after by two mums and two dads.'

'That sounds wonderful,' she said. But how on earth would this work? She had read about similar arrangements in the paper, but she had never thought she would be part of one. No one else she knew was in the same boat. Her life had been so sheltered. Her own grandparents had never been on the scene, and her parents had packed her off to boarding school when she was seven. 'As you haven't got brothers and sisters, you'll make lots of friends there,' her mother had encouraged her. Quite wrongly, as it turned out. All it had done was distance her from the little family she had. As for eight grandparents! That seemed an unmanageable number to her.

'It is. We've talked about it for so long but never dreamed it would happen so quickly. It could have been me.' Her excitement was back. 'We both tried, assuming only one of us would get pregnant. And that's just what happened.'

'What about her job?' She tried to sound interested, not concerned or panicked.

Eve laughed. 'Is that all you can think of? She'll take a year off and then we'll see. This is going to be the best thing. Please be pleased for us.'

'Of course I am.' Sandy stared ahead at the painting of a baroque fountain in a roman piazza on the wall opposite the end of her bed. 'I just wasn't expecting it.'

'I know it's over the phone but I thought if I told you now,

84

you'd get used to the idea before we see you. Dad would be pleased.'

That hurt. 'I'm used to it already...' Not quite true. '...And I can't wait to see you both.'

'Really?'

'Yes, really.' They ended the call promising each other to speak again soon, with Sandy sending her love to Jen. After she'd hung up, Sandy lay quite still. She'd grown up believing that every child needed a devoted mother and father. Having two of each sounded like a recipe for parental disagreement and disaster. While her own parents were distant, they at least had been there and done their best. She and Matthew had rarely disagreed over Eve, both of them adamant she would go to their local school after Sandy's unhappy experience of a minor boarding school stuck in the depths of Derbyshire. He was more lenient than she had been but that was because she had seen the result of careless parenting from all her years of teaching. And experienced it herself. Firm and consistent, that's what was best. But Eve was her only child and – whatever Eve might think – she meant everything to Sandy. All she wanted was her happiness. She couldn't help thinking ahead – that was her nature. Jen was having the baby but what rights would Eve have if they ever split up. What custody arrangements could be made if Eve was not biologically related to the child? Perhaps she was protected by their marriage. But was she as old-fashioned and narrow-minded as Eve accused her of being? She punched the pillow as Matthew's voice came to her. *Live in the present, my love. There's nothing you can do about the past or the future.* If only she could.

She got off the bed and grabbed the guidebook. Her room felt unbearably claustrophobic. Being alone with so many muddled thoughts going round her head was not where she wanted to be. Outside her room, her flipflops slapped against the floor tiles as she walked to the stairs. To her disappointment, the bar was empty. The others must still be out or have gone to bed. Peter and Brit had gone up when she did, but Lia had inveigled Alan out on the pretext of finding some club she'd read about while Alice and Mark had gone for a stroll. She wished she had accepted their invitation to go with them.

The waiter was by her side almost the moment she sat down. Without thinking she ordered herself a brandy. *To celebrate*, she excused herself. A baby! A grandchild! The thought gave her a thrill of excitement until she thought of the circumstances again. Why hadn't Eve taken things more slowly? She wondered about Ian and Daniel: who they were and how committed they would really be to the child. She wondered about Jen's parents and their reaction. Would there even be room for her, after all this? The brandy made her cough.

'Ah, a secret drinker.' Alan was pulling out a chair at the table. 'Mind if I join you?'

'Not at all.' At that moment, Sandy was happy to be joined by anyone.

'We bumped into Mark and Alice so Lia's with them. My legs have had it so I thought I'd come back. Delighted to find you here.'

She waited while Alan ordered himself a brandy too.

'It's cooler here, thank God.'

'Where have you been?'

'No idea.' He laughed so his polo shirt rucked up to reveal his fleshy stomach. 'Just wandering, soaking up the atmosphere, looking for a club that didn't seem to exist. It's buzzing out there. Did you go out?'

'No. I wanted to call my daughter.'

'If you're unsure about going on your own, I'd be happy to escort you.' He tipped his head to one side, his hand out as if he expected her to take it.

She picked up her glass, wishing she had the protection of her wedding ring. 'That's very kind, but not tonight.'

'Please don't think I meant anything... well, you know...
by that.' His face flushed a deep red. 'I was just trying to—'

'No, no, of course. I mean I didn't.' Sandy wished she'd
stayed in her room after all.

'I mean I'd love it if you did but...' He stopped and looked
at her so intently that Sandy had to look away.

'Still up?' To Sandy's relief, Alice pulled out a chair and sat
down. Lia hovered behind her.

'I think I'll go up.' Mark shot a look at his wife. 'Early start.
Beauty sleep.' He laughed.

Sandy noticed Alice stiffen as she spoke. 'Yes, but we're on
holiday. I'll be up in a minute.'

Alan drained his glass. 'Wise man. I need some shut-eye.'

'Me too,' said Lia. 'We'll find that club next time.'

'Thank God,' Sandy said under her breath as they left the
courtyard.

'Have I rescued you?'

'He thought I thought he'd made a pass.' Sandy grinned.
'Look at me! As if.'

'There's nothing wrong with you.' Alice raised her bottle
of water and chinked it with Sandy's glass. 'Cheers. But I can
think of other people I'd rather have make a pass at me. But
did he?'

'I don't know.' Sandy grinned. 'Is asking someone to go for
a walk at night a pass?'

'It might be.' Alice leaned back in her chair. 'At our age. It's
been so long, I don't know. What about you?'

Sandy tried to remember Steven's first tentative suggestion
that they went to the cinema. 'It's been a couple of years.'

'So there is a man in your life?' Alice's eyes lit up with interest.

'Not so much in, as on the edge.' Was that the right way to
describe things? She felt bad relegating him like this.

'Trying to get in?' Alice smiled.

'You could put it like that.' But that didn't describe the situation at all.

'And you're not sure? Sorry. Am I being too nosy?'

'No, no. It's good to have someone to talk to.' She instinctively trusted Alice and felt able to confide in her. 'And you're right, I'm not sure. Steven's a lovely man, but I don't know that I really want a man at all, however lovely. Matthew was enough for me.'

'Your husband?'

'Mmmm.' Sandy ran her finger round the rim of her glass. 'We just sort of fitted together. I can't imagine anyone else like that.'

'Maybe you have to compromise. That's what I've learned. Marriage is bloody hard to get right and compromise isn't necessarily a bad thing, is it? Aren't you lonely on your own?'

Sandy longed to shout, *Yes! Every day I wish I had someone to share things with, but I don't know how to let them in. I've built a protective wall round myself that's impossible to bring down.* Instead she said, 'Not really. I'm used to it now.'

'You don't sound it. Being together isn't always easy either. Mark and I have had our ups and downs.' She looked at her watch. 'But I think we're all right now.' There was a note of uncertainty in her voice.

'But you seem so together.' Sandy downed the last of her brandy.

'We're just out of a bad patch. Maybe I'll tell you another time, because we probably should be sensible and call it a day, tempted as I am to sit up for longer.'

'Deal. Let's get that beauty sleep!'

9

'This is a zoo.' Lia complained as she stumbled into Alice, shunted by a tour leader whose attention was on gathering his flock around him. The others were ahead of them. Gilly's stick with the limp red scarf knotted on top was aloft in a corner of the gallery. Lia had said the name of every gallery of the Vatican Museum out loud as they entered, rolling her tongue round the syllables. '*Galleria Chiaramonti*', '*Sala degli Animali*' and so on until they'd arrived at the '*Galleria degli Arazzi*'. That was the biggest test of all but she managed it, loudly. They pushed their way against the tide of visitors until they reached to the others.

'I never thought it would be like this.' Sandy came to stand beside her. 'So many people. It's like the one time Matthew took me to an Arsenal match. We couldn't go backwards if we tried.'

On they went, pushing through until they reached a set of much smaller rooms adorned with detailed frescoes.

'Is this the . . .' But Lia didn't finish her question thanks to Peter who came to her rescue. 'One of the Raphael Rooms? Yes. His technique is unmistakable. Look at the . . .'

But Lia had turned away to carry on photographing. Brit smiled at her husband and slipped her arm through his as though to say 'mine'. She was as cool and elegant as usual. Her long peppermint green sleeveless shift was the sort of shapeless garment that would make Alice look like a sack of potatoes, but Brit looked as if she'd just walked straight out of *Vogue*. Not even walking with this crowd had made her break into a sweat.

Mark and Sandy were leaning forward, the only two who were listening closely to what Massimo was saying about the School of Athens as he pointed out one scholar after another in one of the paintings. 'And there, in the corner, is Raphael himself.'

'In the black hat?' asked Sandy, apparently as intrigued as Mark in what they were being shown.

'They get on well, don't they?' Lia stood right behind Alice and spoke so quietly Alice barely heard her over the hushed murmur of the crowds.

'Sorry? Who do you mean?'

Lia's face was expressionless. 'I'm just saying that they seem to have found a friend in one another. Same interests. I noticed that yesterday, when you went back to the hotel.' She lifted her camera, focused on them. Click. Her smile was mean. 'I'll email my photos to anyone who wants them.'

Alice wasn't sure what Lia was getting at. 'They're both interested in history and fine art. It's nice that Mark's met someone who can share that with him.' Why was she justifying his behaviour? *Because of what he's done*, came the ready answer. But Lia couldn't know anything about that and Sandy was much older than the other women Alice knew about, so hardly his type. Besides she trusted Sandy, knew she'd found a friend in her. Breathe. Remember he's learned his lesson. He won't do it again. 'I like seeing these things too but I'm not always quite as into the fine detail as they obviously are.'

They pressed on, carried by the tide of people through the contemporary art galleries and finally into the main attraction: the Sistine Chapel. As they passed a couple of guards Alice couldn't help watching Mark and Sandy. They were shoulder to shoulder, staring up at the ceiling, pointing, exclaiming as the crowd pushed them forward into the chapel. All at once, there was a loud 'Shhh' broadcast over a loudspeaker, followed by an announcement forbidding the taking of photos. For a moment the chattering stopped then gradually increased in volume again. Alice wished she could sit on one of the wall seats running down either side of the chapel, but the occupants were so squashed together there wasn't room for any more. No one looked as if they were going to move. Alice's legs were aching and the blister from yesterday was stinging again, despite the plaster and her sensible shoes.

The breath on her cheek turned out to be Alan's. 'Is this the Sistine Chapel, then?'

She looked at him. She might not have Mark's finely honed interest in things cultural, but even she knew why everyone was staring up at the ceiling. 'Yes,' she said trying not to make her incredulity at his ignorance show. 'This is one of the greatest things we'll see in Rome,' she said, hoping that was enough to shut him up.

'Yeah?' He rubbed the back of his neck. 'I prefer a painting you can get up close and personal with. See the detail properly.'

Gilly's red scarf was moving beyond the screen into the less crowded section at the back of the chapel. Alice edged towards her, marvelling at the ceiling at the same time. Lia slung her camera over her shoulder and headed towards the exit without a glance at anything else. If she couldn't photograph it, she wasn't interested.

'Amazing, isn't it?' said Sandy, who came up behind her. 'But so crowded. I can't help thinking what it would be like being here on your own. That would be the way to really appreciate it. It makes me think of the time Matthew and I visited the Sandham Memorial Chapel. Have you been there?'

Alice shook her head.

'It's an amazing small chapel in Hampshire where the walls are covered with paintings by Stanley Spencer. Not as grand as this, but all the same...'

Alice had never heard of Stanley Spencer but watched as Sandy's eyes half-closed as she took herself back.

'We were completely on our own there, just the two of us together with these extraordinary visionary paintings. I've never forgotten it. It was very special.' Her voice caught as she turned away before Alice could say anything.

On the way out of the Vatican they had to run a gamut of retail opportunities. There was everything any self-respecting tourist could desire, from postcards and rosaries to fridge magnets, aprons and spectacle cleaners, even miniaturised copies of the most famous statues they had seen. Alice lingered by a scaled-down copy of the Nile, the great river god swarming with cherubs and river animals. What would you do with that? Ship it back and put it in a corner of the garden? Ridiculous. She followed the others down the spiral staircase that took them to the final exit and the street outside.

Outside, the heat was smothering. She unscrewed her bottle and sipped the lukewarm water. Peter and Brit were sheltering in the shade of Brit's umbrella. She was one of the few women who could turn a man's black umbrella into a fashion statement.

'Wasn't that marvellous?' Mark said to Sandy as they joined Alice. 'I was last here when I was hitching round Europe in the seventies. What a difference the restoration's made.'

Sandy looked dazed, as if the whole experience had left her speechless. 'It was hard to stop and really appreciate things, but I'm glad I've been there.'

'Everyone with us?' Gilly was rounding them up, red ribbon fluttering. Her face was flushed, even her ponytail had lost its swing. 'I know it's hot but we've just got time for the Basilica. Follow me.'

Brushing off the touts offering bottles of cold water, hats, paintings, scarves, they made their way back along the wall of the Vatican, pausing for a second to stare at the uniformed Swiss guards in an entrance.

What a motley crew they made, all except Brit who floated along as if her feet barely touched the ground, umbrella aloft.

Mark and Alice followed her and Peter while the rest of them trailed behind. Alice felt a little guilty when she looked back to see that Alan had caught up with Sandy. She was tempted to carry out a rescue mission but perhaps she was misreading the situation. An archway gave on to a large keyhole-shaped piazza on one side of which was the massive façade of St Peter's. Mark took her hand, humming under his breath, then let go as Lia caught them up.

The vast interior of St Peter's was dark and cool after the midday heat. Sandy made her escape to explore for herself but this was all too dark, too busy, too overblown for her. She couldn't help thinking of the churches that she and Matthew had enjoyed so much when they went to Wales. Each one so modest by comparison, but every bit as beautiful in their own way. She walked dutifully round all the highlights until she finally stopped in front of Michelangelo's *Pietà*.

Mrs R was so moved when she saw the Pietà, she had to sit down. I had to hide my laughing. It's exquisite, I can see that. Her face especially. But nothing made out of marble would move me like that. I have to confess I was dying to get back to the hotel where I hoped to be back in time to catch the others...

'Beautiful, isn't she?' Mark was at her side again. 'Are you all right?'

To her embarrassment Sandy realised tears were running silently down her cheeks. She brushed them away and took a step to the side, not wanting to be disturbed. Mark had walked beside her through the Vatican, and hadn't stopped talking the whole way. He was well-informed and fascinating but reaching the Sistine Chapel, which demanded silence even if it didn't get it, had come as such a relief. Now, all she wanted was to immerse herself in the sadness and devastation on the Virgin's face without having to be polite or to respond to him. All the emotions of motherhood were laid bare right there in front of her. She imagined the pain of losing one's own child – something too terrible to contemplate.

'I understand,' said Alice softly at her other side as she guided Mark away.

When they finally exited into the sunshine, Gilly liberated them to do whatever they wanted with the rest of the day. After only two days of sightseeing, Sandy was exhausted and said she was going to walk back to the hotel, confident she could find her way. Tourism twinned with a restless night, worrying about Eve, had done for her. Gone were the days when her daughter listened to what she had to say. *Quite rightly*, she reminded herself, as she set off on her own, leaving the others planning where to find lunch.

Her own mother had blown hot and cold towards Sandy almost all her life. When as a seven-year-old she had been dropped for the first time at Burnleigh School, she had sat at the window waiting and watching for her mother to come back. She had to return because Monty, Sandy's teddy, was stuffed in the rear seat pocket. He was too scared to go anywhere without Sandy. Eventually she was prised away by Jane, the girl who had been assigned to help her settle in: Jane, who broke the glass over the photo of Sandy's parents; Jane, who tore pages from Sandy's favourite books and once tore her homework to pieces; Jane, who later tried to throw her out of the dorm window. When her mother eventually returned, it was half-term. The first thing Sandy had done was check the car pocket for Monty but he had disappeared and, when asked about him, her mother just shook her head and sighed.

During the holidays, however, she could go overboard, whisking Sandy off to the zoo, shopping or to her favourite, the pictures. Sandy had never forgotten the enveloping warm darkness, the sense of anticipation and the satisfaction of a good film. Sometimes they'd see her mother's friend Esme and her rowdy son, Tom. The two of them would be thrown out into the garden and told to 'play'. She wondered if he had hated it as much as she had as they skulked around looking for something to do. Then, after any of these occasions and without warning, her mother would revert into her shell, shutting herself in her bedroom or burying herself in a book, going for a walk on her own, telling them she didn't want to be disturbed. It became a relief when Sandy had to return to the routine of school. Her mother's moods had always been so disconcerting and puzzling that it was a welcome liberation when Sandy could at last take control of her own life. As soon as she could leave home for university, she had. And yet, despite everything, Sandy had loved her mother, who had come to live near her and Matthew when she was widowed, as if she couldn't quite let go after all. Sandy and Matthew had accepted it.

Her father had been kind but distant, preoccupied by his work as a country GP, a man of his generation. His wife was there to look after him, his only child was not to bother him unless he wanted to be bothered. But at least Sandy had always known where she was with him. Her abiding memory was his smell of tweed and pipe smoke, the way he'd stick together a cut on his finger or hers with Durofix.

If she ever had children, she used to tell herself, she would be a very different parent to her own. There would be love and consistency in spades. Then she had Eve, who taught her that the most important gift she and Matthew could give their daughter was her freedom, along with the knowledge they would always be there when needed. They had discussed what kind of parents they wanted to be and agreed. She bit her lip. Was she letting all three of them down by not giving Eve her undiluted support now? But she had also always set store by honesty. How could she pretend otherwise?

Back at the hotel, she took her diary into the courtyard, where she ordered a cup of coffee and began to write down all she remembered from the day: the sounds, the smells, the impressions. As she wrote, her eyes began to close. She checked the time. Only three o'clock. A quick siesta and she'd be raring to go again.

She had barely lain down when she was woken by a ringing sound. She automatically reached for her mobile before realising it was the hotel phone by her bed.

'Sandy? Good, you're there. It's Lia.'

Sandy was suddenly wide awake.

'The others have all gone off together so I was thinking we might go somewhere. Shopping? Or just wandering. I'd love to see the Trevi fountain.'

Sandy remembered her mother's journal entry, as things began to hot up with Tony.

Took a horse and carriage to the Trevi fountain! Beautiful. Tony's idea as Mrs R gone with Flemings to Tivoli. Stood by the edge and ate ice creams. Tony made us laugh with his stories of the hospital. He's going to be a marvellous doctor. He put his arm round me and kissed my cheek when Fleur wasn't looking. We threw coins over our shoulders into the water to make sure we'll come back one day. Maybe together, he said...

'I ought to write some postcards.' It was a lame excuse but it would do. 'Aren't we doing something this evening?'

'Can't you do that later?' Lia was almost pleading. 'Do come. We'll have fun. I promise not to mention school.'

Maybe they would have fun. And if Lia was offering the hand of friendship then she should accept it. 'I'll meet you at reception in ten,' she said, swinging her legs off the bed.

Lia was waiting for her, camera over her shoulder, map in

hand. 'Look. Once we're over the bridge all we have to do is cut diagonally through here, across the Via del Corso and we're there.'

'You don't think it's too far to walk?' But what else had she to do? They had hours before they were due to meet the others for supper. 'No, no. I'm being silly. Let's go.'

The streets were busy but many of the shops were still shut during the siesta. 'Remember to look up,' said Lia. 'You'll see all sorts of things you're not expecting. Look at that ceiling.' She pointed up at a painted wooden ceiling just visible through a window three floors up.

Sandy bristled. If being patronised by Lia was the price of their new-found 'friendship', the cost was too high. She concentrated on looking out for other pieces of decorative carving, ceilings, shutters, little paintings of the Madonna on street corners. She soon found she was enjoying herself. Perhaps she had been wrong about Lia after all. They stood on street corners, turning the map, trying to work out where they were before setting off again. Whenever they crossed a road, Lia would say, 'Attraversiamo', as loudly as if it were a spell in Harry Potter.

'What are you saying?' Sandy asked after the third or fourth time.

'Let's cross.' Lia looked pleased with herself. 'It was Elizabeth Gilbert's favourite word out of all the Italian she learned.'

Sandy gritted her teeth and stepped off the pavement.

Eventually they found the outsize baroque fountain that dominated its small piazza. Hundreds of people were jostling round the lip of the pool, taking selfies and tossing coins over their shoulder into the water just as her mother had done years before.

'Shall we?' said Lia. 'They say that if you do, you'll come back to Rome.' She began to push her way towards the front with Sandy right behind her. Sandy sat on a step while she got fifty cents out of her purse. There was a sharp whistle and a shout. She looked up to see a uniformed official waving in her direction.

She stood up, and he looked away. 'What? You're not allowed to sit down?'

'Bureaucracy run riot.' Lia took a couple of euros from her pocket.

They were right at the front of the crowd now. 'Let's do this.' Lia turned her back on the fountain, Sandy copied her and they both tossed a coin over their left shoulder. 'And now, let's get outta here.'

As she was inching her way through the crowd, Sandy felt a hand on her waist, a thumb pressing insistently. She was too slow to realise what was happening as the catch on her money belt popped open and the belt was ripped from her. 'Hey!' she shouted as a young girl raced past her, passing the belt to a boy who nipped ahead. 'Come back here.' But her schoolteacher ways cut no ice here. As a man stepped in front of her, blocking her path, she saw Lia take off after the children. By the time she reached the corner of the square, all three of them had vanished. She stood wondering what to do. Fortunately, she had only been carrying about twenty euros, with some small change in her purse. She put her hand in her pocket to check that it was still there. But what if Lia had been hurt?

'Got it!' Lia appeared, flushed and triumphant, the money belt dangling from her grasp. 'When he realised it was empty, he threw it at me and made off round a corner. Bloody kids.'

'But it wasn't.' Sandy unzipped the belt and pulled out a couple of notes. 'Thank you so much. Anything could have happened to you.'

'Nah. They were just kids working the crowd. They'll be on to their next target by now.'

'They could have taken your camera. That was so brave of you.'

'It was just instinct. I'm sure you'd have done the same for me. Glad I got it back for you.'

Being in Lia's debt was an unexpected twist in affairs that Sandy wasn't sure she welcomed. She put the money belt back on and tucked it down inside her waistband, looking around her, annoyed with herself for not having been alert enough. People still crowded round the fountain and shopped at the souvenir stands at the back of the piazza, oblivious to their small drama. Lia went back to shooting a few more photos, trying to find the best angle for the fountain.

'You need Alan,' Sandy joked.

'God, don't! I had enough of him at St Peter's. He thinks he knows everything there is to know about photography.'

'But he hasn't brought a camera.'

'No, because "these modern phones",' Lia imitated Alan's burr, 'do just as good a job. What bollocks.'

Sandy laughed. 'He's chatting you up as well.'

'Think so? He hasn't a hope, although I wouldn't mind someone.'

Sandy was taken aback by the sudden unsolicited confession. 'You wouldn't?'

'Oh, I don't know. Sometimes I think I would and others... not so much.' Lia shut down the conversation with practised ease, clearly realising she had overshared. 'It doesn't matter.'

'Of course it does,' said Sandy, feeling much warmer towards her now. 'If we're going to be on holiday together, perhaps we should get to know each other better. Wouldn't that help?'

Lia looked uncertain. 'Maybe... anyway you really don't want to know.' She turned away, then. 'Ice cream? Look. On the corner. Bar Trevi.'

'Don't tell me...'

'Elizabeth Gilbert? You know what? I don't think she did.'

Sandy smiled. 'This is on me! The least I can do.'

They paid, got a voucher each and went back to join the

queue and dither over their choices, leaving with a tub each containing two scoops of lemon and raspberry sorbets.

Lia turned down a side street then stopped. 'We'd better eat them before they melt.'

'Go on,' Sandy encouraged her, intrigued by the glimpse Lia had inadvertently given her into her private life. 'You might as well.' Out of the corner of her eye, she was alert for pick-pockets. Next time she'd be ready.

'What?' Lia started walking slowly. 'This must be the right direction.'

'Tell me what you think I don't want to know. Try me. You're not married, are you? But perhaps you were once, like me?' She glanced at the twisted band on Lia's right ring finger.

Lia looked up from her tub. 'How did you guess?'

'Your ring.' Sandy licked her spoon. 'Delicious.'

'It was a long time ago. We married straight out of university and it only lasted four years.' She looked to see Sandy's reaction but Sandy was careful to keep focused on her sorbets. No eye contact, more communication. 'We were way too young. I suppose we thought getting married meant we could face the big bad world together and nothing would change. But of course it did. Nothing lasts.'

'That's not very positive.'

'But true.'

'Have you been on your own ever since?' That was a long time for someone to be single. Sandy was increasingly curious. Up till now, she had only seen Lia as a rival at work, without bothering to consider what had made her the person she was.

Lia laughed as she scraped the last of the sorbet from inside of the tub. 'God, no! They've come and they've gone.'

Sandy looked up, noticing the fleeting look of sadness she saw cross Lia's face.

'Oh look, aren't they adorable?' Lia gestured towards two little girls with cascades of gingery curls who were being pushed past them. She bent over as if she was going to say something to them but swiftly recovered herself. 'Let's move on. We don't want to be late for the others.' Her gaze followed the children. 'Adorable but . . .' The words were spoken just under her breath. 'Perhaps I'm not really cut out for that domestic stuff.' Lia held out her hand for Sandy's tub and spoon.

But Sandy had caught the note of longing in her voice. 'Perhaps you haven't met the right man yet.'

'Oh, I met him, but that didn't work out either.' It was as if a shutter slammed down over her face. Throwing the tubs into a bin gave her an excuse not to go on. When she came back, she had regained her composure.

'What about your daughter?'

'What about her?' Sandy went on to high alert. She didn't talk about Eve at work, where she preferred to keep everything on a professional level; especially when it came to her and the younger teachers. She knew she had a reputation for being self-contained, but that was how she preferred it.

'Still single?'

'No.' But if she was asking Lia to tell her about her personal life, she should give something back. 'She's married, and lives and works in London but we still see a lot of each other.

'No grandchildren then?'

'Not yet.' She wasn't ready to share Eve's baby news until she had fully come to terms with it herself. Especially not with Lia who, if past performance was anything to go by, would have it all over the school within hours of them starting the new term. She must remember to be careful.

10

Mark had assumed the role of host in the group; whether by choice or by natural selection, Alice wasn't sure. He and Gilly made sure the glasses were kept filled and that no one was left out of the conversation. She watched as he coaxed Gilly into talking about her engagement and her wedding the following year in some picturesque country pile. He looked riveted when Alice knew he couldn't possibly be, giving the younger woman all his attention.

'And the honeymoon?' he asked.

'Sam's organising it all. He says because I organise people's holidays for a living, he wants to surprise me.' She blushed. 'He's so sweet.'

'But you deserve it,' said Mark. 'He's a lucky man.'

How could he not realise how ridiculous he looked to the rest of them, flirting with someone at least half his age? But to Alice's surprise, Gilly was almost purring with pleasure. 'He's a pilot,' she said, full of pride. 'With EasyJet.'

He moved on to Brit. 'I'm afraid that I've forgotten what it is that you do,' he said with his most engaging smile.

'Peter's a GP.' Brit looked down at her plate.

'And you?' he insisted, his eyes not moving from her face.

'She's involved in researching the function of genes in human embryos,' said Peter. 'Very complex, important and incomprehensible to most of us.'

'Peter, hush.' Brit put a finger over her lips. 'Nobody wants to know.'

'Oh, but I do,' said Mark. 'I'm completely in the dark.'

Brit looked at him, her grey eyes steady. 'In a nutshell . . . There are a lot of genetic factors affecting pregnancy that aren't properly understood. When we understand more then it might be possible to understand pregnancy failure and to improve the success rates of IVF. But I'm only on the periphery of things. There are others who do the real work.'

'It sounds fascinating. So what do you do on the periphery? I'd like to know.'

Mark had absolutely zero interest in anything scientific; particularly, Alice suspected, when it related to women's bodies, but she recognised his technique, had seen him use it umpteen times at parties, had succumbed to it herself. Peter had turned away to talk to Sandy while Mark focused fully on Brit who, with his encouragement, dropped her guard and began to open up.

Then, when he had enough, he deftly moved the conversation on to neutral ground. 'What did you do this afternoon? Anything you can recommend?'

'We visited a couple of churches. Peter always tries to cram in as many as possible. Don't you, darling?'

He nodded. 'The facade of Santa Maria is being restored, but the mosaics inside are quite remarkable.'

Brit agreed, murmuring 'Exquisite,' under her breath as if she didn't want to interrupt her husband, but looking to Mark for his acknowledgment.

As they chattered on, Alice couldn't help noticing the way Mark sucked up his spaghetti, his mouth pursed like a cat's arse. Sometimes, she thought with surprise, he actually repelled her.

The waiter brought the second course, a much-needed distraction. She breathed in the smell of her salmon fillet served with herbs, citrus fruits and broccoli.

'Where's your daughter going for her gap year?' Sandy turned to her. 'I've noticed so many students here, I'm quite envious.'

'She's still planning.' Alice remembered her most recent conversation with Pip, who seemed to be making arrangements to join Holly and Tess's trip to Australia the following month without having finally committed herself. Alice hadn't been able to broach the subject to Mark, only too aware how he'd react.

'I can get a job as a waitress in the winery, no problem. They've said so,' Pip had enthused. 'I only need another two hundred pounds and I've got the fare.' The next step was to delve into the parental wallet, but she hadn't quite summoned up the courage to ask. Instead she was building up to it so that by the time she did, they'd have no choice but to agree. Alice recognised how skilfully she manipulated them.

'Remember the hippie trail?' A wistful smile crossed Mark's face. 'A friend and I bought an old VW van for next to nothing. He painted it purple and orange and we just took off. Our parents had no idea where we were – no mobile phones, just the odd postcard that took forever – and somehow we made it to Goa.'

Alice had heard this story hundreds of times. If he had such great memories of his travels, why was he holding Pip back?

'What about money?' she asked, although she knew the answer.

'We'd saved a bit, worked a bit en route. Things were cheap back then.'

'It's all relative, surely,' said Alice.

'What would you know?' he snapped. 'Did you travel? No.'

She subsided into her chair, bridling. A mouthful of salmon then wine calmed her.

'You drove all the way?' Sandy tried to rescue the situation. But Mark was quick to correct her.

'No, no. We ditched the VW in Germany when it gave up the ghost. After that we threw ourselves on the mercy of strangers. That or public transport. God, the world was a different place then.'

'*You* were different too,' Alice reminded him. Not that they had met till many years later. By then he was a chino-wearing, linen-jacketed university lecturer smoking cigarettes through a holder. In anyone else she would have found it an affectation but, in him, she had found it charming. Back then.

'True. I had long hair, a moustache. I never thought this would happen.' He pointed at his receding hairline.

'I never thought *this* would happen,' Alan patted his paunch. 'I never went to India or Thailand but I worked on an Australian sheep farm, friend of my dad's. Most hellish experience of my life but gave me a taste for beer.' He raised his glass to his lips.

'I worked in the local chicken factory with my sister,' said Alice. 'Horrible. We stank when we came home at the end of the day. And we never earned enough to take us away.' She shook with laughter.

'Or perhaps, you simply weren't brave enough,' said Mark, pouring himself another glass, offering everyone else but her. 'Some people aren't.'

'I was brave enough to take you on.' Alice couldn't stop herself. 'That suggests I might have been brave enough for anything.' She forced herself to smile as if she was joking.

Mark frowned.

'Well said.' Lia clapped.

'Kids seem have a much easier time of it these days,' said Peter, stepping in. 'They expect everything on a plate.'

'Not everyone does, love.' Brit corrected him gently then looked around the others. 'We don't have children ourselves so we can't really talk.'

'That must be why you both look so young.' Mark put down his glass.

'I think Pip would love it here, don't you?' Alice asked Mark, trying to smooth things over.

He stopped twirling his fork in his spaghetti and nodded before turning his attention back to his food. 'Probably. Except that she's got this bee in her bonnet about Australia now.'

'Good for her,' said Alan. 'My sons went on gap years. Did them the world of good. Made them grow up. Worth every penny even though I had to bail them out of South America when their backpacks were stolen.'

'Eve worked in Sainsburys for six months then went off with friends to the Far East,' said Sandy. 'And she was a different person when she got back.' She looked down as if stopping herself from saying more. 'I'd love to have done that but I was too frightened.' She looked at Alice who gave her a sympathetic look.

'I can't believe that,' said Lia, looking round the table. 'You should see her at school. The girls are in awe of her. Firm but fair and never frightened.'

Sandy shifted in her seat as she toyed with her veal. 'That's years of being in the playground. If you're not firm, they'll eat you alive. You know that.' She smiled. 'I've always been pretty unadventurous. And then I met Matthew and we went on being unadventurous together.'

What could be troubling Sandy? Was she wary of giving away too much in front of her younger colleague? There was something else going on behind that composure that Alice couldn't work out. And something about Lia that she didn't trust. Why had she bothered to point out how well Sandy and Mark were getting on? Perhaps she was just one of life's natural troublemakers.

'I'm just the opposite. I've always loved seeing new places,' Lia spoke up. 'You must be the same, Gilly.'

'Ever since I was a kid. My dad was in the foreign office so we were always on the move. I was born in Nigeria, but we lived all over the world. I guess that's what gave me the bug. But maybe I'll stop when we get married.' She flashed her ring at the table.

'Maybe I'll have the bug after this,' said Sandy, hopeful.

'If you don't get it in Rome, you won't get it anywhere.' Mark topped up her glass despite her half covering it with her hand. 'Have you had any luck with your mystery letter?'

Sandy pushed her glass away from her. 'No.'

'What mystery letter?' Lia's ears pricked up immediately. 'Sounds intriguing.'

'It's nothing.' Sandy clearly wished Mark hadn't said anything. 'Just something my mother asked me to deliver.'

'What's the mystery?' Lia bounced up and down on her seat once, like a child. 'Who's it for? You never said anything.'

'That's the point,' said Mark, downing his wine, oblivious to Sandy's discomfort. 'Sandy's got the name but no address.'

'It's not really our business.' Alice stepped in, annoyed by Mark's insensitivity.

'But perhaps we can help,' offered Gilly.

'Oh no no, it's fine.' Sandy brushed the offer away. 'Thank you but I'll manage.'

'Well, if you need anything...' But Gilly's attention had moved on to the tomato sauce she had dropped on her white T-shirt. 'Damn! I'll never get this out.'

'Is this letter important?' asked Lia. The attention of the whole table was on Sandy now.

'No. Really not. It's a private thing I'd rather not talk about. I shouldn't have said anything.'

'OK. I was only trying to help.' Lia was obviously annoyed at being knocked back.

'Thanks.' Sandy gave her an apologetic smile. 'But it's something I need to do on my own.'

This was entirely Mark's fault. The idiot. Alice pushed back her chair and left the table, going down the grubby white staircase to the ladies. There was only one cramped cubicle where she sat, elbows on knees, head in hands, while she peed. However much Mark drove her mad sometimes, she must try not to let it show. For all their sakes.

Sandy was fuming over Mark telling everyone her business. She should have said something about keeping it to himself but she'd had him marked down as being better than that. She'd mistaken him for a man who was considerate, generous with his time and patience. Not a gossip.

She looked down the table at her fellow travellers. Now they were getting to know one another, the mood among the group was changing. New allegiances were being forged as they came out of their couple-bubbles. Even Peter and Brit were beginning to thaw. That was down to Mark again. He had successfully achieved what none of the rest of them had and brought them briefly out of their shells. As she studied the three men, Alan looked up, caught her staring and winked.

She looked away quickly, felt herself blushing, and focused her attention on the other end of the table. Benno and Alex were telling the others about their surrogate twins, Christian and Jenna. Alex's arm was draped round the back of Benno's chair as he held the table riveted, scrolling through his photos of the ten-year-olds to pick the best to show them. 'Benno's cousin carried them for us. She and her husband already had the two children they wanted. Can you think of a greater gift?'

She was dying to ask who had donated the eggs. And what about the donor? Did she have any rights over the children who were biologically hers? Did she know about them? Would she want them if she did? Would the answers to any of these questions ease her mind when it came to Eve?

She sat straighter, glad when Alice came to join her.

'Move down, Mark.' Alice took her glass and sat where her husband had been sitting while he moved to sit next to Lia.

'I'm so sorry about him,' she said under her breath. 'Sometimes he just doesn't think.'

Sandy was glad of her sensitivity. 'Don't worry. I'm probably being over-protective.'

'You're not at all. But if you do want any help, let me know.'

'Thanks.' She was the one person at the table Sandy felt she could trust not to say anything.

'Would you, Alice? Sandy?' Lia spoke loudly from the other end of the table.

'Would we what?'

'Be a surrogate. Have a baby for someone else.'

'It's a bit late for that.' Alice said, laughing.

Sandy hesitated. 'Perhaps if I'd had my own first.' That was the right answer for the situation but it wasn't the truth. 'It would depend who I was doing it for.'

'For God's sake!' Peter jumped in. 'That's not even an option open to most people.'

Sandy turned to him, startled. But before he could say any more, Brit shushed him.

'Time to move on.' Gilly summoned the waiter so she could pay the bill. 'Anyone fancy a walk? It's cooler now.'

The others got to their feet but Peter and Brit stayed put. 'I think we'll stay for a coffee,' he said, rapping his fingers on the table.

'We'll see you all in the morning.' Brit stroked his hair, soothing him.

'Christ! Who rattled his cage.' Lia was in the street waiting for someone to make a decision about where to go next.

'You, I'd say,' said Sandy. 'Not having children must be a sensitive subject for them. Didn't you think about that?'

Lia bowed her head, embarrassed. 'I didn't mean anything by it.'

'Anyone fancy a nightcap?' Alan chipped in. 'The night's still young.'

Sandy realised she couldn't face another minute with them all. The thought of a calm, solitary bedroom was much more attractive. 'I think I'll go back,' she said.

'I'll keep you company,' said Alice.

'I know where we can go. I saw a great-looking place this afternoon.' Lia glanced at Mark. 'Coming?'

'Sure. Come on, Alice. We won't be late.'

'Yes, come,' said Alan.

Alice smiled at them. 'I'm knackered after all that walking. I just want to put my feet up and read my book. You go. I'll see you later.'

So Sandy found herself walking back to the hotel with Alice through the streets of Trastevere, where the energy was infectious. So many people out walking, drinking, eating, having fun. Her mother had felt the same sort of excitement.

Tony furious I'd gone out without him. I sneaked out of my room when Mrs R had gone to bed and met Ignazio at the back of the hotel. We went to a club near the hotel and DANCED! It was wild but I was careful. I know what they say about Italians! But it was all fine and he took me back to the hotel and I was in bed by 1.30 a.m. with Mrs R none the wiser. Yes, we kissed ... under the stars ... just once.

'Cuppa?' Alice said as they reached the hotel gate.

'I thought you wanted to read.'

'I did when I was with them! But really all I want is to relax, chat for a bit.'

'Then, yes, I'd love to.' Though she would forfeit her time with her diary, Sandy wanted to get to know Alice better without Mark hanging over them.

'Excuse the mess.' Alice cleared the clothes from the two chairs, hurling them into the suitcase that sat open on the side. She delved inside it. 'I've got some shortbread somewhere. I've hidden it from Mark because he moans about my weight.' She pulled out a tartan box and held it out. 'Here.'

Within minutes, the tea was ready.

'Let's go on to the terrace,' said Sandy.

Outside, they lay side by side on two sun loungers, staring up at the inky sky pinned with stars. The only light came from the windows of the surrounding houses, and the two dim lights in the stairway. Everything was quite still. The odd shout from the street broke the peace.

'I love it here.' Sandy sat up to drink her tea.

'Me too. If only Mark would . . .' Alice didn't finish her sentence, just stared into the night, taking a bite of her biscuit.

Sandy looked at her. 'Is everything all right?'

Alice's face crumpled. 'Not really. But there's no point talking about it.'

'If it'll help, I'm happy to listen.'

Alice took a deep breath as she made up her mind. 'It's just Mark. He loves being at the heart of the party and I don't mind that, but sometimes he can be so dismissive.'

'I'm sure he doesn't mean to be.'

But Alice wasn't listening. 'We've been having counselling, but it's hard. Really hard. Sometimes I watch him and wonder what's the point. He likes the company of other women and he's bored with me.'

'That's not true.' Sandy hadn't anticipated this and wasn't sure how much she wanted to get involved.

'You know what I think?' Alice sat up and took her tea from the table between them. 'I think he's never got over Sally leaving him. His first wife. She left him and her two children for another man and left the country. She's never seen them since.'

Sandy shook her head. 'That's terrible. Poor woman. But presumably she keeps in touch with them?'

Alice shook her head, 'No. She's completely cut herself off from them. Not a word. Perhaps she thought that was the kindest thing. Mark wouldn't talk about it with the counsellor, but I think he needs the attention of other women to prove something to himself. That's why he's had his affairs. Other women validate him in a way that I don't any more. I'm not enough.' She raised a hand to stop Sandy from contradicting her. 'He needs them to stroke his ego to prove he's not worthless. If I haven't been enough for him and he won't talk about it, I never will be.'

Sandy let out a long breath. 'I'm sorry.'

'Don't be.' Alice gave a small smile. 'It's my problem. It feels better being able to talk about it. Was your marriage . . . ?'

'We were happy together. I don't think Matthew ever looked at anyone else.'

'You're lucky. When I married Mark and took on Patrick and Henry as well, I would never have dreamed it would turn out like this. I gave up everything for them. Don't get me wrong. I wanted to. But now I have nothing else.'

'But it's not too late.'

'To do what?'

'To do something for yourself. Didn't you say you'd been a chef? Why can't you be again? Or train as something completely different. Your kids are grown up, so what's stopping you?' But she knew how easy that was to say and how hard to do. There had been times when she'd had enough of teaching, but she wasn't qualified for anything else. Matthew had always been there to calm the stormy waters, and reassure her the right thing was to stick with something and prove you could handle it. And he had always been right.

Footsteps sounded on the stairs. A young couple Sandy had seen in the dining room appeared, glanced at the two women, then settled themselves with their drinks at one of the tables and began whispering together. As far as they were concerned Alice and Sandy might as well have been invisible.

'I think it's time to go to bed.' Alice got to her feet. 'I've said too much.'

'I'm not going to say anything to anyone else.'

'But it's your turn next time.' Alice picked up the cups. 'I want to know your story.'

II

My favourite flowery dress has got too tight! But Italian food – especially the pasta – is delicious. No tins of lunch meat here... And the other night Tony whispered to me that he liked something to get hold of! I don't think Fleur heard. Mrs R is turning out to be much better company than I first thought. I've unearthed her sense of humour. Quite a feat! Also went shopping with her today. Bought beautiful red swing skirt for tonight. Dreading going to Naples and having to work! Too hot for that and besides, having far too good a time.

Miriam Mackenzie, May 19th 1952 – Rome

Eight thirty in the morning and the market in Campo de' Fiori was buzzing. Sandy dodged to one side as a waiter from a nearby restaurant ran past with a tray loaded with beakers of coffee and a bag of cornetti, delivering them to one of the stallholders. This was like stepping back in time. Surely it had been exactly the same when her mother visited. She hadn't mentioned the market in her journal, but Sandy was increasingly sure that there was much that had gone unwritten about.

The piazza was surrounded by tall terracotta and ochre-rendered buildings, the shutters at the windows thrown wide. Under bleached-out awnings, the stalls were laden with fruit and vegetables that customers picked up and turned over, selecting the best. Aubergines sat alongside beefy tomatoes and courgettes with their papery yellow flowers. There were oranges, lemons, multi-coloured squashes, wheels of cheese, barrels of different kinds of olives, cans and bottles of olive oil, pasta of all shapes and sizes: *bucatini, tonnarelli, spaghetti, gnocchi* – the words danced jigs around Sandy's head. There were stalls devoted to truffle paste and oil; bottles of limoncello in every shape and size; coffee-making equipment; spices piled in colourful displays; sun hats and a few flowers already beginning to wilt. The shouts from stallholders reverberated round the square where local residents were out shopping while the day was still cool. Tourists strolled among them, stopping to look, buy, or take pictures.

'Look at these!' Alice beckoned her over to a stall where packets of every kind of vegetable seed imaginable were on sale. 'I'm going to get some.'

Sandy thought of her own unattended garden: small, and planted so it needed minimum attention; which was as well, given the amount of time she'd been able to devote to it over the last couple of years. Not that gardening had ever been high on her list of priorities. That had been Matthew's thing. When he came home from work during the summer, he'd head straight out there to check everything was as it should be. She'd hand him a drink through the kitchen window and watch as he made his way up one side and down the other, dead-heading, weeding, talking softly to the plants under his breath.

In the distance she spotted Peter and Brit, deliberating beside a fruit stall. He had picked up a couple of peaches, which she took and put back, as controlling as usual. Why did he put up with it?

'Coffee?' Alan came up behind them and pointed towards a narrow road that led off the square. 'I saw a café down there where we can sit outside and it's a bit quieter.'

Alice looked at Sandy, who shrugged. *Why not?* Though she was reluctant to leave the hubbub of the market square.

'Where's Mark?' Alan looked over his shoulder at Alice as he led the way.

'Sleeping it off before the cookery class.'

'Ah. I left him and Lia and the Germans to it. Were they very late?' He turned down a side street where there were some empty tables, got a nod from the waiter and pulled out a chair for Alice.

'No idea. I think it must have been.'

'Let me get this.' Alan went inside the café and came out smiling. 'We're blessed, aren't we? I never thought my life would be like this when I got divorced.'

They all paused as their coffee and a plate of pastries were put in front of them.

'Go on, help yourselves. A third each.' The cream in the *maritozzo* oozed over his knife.

Sandy took the tart topped with cream and strawberries while Alice tackled a fat *cornetto*.

'What did you think it would be like?' Sandy offered the three uneven pieces of tart to the others. She had often wondered whether death or divorce was preferable. At least after divorce, there could still be hope of reconciliation. But perhaps that was worse than knowing there could never be a future together.

Alan thought for a moment. 'Empty probably. June and I hadn't really got on for years before we split up. I had a little brush with cancer so she looked after me and after that fear and inertia stopped us separating.'

'I can understand that.' Alice spoke quietly.

Sandy glanced sharply at her.

Alan helped himself to a bit of broken *cornetto*. 'But I shouldn't have been so worried. Never been happier.' He looked around him. 'Who wouldn't want to be here right now with two such lovely ladies?' He took a bite of the *cornetto*, a couple of flakes getting caught on his goatee.

Sandy squirmed at his clumsy flattery. 'Where's your wife now?'

'She moved to Lyme Regis three years ago, where her sister lives. The kids tell me she's met someone else. And good luck to her.' That had the ring of bravado.

'Don't you speak to each other at all?'

'Not if I can help it!' He forced a laugh. 'Occasionally we have to talk about the boys – if one of them needs financial help or gets into a tight spot – but that's about it. We lead separate lives now.'

'Were they affected by your divorce?' Alice had cupped her cappuccino in both hands.

Alan tapped his spoon on his saucer. 'Perhaps. But not so as you'd notice. They were pretty much all grown up when we finally got round to it. Honestly? I think it probably came as a bit of a relief. Too many warring Christmases under our belts.' His laugh was more genuine this time. 'And most of their friends' parents didn't last the course either. I almost feel sorry for the ones that did, now.'

'I don't think they need your sympathy.' Sandy was sharper than she had meant to be.

'Sorry.' Alan puffed out some crumbs as he realised what he'd said. 'I'm a silly fool. My wife always said I opened my mouth without thinking. I didn't mean to give offence.'

'None taken.' Alice stepped in.

Sandy was thinking with sadness of the Christmases she and Eve had spent without Matthew since his death. Eve had come home as usual, except for last Christmas, when Sandy was too busy looking after her mother to be there. Instead, she and Eve had shared a modest roast chicken and a couple of roast potatoes, but they hadn't the heart for the usual decorations and traditions with her mother so ill upstairs. Eve didn't even stay the night but went home to Jen and their own Christmas. And now that they were having a child, those precious exclusive mother–daughter times that Sandy had valued so much would happen much less. 'Empty'. She understood what Alan meant.

'But look at all this.' He swept his arm out as if to encompass the city. 'If I hadn't come on this holiday I wouldn't have met you.'

'And we wouldn't have met you,' said Sandy. Alice's foot nudged her ankle.

'I'm looking forward to the next ten days, finding out more about you both.' He stroked his goatee, dislodging the pastry flakes.

'I think we should get back, don't you?' Alice downed the last of her coffee. 'We don't want to miss this cookery class. I managed to persuade Mark to do it even though as far as he's concerned, the kitchen's my domain.'

'Matthew and I used to cook together a lot.' Those evenings rushed back into Sandy's mind: she, bent over a cookery book following the instructions slavishly, while he insisted on experimenting and going off piste. 'He was better than me, more instinctive, but I'm hopeless without a recipe.'

'That's me. Instinctive.' Alan gave a wolfish grin.

'Down, boy,' said Alice, flapping her hands to ward him off. 'We're already spoken for.'

'Sandy?' He tipped his head to one side.

'Yes, her too.'

By the time the three of them arrived at the cooking school, the rest of the group were already there, having coffee and homemade biscuits round a long table. Through a doorway at the back, they could see a table piled high with vegetables. 'Just like *Masterchef*,' whispered Alice.

As soon as they sat down, Chef Alessandro brought them coffee. He was dark, slim, charismatic. Now that they were all gathered, he explained the four-course menu that they would be cooking together from scratch. Then: 'OK. Put on your aprons and let's start.'

'This is my idea of heaven,' Alice said as she picked up her red apron. There was barely room for them all in the tiny kitchen but they bunched round the table, waiting to be told what to do. The walls were hung about with steel pans in every size, bunches of garlic, dried chillis, shallots and herbs. Sandy's back was pressed against a large cooking range with Alan pressed up a little too close to her. There was no escape.

Peter volunteered to cut the bread for bruschetti while Brit chopped tomatoes beside him. Alice took on the parsley chopping and when Mark offered to clean and chop the mushrooms, Lia put her hand up to join him. They stood at one side of the kitchen, hunched over their boards, talking and laughing. Benno and Alex chopped courgettes into tiny rounds while Gilly was put to skinning, deseeding and chopping more tomatoes for the ravioli sauce. Teamwork.

'And you, Miss Sandy.' Chef Alessandro turned to her. 'Will you prepare the vegetables for the main course? I think so. Yes, with you Alan. We have carrots, celery and onions to make a *soffritto*. You put them in the pan with olive oil and Gilly's tomatoes. Yes?' He looked to see Gilly's reaction.

'Yes, chef!' Her face was flushed with the effort of working so hard.

'Damn! I've cut my finger.' Lia's voice rose above the others.

Sandy looked up to see Mark, holding up her hand and leading her to the sink. 'Out of the way, please.' The others stood back to make a path for them. He turned on the cold tap and held her finger under it.

Within seconds, Alessandro produced a first aid box. 'Let me see. This isn't too bad. A little of this...' and he dabbed on some antiseptic. 'And this.'

'I can do it.' Lia was back to normal. 'You all get back to work.' She took the padding from Alessandro.

'Let me. It's easier.' Mark took the blue plaster and wound it round her finger. 'There.'

'Everybody OK?' Alessandro was back at the table as Mark and Lia made their way back to their station. 'The knives are sharp here. You must be careful and always cut away from your fingers. All right Miss Lia?'

'*Sto bene, grazie*. Almost done.'

Sandy glanced in their direction, noticing for the first time the demonstration mirror hanging over their station angled so everyone could see what was happening beneath it. In it she saw Mark stroke the side of Lia's hand with one finger. The gesture was so quick, so slight as to be almost unnoticeable. But not quite quick or slight enough for it to be entirely innocent. Nor was the way Lia glanced up and smiled at him before she turned with the bowl of ricotta and spinach they had prepared and put it on the central table. Sandy's conversation with Alice came back to her.

Alice was rolling out the pasta, putting it through the machine three times. 'You've done this before?' asked Alessandro.

'I trained as a professional cook.'

'That was long before we met,' Mark interrupted. 'She hasn't worked professionally for years.'

Sandy caught Alice's eye. Dismissed again. *Go on*, she willed her. *You can do it*. When they were next alone, she would encourage her again.

12

I'm so glad I came to Rome. I don't want to go back to my dreary life as a secretary. In fact I can't go home again now I've experienced this. I can't face Pa and his drinking and morose Mama. Mrs R is a guardian angel beside them. I want to be free. I want to live and do exactly as I want. Think where that might take me!

Miriam Mackenzie, May 22nd 1952 – Rome

When lunch was ready, they sat around the dining room table, removing their aprons and draping them over the back of their chairs.

'We've been on our feet for hours. No wonder I'm exhausted.' Alan lifted his wine glass, registered it was empty, and put it down again. 'I could never work in a professional kitchen.' A waitress came round the table to help him to more. 'A different one with every course. I'm not objecting.' He tasted it. 'Delicious.'

'Did you enjoy that?' Sandy asked Brit.

'I'm not much of a cook.' Her voice was as quiet as if she feared waking the dead.

'Yes, I'm the cook in our household.' Peter chipped in. 'Lucky you, Mark. Gather you get cooked for.'

'I chose to be a stay-at-home mum,' snapped Alice, on the defensive. 'So the least I can do is rustle up something to eat for everyone. And I like cooking. Mark doesn't. But the jobs around our house are pretty evenly distributed beyond that.' She ripped a piece of bread in half.

'This bruschetta is amazing.' Mark held up the one topped with courgettes. 'Come on, everyone – try them.'

The plate was passed round and Sandy tried again with Brit, managing to elicit that this was her second marriage and she'd had no children from either.

'That's all right though,' she added as if to prevent Sandy being embarrassed. 'We've come to terms with it as best we could. I couldn't have given so much to my work if I had.'

'Tell me what you do again.'

'I'm a medical researcher. And Peter's a GP,' Brit finished off for her. 'He's a senior partner in the local practice and very highly thought of.' She lowered her voice so Peter couldn't hear. 'He had a breakdown a couple of years ago, burned out by the pressure, so he's thinking of retiring soon. It's a job that's getting tougher every year. I try to ease things for him when I can.'

All at once her behaviour was explained. She wasn't controlling but caring. Sandy should have thought there might be another explanation.

'We're looking forward to doing much more of this.' Brit's wave of her arm included the whole room.

'What? Cooking or travelling?'

'Both. And being spontaneous. I saw this advertised and we made a snap decision to come. I'm so glad we did.'

'I should think so,' said Peter, catching the tail end of the conversation. 'Small group travel doesn't come cheap, even when there's so much free time factored in.' For the first time Sandy noticed the very slight tremor in his left hand.

'But you've enjoyed that, darling.' Always appeasing, Brit leaned back as her plate was taken away.

'Another course, another wine,' crowed Alan, as a straw-coloured white was poured into his glass.

'Not for me, thanks,' said Sandy.

'Let yourself go. You only live once.' He raised his glass in a salute.

'It is very delicious,' added Alice.

'You can have a sleep afterwards,' Lia joined in. 'I know I will.'

'Me too,' said Benno.

Alex touched his shoulder. 'The benefits of not having the children with us.'

They caught each other's eye and smiled.

Mark beckoned the waitress back to do the honours. Sandy watched as the wine was poured a quarter of the way up her glass. They were right of course. How often was she going to be in a Roman kitchen, having cooked a proper Italian meal? The occasion deserved celebrating, so why not let go and join in?

As the meal went on and the four different wines were tasted, the group got louder. Sandy found herself getting pleasantly tipsy as the conversation whirled round her, darting in and out of different topics, never stopping long enough to get too contentious.

Alan was in full flow, announcing his support for Brexit before he realised the majority of the people at the table profoundly disagreed with him. 'You're just all card-carrying *Guardian*-readers from the South,' he said. 'You have no idea what life in the rest of the country is like.' He made a sweeping gesture on their behalf and his hand caught Brit's glass of red wine. As it tipped, the wine flew from the glass across the table and on to her pale linen dress, where it leached into the fabric. She stared down at it in shock.

'You idiot!' Peter was on his feet so fast, his chair crashed to the floor behind him.

Everybody froze.

'My God, I'm so sorry.' Alan passed over several paper napkins. 'I didn't see it there.'

'It's fine. It's an old dress.' Brit dabbed at the mark. ' Sit down, Peter. I'll quickly go back to the hotel and change.'

'I'm coming with you. We'll give you the cleaning bill, Alan.' Peter's face was puce. 'You, you ... Brexiteer!'

'Of course,' said Alan. 'I was going to offer anyway.' He drained his glass of wine.

'No need,' said Brit, emollient as ever. 'I can be back in a few minutes.'

'I'm coming with you.' Peter righted his chair and snatched his sunglasses from the table. 'Thank you, Alessandro. That was a marvellous morning.'

Gilly glanced at the clock on the wall and exchanged a look with Alessandro, who gave a brief nod.

'It's time for us all to go, anyway.' Gilly stood up. 'It's gone four and Alessandro has given us enough of his time. So if you want to settle your drinks bills or buy any of his jams and chutneys ...' She gestured towards the rows of prettily labelled jars on the shelves on one side of the room.

One by one, they drifted into the street, the heat of the day wrapping round them like a comforting blanket after the over-air-conditioned dining room, the shadows sharp on the cobbles and against the walls.

'What an overreaction.' Alan followed Sandy out. 'You'd think I'd done it on purpose.'

'I wouldn't worry. It'll all have calmed down by this evening. At least we're not eating together. I couldn't eat another thing.'

'Bloody good, wasn't it? That tiramisu ...' He patted his stomach. 'But now what?'

'I'm going back to the hotel to recover,' said Sandy, looking forward to being alone with her diary. She wanted to look at her mother's again too.

'Would you like some company?' The words slurred together in the middle.

'I'm sorry?' He can't have said that.

'Would you like—' He staggered over the curb.

'I don't think that's a very good idea.' Sandy tightened her grip on the strap of her bag, adopting the expression she used to silence a room.

'You needn't worry. My prostate's done for me.' He raised his hand to his mouth. 'Oops! Too much information. But I wouldn't be any trouble. Just a cuddle.'

She could smell the drink on his breath, see his half-closed eyes. 'Alan, when will you understand? I'm on holiday on my own for a reason. I'm flattered by your suggestions of course, but don't harbour any hopes, because they aren't going to come to anything.'

He looked like a whipped puppy before rallying. 'You can't blame a chap for trying. A beautiful woman like you.' He stumbled over the uneven cobblestones. 'We could both do with a bit of affection.'

'I think we should sleep it off.'

His face brightened.

'Separately,' she said, just to be clear.

As they reached the gates of the hotel, Alice and Mark caught them up. 'Great minds.'

'See you later.' Sandy took the opportunity to break away and headed alone to her room.

Later that evening, Sandy was sitting alone in a bar in Piazza Santa Maria in Trastevere. She had brought her iPad and diary along for company but was enjoying watching the people strolling past, some stopping to watch the spray-painters who were working under spotlights. Children rushed after the small feathered contraptions that the sellers catapulted high into the air for them to float down to the cobbles, while knots of students gathered round the central fountain as a constant stream of people threaded their way from one side of the square to another.

Before coming to Italy, the catastrophist in her wouldn't have dreamed she would sit alone like this and feel so relaxed, so unthreatened. She would have concocted every kind of disaster. But she had been pickpocketed and survived. She enjoyed being in the group, although the changing dynamics were wearisome. Being thrown together over a short time meant tensions formed; and with such close contact, relationships were fast-forwarded. Friendships and enmities were deepening. More than that, Sandy was beginning to sense a bond with a side of her mother she hadn't known, enjoying their appreciation of the same things, while her mother's journal gave an unexpected glimpse into her past.

She tapped her iPad so it came to life and went straight to her emails. At the top was one from Steven. Below it, one from Rosemary, her head teacher, headed 'Results'. She had a sip of wine and opened it first.

Hello! Hope you're having a really great and restorative time. I'm writing just to let you know that your girls have performed even more brilliantly than ever. A*s As. All of them should get their uni places, except for Charlotte Betts and Lucy Holden who have dropped their grades in French.

Sandy looked back at the square, magical in the dark. She should be at home celebrating with her girls, showing them how proud she was of them. They had been a particularly good year, one that she had genuinely enjoyed teaching. She looked back at the screen.

So now I want you to forget about us, and enjoy the rest of your well-deserved holiday. I'll see you just before the start of the new school year, when I hope I'll have some news for you. Till then. Rosemary

Some news. What did she mean? Good or bad? But surely she wouldn't mention it if it was going to be bad. And if it was good, perhaps the decision had been made about the deputy headship in her favour. She opened Steven's.

Just curious to know what you thought of the Bernini statues? What did you make of Apollo and Daphne? The expression on her face – so much emotion. I expect you're tied up, having a wonderful time. I won't bother you too much – I know you want some you-time – but I miss you, and think of you often. Sx

She stared at it for ages. Why was she even hesitating over a man whom most women would welcome into their lives with open arms? What was wrong with her? Moving on from Matthew was not disloyalty or infidelity after all this time, it was what she had to do if she was to have a life of her own now. So why was she hesitating?

'Mind if I join you?' Alice was standing on the other side of the bushes dividing the café from the square.

'Of course not.' Sandy was pleased to be distracted. 'Come and have a glass of wine.'

Alice walked round the corner of the bar and twisted her way through the tables to reach Sandy. '*Vino bianco, per favore*,' she said to the waiter. 'I always learn the essentials,' she said to Sandy's surprised expression. 'But never use them because Mark always mocks me.'

'Where is he?'

'He's walking with Alan and the boys to see St Peter's at night. I haven't got the energy. Lia went though.'

'Maybe she and Alan will get together.' Then she remembered what he'd told her.

'No chance. His sights are fixed on you.'

'You should have heard what he said after lunch.' As she

went on to repeat their conversation, Alice began to smile. 'You've got to hand it to him – at least he tries.'

'Booze-induced. Poor old sod. But I'm too preoccupied with Steven to take on anyone else.'

'Why so complicated? You're single. He is too – yes?'

Sandy nodded.

'Although, from where I'm sitting,' Alice pulled her seat nearer the table. 'I can't think why anyone our age would want to embark on a new relationship. Sometimes being single seems pretty enviable.'

'But it can be lonely too. Steven's a kind, thoughtful man who wants commitment.'

'And you're afraid of giving it?'

Sandy hesitated before answering. 'Two things. I still love Matthew is one. And two, I'm afraid that if I do, it might not work out. But if I don't I'll be single for the rest of my life. And I don't want to be a sex-free zone for evermore. Imagine.'

'Actually I can – quite happily.'

Sandy laughed. 'You're just saying that.'

'Well yes, I suppose I am. But as for Matthew – wouldn't he want you to find someone else, to have happiness? Loving him isn't the same as loving Steven. Can't you do both?'

Sandy thought about what Alice meant. 'Mmm. Maybe.' Of course she was right. Being faithful to a memory couldn't sustain you.

13

*Went to the Villa Borghese with the Flemings. Bernini
statues extraordinarily beautiful but we were dying to
get into the park. Bumped into Ignazio (barman) and his
friend Niccolo. Pretended not to know them or Mrs R would
have had a blue fit. Lay under the umbrella pines and
stared at the sky. So blue. Bliss. I do really like Tony ...*

Miriam Mackenzie, May 23rd 1952 – Rome

Sandy had gone ahead of the others as they made their way
down from the top floor of the Villa Borghese and slipped
back into the elaborately ornamented downstairs room so she
could have a last look at the statue on her own. *The Rape of
Persephone*. That it was possible to capture such energy and
emotion from a material as cold and unforgiving as marble was
astonishing. The genius of Bernini had mesmerised her just as
Steven had said it would. Just as it had mesmerised her mother
before her. The white marble seemed as soft as flesh – she stared
at Pluto's hand, his fingers pressing into the woman's thigh; the
tears on Persephone's terrified face; the agony in her expression;
the determined glee in his. The detail was perfect. The photo
in her guidebook came nowhere close to conveying the power
and beauty of the thing itself that so moved her. As she walked
round the statue, she rather enjoyed knowing that she shared
her pleasure with them both.

'Mrs Johnson?' The voice came from behind her. 'Mrs Johnson.'

She turned to see a group of young women standing there, three of them staring straight at her.

'Mrs Johnson.' The one with the shortest shorts and heavy biker boots took a step towards her. Her face was familiar but Sandy couldn't place her.

'It's Emma. And Flora.' Both with long blonde hair, wide smiles and few clothes.

'And Charlotte,' said the one with unruly dark hair that didn't look as if it had seen a hairbrush for days. She was wearing three vests of different sizes and colours draped over her skinny frame.

Sandy raced through her school registers in her mind. They must be Ecclesworth girls but out of context, she couldn't immediately place them. Without their uniform, they looked very different. She prided herself on remembering all the girls who she taught, although as the years went by it was increasingly difficult.

'How lovely to see you, Emma,' she said, hiding her confusion. 'What are you doing here?' She hoped a clue would emerge from the answer.

'We're on holiday.' Flora offered the information as if was a revelation. 'Thought we ought to come up here.'

Sandy smiled. Shades of her youthful mother's reaction to the prospect of classical art.

'You're at uni now, aren't you?' Sandy tried again.

'Yeah, I'm at Leeds doing English and History,' said Emma. Of course! In a flash Sandy recognised the girl who had endured all that extra coaching at her parents' insistence, so determined were they that she should go to Oxford or Cambridge. Their disappointment and Emma's relief when she didn't had been equally matched.

'Enjoying it?'

'Totally. Flora's there too, doing Italian. And Charlotte's doing Geography.'

'You remember us?' said Flora as if she would be invalidated if Sandy didn't.

'Of course I do.' They were coming back to her now. They had left the school two years earlier. Wasn't Charlotte the one who'd attached the two rape alarms to helium balloons, set them off and let the balloons float to the ceiling of the school hall, where they'd remained, screaming, until the caretaker could get them down? The head had gone ballistic. 'It's seeing you out of context that threw me. Are you enjoying Rome?'

'Totally. Like we're only here for three days and then we're heading up to Florence on the train.' And Flora was the one whom she had once caught smoking in the school toilets after a history exam.

'We've seen some amazing things.' Charlotte looked around the elaborately decorated room they were in. 'We've been to Poland, Hungary...'

Perhaps they weren't such cultural heathens after all. Sandy was pleased about that.

'There you are.' Lia came up behind the girls. 'We've finished upstairs, so I've come to find you. We're going into the gardens.'

The three girls turned at the sound of Lia's voice.

'Miss French!' said Flora.

Lia looked almost as bemused by their appearance as Sandy but she managed her way out of it differently. 'Good God! Flora and Emma! Can't we ever get a break from you lot?'

The girls gave awkward smiles as if they weren't sure whether she was serious or not.

'Are you here together, then?' Flora asked what all three girls were obviously wondering. Sandy saw Emma and Charlotte catch each other's eye. Something passed between them.

'We're in the same tour group, yes,' said Lia, dismissing any implication that she and Sandy were close.

'It's a complete coincidence.' The moment she said it, Sandy knew how unlikely that sounded. This was mirrored in the girls' faces.

'Whatever,' said Emma. 'Hope you enjoy it.'

'We shouldn't keep the others waiting.' Lia jerked her head in the direction she'd come from, encouraging Sandy to follow her. Now.

'Well, great to see you, girls. Have a good holiday.' Disappointed not to be able to stay in the room any longer, Sandy followed.

'Little witches,' Lia muttered.

'They're not that bad.' Sandy was shocked by the venom in Lia's voice.

Lia stopped at the door. 'They're every bit that bad. You know what they were implying? "Hope you enjoy it."' Her imitation of Emma's accent was faultless. 'That we were together.'

'But we are. Oh!' The penny dropped. 'Together, like that! Were they? Are you sure?' The idea was so unlikely that Sandy began to laugh.

'Perhaps I should go back and explain,' suggested Lia. But when they looked back, the girls were nowhere to be seen.

'What could you say? Anyway, what does it matter what they think?' The last person with whom Sandy would ever be involved was Lia. 'It's quite funny really.'

'Yes, well.' Lia's feathers were clearly ruffled. 'Today, another lot are being released into the world, God help us.'

'I miss being at school to congratulate them. Don't you?'

'You always turn in such good results. I always dread them.' This was the first time Lia had admitted to a more vulnerable side. 'But apparently I haven't got any fails this year, so that's something.'

'But the students love your subject. It's so much more relevant than mine.'

'True.' Lia walked out into the portico.

Sandy had only demeaned History to make Lia feel better. She hadn't meant her to agree.

'At last!' Peter glanced down at his watch. 'We were beginning to think you'd been spirited away.'

'My fault, I'm sorry. I wanted to take a last look at *The Rape of Persephone*. I don't think I've ever seen anything as beautiful.'

'And we bumped into some girls from school,' Lia added. 'Something I always dread.'

'Same with my patients,' said Peter. 'There's always one somewhere. And they usually want an on-the-spot consultation.'

'At least we were spared that,' said Lia.

Gilly was holding open the door to the outside, and just raised her eyebrows. 'Let's wander round the gardens. The minibus will pick us up in a couple of hours, so we can meet here.' She pointed at a spot she had ringed on a small folded map. 'I'll give you each one of these.' She handed them out.

'Look!' said Alice, holding up the map so they could all see how the park made a green heart shape. 'Look at it. The beating heart of Rome.'

'Oh, Alice, you're such a sentimental soul.' Mark took the map from her. 'Down here, I think.' He drew his finger down the road cutting straight through the middle. 'Let's go.'

They meandered through the park beneath the shady umbrella pines, going off onto the sunburned grass, crunching the pine needles under their feet so the air was scented with resin. Somewhere up high, parakeets shrieked in the branches, while the roadways were wide enough for dog walkers, joggers, cyclists and people, like them, just wandering, finding respite from the bustle of the city. Every now and then, they'd pass a kiosk selling refreshments.

'Oh my God! That's the statue.' Lia crossed the browned grass to several benches arranged around a fountain with a centre-piece of a faun and a woman tussling over a child. But the fountain was dry and dead leaves lay in the grubby blue bowl surrounding the figures. A spider's web strung between the mother's and child's heads glittered in the sunlight.

'Elizabeth Gilbert, I presume.' Sandy took a perverse pleasure in seeing one of Lia's highlights failing to live up to expectation.

'Again?' Alan was bemused by Lia's crush on this writer he'd never heard of.

'Well, I don't see why this was her favourite fountain in Rome.' Despite her disappointment, Lia walked around it, taking photographs from every angle. Then she turned away. 'Why don't we hire a rowing boat? Come on, Alan.' And off she went.

'I'd follow you anywhere.' He gave a throaty laugh and trailed after her.

Sandy stopped for a moment. It was too hot to rush. Walking through the gardens into this fenced-off section where Segways and bicycles weren't allowed had tired her. Her cotton trousers stuck to her legs, her shirt to her back. Her bottle of water was almost empty.

While the others took to the lake, she and Alice found a bench looking across the water to an island folly of a Greek temple. Above them the trees moved in the slight breeze, their shadows black on the sunlit ground. The path round the lake was dry and dusty. Alice stretched out her feet and tipped her head back. Not far from them, a busker was playing a run of tunes from the fifties. Had her mother heard the same songs when she lay on the grass here too?

'What a magical place.'

'Mmmm.' The sun was warm on Sandy's face and chest, and she allowed herself to relax. 'If it weren't for the music.'

'I think it's rather atmospheric. "*Volare, oh, oh. Cantare...*"' she sang. A couple of people on the next bench turned to see.

'"*Oh, oh, oh.*"' Sandy joined in, as they shouted the refrain together, then swayed side to side to the rest of the music, humming and laughing.

'So how were Pip's results? Have you heard?' Sandy hadn't dared ask till now.

'Not yet. I'm sure she'll call when she's got them. My fingers are crossed.'

'Alice!' A shout from the other side of the lake made them both sit to attention. Mark was with Lia, Alan and the boys by the boat hire, waving his hat.

Alice lifted an arm in a return salute, gave a thumbs up. 'You don't like her, do you?'

'Is it so obvious? I thought I was hiding it.' Sandy watched as the group took a couple of rowing boats and pushed out into the dark green water, making a pair of ducks take to the air. 'Rescuing my money belt has meant I'm in debt to her.'

'You are. I was only wanting to have a moan.'

Sandy looked at her quickly, surprised, but Alice's face was relaxed behind her dark glasses. 'Why?'

There was a shout as Alex lost his balance and fell backwards in his boat, which rocked as Benno hauled him back on to the seat. Their laughter reverberated across the water.

'I don't like the way she hangs round Mark. Look.' She sat straight and watched them making slow progress across the lake.

'What do you mean?'

'She's flirted with all the guys, but with Mark it's different. I don't trust him not to respond.'

'And you trust Alan? Anyway Mark wouldn't when he's on holiday with you, surely?' Alice couldn't distrust him that much.

'You don't know him.'

'She's a man's woman. Some women are like that.'

They could see Lia gesturing at Alan, trying to show him how to row in a straight line. Mark's threw his head back as he laughed.

'She likes being liked. Don't we all?' Sandy tried to be re-assuring.

'Then why did she take the trouble to point out how well you and Mark were getting on?'

'When?!'

'In the Vatican.'

A laugh burst out of Sandy. 'That's just silly. He was being kind, explaining when I didn't catch what Massimo said, sharing his knowledge. I was interested.'

'That's what I thought, but you don't know Mark. He'll take any encouragement and turn it into something else, and some people respond.' She gave a deep sigh.

'One, I wasn't encouraging him.' Sandy was appalled Alice might think so. 'And two, I'm a much harder nut to crack than that.' She wondered whether to be insulted by the idea that she would be so easily susceptible. 'And three, I've got too much on my plate at home to want to make things any more complicated.'

'I know that now.' Alice took off her glasses and rubbed her eyes. 'I might as well tell you the whole story, then you'll understand. The year before last, Mark had an affair with one of his students. She got pregnant, accused him of rape and her parents got involved. It's been a nightmare. But... we got through it. She had a private abortion that Mark paid for. But it wasn't the first time. The affair I mean – not the student or the pregnancy. Until then he'd managed to restrict himself to a couple of members of staff – the younger ones.'

'How awful.' Sandy wasn't sure how to react. 'But you really don't have to worry about me – I'm no threat.' The idea was laughable.

'I never really thought you were.' Alice turned her head and smiled. 'I shouldn't have said anything.'

'What happened?'

The authorities couldn't ignore it. He was cleared of rape

but you can imagine the scandal. He decided to take "early retirement"...' She put inverted commas round the words in the air. 'His career's over.'

'But isn't he working on a book?'

'So he says. But whether he'll finish it or get published, who knows.'

Rape. The word hung between them.

'Of course he wasn't guilty,' Alice said hastily. 'He wouldn't do anything like that and that's what the court found. I do believe him when he said it was a hundred per cent consensual. Not that I like hearing that either.'

'But you're here together now, so you've managed to come through it?'

'I hope so. I don't know.' Alice paused. 'I wouldn't confide in anyone like this at home.'

'Sometimes it's easier to talk to a stranger. I'm not going to judge or gossip. But if you're worried about Lia, then shouldn't you say something?'

Alice looked sad. 'What's the point? He'll only deny it. Despite all the conversations and apologies and reassurances, I don't know if I can trust him any more. I want to, but...'

They sat in silence, Sandy wondering. She bent to pet a black-and-white puppy that had stopped to sniff the leg of their bench then jumped up to say hello. When its owner called, it ran off, leaving dusty paw prints on her trousers.

'In truth, I'm not even sure how much I care any more,' said Alice almost as if she was talking to herself. 'I can't go through that again.'

'You don't mean that.' Matthew had never given Sandy any reason to doubt him, but that sort of uncertainty must be horribly unsteadying. She wondered if it was easier to get over infidelity when you were further down the line in a relationship, when the life you had shared together mattered more than an indiscretion? The children; the companionship; the life ahead of you.

'Actually I do – if it weren't for the children, Pip especially, and the thought of a lonely old age. But you don't want to hear all this. I'm sorry.' She reached her arms out in front of her, flexing her wrists.

'Of course I do.' Sandy knew the relief of releasing bottled-up emotion. Steven had become such a reliable sounding board whenever she was worried about Eve or her mother, as Matthew had been before him. Steven. What would they be doing if they had come here together? Would they have taken another of the rowing boats? Perhaps they'd have struck out on their own, hired a rickshaw and pedalled round the gardens together, stopping at the museums, having a coffee or an ice cream at one of the kiosks. They might even lie under the trees, staring up at the sky like her mother and her friends.

'Thanks.' Alice stood up. 'But I don't want to spoil all this by droning on about Mark and me. I've been thinking about your letter,' she said. 'Don't you think your mother might want you to open it if there's something in there that would help get it to where it's meant to be?'

'You didn't know my mother. She never said what she didn't mean. If she'd wanted me to read it, she wouldn't have bothered with the envelope.'

'Really? She sounds terrifying.'

'She wasn't really. She was just herself.' Sandy hesitated. How could she best describe her mother? 'It's harder for me to talk about her now I've had a glimpse of her as a young woman writing in her journal. In it, she's so at odds with the woman I knew. But certainly when she was older, you wouldn't want to get on the wrong side of her. She could be so moody. I've no idea whether she was always like that. She didn't have any family, so there was no one to ask.'

'No one? Not even your grandparents?'

'Nope. She used to say there'd been a rift when she married Dad. Apparently they never spoke again. God knows why.

Mum and Dad wouldn't talk about it, said they'd always vowed not to – even to me.'

'And when you got older?'

'Even then. They dodged the question until I eventually stopped asking. That was just the way it was.' She remembered the way her mother's face shut down when asked. 'She taught me to respect that.'

'No clues at all?'

She should have been more curious, but it was hard to make someone else understand what her parents had been like. After her mother's death, she had frequently been ambushed by regret over all the questions she hadn't asked her, some of them questions she hadn't even thought of until it was too late. She would never find the answers now.

'My parents were so closed up and unemotional. They only said what they wanted me to know, and I accepted that. How stupid I was.' In retrospect, she had become aware how undemonstrative they were compared to some of her friend's more overtly loving parents, but then she had been too busy with her own life to let it worry her unduly. She just accepted that was the way they were. 'I remember being bewildered by her lack of love when I so wanted it. I thought it must be because I was unlovable. I really believed that until I met Matthew. If it weren't for him . . .' She felt tears welling and had to stop, take a breath. 'Actually I did find one thing when I was sorting out her stuff.'

'What?' Alice was sitting up, concentrating on what Sandy was telling her.

'A box labelled "Italy".' She had found it in the spare room chest of drawers, The room had been unused for so long it was more like a junk store than a bedroom, stacked high with old newspapers, suitcases, undisplayed pictures and ornaments, furniture and furnishings such as her childhood bedroom curtains that her mother didn't want but couldn't throw out. To waste things was a sin.

'And?'

Alice's interest made Sandy feel less alone. Perhaps she should have told Steven ages ago, but bringing him in on it would have involved him even more in her life before she was ready. Talking to someone sympathetic whom she barely knew and might never see again seemed so much easier.

'Not much.' She had taken the box downstairs and opened it on the dining room table. 'Two old photos – those tiny faded Kodak squares with the deckled white edges. Remember them? One's of a house that could be anywhere but, given the box, I guess it must be somewhere in Italy. And the other's of a woman leaning over a pram. For a moment I thought it was Mum and me, until I turned it over – and it just says Anna.'

'So you know what she looks like?'

'This must have been taken at least sixty years ago – so it's not much of a guide!'

'But it gives you another clue.'

'Unless the photo's of Mum and it's from Anna. It's in my wallet. Hang on.'

Alice got out her reading glasses and waited till Sandy held the photo out to her. 'Yes, I see what you mean. It's hard to make out her features. But all that curly hair. Perhaps that's a clue.'

Sandy felt as if she was handing over the family silver, but at the same time, she was pleased to be able to share her speculations at last. 'Mum's was like that. So it could easily be her.'

'You said there were a few things in the box. What else?' Alice handed back the photo so Sandy could slide it back into its pocket.

'A travel journal. She came here when she was about twenty. Here and Naples.'

'No!'

'Yes, really. I had no idea. She mentions coming to see Anna in Naples but she gave up writing it not long after she got there.'

Alice laughed. 'I remember that. Diaries begun with all good intentions then I'd get bored after a week or two. So you're following her footsteps?'

'It didn't begin that way but now it's a bit of a personal quest for me, one I was too nervous to make alone.' That sounded so feeble. 'Before I came, the thought of finding Anna, whoever she is, seemed overwhelming. But in her journal Mum seems such a different person to the woman I knew: younger, obviously, less buttoned up, more carefree. I want to know more about her. Maybe if I find this Anna, she can tell me. And if I don't find her this time, perhaps I could come back on my own to try again.'

'Naples is meant to be very different from Rome, though.' Alice looked doubtful. 'Anything else?'

'Not much. A scrap of fabric, a dried sprig of leaves and a flower. Possibly from an olive tree. A Christmas decoration. At least I think that's what it is. And an appointments diary.'

'A diary?' That caught Alice's interest.

'There was very little in it.' Why her respect for her mother's letter hadn't extended as far as the diary or the journal, she didn't know. 'One of those tiny pocket diaries with just the odd name or place and time scribbled in. I only know it was Mum's because it had her maiden name at the front. Miriam Mackenzie. Otherwise it could have been anyone's. All meaningless.'

'Which year?'

'Same as the travel journal. But please don't tell the others. I don't want them involved.'

'You have my word.' Alice waved at the others who were back on dry land, their time in the boats having expired.

14

Alice couldn't help watching Lia as she descended the Spanish Steps in front of her. Sidestepping a couple who had stopped to kiss and were oblivious to any obstruction they caused, she reprimanded herself for being so suspicious. While she was there, any flirtation between Lia and Mark could only be a game. Lia was sassy, good company, fun, even if she drove people mad with the constant clicking of her camera. And, yes, younger and slimmer than Alice. What was not to like about the woman?

Well, clearly, there was something not to like. She had picked that up from Sandy. Even Mark had noticed there was little love lost between the two women. The previous evening at dinner, Alice had noticed Lia's dismissive expression when Sandy admitted she wasn't on WhatsApp. Similarly, Sandy's exasperated sigh when Lia insisted on reading the menu out loud *again* 'to practise my Italian' had not escaped her. As the two single women in the group, they were thrown into each other's company and were trying to rub along for everyone's sake.

Alice was pleased to have found a friend in Sandy. Meeting a kindred spirit rarely happened on these trips and she wished she hadn't doubted her. Below her, Sandy and Lia were smiling at something Alan had said. Lia tucked her arm through his and huddled up to him. She turned round and gave a little wave at Alice and Mark when she saw Alice looking in her direction.

Below them in the piazza, tourists milled around the fountain, the blue of the water bright among the shadows.

'Enjoy that?' Mark had been silent ever since they had left the Borghese Gardens.

She turned her full attention to him. 'Absolutely. What a collection.'

'Have you heard from Pip?'

'Nothing.' She tried to hide her anxiety. 'She'll be at work.'

'I suppose she'll phone and let us know her grades when it suits her.'

'I expect so.' Change of subject. 'So – favourite painting?'

He laughed. 'That's too hard.' They played this game wherever they went: an old family habit that started with the kids. Favourite painting. Favourite place. Favourite meal. Favourite person. 'You go first.'

She raised her bottle of water to her lips as she thought. Then she said, 'I loved the Caravaggio boy with the fruit. Perhaps that. You? Go on.'

'Well . . .' he considered for a moment. 'I guess it has to be Titian's *Sacred and Profane Love*.' He reached out for the bottle.

A little bit more of her died inside. Its brilliance aside, how apt a choice for a man who had so often been torn between his wife and another woman.

'Let's peel off from the others,' he said. 'I can't bear the sound of Alan's voice for another second. Or listen to Peter and Brit. All that mollycoddling she does. I don't know how he stands it.' Below them, she could see Alan with Lia and Sandy at the foot of the steps.

'Isn't that the Keats Museum?' she asked. 'I'd like to see that.' As a teenager she had fallen in love with the Romantic poets, and the story of Keats' early death had seemed unbearably tragic. She was curious to see where it happened.

'Let's go later when they've gone.' He started to walk in

143

the opposite direction. The way he made decisions for both of them could be maddening. However – she took a deep breath – taking some time out with him away from the rest would do them both good. She was not giving up on her marriage yet.

'You guys going off on your own?' Gilly called down to them.

'Yeah.' Mark raised a hand. 'See you later.'

Within moments they had escaped the crowds and were walking past a kiosk selling postcards under a group of spindly palm trees towards an elegant-looking shopping street. As soon as Alice saw the words Dolce & Gabbana, she knew she would be window shopping only.

'Let's get a postcard to send home,' she said, stopping by the display.

She dithered over a view of St Peter's and one of the Colosseum, then plumped for a street scene.

'Less of a cliché,' was Mark's deciding contribution, as he handed over some change.

For a moment Alice felt that nothing had happened to divide them, that they were as happy as they had been when they first met. Was it her fault things had gone wrong between them? Had she not paid him enough attention? Had she mothered him too much? Questions, questions. Then she remembered Joanna, the student, and the night she took the call from the young woman's furious father, demanding to speak to Mark. She hadn't meant to pick up his phone but hadn't bothered to check whose it was when she answered. What a way to find out.

'Look at this.' Mark pulled her from a window full of the most exquisite underwear that she would never need or be able to afford even if she could fit into it. He took her a couple of shopfronts down.

'A man's shop. Do you want something?' she said. Mark was very particular about what went into his wardrobe.

'Not just any old men's clothes. Fine Scottish tweed. Have you ever seen anything more incongruous? Look at this place. It's like stepping back in time and into another country. Shall we go in?'

Inside, the shop was panelled like a Scottish men's club. On the walls between the pictures of Edinburgh and various Scottish landscapes were several stags' heads of different sizes. Tweed jackets, panamas, bow ties, ties on racks, socks in open suitcases, button-down shirts piled high on mahogany tables – everything an English or Scottish country gent could need.

'Why don't we get you a shirt? Shall we go in?'

As they walked through the door, something clicked in Alice's brain. At various points along the walls, the name of the shop was written large. 'Mackenzie dal 1901'. *Mackenzie*. Wasn't that Sandy's mother's maiden name? She was certain that's what she had said. Twice in two days. How funny.

'What's up?' Mark must have heard her intake of breath.

'The name. Mackenzie. It's just that Sandy mentioned that was her mother's maiden name. And that her mother came to Italy when she was young. But they couldn't be connected, could they?' Too late, she remembered her promise not to mention any of this to anyone. But this was Mark; he wouldn't pass it on if she asked him not to. 'You mustn't say anything to the others about her mother. She doesn't want everyone picking over her family history.'

'Are you serious?' Mark picked up a pale blue shirt, just like the many others he had in his wardrobe. His eyes were cool when he looked at her.

'Why not? It could be the Italian connection she's looking for.' Yes, it was a tenuous link but all the same . . .

'Have you any idea how many Mackenzies there are in the world?' He put the shirt down and picked up another so similar it was indistinguishable. 'It must be one of the most common Scottish names there is. That's taking jumping to conclusions to a whole new level.' He gave a dismissive laugh.

How he could belittle her so effortlessly. But she wouldn't rise to the bait. 'I do know, actually. But I just thought . . .'

'That you'd get the poor woman racing down a blind alley. I think I'll get this one.'

'You mustn't say anything.' Alice was anxious now. 'She asked me not to tell anyone.'

Just then she heard her phone buzz. Pip? Her heart racing, she pulled her phone from her bag to check.

Got the grades! Off to Bristol! Btw have booked ticket and am going with Holly and Tess to Oz. All sorted. Will call and explain. xxxxxx

She experienced a cocktail of elation and alarm, slipping her phone back in her bag before Mark noticed.

'Who was that?'

'Pip. She's got her place.'

'What does she say? Let me see.' He held out his hand.

'She's had a change of plan.' She opened Pip's text and passed him the phone, then waited for the explosion.

But of course Mark wouldn't make a scene in a public place. 'Oh,' he said. ' Stupid girl. I might have known.' He put down the shirt.

'They've got it all worked out. She may even have a job to go to.' She rushed over the words without thinking.

'You knew and you didn't tell me?' His outrage was matched by his disappointment in her.

'I was going to. There just hasn't been a moment. I'm sorry.' Though of course she could have made a moment had she not been frightened of his possible reaction.

He picked up the shirt again and headed towards the counter. 'We'd better find a moment then. I'd like to hear my own daughter's plans.'

Sandy had walked back to the hotel again, and was in her room, thinking about her conversation with Alice that morning. Perhaps Alice was right. Perhaps opening the letter would help her find the mysterious Anna Viglieri.

'Why did you leave me with this, Mum?' she said aloud. 'You could have talked to me and we could have found her together.' After Matthew's death, it would have been something to preoccupy them. Better than the endless jigsaw puzzles that her mother was so fond of. She turned the letter over in her hands yet again.

What would Matthew do?

I'd open it, he'd say. *But it's your decision.*

Eve?

Give it to me. Quick. She would be ripping the envelope from her hands and opening it herself. Which of course was exactly why she had never told her about it.

Steven?

It had nothing to do with him. Why was she even thinking about him? But what would he say?

Would you like me to open it for you? You need all the help you can get with this.

But if she opened it and went on to find this woman, it would be obvious the letter had been read. *Not if you put it in a new envelope*, she said to herself. *Whoever she is and whatever she's done, she won't be examining the handwriting on the front in forensic detail.*

Sandy slipped her finger into the tear that she had made the previous evening. 'Sorry, Mum. But I'm doing this for you,' she said out loud. Then she ripped the envelope open.

Inside was a single sheet of paper, her mother's address at the top, her signature at the bottom.

Sandy waited a moment before she began to read.

Anna
I'm dying. I've been diagnosed with cancer and I haven't
got long left now. But I can't go without sending you a
message. I don't know if you'll ever get this – perhaps you
have gone before me, but I hope not. I will ask my daughter,
Alexandra . . .

Sandy stopped reading. Her mother hadn't called her by her full name for as long as she could remember. Why now?

. . . to find you. Yes, I did marry a few years after I left
Naples – perhaps you heard, but why would you – and
we had a daughter. If she succeeds in tracing you and
you agree to meet her, I hope you'll like her. She has been
everything to me.

Something fractured in Sandy's head. Despite appearances, her mother had loved her. She removed her reading glasses. At so many times during her life, that was not how she had been made to feel. That time when she had run up to her after breaking the school high jump record only to find her mother had been chatting and missed the whole event. The crushing feeling she had never forgotten from that day had been repeated often until Matthew had rescued her. After that, her mother's apparent lack of interest didn't seem to matter so much and they established a friendly distance that only changed when Matthew died. Then they mysteriously became closer, like two sailors clinging on to the same life raft. And yet, they still never addressed the questions that Sandy now wished she had asked. Was her mother really unaware of how chilly she had seemed at times, how uninterested? Was she trying to make up towards the end? She'd never know. She returned her attention to the page.

I am so sorry. There. Four short words that are inadequate to sum up everything I've felt all these years. What I did was so wrong. I've spoken to no one about what happened and how it divided us. And I won't now in case someone else reads this. I'm not coming to look for you myself because I'm too ill now, and the disappointment if you wanted to continue having nothing to do with me would be too great.

It was as if her mother was looking over Sandy's shoulder, rebuking her.

I've thought about you so often, wondered what you would say if I tried to contact you. Believe me, I've been so punished. Every time I look at my daughter, I'm reminded of what happened. Sometimes that's been so hard and I know I've pushed her away as a result. But there's no point trying to explain to you. Just try to imagine how I've suffered for yourself. I'm not blaming you – how could I when it was all my fault? – but I want you to know I've never forgotten. And this isn't about me, but about us.

My last wish is for you to find it in your heart to forgive me, Anna. If you can't, then at least know how much I regret what I did. If I could go back and do things differently I would. Please believe me.

Ever yours

Miriam

Sandy read the letter again before laying it on her lap. This was a cry from the heart that didn't tally with the mother she had known. But what had her mother done? Nothing in their life together had suggested what it might be. She wondered if her father knew. But she'd said she had told no one. *'Every time I look at my daughter, I'm reminded of what happened.'* Did that explain the way she used to withdraw affection sometimes? ... *I've pushed her away* ... Whatever had happened between her and this woman had clearly burdened her for years.

There were no clues here to tell her where she might find Anna Viglieri or who she was, but only new questions. What had her mother done to this woman that had so divided them and needed forgiveness? And when had it happened? Before her own birth, if Anna had to be told of her existence. But that was almost sixty years ago. What could go so long unbroached and unforgiven? As far as she could see, there was no clue in her mother's journal, either.

Reading the letter made her more determined to find Anna Viglieri when they reached Naples. She wondered about the shop that Alice had mentioned when they had bumped into each other in the courtyard earlier.

'I'm so sorry I mentioned it to Mark. It came out without my thinking. I was so surprised by the coincidence.'

'But maybe it isn't. Mum mentioned a shop in her journal, maybe that's it. It's just chance you passed it.'

Shopping with Mrs R again. Wanted to get a new suntop. We found the family shop. Fancy naming it after your family. How unimaginative. She bought ties to take home as a present for Niall – just to prove she'd been there. Almost time for her to leave for Florence and me to go to Naples. Freedom beckons! Longing to see Anna though anxious about looking after children. I'll probably miss Tony and Fleur, too, though getting a tiny bit bored with them now.

Miriam Mackenzie, May 24th 1952 – Rome

She had assumed the shop had something to do with Mrs Robson's family. But perhaps it was a connection between her mother's family and this country? But she didn't remember anyone ever mentioning it. Her parents had never visited Italy together, and she was certain they had never mentioned a family business. The next day she would phone Mackenzies. It might not be the lead she wanted, or indeed any lead at all, but she would find out.

She pulled out the postcards she'd bought in the Keats museum. This was the sort of old-fashioned holiday communication she preferred. She and Matthew had been assiduous in choosing and sending cards within the first days of their holidays to show they hadn't forgotten despite their absence. First to Eve. A photograph of the Colosseum.

I'm thrilled about the baby. So looking forward to
seeing you both when I get back. One more week of
Italy. It's been a revelation. Love, Mum x

For Steven, she had chosen a postcard of Bernini's *Apollo and Daphne*. He would appreciate that.

You were right. The Bernini statues were marvellous.
The sun goes on shining, food delicious. I love it here
but we're almost done in Rome. On to Naples tomorrow.
See you very soon. Love xx

She stared at the words. Was that enough? Or too much? It was enough. Meeting Alan had made her aware of how lucky she was to have Steven.

Her thoughts returned to her mother. They had been in a pub garden not long before her cancer was first diagnosed.

'Do you ever think how your life could have been different?'

Matthew had died not long before and Sandy's thoughts were full of what-ifs.

Her mother had put down her cider, the sun on her face. 'Often,' she said, sounding wistful. There was a long silence. 'But regret's pointless. We can't undo the past.' Then she recovered herself and changed the subject. If only Sandy had pressed her to explain. But she had let it go.

The following evening she would be in Naples at last. She looked at Miriam's final entry for Rome and first for Naples. The magic of her new friends had worn off and she was on to the next big adventure.

Left Mrs R at the hotel. Quite sad to say goodbye to the old trout. I rather enjoyed being with her in the end. Tony and Fleur took me to the station and waved me off. Not a tear from any of us. Train to Naples. Anna met me at station and we went straight to Stuart's so I could leave my things in my room and meet the girls. Poor little things. How awful to have lost their mama so young. Also met Anna's fiancé – what a dish. Very dark and handsome, like a film star. She calls him il Capitano. Yes, he has a boat! She's never going back home she says.

Miriam Mackenzie, May 26th 1952 – Naples

Who were these people? Were they the ones who had such a traumatic effect on her mother's life?

By the time Sandy got down to breakfast the following morning, a number of cases were lined up outside the reception waiting for collection. The group was having breakfast at separate tables in the courtyard.

'*Buon giorno*, campers.' Lia appeared from her bedroom door in the cloister. Sandy had to hand it to her. She did look good in those shorts, the sort of thing that Sandy had long ago given up any thought of wearing. And instead of heavy walking shoes, she wore walking sandals that on anyone else would look orthopaedic but on her became a fashion statement, teamed with a matching shirt. 'Have I got time to get a new pair of sunglasses? I can't find mine.'

'Sure. We can wait for you.' Gilly tapped the top of her boiled egg.

'I'd have loved to have taken the train,' Peter said in a mumble that everyone could hear, including Gilly.

'No, you wouldn't.' Brit looked up from her croissant. 'This will be much more comfortable.'

Gilly put down her fork laden with fruit tart, and with a supreme effort at self-control said, 'If I'd known you wanted to catch the train, that could have been organised. If you and Brit want to take your cases to the station and make your own way, that's up to you. The rest of us will be driving and taking a minor detour en route to have lunch in a first-class restaurant in a delightful town with superb views. We wanted to give everyone the briefest taste of rural Italy, since the rest of your trip is mostly devoted to the two cities.'

Everyone else was concentrating on the food on their plates, embarrassed.

'Let's do what Gilly's got planned,' said Brit. 'I'd like to see something of the countryside. It won't be the same through a train window. You'll enjoy it.'

'And your cases will be taken from here to the next hotel without your having to touch them,' added Gilly, before returning her attention to her breakfast.

'A big plus,' added Lia. 'Come on Peter. Loosen up.'

Surprised, Sandy looked up from her fruit and cereal. Since when had Lia and Peter had been on such familiar terms?

Peter visibly relaxed. 'I'm sorry. I shouldn't have said

anything. Of course we'll stay with you, and look forward to the lunch.'

'Great,' said Gilly as if nothing had happened between them. 'I have a feeling you'll be pleased you did.'

Just then, a large orange fell to the ground with a thump, missing Peter's head by inches, and burst on the pebbles. 'Christ!' He put his hand on his head as if he'd been hit.

Brit leaped to her feet. 'Are you all right?'

'You've just been Tango'd,' said Lia with delight and everyone began to laugh.

'I just want to make a phone call before we go.' Sandy stood up. 'Can you give me a few minutes?'

'We're not in a hurry.' Gilly repositioned the tart on her fork. 'It's not a tremendously long drive. If anyone wants to have a last-minute stroll around – do.'

Peter perked up. 'Then I'd like to walk up to that fountain on the hill. Brit?'

'Mind if I tag along?' Alan pushed his chair back at the same time as Brit stood up.

'Sure.' They didn't look exactly keen at the prospect of his company but didn't complain.

What was going on? The allegiances that Sandy had thought were being formed were changing again. She looked over at Alice, who shrugged.

'We'll meet here at eleven-thirty. Bags packed, extras paid for and ready to go. That should give you all enough time.' Gilly poured herself more coffee.

'In which case, I'll go for a last stroll,' said Mark. 'Coming, Alice?'

'I'd love to but I'd better pack and get those postcards written. There's no point sending them from Naples.'

Alice and Sandy watched Mark and Lia walk together towards the gate, their hands close but not touching. He said

154

something that made her raise her hand to her mouth as if she was brushing away crumbs.

Alice coughed. 'Pip called last night. She's got Australia all sorted.' She spoke proudly but quickly as if she wanted to take her mind off what they'd just seen. 'Her friend's uncle is giving them all jobs on his wine estate, so that's where they're going to start. And the job means she can fund herself.'

'But that's great. How did Mark take it?'

'When I first told him, he was livid but then, when he stopped to listen, he was so surprised by her organisation that he couldn't object. She's always known how to get what she wants. Whatever he thinks, she has him round her little finger.'

'And you? How do you feel?'

'I'll worry when she's so far away, but I can see it's inevitable. I'm happier about this than I am about her wandering aimlessly through India, which was her first idea. So for the moment, all is good. Anyway, I'd better get on. Have you phoned Mackenzies yet?'

'I'm going to do that right now.'

A few minutes later, Sandy looked up the number of the shop on her phone and dialled, wishing as she did so that she had asked Italian-speaking Gilly or one of the girls at reception to do it for her.

The call was answered with a flood of Italian.

'Speak English?' she managed, wondering at her own sudden inability to speak it properly either.

'*Momento*.' That at least she did understand, and hung on while she heard a man's name being shouted. '*Giancarlo! Vene qui!*'

'Can I help you?' Though heavily accented, his English was clear and confident.

'I . . .' Sandy stopped. What could she say that would explain what she was looking for when she didn't know herself?

'Hello?'

'I'm sorry. Is there a Mr Mackenzie I could speak to?

'Mr Mackenzie. Is this a joke?

'No. I'm trying to track down someone in my family, and I think she might have something to do with your shop. Maybe from a long time ago.'

'Ah. But there is no one Mackenzie here. Maybe in Naples shop. But I don't think so. That's where is the first shop. In Via Toledo. You know it?'

There was a shout for him in the background.

'Thank you. I'll try that.'

Their call was cut off and Sandy sat on the edge of the bed staring at her phone, disappointed. But what had she expected? That Anna Viglieri would answer the phone and her mother's past would be unpicked at a stroke? If only life were that simple. But she would be in Naples in under twenty-four hours, and that's when her search would really begin. She took the photo out of her wallet and stared at it.

'Who are you, Anna Viglieri? And what did you mean to my mum?'

15

When Mark got back from his stroll, the cards were written and the bags almost packed. Alice would have liked a last chance to wander through the maze of Trastevere streets with their abundant graffiti, overflowing restaurants and bars, and creeper-covered facades that oozed history. Instead she'd spent the last half hour or so trying to fit their clothes back in the suitcases that seemed to have shrunk since they left home.

'Nice walk?'

But he'd disappeared into the bathroom.

'Where did you go?' She raised her voice only to repeat the question when he came out.

'I heard you the first time.'

'Then why didn't you answer?' She flung a pair of his pants that had been kicked under the bed into his case.

He folded the pants and then began to reorganise his packing that she'd just done. 'Those streets are so confusing. I just wandered in a vague circle till I found my way back here. You should have come. Have you packed my shirts?'

'I was leaving them to you.' He always complained about the way she folded the sleeves, even after all these years of marriage.

As he took them from the wardrobe and began folding them, she watched, still unable to detect the difference between her way and his. If only she could magic back those days when folding shirts was one of their last considerations. Although her marriage seemed to be slipping from her grasp, she still wanted to rekindle the feelings they once had for each other.

But perhaps she had to come to terms with the fact that if they were to survive together, they had to fashion something new that was nothing to do with the past. She wondered if that was possible.

By the time they reached the minibus, pulling their cases behind them, the others were piling in. With the cases in the boot, they went round to the door, feeling the heat of the sun reflected off the gleaming grey vehicle. Inside, Alice screwed up her nose at the strong smell of air freshener. Peter and Brit had the best seats for views, behind the driver, just across the aisle from Gilly. The others were behind them, apart from Sandy who was nowhere to be seen. Mark went to sit in front of Lia and, instead of standing aside to let Alice go by the window, which he knew she preferred, he sat down and shunted himself into it.

'Hope they've got good aircon, or we're going to fry alive.'

Alice tried not to mind Lia's hand on the back of their seat.

Sandy appeared at the open door, looking hot and flustered. 'Sorry to be late. I couldn't get my case closed. I think the lock's broken.'

'Lock?' Alan half stood as she climbed in. 'Time you updated and got something with a zip.' He sat down again and patted the seat beside him as if expecting her to sit there.

'That's so kind of you Alan, but I think I'll sit in the back. I didn't sleep well last night.'

Alice returned Sandy's smile as she went past.

'Like my new glasses?' Lia addressed the whole bus. She had put on an enormous pair of round, white-framed and very black sun specs.

'Yes, they're very, er – striking,' said Benno.

'Mark persuaded me they were retro film-starrish.'

Mark turned his face towards the window, away from Alice.

'You didn't mention that, darling.' *Why not?*

Lia took them off and put them in their case. 'I usually take ages to make up my mind.'

'Mark's good on snap decisions,' said Alice, staring straight ahead of her.

'He certainly is.' Lia gave a laugh which seemed loaded with meaning that Alice didn't understand. Or didn't want to.

'So where are we going, Gilly? Put us out of our misery, or is it a mystery tour?' Peter had recovered his good mood, and a map was spread across his and Brit's knees.

Gilly turned round as the driver took his seat and started the engine. 'No mystery tour.' She fanned herself. Anyone else want the aircon up a touch till we get going? No, in fact we're going in the direction of Campodimele.'

'Field of honey,' translated Lia, smug as ever.

Alice understood exactly why Sandy got so irritated by her.

'Well, not *to* it exactly, though if there's time, we could drive up there. But on the way there's a restaurant that does a great lunch with views. I think you'll like it, especially before we plunge into Naples. It's quite a contrast.'

Through the window of the minibus, Alice could see the lines of traffic at a standstill on the opposite bank of the Tiber. Mark had shut his eyes as if whatever was going on inside his head was more interesting than the view outside. Whatever it was, she didn't want to know. This holiday had been a horrible mistake. She should have known better than to go along with it. He said he wanted to make it up to her, but he wasn't strong enough to resist temptation. Lia was too great an attraction. She understood that now. They weren't ready to leave the safe havens of their home and Jane's therapy room. When they were there, at least Pip and the boys acted as some kind of brake on him. He didn't want a repeat of their scorn and hurt when they found out he'd been having an affair – the only one they knew of.

'Pregnant! How could you do that to Mum?' Pip's outrage had been shrill.

For the first time, Mark had looked ashamed.

'Dad, that's pretty gross.' Hugh had turned away.

She hadn't wanted to tell the children at all but after talking with Jane, Mark had decided having everything in the open was the right thing to do. There would be no more lies. And the ridiculous thing was that Alice had believed him. She had honestly thought he was in control of whatever impulse led him to risk everything he had once held dear. And she had to believe he still did so, otherwise the last twenty years of her life had been a sham. Ever since Sally had left him and the boys, he needed to show that although she might not have wanted him, there were others who did. That validation gave him the self-confidence he needed and in turn that made him attractive.

Buying sunglasses with Lia was not suspicious in itself, but why hadn't he mentioned it? Because he felt guilty? On the other hand if there was something to it, why had Lia mentioned it? What Lia took as innocent flirtation could be interpreted by him as something more. How could he be so stupid?

'Mark, can you explain your behaviour in any way so Alice can try to understand?' Jane had once asked.

I don't want to understand, she cried inside. *I want you to stop. Don't you ever think about how worthless it makes me feel?*

And Mark had been unable to reply.

Once out of the historic centre, the outlying areas of Rome were nothing special. Alice gazed past Mark at the streets, watching everyday life go by, letting her thoughts whirr through her brain. Behind her she could hear Lia reading out names of restaurants and snatches of advertisement hoardings under her breath, and the occasional click of her camera. The others were chatting to each other but she couldn't really hear what was being said. She heard Sandy and Alex laugh at something but didn't turn round.

When they reached Naples she would talk to Mark. She couldn't go on pretending nothing was happening. She had to speak up and stop things before they went too far.

After an hour, they turned off the motorway to drive through farming country, heat haze rising from the tarmac in front of them, mountains smudged blue in the distance. Finally they pulled off the road and parked under a split-bamboo shelter. A ginger cat was curled up by the front wheel of another minibus parked two spaces away.

Climbing stiff-legged out of their air-conditioned luxury, they were hit by the heat they were now familiar with. Alice drank from her bottle of water.

'This way.' Gilly ran ahead, ponytail bouncing, assuming the group would follow. The front door of the building led into a dim dining room, cream walls and dark wood furniture, tables laid but only one of them occupied by an elderly couple. Gilly was greeted warmly by a middle-aged man with a set of menus under his arm. He stood back, his other arm outstretched to guide them through another door. Along a short passageway, past the kitchen where an old woman was bent over pasta-making and two younger women stirred and chopped beside her, the sound of pans clattering accompanied delicious herby, meaty smells that made Alice realise how hungry she was.

Outside, two long tables were laid in the shade of a vine-clad pergola, each with a view that stretched away to another hazy range of hills. One was occupied by a group of Germans, the other was for them. Below them olive trees stood silvery under the sun, black nets at the base of their trunks. A couple of butterflies danced past them towards the flaming red bougainvillea at the side of the house while bees busied themselves among pots of bright geraniums.

'Sit down, sit down.' Gilly took a seat with her back to the view. 'I've seen it before. You must enjoy it. Let's order some wine and water. Giovanni!'

There was an awkward dance round the places as Peter and Brit and Benno and Alex tried to sit together while the others tried to escape each other. Alice found herself between Alex and Brit while across from her Sandy sat between Alan and Mark.

'Vino? Birra?' Giovanni held out the wine list. Mark was nearest so took it and trailed his finger down the page, his face a picture of concentration.

'Need any help?' Peter's pride in his knowledge of wine had come out before. He reached across the table.

Before Mark could refuse, Giovanni passed Peter a list of his own.

'Any suggestions, Gilly?' Mark obviously hadn't seen anything he recognised.

'Surely the Lacryma Christi?' suggested Peter, the list shaking slightly in his grasp. 'The name's too good to ignore. Brit?'

'Honestly?' said Gilly, dabbing her forehead with her napkin. 'The house wine is very nice.'

'Well, we're happy with that, if you recommend it,' said Mark. 'Aren't we Alice? A couple of glasses, please.'

She nodded, annoyed that he had spoken for her without even showing her the list. She had spent years pairing food and wine but he always insisted on choosing himself.

After a few minutes, Giovanni returned with the drinks. 'Your food will be with you very soon.' His bowed his head.

'But we haven't ordered. I was hoping to have . . .'

Peter was stopped from saying more by Brit's quiet 'Wait a second, honey.'

'Oh, didn't I explain?' Gilly downed her water. 'The kitchen's run by Giovanni's *nonna*, his mum and sister. They cook a set menu every day depending on what's available. This is traditional home cooking that's hard to find. The real thing.'

'Good to have the decision taken out of our hands. Sounds wonderful, doesn't it?' Brit spoke for her and Peter. He nodded. Alice had seen this before. Why did women feel bound to make up for any awkwardness caused by their more socially inept husbands?

But a family kitchen – this was the sort of home cooking Alice adored. The food came in a steady flow. The rough bread and olives were followed by caprese salad, spaghetti carbonara with black truffle, then meatballs. The smells, the tastes, the textures. She was in seventh heaven.

As they ate, Gilly prepared them for Naples. 'So many people stay there a couple of days and use it as a stepping stone for the sights around it, but the city itself is a joy. Yes, it has a reputation for being dangerous but I've never had any trouble. You just need to be as careful as you would be anywhere else.'

'Especially with your money belt.' Lia pointed a finger at Sandy who looked away as the others laughed.

'But it's a city I love,' Gilly continued. 'It's not a tourist showpiece, like Rome. This is a city that feels real. You'll see.'

By the time Giovanni brought out the poached cherries and mascarpone, everyone had relaxed, tensions had been forgotten in the face of the delicious and unpretentious food and drink. Somehow the dessert slipped down into the minuscule gaps left by the earlier courses.

'I may never eat again.' Sandy leaned back, leaning forward again as soon as Alan leaned back beside her.

'So good,' said Alice, sipping her wine, feeling at peace. Perhaps that talk with Mark could wait till they were back at home after all.

'And now Naples,' he said, hitting the table with the flat of his hand. 'I'm ready.'

'Me, too,' said Lia.

'What about you, Sandy?' Mark turned down the table to look at her. 'You ready?'

She gave him a puzzled look. 'Yes, of course.'

'Now you're close to unravelling your little mystery, you must be excited.' He had ordered himself a small carafe of wine without offering any to the others. Alice realised that although no one else but her might pick up the signs, her husband was getting drunk. The heat, the wine, the time of day – and she could see disaster round the corner, but she was sitting too far from him to be able to place a Brit-like hand on his arm, or to kick him hard under the table. But perhaps no one would notice.

Sandy bent her head as she twisted her napkin in both hands. 'I'd rather not talk about it.' She gave him the sort of glance that must have intimidated many a child. But Mark wasn't a child. And the children it might have intimidated wouldn't have been drinking.

He looked around the table, pleased to have found such an eager audience. 'But a mystery woman known to your mother and a secret message. What could be more intriguing?'

'Mark! That's enough! It really isn't our business.' Alice finally found her tongue. But too late.

'Have you still no idea who she is?' Lia was agog. 'How thrilling.'

'No, I haven't,' said Sandy with icy calm. But if she'd hoped to close down the conversation, Mark had other plans.

'But Alice made a connection between Mackenzies – a men's clothes shop we found,' he explained for the benefit of the others. 'And Sandy's mother. They have the same name. Though what are the chances?' He laughed. 'I mean, really!'

Alice wished she could curl up under the table and die. She had been so clear that she shouldn't have mentioned it to him, that he must forget she'd said anything. Sandy would never forgive her. Indeed, when she looked up, she saw her look of hurt and surprise.

'But this is Sandy's business.' Benno moved the carafe out of Mark's immediate reach. 'Not ours.'

'But what if they are connected?' Lia asked. 'Maybe Alice is right.'

'They're not,' Sandy cut off any further speculation. 'Look, thank you for being interested but this is something I've got to sort out myself. It's something I owe my mother that's between her and me.' She glanced down the table at Alice, frowning.

'But we're all friends now.' Alan raised his glass. 'And friends help each other.'

'Exactly,' said Lia. 'Tell us what we can do.'

'I think you should all leave Sandy alone.' To everyone's evident surprise Brit spoke up. 'I agree with Benno. This is her business. If she wants us to help, she knows all she has to do is ask.'

Alice saw the look of gratitude Sandy sent Brit and wished she'd spoken out herself. 'I agree,' she said, wondering how she could make up for her stupid lapse of discretion. She would have to get Sandy on her own when they reached the next hotel.

'Well then, that's sorted.' Gilly pushed her chair back. 'Anyone for coffee?'

16

Have meant to keep up journal but having such a good time. Don't know if I want to take on looking after the girls for long though. Too much like hard work. As for Anna and il Capitano – they take me all over the place when they can. At weekends we go on the boat when il Capitano isn't working. He's gorgeous – wish he was mine.

Miriam Mackenzie, June 15th 1952 – Naples

Without enough space to park, the minibus pulled up at an angle outside a grand gateway.

'Everybody out! We've arrived.' Gilly and the driver were already halfway down the steps as the others roused themselves from their post-lunch torpor. By the time they were in the street, the cases were waiting for them. A couple of doors down, music pulsed into the street from a bar. Immediately Sandy could sense the difference from Rome. The heat was more intense, the graffiti bolder, the atmosphere edgier. Just down the street from where they stood was a small square lined with bars and restaurants. Gilly saw her looking.

'We're right by the historic centre here. It's smarter down by the sea, better views maybe, but here we've got the real gritty Naples on our doorstep.'

Sandy wasn't sure how much the 'real gritty' anything appealed to her. But, she reminded herself, this was the city she'd wanted to visit: the place where her search for Anna Vigneri might come to something.

Gilly pressed a bell and announced herself on an intercom. The small gate in a larger one swung open. They went through one at a time to find themselves in the courtyard of a dilapidated palazzo that looked as if it had been divided into apartments. Gilly led them across the cobbles to the back of the yard, where a hidden door opened at the touch of another buzzer. All at once they weren't in the throbbing heart of Naples at all, but in a second, smaller, more elegant courtyard where shrubs and palm trees sheltered a kidney-shaped swimming pool, surrounded by loungers. Some steps took them up past a terrace and into the hotel reception area.

One by one, room keys were given out as everyone was signed in. Sandy sat on one of the white leather sofas waiting for Gilly to call her name. Inside, she was buzzing with excitement and trepidation. As soon as she got to her room, she would phone the Naples branch of Mackenzies, the only possible lead she had so far and as good a place to start as any. The others disappeared to their rooms until only Lia, Alan and she were left. Sandy looked around her at the modern art on the light-coloured walls, the glass case of local food products, the sleek leather sofas and chairs. She could see some agitated chatter going on between Gilly and the receptionist, who was looking alternatively upset and resigned. Eventually Gilly came over.

'I'm so sorry but there's been a misunderstanding over the booking. They only have two rooms left. They can give us a third after lunchtime tomorrow but until then there are only two.'

'Surely there must be another room somewhere.' Lia stopped fiddling with her phone and stood up. 'For God's sake.'

'She's said she'll phone the neighbouring hotels, but isn't hopeful this late in the day.'

'Well, ladies. Looks like it's my lucky week. I'll very happily share with one of you.' Alan put his hand out for a room key.

Sandy and Lia exchanged a look. This at least was one thing they could agree on. Neither of them was going to share with him.

'I was wondering if the two of you would mind sharing for one night.' Gilly looked mortified by having to ask. She caught a finger in the thin chain of her necklace, running it back and forth.

'Sharing!' Sandy blinked. Gilly couldn't be serious.

'I know it's not ideal but it would solve the problem.' Gilly's eyes shut as she spoke, aware of how much she was asking. 'And it's just for one night. I'll make sure you're refunded.'

'I think I could do that if there really isn't an alternative,' said Lia. 'Don't you, Sandy? Don't look so appalled.'

The idea of sharing a room with anyone was bad. The idea of sharing with Lia was much worse. Equally, Sandy didn't want to be difficult. Up till now, Gilly had run things so smoothly that this almost certainly wasn't her fault.

'I'd prefer to have my own room if possible but if there's really no choice...'

'It'll be fine. We can pretend we're on a school trip – just for one night.' Lia bounced up and down on her heels. 'It won't be so bad. And presumably we'll get some kind of compensation on top of the refund.' Her voice lifted at the end of the sentence to show it was a question.

'Of course.' Relief edged into Gilly's face. 'I'll have to work something out with the office at home.'

Sandy had never enjoyed school trips, not even the short weekend ones where she'd had to sleep in scout and guide huts on rickety camp beds. Not even when the only consolation was a bottle of warm white wine smuggled in by one of the more risk-taking teachers without the pupils or the head seeing. Even cheap hotel rooms, when teachers doubled up for economy, were agony to her. She put a high price on her privacy.

'Sandy?'

They were waiting for her. Now Lia had come round to the idea, refusing might cause the sort of offence that would infect what was left of the holiday, never mind the new school term. Things were bad enough without that.

'All right,' she agreed, having a nasty feeling that those two small words would cost her. 'But as long as it really is only for one night.'

'I promise,' said Gilly. 'And I'm so grateful to you both for taking it so well.'

Sandy didn't feel she was taking it well at all. Her efforts to master her dislike of Lia were failing miserably. She tried again as the flustered receptionist handed her a key in exchange for her passport.

'Room 202,' said the receptionist. 'If you wait one moment, I show you the way.'

'At least we're getting special treatment.' Lia embarrassed Sandy by speaking so loudly. But she flashed her a quick conciliatory smile and hoped that would do.

Room 202 was at least large. 'Our family room,' the receptionist announced as if that would make things better.

Lia went straight to the window and drew open the floor-length swag curtains. 'Naples!' she said with a flourish to the view of the flat-fronted building across the street.

Sandy laughed. 'I hope it gets better than that.' The wall made their room feel more cell-like than ever. Lia threw herself onto the double bed, owning it, the contents of her bag spilling out round her camera. 'Which bed do you want?'

The double, obviously, but Sandy said, 'I'm OK with the single.' At least it was by the bathroom door.

'You sure?'

'Yes, don't worry.'

Lia sprang from her bed and opened a cupboard under the table. 'Ah ha! As I suspected. The mini-bar. There's no point unpacking if we're going to be in different rooms tomorrow. So let's celebrate our having got this far. Prosecco?' She brandished two miniature bottles in one hand and a couple of plastic champagne flutes in the other. 'Class.'

'Don't mind if I do.' Sandy packed away any resentment and possible embarrassment, saving them for later when they would have to go to bed. Lying propped up against her headboard, she studied her roommate, who was pouring out the drink and handing it to her. Enthusiastic, headstrong, wilful but fun were all good ways to describe her.

'God! If the girls could see us now.' Lia flopped back on her bed, careful not to spill a drop. '*Salute.*'

'Cheers.' Sandy raised her glass and tasted the spritzy sweet drink, letting the bubbles tickle the back of her throat. 'To us in Naples.'

'And to you solving your mystery.'

'Let's not talk about that.' Sandy sounded stuffier than she meant to.

'Oh, come on.' Lia settled herself in the middle of her substantial bed. 'I might be able to help. I'd like to.'

Never had Sandy been so grateful for the buzz of her phone and the sight of her daughter's name on the screen.

'Eve! How are you?'

Lia had picked up her own phone and was working it to death with her thumbs. She was making a good show of not listening but Sandy guessed otherwise.

'Hey, Mum. I thought you'd have called me back before now.'

Calm. Deep breath. 'I've just sent you a postcard.'

Outrage fizzed down the line. 'I was hoping you'd call me to say you'd come round.'

'I am "round". Really. I'm thrilled.'

Lia lifted her head, glanced at Sandy, interested.

'Mum, I know you. I can tell you're not saying what you think.'

'This is a bit of a difficult time. Can I call you back later?'

'Mum! This is important.'

'I know. It is to me too. But I'm with someone at the moment.' Despite the hint, Lia didn't move. 'Hang on while I go outside.'

Shutting the door behind her, Sandy slid down the wall of the windowless corridor until she was squatting. 'I am so pleased for you both, darling. Honestly. And I'm dying to be a grandmother.' Except it would never really be her grandchild – not one gene or chromosome of it. 'It's just . . .'

'Just what?'

She shrank from the edge of hostility in her daughter's voice. 'Nothing important. We can talk when I'm home. It won't be long now. But give Jen my love and congratulations.'

'You'll have to get out the knitting needles.' She had been forgiven. For now.

As she went back into the bedroom, Lia focused her camera in Sandy's direction. 'I always take a photo of every room I stay in. You don't mind?'

'Er, no.' Sandy stepped to one side so she wouldn't be in the picture.

'Trouble at home?' Lia was snapping the room from several angles.

'Only my daughter. It's nothing we won't get over.'

'You're so lucky to have her.'

'Sometimes I wonder.' Sandy gave a wry laugh, then felt guilty. 'No, of course you're right. She's still the most important thing in my life, even though she's grown up and has a life of her own now.'

'More important even than your job?'

'Of course. What a strange question.'

'I'm jealous.' Lia clicked the lens cap back on the camera. 'I'd give anything, absolutely anything, to have a child of my own.'

Sandy took a sip of Prosecco while deliberating how to answer. 'I thought you said the other day you weren't cut out for it.'

'I tell myself that to persuade me, but I'm not too old,' Lia said, reading Sandy's mind. 'Not quite. There's not all that much time left on the old biological clock, so I've got to be quick. Of course I could try all sorts of things but I'd prefer to know who the father is and have some kind of relationship with him. Perhaps. But I'm not fussy any more: I've given up looking for the perfect relationship. I haven't got time. I just want someone intelligent and amusing. I don't care how old they are. I don't even care if they're married.' She stopped, looked at Sandy over the rim of her plastic glass. 'Have I shocked you?'

'No, you haven't. But the baby? Don't you mind that you'll be its only parent?' Sandy was genuinely interested.

Lia's expression shaded with doubt. 'I don't think so. Plenty of people do it. All I know is that I need to have a baby.' She paused. 'I can't explain but the feeling's so strong.'

There was an answering echo in Sandy. She remembered so well how the hunger to have a child overrode almost everything else when others never felt it at all. Fortunately Matthew had felt the same, perhaps for different reasons but he wanted a child. They had talked about it soon after they had met, even though they were still at university. They had known even then they were going to spend the rest of their lives together. He would have liked a bigger family but it wasn't to be; so they decided they would accept and enjoy what they had, not destroy themselves with longing for what couldn't happen. That was the best decision they made.

Lia peered at her. 'I think you understand.'

Did she? The urge, yes, but not the determination to do anything at all to satisfy it.

Sandy composed her features, trying not to show any reaction. Surely Lia couldn't have her eye on Mark as a candidate. She wouldn't. 'I do. I remember how much I longed for Eve. But you're not planning on doing anything about it while we're here, are you?' Alice would be devastated.

'If the opportunity presented itself . . .' Lia stopped and laughed. 'Your face! Don't worry, I'm not that bad. Anyway who with? Alan? Peter? Or Mark?' She ticked them off on her fingers. 'But you'd never unhave your daughter, would you? That's what I'd like in my life: that all-consuming unconditional love.'

'But you can have that without involving a man, can't you?' Sandy thought of those few women she knew who had turned to fertility clinics for help.

'Like I said, I want to know who the father is, even if that's as far as it goes. I'd forfeit a relationship for a baby.'

That went against everything Sandy believed in. She gave a short laugh. 'It's not always plain sailing. Eve and I have had our ups and downs.'

'So I gathered.'

'She's having a baby but it's complicated.' What was she doing telling Lia, with whom it had nothing to do?

'But that's fantastic. What's the problem?'

'Long story.' *And none of your business.*

'Is she married? Or still too young?'

'Yes. She's married.'

'Do you like him? It must be awful not to like your child's partner. My mum loathed Jonny, my long-ago ex. She never said a thing but she made it perfectly obvious. Looking back, I wonder if I didn't marry him just to get at her. But turns out she was right. He was a shit. Left the marriage with everything he could, leaving me with nothing.' She stopped for breath and looked at Sandy for a reply.

'Her, in fact. Eve's—'

'Gay!' Lia's eyes were avid for gossip she could take to the staffroom.

At once Sandy remembered what happened at school, the gossip that went round the staffroom like wildfire, the fact that she and Lia were not friends in their other life. For a moment she had thought discussing her reservations with someone younger might help. She quickly readjusted. 'That's right.'

'And you're OK with that?'

'Of course. Provided she's happy. I don't mind who she has sex or falls in love with, it's none of my business.'

Lia looked taken aback by her sudden sharpness. 'It's just not what I was expecting. That's all. Sorry.'

Sandy swung her feet on to the floor, noticing her shoes had pulled out some threads in the glittery bed runner. 'Think I'll freshen up a bit before we go down.'

'I didn't mean to offend you.' Lia almost looked worried.

'You didn't.' Sandy reassured her. 'I'm used to it.' Her mother and her mother's friends had found Eve's coming out very difficult to accept. When that happened, Sandy was strong in her support of her daughter, not for one moment wavering in the face of prejudice or lack of understanding. Thanks to her insistence, her mother had come to a gradual acceptance of Eve's sexuality. Now, Sandy realised how much she wanted to talk about the baby with another woman, to discuss the issues surrounding its birth so she could sort out her own prejudices. Because that's what they were and she had to recognise that to move forward. Eve sensed her anxieties but Sandy didn't want to discuss them over the phone. She should say that to Eve, of course. But Lia was not the audience she wanted.

Just as she was about to get into the shower, Lia called through the door. 'You haven't got a needle, have you? The button's come off my shirt.'

'In my case. There's a little tin in the pocket. There should be a safety pin in there.'

One night only. She could do this.

When she emerged from the bathroom, she was beginning to see the funny side of things. Nobody at school would believe she had shared a room with Lia French. And in less than twenty-four hours this would be over. She zipped the lid of her case, catching sight of her mother's letter and journal. As soon as she could, she would call the shop. But not in front of Lia. For the next little while before they went downstairs, she would restrict the conversation to the A-level results and how Lia's pupils had done, making sure to steer well clear of the deputy headship question. That was hers and she would not let it go easily.

'Oh, you had a call,' said Lia, offhand as she leaned towards the mirror to put on her mascara. 'Steven. He asked you to call him back.'

'You answered my phone!'

Lia turned, her eyes heavily accented. 'Well, it rang and, as you were in the shower, I answered it in case it was important.' She turned back to the mirror.

'And was it?'

'I don't think so.' She titivated her hair until it was just as she wanted it. 'Who is he?'

'A friend.' Sandy snatched up her phone.

'I didn't think you had a man in your life.' Lia stepped back from the mirror, satisfied with what she saw.

Momentarily stunned, Sandy replied. 'That's because I don't talk about my private life at school. I try to keep them separate.' She tried to adopt the voice she used when the kids were playing up. If she got angry, they only behaved worse.

'Yes, but it's different now we're here and sharing a room.' Lia was nonplussed. 'I thought we were friends. Otherwise I wouldn't have told you about how much I want a baby. I don't want that going round the staffroom either.'

'No, I don't suppose you do.' Sandy didn't like the idea of

exchanging confidences with someone she didn't really trust. However, given the circumstances, and that she had been made to feel guilty by what Lia said about being friends, perhaps she should give a little.

Lia was staring at her. 'So, go on then. Who's Steven?'

'He's someone I met at the choir I sing in.' Sandy took a breath. *Come on.* 'He's been a big support to me, particularly over the last few months while Mum was dying.'

'I'd always imagined you lived on your own, like me.' Lia slid off her wedding ring and put it back on her other hand. 'That was one thing I thought we had in common.'

'But I do. Steven and I live separately and it suits us well.' She spoke from habit, wondering as she had done several times whether she really believed that.

'Really? I like the idea of sharing everything with someone else, even though I've come to terms with the fact it might never happen.'

'We both like our own space.'

'More fool you,' said Lia, turning back and forth in front of the full-length mirror. 'But I guess we have to do what makes us happy, whatever anyone else thinks. God! This dress! Linen only looks good if you never sit down.'

'You go on. I'll catch you up. There's a call I need to make first.'

'Oh, by the way. I don't suppose you'd let me borrow that scarf that's in your case? The green would go perfectly with this dress. A bit Brit-like, in fact!'

17

Alice sipped the glass of water that had come with her coffee. If she didn't say something soon, they would be joining the others for supper and she'd be watching Mark flirt with Lia again in front of everyone else, and she wasn't sure she could bear that. He was studying the map of Naples with his guidebook open in front of him. Rather than stay in their room, they had come out to one of the cafés near the hotel. Usually, Alice liked nothing more than people-watching in a strange city, but for once she was too preoccupied to enjoy it.

'Mark.'

'Mmm.' He looked up from the map. His eyes were as blue as they had ever been, his gaze as intense. This was the face that she had fallen in love with, although it had changed with time. His jawline had softened and the wrinkles round his eyes and mouth had deepened but not to any detriment. His lips were thinner but the smile was the same. 'Pompeii – the bit I'm looking forward to most I think.'

'It's going to be so crowded.' It was possibly the part of the trip she was looking forward to least.

'Probably, but we managed the Vatican, and it can't be worse than that.' He picked up the guidebook and pointed at a picture of the ruins. 'We can't possibly miss it. What were you going to say?'

This was going to be difficult. When they were alone together, they got on well enough for her to wonder whether she was mistaken. He was dismissive of her only when they were in public or even sometimes with friends, showing off to them. Remembering that gave her the courage she needed. 'I wanted to talk to you about Lia.' She reminded herself to look at him, not at the ground. She must be strong.

'What about her?' Still staring at his book, he pushed his specs back up his nose. His mouth clamped shut.

'It's just that after everything we've been through, after all the promises we made each other, I don't want things to go off track now.' She mustn't sound too emotional. If she did, he would switch off.

He turned a page in the book and ran his finger down the page. 'I'm not sure what you mean.'

Was he going to make her spell it out? 'Mark, you do know. Don't make this more difficult that it already is.'

Finally he looked up at her and took off his glasses and tapped them on his knuckles. 'What?'

By being deliberately obtuse he was forcing her to make more of an issue than she wanted. This was his way: to make his problem someone else's. But this time she would not be intimidated into silence. Exasperated, she flicked a fly from the edge of her cup. 'You know perfectly well. Everyone's noticed you and Lia flirting with each other. They've all been talking about it. It's humiliating for me, and you're embarrassing yourself.'

He snapped shut the book and banged it down on the table. 'You're imagining things.'

She wouldn't be put off by his unbearable condescension. 'Well, then why didn't you tell me that you'd helped choose her sunglasses?'

'I didn't think you'd be interested. You don't usually want to know about the duller minutiae of my day. If you do now, things are going to get very boring.'

'Of course I don't.' Alice's eyes were stinging but she blinked the tears back. She was not going to give in. 'You know exactly what I mean. I can't go through this again.'

'Is that a threat?' He clasped his hands behind his head and leaned back, looking down his nose at her.

Alice had a vision of herself running a dagger straight between his ribs to his heart and twisting it hard, but all there was to hand were some wooden cocktail sticks on the table. 'Mark, please. If you won't think of me, think of the kids.'

'But they're not here.' He brought his arms down and began pulling his fingers and cracking his knuckles. One. Two. Three. Four. He knew how much she disliked the habit.

'But *I* am. I know it's flattering when someone flirts with you . . . but what was the point of all the counselling and heartache we've just been through, if you're just going to let it happen again, especially right under my nose. I'd like us to talk about it and, if you won't, then I'm not going to sit back and watch it happen.'

He straightened up, hands on the arms of his chair. 'Alice. Nothing is happening. You're making a mountain out of the very tiny molehill that is me getting on well with someone we've just met. There's nothing more to it than that.'

Alice's shoulders sagged. If he was going to deny it, there was nothing she could do. He wouldn't admit there was something more fundamentally wrong in their marriage, and wasn't prepared to discuss it. She stood up. 'If you won't talk about it, then I'm going back to the hotel.' Perhaps the time had come at last when she would have to make some decisions of her own. But she was afraid: afraid of doing something she might regret and be unable to reverse. He was banking on that fear keeping them together.

'You do that.' He picked up the guidebook and opened it.

'The Neapolitans claim any pizza outside Naples isn't real pizza. So today that's what we're having.' Gilly was leading them down a street in the old town, crowded with night shoppers, little shops that sold anything from plastic buckets and groceries to cakes, ice cream, tourist tat and junk.

'Not . . . San Michele?' Lia was walking just behind her, her hand on Sandy's green scarf, which did indeed go with her dress. Sandy hadn't known how to say no, although she had been astonished by Lia's cheek. 'Elizabeth Gilbert says their pizzas are something else. I really want to go there. For a margherita with double mozzarella.'

'No, not tonight. It's got so famous, they queue round the block to get in. I didn't think you'd want to do that,' said Gilly, stopping outside a restaurant where a modest queue stretched back from the door. 'Oh. But I'm sure we won't have to wait for long.'

Sandy could hear Brit muttering something about not wanting a pizza and calories, and being shushed by Peter. An interesting reversal. She couldn't help thinking of Miriam's words again as she queued to repeat her experience.

Pizza is quite the thing here. Tomatoes, cheese and doughy base. Simple but so delicious. How do the women stay so slim?

As they walked, she had kept her hand clutched tight on the cross strap of her handbag just in case someone tried to rip it from her. She was not going to be robbed again. Disappointed by the outcome of her phone call to Mackenzies, all she wanted was to get into the cool of an air-conditioned dining room and have a drink in her hand. The whole idea of some kind of link between her mother and the shop was obviously a complete red herring after all. Mark was absolutely right.

Within thirty minutes of waiting they were inside a square room, noisy with customers and full of the smells of pizzas cooking. Wooden beams crossed the ceiling, pictures and cooking implements decorated the walls. They edged round the red-clothed table that had been set up for them, each one trying to sit near their favourite people and avoid those who weren't. Alice and Gilly took the two heads of the table. As soon as Sandy saw Lia take a chair by Gilly, she made sure she sat at the other end. Drinks were brought and pizzas ordered while Gilly began to talk about what they'd be doing in the time they had there.

'I've said before that most people use Naples as a stepping-off point for everything there is outside the city – Pompeii, Herculaneum, the islands and the Amalfi coast – but we're here long enough for you to get to know the city a little better than that. Tomorrow we'll do two walks – nothing too strenuous, not in this heat – and then the next day we'll have Pompeii.'

As everyone began to talk about where they particularly wanted to go, Sandy allowed herself to drift off, rerunning the disappointing conversation with Mackenzies in her head.

'Are you OK?' Alice leaned towards her so the others couldn't hear.

'I feel a bit let down, that's all.' The responsibility her mother had placed on her was turning into a burden.

'You can tell me, you know.' Alice paused. 'I'm so sorry I mentioned the Mackenzie connection to Mark. It seemed such a weird coincidence that I blurted it out without thinking.'

Alice wasn't like Lia. There was something in her that Sandy instinctively trusted. 'There's no harm done. I shouldn't have made it into such a big thing. What does it matter if everyone knows? Nothing's going to come of it.'

'Why do you say that?'

They waited as the pizzas were put in front of them. Large, bubbling, tomatoey, cheesy, thin-crusted margheritas. 'Oh my.' Alice began to cut into hers. Sandy was slower. After a minute or two with her eyes shut and an expression of bliss settling on her face, Alice came back to earth. 'Sorry, but this is one of the things I've been really looking forward to. The real deal. But why won't you find your mystery woman?'

Sandy put down her knife and fork. 'Because it was ingenuous of me to imagine that I ever would. How would you go about tracking down someone in London or Birmingham – it's like looking for a needle in a haystack. She might not live here any more. She might not even be alive. I don't know the city and I don't even speak the language. All I know is that someone called Anna lived here nearly sixty years ago with a boyfriend she nicknamed *il Capitano*. Not helpful. And that Mum came here to see her and to look after two little girls.'

'What happened when you called the shop?' Alice sawed through her pizza crust.

'They found a young guy who spoke English and said he had never heard of an Anna Viglieri, that he couldn't help at all. I heard him asking around in the shop but nothing. I'm afraid Mark was right and the Mackenzie name is just a random coincidence. I stupidly let myself believe that it might be the first step to finding her but I was wrong. And now I'm here, in Naples, I haven't a clue how to go about this. I don't want to let Mum down . . .' She started to cut herself a piece of pizza. 'But she must have known she was asking the impossible.'

'I wish I could help.'

'That's kind but I should forget about it and enjoy being here, although I can't quite let go. Mum would be so disappointed.' Sandy was surprised by how delicious, light and crisp the pizza was.

'But you've tried. You can't do more than that.' Alice leaned forward again to make sure she wouldn't be overheard. 'And now you're sharing with Lia? How's that?'

'Let's just say I'm looking forward to tomorrow when I'll have my own room again.' She remembered the conversation about the baby and looked down to where Lia was telling a long story that had the other end of the table in gales of laughter. Mark was hanging on her every word.

'There's something about her that doesn't sit right. Look at her now. Just what you said: a man's woman. She's flirted with all of them. Only Alex and Benno are safe.'

'I wouldn't bet on it!'

Every now and then Lia glanced towards Mark, whose eyes only left her when he had to reply to something said to him. Sandy couldn't hear what the two of them were talking about but he hadn't addressed a word to anyone else since he'd sat down unless he had to.

'Don't worry about her,' she said to Alice. 'She's honestly not worth it.'

'I can't help myself. I want to trust him, and for years he's been like this: flirting and fun. I used to think it was funny but now I see it for what it is: humiliating and hurtful. I've got to think of myself, now. I'm in my fifties and now the kids are leaving home, I've got a chance to do something new, branch out. I can't live the rest of my life under his thumb.'

'What are you going to do?' Sandy scrutinised Alice's face which she had never seen so serious.

'I'm going to do something for myself.' Her eyes had lit up.

'Like what?'

'I'd like to work again. I loved chefing before and still love cooking and experimenting with food. So why not go back to it? I've spent the last twenty years entertaining Mark's colleagues and our friends, so I might try to do something with that.'

'You're not going to leave him then?' She was relieved. Ending a marriage on the basis of a suspicion seemed hasty.

Alice laughed. 'We've been through too much for me to throw the towel in just yet. But if he had another affair, then things would be different.' She looked down the table. 'He's always been set on my being at home to look after the kids and I've always been happy doing that. His boys were such lost souls when I first met them and desperately needed me to be there, and then of course there was Pip . . .'

'But now they're all grown up.'

'Exactly.'

'What are you two talking about?' Mark swivelled round in his chair as Brit took over his conversation with Pete. 'These pizzas aren't bad at all.'

'The children.' The words snapped from Alice.

'Why? Have you heard any more from Pip?'

'Nothing. She'll be earning what she can and organizing her departure.' Alice frowned. 'I hope it'll all be OK.'

'Why wouldn't it?' he said.

'I thought you were against her going.'

'I wanted her to stick to her plans, but she seems to have this trip and how she's going to finance it pretty well worked out. And Holly's a sensible girl. It's time Pip spread her wings, even if it's not in the way I'd prefer. This is what happens. Don't you agree, Alex?'

Alex had been talking quietly to Benno and looked up. 'What's that?'

'You have to let your children fly the nest when they're ready. My parents couldn't wait to get rid of me.'

'I can't imagine reaching that stage, can you?' Alex turned to his husband with a smile.

Benno shook his head. 'They're so young. I hate the idea of them growing up at all.'

'You see,' said Alice, slapping the table top with the flat of her hand to emphasise her point. 'They understand. Of course they have to lead their own lives eventually but when they're battering on the door to get out and you're not convinced they're ready, it's even harder.'

'You're too sentimental.' Mark took a long draught of his beer. 'If they don't get a chance to experience life on their own, they'll never stand on their own two feet. That's what Pip needs.

Holly's got her head screwed on and it sounds as if her uncle will give them the start they need. Sandy, you must have a view. You see hundreds of kids reach this age. What happens?'

'It's up to the parents, I'd say.' Sandy had no wish to be involved in their disagreement. 'Some kids are more mature than others, others need more time before they're ready. There's no right or wrong'

'Very diplomatic.' Mark banged his glass on the table. 'And if the parents don't agree?'

'You can't expect her to answer that.' Alex stepped in. 'This is for them to sort out.'

Sandy was grateful he had stepped in. 'I don't know your children and I hardly know you.' What had she and Matthew done when Eve was that age? They had muddled through just as everyone else did, hoping for the best for Eve and often getting it.

'Time to go, guys.' Gilly came over to their table, a waiter standing at her shoulder. 'They want the table for the next group.' She gestured towards the door, where they could see people waiting.

'Now what?' Lia rubbed her hands together, looking up and down the street.

'I'm turning in.' Gilly took a couple of steps in the direction of the hotel. 'But up to you. If I were you, I'd leave exploring the old city until you've got your bearings after tomorrow. But there are plenty of places to drink in the Piazza Bellini or, if you want something quieter, in the Piazza Dante. I'll show you on my way back.'

'Sounds good to me,' said Alan. 'Anyone for a nightcap? Sandy? You'll come?'

Anticipating Lia's acceptance of the invitation, Sandy thought of having their room to herself and the calls she could make. But Lia would only wake her up when she came in, so she might as well join them. 'Why not?'

'Good woman. Who else?'

They walked back in the direction of their hotel. The Piazza Bellini was heaving with students drinking outside the bars, filling the pavements and spilling over into the road. Above them, light shone from windows and people sat on tiny balconies looking down at the proceedings below. By an alleyway, a knot of young men in African football shirts looked as if they were hanging out, waiting for something. Sandy watched one of them approach a couple, who walked swiftly past. The next person he tried, a man, went with him into a doorway where something changed hands before he walked away.

'I don't suppose you'd rather go back to the hotel for a drink,' said Alice. 'It's much quieter there.'

'Don't be so antisocial,' said Lia as she overtook them. 'The night is young.'

'Let's go with them. I'm curious.' Sandy had no intention of going back now. She loved the atmosphere, the heat, the street life that made her feel energised, alive. Besides, didn't Alice want to keep an eye on Mark, who was walking between Alan and Lia, laughing at something Alan had said. He didn't turn once to check whether Alice was there.

18

Il Capitano took us into the old part of Naples today.
Narrow dark streets with tiny shops. Washing hanging
everywhere. Felt rather threatening except in the churches.
Far more intimidating than Rome. Anna and I stand out
with our pale complexions. Glad il Capitano was with us.

Miriam Mackenzie, June 22nd 1952 – Naples

The following morning they returned to Piazza Dante. The square was thrumming with city life before the day got too hot: kids on bicycles, playing football or racing about; mothers with prams, chatting; tourists figuring out where they were going. The entrance to the Metro was black with graffiti. Large cream parasols shaded the tables of the cafés and restaurants that encroached from the sidelines. They were quiet now, very different from the hubbub of the night before. Unlike anywhere Sandy had visited in Rome, this was grimy, dusty and urban with no pretensions. She stopped to buy a cold bottle of water at one of the kiosks, running it up and down her arms before she opened it, relishing how cold it was. Ahead of her, the group was pressed together in the narrow strip of shade provided by Dante's statue. She looked behind her at the curved palatial building, topped with statues on either side of its central clock tower, then crossed over to where they stood.

'Hot enough for you?' Alan grinned.

Brit had her umbrella aloft in one hand and with the other was fanning herself with a painted paper fan.

'Oh, I could take a few more degrees,' said Sandy with a smile, unscrewing the cap of her water bottle. Gilly's face was glowing as she gave them a potted history of Naples. 'Three thousand years in three minutes' was what she promised and delivered. Her lacquered Japanese parasol was brilliant yellow, decorated with a pair of green and pink lovebirds, and stood out in the surrounding dust and grime. Back through the Porta Alba and they were in a covered alley lined with bookshops that spread on to stands in the street. At one end a tiny pizza shop sent out cooking smells that drowned the occasional but unmistakable smell of piss.

Gilly led them down the Via Tribunali, past where they had eaten the previous night, pausing at the one and only Banksy in Italy, a madonna with a pistol hovering over her head. They stroked the gleaming nose of the brass head of Pulcinella for luck and stared up at the massive hyper-real mural of San Gennaro, patron saint of the city, that dominated a church wall close to the Duomo. They climbed the steps to the Duomo itself, laughing at the small boys playing on one of the stone lions that flanked the doorway, and strolling round the vast ornate interior before resting in the pews of a side chapel gazing up at the putti playing high over an altar. The constant clicking of Lia's camera accompanied them every step of the way. They walked down 'Christmas Alley' where the shops were devoted to all sorts of Christmas kitsch, decorations, lights and figurines for the elaborate nativity scenes and tiny replicas of daily life in the city that were sold in specialist shops. Above their heads hung painted tambourines, puppets and more decorations. Sandy bought a bright red chilli pepper charm as a talisman to give to Eve. Then she went back and bought herself one too.

'Perhaps you should get one for Pip,' she suggested as Mark and Alice caught her up.

'You don't believe in all that superstitious nonsense, do you?'

She bristled at Mark's tone. 'Of course not, but I love the colour.'

He shook his head and waited as Alice decided which size of chilli pepper Pip would prefer. On they went past pizzerias, bakeries, and shops selling everything you could think of from groceries and souvenirs to football paraphernalia or virulent-coloured slushy drinks. Washing was strung between the balconies in the streets that laddered off to either side, buildings too high and close together to let the sun in. Despite the draining heat, the energy of the place was infectious. Sandy's grip on her bag had loosened, she almost felt at home.

'If we don't stop for a coffee soon, I think I'll die.' Alice's face was a pink that clashed with her shirt. 'And I can't wait to try one of those shell-shaped pastry things. I've seen them everywhere.'

'*Sfogliatelle*,' said Gilly. 'And you've got to try a *baba* too. They're sort of syrupy brioche things and my favourite.' She gestured them over to two tables under the parasols labelled Gran Caffè Neapolis.

'Oh, thank God.' Alice took the nearest seat to her.

Immediately a man came up holding a terracotta begging bowl. Before anyone could do anything, a waiter had chased him away.

'This poverty makes me feel so uncomfortable.' Alice stopped digging in her bag and put it under her chair. 'I mean, look at that dog.' She nodded towards a big old grey dog with a matted coat that lay in shade by its master and two small bowls: one full of water, the other of coins.

'You're such a softie.' Mark slipped his arm round her.

'I can't help it.' She gripped his hand, obviously as surprised as him by this spontaneous burst of affection.

'The trouble with you is that you'd like anything offensive kept under wraps so we don't see the real life of a city.'

'That's not what I meant at all.'

Sandy didn't like the scorn she heard in his words, and was conscious of the others looking away, embarrassed.

Click. 'You don't mind do you?' Lia took the last chair at their table.

Nobody objected although they all knew what the rest were thinking. There had been enough muttered complaints among them about Lia's frequent photographing of them.

'But this is so ... I don't know ... exhilarating ...' Sandy stopped as the waitress stood beside her. '*Un tè freddo, per favore.*'

They all looked at her.

'What?!' She laughed. 'I'm learning the basics. Just the odd word or two. You know.' This rush of new confidence was as intoxicating as it was unexpected.

'Did you talk to Steven?' Lia leaned across Mark to get the sugar, brushing against him.

'Not yet.' Sandy was aware of Alice watching the other woman. She was about to say something more when her chair was shoved from behind amid the sound of shouting.

'*Vai!*' The waitress yelled at a street vendor with a tray of lighters who was in the midst of the tables. '*Vai!*'

Sandy recognised the man in the football shirt from the night before standing just behind him.

Instead of going, the man tried to push the waitress out of the way so he could carry on his conversation with another table. His mistake. From the doorway of the café rushed two waiters, but the lighter seller was faster, dodging between the customers and making a run for it before they could get to him. Sandy watched as the furious waitress persuaded them to run off in pursuit. When she looked back, the football-shirted man had disappeared too.

Alice scraped her chair back on the cobbles with a shout. 'No! Someone's taken my bag!'

There was a flash of colour as the football-shirted lad shot round the nearest corner and disappeared.

'Down there.' Sandy stood and pointed after him.

Mark stood too, staring around him as if he expected the thief to come back. 'There's no point. We'll never find him.' He sat down again. 'You didn't leave it on the ground?'

'I thought it would be safe under my chair. I was so hot, I didn't think.'

'Don't tell me you had your passport in it?' He shook his head in despair.

'I'm not a total idiot.'

The others looked away, as Sandy and Brit checked their own bags were safe on their laps. On the other table, the rest of the group went back to chatting as the waiters returned from their manhunt empty-handed. Lighter man had escaped. And so had Alice's bag.

'Was there anything important in it?' Sandy tried to restore the conversation to a more manageable level.

'Some euros. Guidebook. That's it. Oh, and the chillis I just bought.'

'Do you want to report it?' asked Gilly. 'I'm not sure...'

Mark groaned and put his head in his hands in an unnecessarily theatrical way.

Alice looked as if she would like to throttle him but kept her voice level. 'No. There's no point. We'll never get it back and I haven't lost anything important.'

'Thank God for that.' Mark lifted his head. 'Have we time for another drink?'

'Sure.' Gilly relaxed back into her seat. 'I thought we'd go to San Sepulcro and Santa Chiara, then break off until it cools down a bit.'

'I'm dying to go underground. Are we doing that? I saw the

sign back there somewhere. *Napoli Sotterranea*.' Lia pulled her chair over to sit next to Gilly.

'One of Elizabeth Gilbert's places, I'll bet.' Alan's whisper was loud enough for everyone to hear.

Lia looked daggers at him.

'That's not on our schedule but you can go in your free time.' Gilly had adopted a new approach to Lia's demands – just roll with them, don't rise to them. 'We won't go on our second walk until the day's begun to cool down a bit.'

'Great. Is anyone else up for it? Boys?'

'Definitely,' Benno said. 'It's meant to be—'

'One of the highlights.' Alex finished his sentence.

'Not me,' said Alice. 'I've got an appointment by the pool this afternoon.'

'Me too,' said Sandy. 'I'll come out later.' The thought of going underground didn't appeal at all.

'Oh, come on, ladies.' Alan came over to their table. 'You may never come back here.'

'But I can live without,' said Sandy, picturing dark tunnels, foetid air, nothing much to see, an overwhelming sense of claustrophobia. 'I'd rather stick to what's above ground.'

Alice received her lemon granita and sfogliatella with a smile. 'Thank you.'

'Mark? Or are you welded to the missus?'

'Not at all. I'd be up for it. If I wanted to lie by a pool, I'd have gone to Greece.'

'It's meant to be a holiday, darling, not an endurance test.' Alice remonstrated gently.

'Hear hear,' said Brit. 'Pete, you don't want to go do you?'

'Actually, I will, but I don't mind if you want to stay by the pool.' Sandy and Alice exchange a quick glance. This was a first.

And so it was agreed that Lia would go underground with all the men of the group. How very apt, thought Sandy, wondering what those men would say if they ever got wind of their conversation.

The Sansevero Chapel was as memorable as Gilly had led them to expect. Afterwards the three women strolled back to the hotel, stopping only to pick up three sandwiches on the way. Before they did anything else, Alice helped Sandy move her things into a room of her own.

'I'm never sharing again,' Sandy said, as she threw her bag on to the bed. 'There are some things about other people it's better not to know. The snoring is all I'll say.'

Alice had been glad to have something to take her mind off her stolen bag. Not that the bag was important, or its contents, but their loss had a greater significance than just the physical. Somehow it felt like yet another thing unhooking her from the life she knew. She was as unable to retrieve the bag as she seemed unable to retrieve Mark. There was no doubt that however hard she tried, they were slipping apart again. It could have been so easy to compromise and do something together this afternoon instead of going their separate ways. But he seemed under Lia's spell. Whatever they did, wherever they went, the reality was turning over and over in her mind. One moment she was thinking about them separating, the consequences, the next she was trying to work out how to patch things up. After this holiday she would try to persuade him to go back to Jane. Perhaps that would be enough. But in her heart, she knew that their problems went too deep for that to be a simple solution.

At about three o'clock she went downstairs to find Sandy and Brit already by the pool, deep in conversation.

'We just had to accept that our life wasn't going to be the one we had pictured for ourselves,' said Brit as Alice reached them and sat on a lounger.

'Just as we had to.' Sandy was lying on her side resting on

her elbow. 'But at least we had Eve. It must have been so much harder for you.'

'Yes, it was tough. I just never got pregnant.' Brit's voice tailed away, then she rallied. 'Peter has been fantastic though. We met in university and always knew we'd have a family together. When we had to accept it wasn't going to happen, we were both broken-hearted.' She looked at them both then removed her dark glasses. 'And although you have to accept it, that feeling never completely goes away. It creeps up on you and hijacks you when you're least expecting it – in a shop, a park, when you see something on the TV or a film. When your friends have children, it hurts. Then, when they have grandchildren, it hurts all over again.'

Neither Alice nor Sandy knew quite how to reply to such an unexpected personal confession. Brit had seemed so buttoned up. Alice couldn't think how they had got on to the subject. But Brit hadn't finished.

'It's a kind of grieving, I suppose.'

They nodded, sympathetic.

'And then we went through a terrible patch when we threw ourselves into our work, barely speaking to each other. I was terrified that Peter would leave me for someone who'd be able to have children with him, but somehow we got through and here we are.' She rounded her story off quickly as if she was afraid of boring them, or saying too much – it was hard to know.

'And you have a good life together now,' observed Alice.

'We do.' Brit smiled. 'We made a conscious effort to throw ourselves into a life we hadn't expected. We've worked hard and we've enjoyed ourselves. And we're close to our nieces and nephews too – all seven of them. I love it when they come and stay.'

'All together?' said Alice, wilting at the thought of so many children at once.

'God, no!' Brit laughed. 'One or two at a time. But they've stayed with us since they were young, so we know them well. They like coming to us, I think.'

'They're lucky to have you, then.' Sandy rolled on to her back. 'That sounds pretty perfect. I miss not having any brothers or sisters, never mind a welcoming aunt and uncle.'

'But you have your daughter,' said Brit. She didn't sound envious or hurt, but she replaced her sunspecs, signalling the conversation was over.

Sandy picked up her notebook.

'Only mad dogs and Englishwomen . . .' Alice spread her towel on the sun lounger and lay flat. Above her, the three palm trees were motionless against the blue sky. Beside her, Sandy was already scribbling. 'I've got so behind,' she said. 'You don't mind?'

'Of course not. I'm just glad to relax. I've got my book.' She picked up her Kindle. After about twenty minutes, still not gripped and baking in the heat, she got to her feet and crossed the hot tiles to the pool. Stepping into the water, she held out her arms, feeling the sun's burn. 'That's better.' She dipped her head under and swam the three or four strokes it took to get to the other side. How strange it was to be in a pool overlooked by so many tall city buildings, but the relief from the heat made her not care.

Sandy put down her notebook and looked up. 'Nice?' She stood up, pulling down the bottom of her own swimsuit. She was a good-looking woman who had obviously looked after herself, thought Alice. She couldn't help comparing Sandy's with her own less than perfect body. *But you like eating*, wailed her inner foodie. *Does being a bit overweight really matter?*

The two of them supported themselves with their arms hooked on to the edge of the pool behind them, lazily kicking a leg or two every now and then.

'How are things?' Sandy asked at last.

'I'm so glad to have an afternoon like this.' Alice batted away a fly. 'I talked to Mark about Lia.'

Sandy looked surprised. 'What did you say?'

'I asked him straight out and he said nothing was going on. Of course.' How awful it was not to trust the man in whom she had put all her faith twenty years ago. 'I never thought I would ever be talking to a stranger about my husband.'

'I'm not a stranger, we're friends now.' Sandy tipped her head back to the sun. 'Even if we haven't known each other for long. Anyway she's with all the men now, so I think Mark's safe for the moment.'

'Sandy!' Lia's voice broke into their conversation. 'Look what I've found.' She ran over from the gate to them. In her hand was a paper carrier bag. 'You've got to see this.'

'Let me get out first.' Sandy swam back to the steps.

Alice could hear how irritated Sandy was to have their afternoon's peace interrupted. She swam beside her and climbed out too. As they returned to their loungers, Lia was bouncing with excitement.

'Whatever you've got in there had better be good.' Sandy dried her arms, then sat down. Lia came to sit beside her, making her shift along. By this time, Brit had woken and sat up to watch what was going on. From the gate they heard the sound of the men talking. 'Is it too early for a drink?' Alan led the way in and, ignoring the women, sat on the terrace behind them ready to order a beer. 'Anyone else?'

'Have you had a good afternoon?' Mark came over to Alice. 'That was extraordinary, fascinating, but I think you'd have hated the bits where it got really narrow. One woman couldn't hack it and had to be taken back. But otherwise . . .'

Alice tried to give him her attention but couldn't help looking across to where Lia was pulling something out of the bag. 'You know those junk shops?' she was asking Sandy. 'We've seen a few of them. Well, I can't resist. I'm always intrigued by those old photos of people that can't mean anything to anyone any more or they wouldn't be there. There's something so sad about them.'

'She dragged us all in,' said Peter, but with an indulgent smile. So Lia had charmed him too. 'It was fascinating, actually, and I got something for you.' He passed a little box to Brit.

'Oh, isn't it gorgeous?' She took out a bright blue micro-mosaic brooch with a bunch of flowers at its centre and showed the others. 'Thank you, darling.'

Visibly pleased, he kissed her cheek.

'But look what I found,' Lia insisted, brandishing a picture frame that she handed it to Sandy.

'A picture of Mackenzies,' said Sandy, her voice flat. 'It's nice of you to remember but I'm afraid it's a dead end. I've checked.'

'Are you sure?' Lia's excitement was so infectious, Alice got up to have a look. 'See here.' Lia pointed at the small print under the photo.

'Where?' Sandy was impatient.

'Here. Look who it is. Roberto Viglieri!'

There was a silence.

'Viglieri!' she repeated. 'Outside Mackenzies. Viglieri and Mackenzie! It must tie up, mustn't it? It's part of your jigsaw.'

Sandy frowned. 'How do you know?'

'How do I know what?' Lia's turn to be puzzled as Sandy still didn't look at the picture.

'That I'm looking for someone called Viglieri.'

Lia was immediately defensive. 'You told me.'

'No, I didn't,' insisted Sandy. 'I was careful not to, quite deliberately. There's only one way you can know that and that's because you've seen the envelope. Unless someone else told you.' She looked at Mark who shook his head and walked over to join Alan on the terrace.

Lia looked down at the picture. 'Well, yes I have. I couldn't help seeing it when I got out your sewing tin. Remember?'

'But you must have taken out the envelope too, if you read what's written on the front.' Sandy drummed her fingers against the glass covering the photo. 'Did you read the letter too?'

'Of course not!' But she looked shifty. 'Have the photo anyway.'

'Thank you.' Sandy put it in her bag, collected up her stuff, slipped on her dress and walked back into the hotel without another word.

'Well,' said Lia. 'I thought she'd be pleased. Some people.'

'But if you looked through her things . . .' Alice began.

'Of course I didn't.' Lia looked straight at her. 'I would never do anything like that. I saw the envelope and took it out by mistake.'

But Alice didn't miss the uncertainty in her smile, the tremor in her hand as she folded up the paper bag she had brought the photo in.

19

Not sure about Naples. I don't like it as much as Rome. I don't feel so safe here. But the coast is beautiful. Villages hugging the cliffsides, the sea sparkling in the sun, lemon groves, donkeys. I've never seen anywhere like it. Got new bikini – very racy. Ma would die if she knew ... but she never will

Miriam Mackenzie, June 26th 1952 – Rome

Sandy sat in the chair by the window, looking down on to a motorbike repair shop below. How different her experience was from her mother's. Her breath caught as she tried to control her anger with Lia for poking about in her things. The scarf had been bad enough. Leaving the photo on the bed, she went over to check her half-unpacked case. The envelope and its contents were still there, the writing on it hidden by the pocket. To read the name, Lia must have removed and replaced it without saying anything. She had invaded Sandy's privacy even though she knew how highly Sandy valued it. Had Lia read the letter? Had she had enough time? Sandy quickly went through her things but nothing seemed to be missing.

Still reluctant to look at the photo, she went into the bathroom and turned on the shower. She would still rather no one else was involved in this search. She closed her eyes, letting the water beat down on her as she concentrated on letting go of her fury.

After five minutes, she was feeling calmer. She wrapped herself in a towel, making a turban of a smaller one for her hair, and returned to the bedroom.

Taking her reading specs from her bedside table, she finally picked up the frame from the bed, a flicker of excitement igniting inside her. As much as she didn't want Lia's help, perhaps this really would take her closer to her goal. The picture was a grainy old photographic print showing a line of men, suited, black hair slicked down, staring unsmiling at the camera. They were standing in front of a shop with 'Mackenzies' written in large script above the doorway. Together they looked like something straight out of *The Godfather*. Underneath was printed 1955 and the names of the men. Sure enough, third from the left was a Roberto Viglieri. Dressed almost identically to the others, in dark suit, waistcoat and dark tie, he was straight-nosed with a generous bowed mouth, his eyes staring straight at the camera. There was a definite look of Al Pacino about him. Could Lia have hit on something? Surely this had to be another coincidence. She rested the photo on her lap. But there must be some sort of link between the Viglieri family and Mackenzies, the shop. But did it mean her mother's family had something to do with them too? If only she hadn't got bored with her journal the moment she got to Naples. If there was a link between them all, Sandy would be in Lia's debt again. Not where she wanted to be.

Three soft taps sounded at the door.

'Hang on.' She propped up the picture by the TV and crossed the room. 'Who is it?'

'Me. Alice. Are you OK?'

Sandy opened the door, standing behind it so no one in the corridor would see her in her towel. 'Come in.'

Alice had changed into a bright summer dress with a necklace of big coloured beads and several bangles on her arm.

'Do you mind if I quickly get dressed?' Sandy asked. 'It'll take me a second.'

'Of course not. I'll sit here.' She took the chair by the window.

'Have a look at this.' Sandy passed her the photograph. Minutes later she was back, having slipped on a loose top with a pair of Capri pants and combed her hair. 'What do you think?'

'Handsome lot, aren't they? Look at him.' She pointed at a man two along from Roberto. 'Did you see that film . . .'

'You know what I mean.' Sandy sat on the end of the bed opposite Alice, pressing her heels back against it. 'Could there really be a connection? Isn't it just too unlikely?'

'There must be, surely. But the question is, what are you going to do about it?'

'I don't know. Look up all these names in the Naples white pages?'

'But they could be dead or not live here. Shouldn't you go back to Mackenzies with it and try again? Someone must know something about the people who've worked with the shop at a senior level even if they're not there any longer. There must be records.'

'Or a little old man who's worked there for ever that they keep in a back room.' Amused by the idea, she grinned. 'If only I could speak Italian.'

'But Gilly can. Why don't you explain to her? I know you didn't want to involve anyone else but we all pretty much know anyway, and now this has happened, you might as well. For your mum's sake.' She held out the photo to her.

For her mum's sake. The words hit home. Sandy was immediately transported back into her mother's bedroom, the pink walls, the floral curtains, the faded watercolours. She could hear her mother's laboured breathing, smell her Chanel No 5 perfume, feel the warmth of her breath on her cheek as she tried to whisper what she wanted Sandy to do. 'Find her . . .'

'I know, I must. I did read the letter when we were in Rome, thanks to you.'

'You never said.'

'No. I didn't know what to make of it, that's why. Let me show you.' She went to her case and got out the letter.

'You don't have to.'

'As you say, it doesn't matter any more. I'm assuming Lia's read it, and, if I'm ever going to deliver it at all, perhaps I should accept any help I can get and stop being so stubborn.'

'No.' Alice was firm. 'I don't need to read it too.'

'But I'd like you to.' Sandy had meant what she said. For the first time since Matthew's death, she found herself wanting to ask for help.

Alice took the letter with some reluctance then concentrated as she read it straight through. She looked up at Sandy when she finished. 'I see why you didn't want to talk about it. This is so personal, so painful. "What I did was so wrong",' she read aloud. '"I've been so punished", "how I've suffered", "please forgive me."'

Each phrase made Sandy more determined to fulfil her mother's wish.

'What could she have done that was so terrible?' Alice folded the letter slowly. 'You have to deliver this.'

'I know, and I think Gilly's a good person to ask.'

'Do you really think Lia read it?' She handed it back.

Sandy held it close to her heart. 'Who knows? If she was hoping to find something that she could use against me, why would she have been so pleased to have found this?' She laid a hand on the photo.

'Why would she want to use anything against you?' Alice frowned.

'In a couple of weeks, we'll be back at school as if none of this had happened. One of us is almost certainly going to be appointed deputy head.' Instead of feeling her usual determination to win, she felt an indescribable weariness.

'You're in competition?' Alice's eyes widened.

Sandy nodded. 'But we've agreed the subject's off limits while we're here. Otherwise it would be impossible.' Even so, she felt sick at the thought of the battle ahead. This holiday had shown her that, if anything, Lia had no scruples. Sandy couldn't bear to think what she would be like if she didn't get the job.

'Well, then we'd better find Gilly.' Alice held out the picture. 'We're not here for long so if you'd like me to help, I'll do my best.'

Through the window at the front of the hotel Sandy could see Mark sitting with Alan, Peter and Brit on the terrace, drinks on the table in front of them. She was about to go out to ask if any of them had seen Gilly when she heard the sound of someone running downstairs. Gilly turned the corner, hair down for once, looking cool and ready to go. 'Hi ladies. You going outside?'

'Actually we were looking for you. Can we sit somewhere private so I can explain?'

Gilly's eyes narrowed. 'You're not making a complaint, are you? When someone asks to talk to you in private, it's usually trouble.' She gave them her perfect orthodontically corrected smile.

'Not this time,' said Sandy. 'I'm hoping you might help me.'

'We can go to the residents' lounge. In here.' Gilly led the way into a small room where the walls were lined with books in different languages, holiday reading left behind by previous guests. On the lowest shelves were magazines and a couple of chessboards and backgammon sets.

They sat down and Sandy plunged straight in. Telling the whole story with all its odd connections took time, especially since Gilly kept stopping her to ask questions, making sure she understood.

'So you need an Italian-speaker to try to find out the connection between the man in the photo and the shop? I don't think my Italian's quite up to the phone but I can explain to Paola, the manageress. I don't need to tell her the whole story, just to find out if and how this Mr Viglieri was connected with Mackenzies. Right?'

'If you don't mind.' If nothing else, Sandy would be able to discard this line of investigation. 'And then if he was, I need to find Anna. She could be his wife or sister.'

'Or any female relation at all! I'd better get on with it then. I'll do it right now.' In her eyes was the expression Sandy had seen in Alice's when she first heard about Anna Viglieri. The thrill of the chase. But now, instead of defending herself against their involvement, she was grateful they were so prepared to help her. Gilly got to her feet and, in the doorway, she turned around. 'Don't move. I'll be right back.'

Sandy could think of nothing she wanted to do less than move. The room was beautifully cool and her drink was hitting the spot.

'Did you mean what you said about Lia the other day?' Alice was leaning back, eyes closed, hands behind her head.

'What did I say?'

'That she just likes to be liked, that she didn't mean any harm.' There was a catch in her voice that didn't go unnoticed.

'Did I say that?' But of course Sandy remembered the conversation.

'You did.' Alice sat up with a rattle of bangles.

'I don't know any more. She's a strange mix: selfish, maddening, determined to get what she wants...' Sandy paused, thinking of the job, the baby... Mark, perhaps. 'But at the same time she's entertaining and thoughtful – what else was getting the photograph but thoughtful?' The last in answer to Alice's incredulous expression.

'Interfering?'

They sat in silence for a moment.

'You're still worried about Mark?'

Alice sat back in her chair and blinked hard a couple of times. 'More than ever. The way he denies everything almost confirms it to me. He did the thing he does so well of making me feel so small and petty-minded for even allowing the thought into my head.' Her face crumpled as she took the screwed-up tissue Sandy passed to her and blew her nose.

'What are you going to do about it?'

She took a long sip of her drink. 'I keep changing my mind. One minute, I think I'll hang on and everything will be better when we get home. The next, I'm making plans for a life on my own.'

Sandy sat up. 'Seriously? You'd leave him? What would you do?'

'If I left him?' She shut her eyes as if she was imagining a new life. 'What I'd like to do whatever happens. I'd go back to cookery school, or I thought last night that I could ask my friend who's got a small chain of restaurants if I could work for her. I'd want to work with food again.' She patted her stomach. 'I like food.' And laughed.

'Right!' Gilly's announcement made them turn to see her framed in the doorway again. 'Paola's calling them right now.'

Sandy felt unaccountably nervous. 'Thank you.'

'Don't thank me till we've got somewhere.' She came over and sat with them without noticing Alice's expression that said she would rather they were left alone. But theirs was a conversation to be had later. Sandy's first priority lay with her mother even if it meant a few minutes chatting about the shoes Gilly had seen that day.

'They'd be perfect for the wedding. Sam loves a high heel.' She gave a wicked grin.

Sandy and Alice listened as she described them.

Eventually Paola walked in, full lips bright with red lipstick, her voice expressive. She spoke rapidly, hands moving, before passing Gilly a piece of paper and nodding at the two women. 'Good luck.'

'Good luck why?' said Sandy, hope finding a foothold inside her. 'What did she say?'

Gilly inched to the edge of her seat so she could pass the paper across. 'She talked to the manager, who said they don't keep any records in the shop itself, but that the head office may be able to help. He gave her their number, so she called and made an appointment for you to see someone there tomorrow afternoon.'

'Not before?' She took the piece of paper and stared at the writing. A name, an address and 5.30 p.m.

Gilly shrugged. 'That's the best she could do. We'll be back in good time.'

Sandy could feel that tiny kernel of hope taking root and sending out shoots of excitement. There was a gleam in Alice's eye too. 'Twenty-four hours. I don't think I can wait. And how will I make myself understood or understand what they say?'

'I'll come with you.' Gilly slapped her hands on her knees. 'My Italian should be good enough. It's just shaky over the phone.'

'You will? But that's—'

'That's my job.' She stood up. 'Well not exactly, but I'm curious.'

After dinner in the Quartieri Spagnoli, Sandy walked back to the hotel with Alex and Benno. In her room, she sank on to her bed, glad to be on her own again. There was only one person she wanted to talk to. She picked up her phone.

Steven answered immediately. Hearing his voice was comforting, as if she had come home. She had almost forgotten how good that felt and found herself relaxing as they talked.

'How's it all going?'

'I've got so much to tell you.' Sandy wanted to share with him everything that had happened. She wanted him to be part of her search too.

'Why didn't you tell me before you went?' She could hear how disappointed he was that she hadn't confided in him.

'I had this daft idea that telling anyone at all was disloyal to Mum, that it was our secret. I didn't even tell Eve. It's hard to explain.' How to tell him that she had put herself second to others for so long, she had needed something purely for herself. 'But you're right, I shouldn't have. I should have told you.'

'I'm glad you have now.' His voice was so clear, she pressed the phone to her ear as if it would bring him closer to her. 'I wish I was there to help you.'

'But there's nothing...' All at once, Sandy wished he was too. Not because she couldn't do this on her own, but because having the sort of support she had missed since Matthew's death would make everything feel easier. And she would love to be sharing her Italian experiences with him, she realised. 'So do I.' She surprised herself.

'You do?' Him too.

'Yes. I have a sense that I'm getting closer, even though I may be about to hare off down a blind alley.' But how comforting it would be to have him beside her when she hit the wall at the end.

'But at least you'll have tried. You can't do more than that.' There was a pause. 'Eve called me.'

Immediately Sandy was on her guard again. 'Why? What did she want?'

Eve liked Steven, they got on well, and more than once she

207

had dropped hefty hints about what a great match he'd make for her mother.

He sighed. 'She's worried you're unhappy about the pregnancy.'

'But I thought we'd sorted that out.'

'I know, but she still thinks you might have reservations.'

'And I thought I'd hidden them so well! I'm only worried about what would happen if they split up. I don't want her hurt, that's all. Will she have any rights over the baby?' She heard how negative she sounded, decided not to mention how not being a blood relation to her grandchild made a difference to how she felt.

'Why ever should they? Besides, they're married so presumably yes, she will. So you dripped cold water on her excitement?'

Sandy stiffened. Usually she liked his no-nonsense reactions. He always shot straight from the hip. And this time, as usual, he was right.

'Was that wise?' He didn't sound as if he was criticising her so much as trying to get her to see things from another perspective. 'Whatever you think isn't going to stop her doing what she wants to do. I should know.' His son Martin had travelled to Afghanistan against all sane advice, only to be killed during an armed attack on the Kabul guest house where he was staying.

'Oh Steven, I'm so sorry. You're right. I didn't mean to but I was only thinking of her.'

'And you went straight to the worse-case scenario. What's the point? It may not happen. For now, can't you share their joy? That's all she wants.'

'Don't rub it in. But there are so many people involved. What if . . .'

'If, if, if.' His voice was gentle. 'This is your decision. I'm not going to make it for you but you don't want to lose your only daughter. If she and Jen stay together – and they've got as good a chance as anyone else – you're going to distance yourself from that baby's life and Eve's.'

'But it's not her baby.' She was on shaky ground now.

'It doesn't matter. It is to her. Think about it, that's all.'

20

As they left the ticket office area and began the walk up the hill towards the ruined city of Pompeii, the heat was stifling. Umbrellas up, hats on, water bottles and sunscreen at the ready. Shuffling along in the crowd, peering towards the city walls, Alice watched as Lia held back, waiting for Mark then pointing and saying something she couldn't hear but that made him laugh. She saw Sandy catch up with them and interrupt their conversation. She should have done that herself but something held her back. It was as if she wanted to test him, to see how far he would go. Perhaps the heat contributed to her overwhelming weariness when she considered her marriage. It was almost as if she didn't care. What excited and terrified her in equal measure was the thought of a life without him. Her ambition to cook professionally again was simmering away. She pictured herself in the heat and frenzy of kitchen service again. Far from her heart sinking, it rose and took wings.

'Don't stop!'

She turned to find Benno right behind her.

'We must keep going till we get through the gate and in the city, then we can stand still. Otherwise we're going to get walked over.' He turned round to impress on her the number of people behind them.

'Sorry, I was a million miles away.'

'You are watching your husband with that woman Lia?' He shook his head. 'She has no shame. You must be careful.'

'What do you mean?' As she had told Mark, everyone else had noticed, too.

'You know.' His look was loaded with sympathy. But the last thing she wanted was pity.

'There's nothing going on, if that's what you're thinking. He wouldn't.'

She heard Lia's laugh above the chatter of the crowds. How could Mark embarrass her like this? The others were probably all talking about them, speculating, thinking she was a fool not to be more assertive like Brit. But her husband had always been a flirt. A bit of harmless fun had never interfered with their marriage and had even added some pizzazz at times, but things had changed. It was only when she discovered that he'd taken things further that her heart had broken.

She and Benno caught up with the others in the Forum, where they had been joined by a man with a lanyard round his neck, a clipboard in his hand and a smile pinned on his face. He looked like a young starlet straight from Cinecittà, as well as someone used to waiting. He took the role that Massimo had in Rome: their specialist guide.

Alice edged round the others to stand beside Mark. On the spur of the moment she took his hand. Old habits. But the look on his face! As if something had burned him. Swiftly readjusting his features, he smiled down at her then looked away, but not before she'd registered the guilt in his eyes. Sandy stood close to the new guide. Her excitement at being here was visible. She was completely focused, concentrating on his introduction to the city. Beside her, Peter and Brit were equally involved. Mark too. Benno and Alex were standing to on side of the group discussing something in low voices, referring to Alex's phone. Lia and Alan listened politely but they were looking around, keen to be on the move. Alice took a bottle of water from her bag and swallowed some of the lukewarm liquid, then tipped the brim of her hat over her face.

When the guide had finished explaining the importance of the Forum, they moved away from the majority of the crowds and down the Via dell'Abbondanza. Even there, knots of tourists stood on street corners, outside the ruined houses of interest, making it hard to see much. However, Alice caught the excitement from being on those heavily slabbed roads, cut through with ruts from cart wheels. Ahead of them, as they followed their guide into the Terme Stabiane, Lia's laughter rang out yet again. Two stray dogs were mating in the middle of the crowd, quite oblivious to the people skirting round them to get to the warm and hot rooms.

'What are they doing, Mom?' a small voice piped up before its owner was hastily ushered out of the room by their parents.

The dogs were oblivious to the tourists who circled round them to get into the next room. Lia had stopped and was watching, unabashed, as she lifted her camera, while Alan said something in her ear that made her laugh again.

'There's no ceremony or shame for some.' Benno said close to Alice's ear. She turned to see if his expression betrayed a second meaning, but he was poker-faced. They went in and out of the ruined houses, admiring mosaics, frescoes, eventually walking through a garden that took them out into a long street shaded by two rows of pine trees. The crowds had thinned out completely, just a couple sitting on the steps in front of a closed door and a family slightly ahead of them. They stopped to have a drink and hear about where they were going next.

Inside the amphitheatre, the temperature was fiercer still. Everyone in there was flushed with heat, bottles of water in their hands. Alan took the top off his and tipped the contents over his head. Lia screamed as he shook himself like a dog so water sprayed over her. They walked quickly through the arena and stood in the tunnel at the far end, glad to be in the shade.

Gilly was waiting at the exit with the guide as the party made their way up the slope.

'Where have Lia and Mark got to?' asked Gilly, looking around.

'And Peter and Brit,' Alice added quickly. She had seen Mark go ahead with them.

'Perhaps they went into the Pink Floyd exhibition in those tunnels on either side of the exit?' suggested Alan.

'I thought Mark was ahead of us.' Alice looked towards the Large Palaestra, next on their list. 'Mightn't they be in there?'

'I'll go back and have a look,' said Alan, earning grateful looks from the rest of them.

After a few minutes he returned with the others.

'Brilliant exhibition,' said Mark. 'Took me back. I saw them live once. Knebworth 1975.' He walked across to Alice. 'You should have come in.' But his eyes left her face as soon as they met hers. Again.

Alice noticed how Lia walked away from Mark to stand alone on the other side of the group, looking pleased with herself.

'Now where?' Alex asked.

Benno pocketed his phone. 'Can we have a word?' He drew Alex to one side to have an intense exchange in German.

Gilly looked at her watch. 'We'll go back past the brothel.'

'Now you're talking.' Alan looked around for an amused reaction that he didn't get.

Gilly carried on, presumably inured to the obvious jokes. 'And then we'll cut through to the House of the Faun and the House of the Tragic Poet before walking through the sepulchres to the House of Mysteries. The minibus will meet us at that gate, in case you're worried about having to walk back. By then, you should have a real sense of the place.'

And until then, Alice thought, she would stick close to Mark. She was not going to be made any more of a fool.

*

Sandy felt exhilarated. She couldn't remember ever having been to a ruined city that gave such a vivid impression of what life must have been like there. The shops, the inns, the houses that must have been breathtaking when the water in the fountains and ponds was running, when the walls were fully painted, the gardens tended. In the amphitheatre she had been able to hear the roar of the crowd, in the Terme Stabiane she had heard the chatter of the men and women and the splash of their separate hot and cold baths; the streets had been alive with people on the pavements, drinking from the water fountains, eating at the inns, stepping onto the pavements as wagons rattled by. Seeing the plaster casts of people and animals in their death throes had brought her close to tears. If only . . . she paused her thought. She had been about to wish that Matthew was with her but a voice somewhere inside her spoke: *Move on. It's time.*

Her mother's summing up had been a masterpiece of understatement.

Pompeii – hot but extraordinary. The atmosphere there.
To think of all those people wiped out at a stroke. What a
tragedy.

Miriam Mackenzie, June 27th 1952 – Naples

All at once she understood that it wasn't Matthew she wanted to share all this with. It was Steven. The realisation made her stop dead. He was no historian but, like Mark, he appreciated the culture of a country and was interested in learning. Yes, it was him she was missing. The time had come to let go of the past and start looking towards the future. The understanding came like a body blow. Matthew would never have wanted her to preserve herself in aspic for his sake. If only they had been able to have those final conversations instead of him being taken away so suddenly. He would have encouraged her to take the second chance that she was being offered. He would have wanted the best for her.

You can't rewrite history, my love. She could hear his voice.

All at once she knew the time had come. She had to let go at last.

Goodbye, Matthew. She said the words silently and shut her eyes. *Goodbye.*

A breath of wind touched her cheek.

When she looked around her, nothing had changed, and yet everything had. Sandy felt lighter, stronger, as if a burden had been lifted from her. She looked around for the others.

Ahead of them was the bluish silhouette of Mount Vesuvius in the distance, the ominous backdrop to the city it had destroyed. A long queue stretched down a narrow side street that ran off the Via dell'Abbondanza, people filling the width of the road.

'This is one of the favourite attractions since its restoration,' said their guide. 'But the place is small and the queues are long. Many of the best pictures hang in the National Archaeological Museum.'

'Then why don't we see them there?' suggested Brit with a twirl of her umbrella. 'I'm going to roast alive if we stand out here for long. And I'm worried about Peter in this heat.'

'Don't be. Nothing's going to happen to me.' He leaned against the wall of a house and gave her a wan smile. 'I'm a doctor, remember.'

Sandy saw Alan raise his eyebrows at Alice. He didn't know about them, about the tragedy that perhaps explained why she infantilised him. A substitute for what she never had.

'What about the rest of you?' asked Gilly, though it was clear from the way her face had lit up what she hoped the answer would be. 'The tiny rooms just have stone beds and pictures showing what's on offer. It's a curiosity but there's lots more in the museum.'

The majority vote was to move on, with Alan the only dissenter. As they turned back down the street, Sandy remembered throwing her coin into the Trevi fountain with Lia. Then, she had thought she would never return to Italy. Now she was determined to return as soon as she could. And when she did, she would come back to Pompeii out of season and really familiarise herself with the place.

'Perhaps I've seen enough for one day.' Alan had hopped off the pavement and was walking up the middle of the road beside her. 'I mean, this is OK but it's only ruins after all.'

She turned to him, puzzled. 'I'd love to spend longer here. This is such a whistlestop tour. 'We haven't seen half the place.'

'I didn't mean Pompeii,' He elbowed her and nodded towards Mark who, with Alice, was talking to Gilly. 'Know what I mean? Nudge, nudge.'

'No, I don't.' She looked away from him. 'I haven't a clue what you're talking about.'

'When I went back in the amphitheatre, remember?'

'Of course.' She knew immediately what he was going to say. Mark and Lia. Oh, Alice.

'I found Mark and Lia kissing.' He winked and tapped his cheek with his finger. He really was a horrible man.

Sandy concentrated on not tripping on the large uneven boulders that made up the road. If she looked up, he would see how horrified she was. Part of what Lia had said to her was bravado that bigged her up in front of Sandy, whom she clearly considered inadequate and dull. But she had also betrayed that all-consuming ache she had for a baby, which might drive her to anything. She should have taken her more seriously. From what Alice had said, Mark wouldn't need much encouragement.

'I wouldn't say anything, if I were you,' she said.

Alan was all innocent. 'But of course. I just thought you should know since you and Alice seem to get on so well.'

'And what do you think I'm going to do now?' This was knowledge she'd rather not have.

'I thought you might say something…' Alan stopped as Lia approached them, and he began to walk ahead.

'Sandy, please can we clear this up?' Lia stood in front of her so she couldn't pass. 'You've been avoiding me since yesterday afternoon. I'm sorry if I've done something wrong but I honestly thought I was helping you.'

'What? By going through my things?'

She looked embarrassed, kicking the kerb with her sandal. 'I'm sorry.' She looked up. 'I really am. It was a spur of the moment thing. I shouldn't have.'

'If I did that to you, how would you feel? You wouldn't trust me. What did you think you'd find?' Sandy felt as if she was telling off a sixth-former. This was not the person she wanted to be out of school, so she relented. 'OK. Let's put it behind us. And the picture is an extraordinary find, so something has come out of it, and I'm grateful.'

Lia looked smug. 'So it's all for the best then.' She began to pull away from Sandy in the direction of Mark and Alan.

'Just one thing.' Sandy grabbed at her chance to say something.

Lia turned, the smile still on her face. 'Mmm?'

'Leave Mark alone.' She whispered the words, but Lia heard them.

Her smile vanished and her eyes hardened. 'Just because we work together, doesn't mean you have any say over my private life. You've just told me off for snooping in your affairs, so do me a favour and mind your own business when it comes to mine.'

'That's rich.' Sandy gave a half laugh. 'I've no intention of repeating what you told me the other night but I like Alice. If you really can't help yourself, at least do it so Alice isn't hurt any more than necessary? Can't you at least wait until we're back in

217

the UK?' By then, Alice might have made up her mind about her own future too.

Lia raised her chin. 'You have no idea. It's not all one way.'

'What are you two so engrossed in. Not the ancient Romans, I bet?' Alan had hung back to wait for them.

'Not exactly,' said Sandy. 'But we can finish off later.'

'I don't think there's anything left to be said.'

'We've gone into the café over there,' Alan indicated the one modern building in sight.

Lia crossed the road and went into the café, where Sandy could see her taking something from one of the fridges and queuing to pay.

'Did you say something?' Alan's breath smelled of peppermint.

'Not really.' She didn't want him to think they were in league together. 'You coming in?'

The relief of being in the cool, however crowded, was heaven sent. Sandy shook Alan off by following the signs upstairs to the ladies. Nonetheless, when she came back he was waiting for her with two bottles of iced tea, one of which he held out to her. 'Thought you'd like this.'

'Thanks.' Much as she wanted a drink, she rebelled against the prospect of his company for the rest of the day. She'd prefer to stick to Gilly and the guide, losing herself in the history of the city again so she could forget the problems that came with the present.

'The others are waiting outside.' He stood back so she could leave first. She found them standing round the corner in the shade of the building.

'Now there's a bit of a walk, but I promise it's worth it. Has everyone got water? Suncream?' Underneath her parasol, even Gilly's ponytail was limp in the heat. They set off again, Sandy near the front and Lia hanging back with Gilly and the boys, who had been distracted every time Sandy had looked in their direction. Either they were huddled over one of their phones, texting, or Alex was speaking to someone on his. They had paid little attention to the guide and barely looked at what they were passing in any detail, which was very unlike them.

Enough. One of the reasons for coming to Italy had been to get away from everything, not to involve herself in a whole new set of problems. She had made some decisions about her own life and was involved enough with Alice's. She didn't need anyone else's. Whatever was upsetting them had nothing to do with her.

'Is anything wrong?' Alice had crossed the road to join her.

Should she say anything? Listening to Alice was one thing. Actively interfering between her and Mark would be something quite different. 'No. Not at all. Look, here it is. The House of the Faun. Shall we?'

Inside the gateway the group gathered close to the small statue of the dancing faun in the atrium, listening to the history of what was once a substantial house. Afterwards they wandered freely before meeting back at the same spot to continue on their way. At last Sandy was on her own, envisaging the horror as Vesuvius erupted. Perhaps she would ask Peter if she could borrow the book she'd seen him reading: Robert Harris's *Pompeii*. He'd mentioned how good it was.

When they finally arrived at the Casa dei Misteri, outside the city walls, Sandy was desperate to get into the shade. Being under a roof was so welcome but the frescoes... The colours were rich and vibrant and depicted some kind of Dionysian cult – or so Gilly said. As the others made their way over the bridge and up the hill to the waiting minibus, Sandy hung back. Thinking she was alone, she was surprised when Mark stepped up behind her.

'Aren't these something else?' she said. 'Do you know any more about them?' He had been so knowledgeable in the Vatican, perhaps he could help here too.

He stared ahead. 'I heard you warned Lia off.'

'I'm sorry?' Sandy was taken aback.

'Take my advice. Don't try to interfere with something that has nothing to do with you. I don't know what Alice has told you but remember that there are always two sides to every story.' He turned on his heel and walked away, leaving Sandy stunned. She watched his back as he rejoined the others, and took a couple of calming breaths. Jesus! Who did he think he was? She was right to keep out of it.

Oh, il Capitano! If only . . .

Miriam Mackenzie, June 29 1952 – Naples

The hotel receptionist took Sandy's key from its box and with it a folded piece of paper. 'Your meeting has been changed,' she explained as she passed it over.

On the paper was a new time of seven o'clock and a name. Giancarlo Frumetti. She popped it in her pocket as Gilly approached. 'The meeting's been changed to seven.'

'That's good. I'm going up to the museum at about four with some of the others. Coming?'

'Yes please.' Apart from the cold shower she was about to take, she could think of nothing she would like more. She would spend her siesta reading up about Pompeii and preparing herself.

The trouble was every time she turned a page, she thought of Alice. Her new friend might be trying to find a future for herself, but that future might still be with Mark. Despite his warning and her misgivings, should she tell Alice what Alan had seen? Would that information make a difference to Alice's decision?

Late afternoon, they left Brit and Peter by the pool, and Alex and Benno at one of their long siestas. During the short walk to the museum, Alice insisted on buying a melon from a small stationary van loaded with them. 'Look at these. I bet they're delicious.'

'Ridiculous!' muttered Mark. 'You're going to have to carry it round with you.'

'I thought we'd take turns,' she said, passing it over with the sweetest smile.

'I don't think so,' he said, passing it back so roughly that it dropped between them and burst on the pavement. He kicked it into the gutter. 'That's that decided then.'

They walked apart for the rest of the way, the others making awkward conversation, trying to pretend nothing had happened.

Seeing the model of Pompeii and the frescoes and mosaics rescued from the city only emphasized to Sandy how extraordinary the town must once have been. These were so colourful and in much better condition that those left in the ruins.

Gilly took them round as if she were showing off her own home – 'You must see this. Look at that. I don't want you to miss this.' – until finally, she stopped at the top of some steps where they could see some exquisite mosaic work. Beyond was the wrought door to the Secret Cabinet. 'This is where all the erotic art from Pompeii is. Hold on to your hats.' Gilly gestured them in.

'This is what I've been wanting to see,' said Alan. 'I'm intrigued by what those ancient Romans got up to.'

The last thing Sandy wanted to do was go in with him. Seeing the statue of Pan copulating with a goat on the floor above had been enough for her. Not that she was a prude or anything, but... Instead she turned into the room on the right to look at four deep-blue and green mosaic pillars. She moved on to the wildlife mosaics on the walls, admiring the detail. Eventually, she was ready for the Secret Cabinet. At the door of the room, Alice caught up with her. On a table immediately to their left were two giant stone phalluses.

'Gosh,' said Alice under her breath. 'I don't know what I was expecting but it wasn't those!'

They followed the arrows, wandering past the exhibits, reading the labels, exclaiming.

Ahead of them, Lia laughed.

'Well, I guess they knew how to have a good time,' said Sandy as they stopped in front of a fresco of a woman with her knees over her partner's shoulders.

'Looks bloody uncomfortable to me,' said Alice.

'You mean you don't...?'

'Not if I can help it!'

They laughed.

'I'd be happy to compare.' Lia's voice floated round the corner of the exhibition. 'You'll just have to let me see.'

Sandy raised her eyebrows at Alice, who returned it with what-can-I-do shrug. 'Perhaps she's talking to Alan.'

'Bet he's loving it.'

They passed a smaller statue of Pan and the goat and turned the corner of the gallery. Lia and Mark were standing together in front of a cabinet in which were displayed fertility figures of such exaggerated priapic splendour that Sandy and Alice could see them quite clearly from where they stood.

'With bells on,' said Mark, nodding towards a winged penis hung about with several of them.

Lia laughed again, her fingers in front of her lips, her camera forgotten for once.

Sandy's cough made them both turn. Lia, looking straight at both women, stepped away from Mark and turned to the pictures behind her. 'Have you seen these, Alan?'

'What?' Alan was ahead of them, reading the label, which Sandy could see read *Sex as a Talisman*. 'The Romans believed phalluses brought them luck. They were all over Pompeii according to this.'

'Well, lucky for some, is all I can say.' Lia's face was hidden behind her camera again.

Sandy remembered her mother's heartfelt journal entry: *Oh, il Capitano! If only...* She didn't need to say more for her meaning to be clear. At this point in her account of her travels, Sandy was wondering how much she would have liked this young woman had she met her then.

Gilly and Sandy talked all the way back to the hotel. Alice was conscious they were trying to lift her spirits and was grateful. But she knew they had seen what she had. Lia and Mark were getting closer, and it was as if he didn't care who noticed. Lia certainly didn't. Alice needed to think. Had she got the guts to leave him? Could she do that to the kids? Was that what she wanted?

As they approached the long line of garbage bins on the opposite side of the street from the hotel, Sandy slowed down. 'Can we talk?'

'Can we later?'

'But there are a couple of things...'

Alice felt sick. If Sandy wanted to talk about Mark... But perhaps it would help her see things straight even though she wasn't ready to make a final decision. She had little time for people who hesitated, but what about Pip? What about the boys? What about her future? All these unanswered question chased through her head. 'Let's have a quick coffee, then,' she heard herself saying.

After agreeing with Gilly that they would meet in forty-five minutes, Sandy took Alice into a café. They sat at a table away from the window where the others wouldn't see them if they passed, and waited till the coffees were on the table.

'Go on, then.' Alice felt Sandy was having second thoughts about saying whatever she had to say. 'I think I know what you're about to say.'

'Some of it maybe, but not all. I could see what you were going through in the gallery, and that made me think I should say something, although this really isn't any of my business.' She closed her eyes and tapped the table.

Alice tried to stem her rising tide of panic. 'Perhaps just get it over with?'

Sandy took a sip of coffee, returning the cup to the saucer and rotating it so the handle was exactly at right angles to her. 'It's Lia.'

'I had a feeling it might be.'

'Perhaps not quite in the way you think. The night we shared a room, she told me that she was desperate to have a child. She feels time's running out.'

The pieces slotted into place quicker than Alice would like. 'What? And you think she's got her eye on Mark to . . .' she couldn't finish her sentence.

'She didn't say so, but it's possible.'

'Can't she get artificially inseminated or something – like a cow?!' Alice's voice rose so the other people in the café turned to stare.

They caught each other's eye and laughed briefly.

'She wants to know who the father is even if she's not with him. And maybe it's that thrill of the forbidden too.' said Sandy. 'She's competitive – I know that from work. She likes winning.'

'If she has to win something, what's wrong with Peter or Alan?'

'I think we both know the answer to that. Peter only has eyes for Brit, and Alan . . . well, isn't he the booby prize? She's going for the one she fancies most.'

'As anyone would.' Alice's voice was dry. 'But Mark!'

'Oh, come on. He's attractive, he's intelligent, he's got a sense of humour. If you were choosing one of the three, I know who I'd go for.'

'Except that he's married.'

'That doesn't matter to her.'

'Well, thanks for the heads up. At least I know what I'm up against and that it's not my fevered imagination.'

'I don't think it is. I was wrong and I'm sorry. Alan told me he'd seen them together in that tunnel. That's the other thing.'

'So what?' She didn't want it to be true.

'They were kissing.' Sandy looked stricken, as if she wanted to take the words back.

But it was too late. Alice felt pinioned her to her chair. She couldn't even move her hand to lift her cup of coffee. Outside the café, the world was going on as normal: traffic and passers-by going about their business, none of them aware her life might be falling apart.

'Oh my God! I didn't mean . . . you've gone as white as a sheet.' Sandy's voice penetrated the rushing in Alice's ears. 'Alice! Have some water.' She was holding out her glass.

Shutting her eyes for a moment, Alice shook her head, waiting for the noise to subside. When her head had cleared she was able to speak. 'I could see it happening, but when I brought it up he denied everything. He still won't be honest with me.' She was *not* going to cry.

'Lia made up her mind and went out to get him despite all of us watching.'

'But that's what you said, isn't it? She likes the competition. She wants what isn't hers to have. And this time she's picked on Mark, who's pathetically flattered when a woman takes a shine to him. It proves to him that he's still got it, that he's not written off yet.'

'After seeing them together in the Secret Cabinet, I had to tell you. I couldn't bear to see him treating you like that any more.'

'I'm grateful.' Alice turned her bangles around her wrist. 'I am, however weird that sounds. It's better to know than not.'

'What will you do?'

'Have it out with him, one last time. And this time I mean it. Final warning! If he's not going to do his bit to look after our marriage, then there's no point in me doing mine. I'd rather have waited till we got home, but how can I? Not with Lia sniffing round him like a bitch in heat.' She looked at Sandy's face. 'Sorry.'

Sandy gave a sympathetic smile, noticing the blue shadows under her eyes. 'Don't be. I'm furious with her, but I don't know what I can do.'

'You're not her keeper. It's certainly not your fault. And this was always going to happen. I just never thought it would be so public.' Her strength was returning. 'So humiliating.'

'You shouldn't feel humiliated.' Sandy shook her head. 'If the others have cottoned on to what's going on, they'll be sympathetic.'

'But that's the point. I don't want sympathy. If this had happened soon after we married, I'd still have been independent and strong enough to deal with it. But the last twenty years have made me as complacent as they have him. We've taken each other for granted.' As she spoke, the truth of what she was saying hit her. 'I've got to find the strength to stand up for myself. Something I haven't really had to do for years. I was too busy focusing on the children, thinking of them.'

'And now?'

'Now it's time to think of myself.' She waved over the waiter. 'Let's pay. I need to get back to the hotel.' While they waited for the bill, Alice looked straight at Sandy. 'Thank you. Really. That can't have been easy but I do appreciate it.'

After she'd showered, Alice took her favourite dress off the hanger. It didn't exactly slip on to her, but with a tug here and there, it was fine – perhaps a little tight on the bust and waist... and hips... but smart enough. Time had been reasonably kind to her although her love of food and her inability to diet meant that she was more rounded – yes, rounded – than when she and Mark had first met. She was not looking forward to Mark's return. But she wanted to be ready and to look her best. When she had finished her minimal make-up, she put on her glasses and studied herself, smoothing a little here and there until satisfied with the results. At least he would see what he would be missing. She lay on the bed, staring into space, rehearsing what she wanted to say until she felt she could face him.

Her eyes opened at the sound of the door handle turning. Mark came in, looking hot and bothered. 'Feeling any better?' He came and sat on the bed, close enough so she could smell his sweat. He cracked his knuckles one after the other.

'Much.' Deep breath. 'But we need to talk.'

He rolled his eyes to the ceiling and stood up. 'Not again.'

'Don't deny it this time. You've been seen.'

'Seen doing what?' He crossed his arms over his chest, defensive.

'Kissing Lia in Pompeii. Flirting with her.'

Alarm registered in his eyes but vanished almost immediately.

She sat straight. 'I can't go through this again, Mark. Not I can't – I won't.'

'For heaven's sake, it was nothing. She came on to me, and I . . .' He shook his head to emphasis how little it meant, raising his hand to pull at his earlobe. 'Nobody should have seen. I'm so sorry they did.'

'You're sorry they saw, or you're sorry that you're going back on everything we promised each other again?'

He looked confused. 'Both, of course. I didn't want to hurt you. I didn't think . . .'

'But you never think. That's the problem. At least if you do, you think about you. Never me and the kids. Why not?'

His head dropped. 'I don't know.'

'Even after all those sessions with Jane? Don't you remember anything? We talked about how being the centre of someone's attention builds your confidence that was so damaged by Sally's departure, and your mother's before that.'

'Cod psychology,' he muttered. 'This has nothing to do with my mother.'

'You've taken me for granted for years now. I've always been there to look after Patrick and Henry and Pip. I've entertained your boring colleagues and students without complaining once.'

He looked taken aback by the 'boring', but Alice hadn't finished.

'I've been as good a wife and mum as I know how to be. And I'm still trying. I know we agreed to put the past behind us, but with this—' she struggled to find the right word '—"flirtation" with Lia, you've really crossed the line.'

'But there's no harm in a little flirtation.' He raised his hands in his defence. 'As long as no one gets hurt. You've never minded before.'

'Christ, Mark. You really don't get it, do you? Can't you see how impossible this is for me? Can't you imagine for one moment how it makes me feel?'

He shook his head as if he'd heard this a thousand times before and there was no answer.

'You're making a complete fool of yourself and a fool of me.'

'Is that what matters now? Other people's opinions?'

'No!' She was shouting now. 'You and me. That's what used to matter. You and me and the kids. Yet you seem determined to destroy everything we've built together. Family. Remember?'

At the mention of family, his face changed. He closed his eyes, rubbed his forehead and heaved a sigh. 'I'm sorry, Ali. I am, really. I don't mean to hurt you or them. I just . . .'

'Can't resist, I know. And I've put up with it because I loved you and I stupidly believed you'd never go further. But women like Lia see you coming a mile off. You're prey to women like her.'

'It's only a bit of fun.' His bluff and bravado had returned.

'You're impossible!' She got off the bed, resisting the temptation to slap him. 'All I'm saying is that if you don't get your act together, then I'm going to have to do something.'

'Again.' He made himself sound infinitely world-weary. 'You've made that threat before.'

'No, not again.' She had to get out of the room before she exploded and said something she'd forever regret. 'This time I'm giving you a long-deserved ultimatum. So please stop – for all our sakes. Can't we try to enjoy the last few days here? Somehow.' She put her hand on the doorknob. 'I'll be on the terrace.'

He held out his hand for her to take. 'All right. I still think you're making too much of it. But yes, let's. I will try harder.'

The way he said the last four words, mocking, as if he was reading a school report, was not lost on her. But she had tried, and she wasn't going to try again. This time, it was up to him.

22

Why is that Anna gets everything that I want? Sometimes life is unfair. And sometimes one has to borrow or take what one wants. Dare I?

Miriam Mackenzie, July 5th 1952 – Naples

Ascending through the Via Toledo metro was like rising up through an incredible blue mosaic heaven. Never had Sandy been in such a beautiful metro station, and one of the very few places in the city that hadn't been scrawled over with graffiti. She and Gilly emerged into the busy pedestrian shopping street and walked until they found Mackenzies. It was an old-fashioned store, all dark wood and plate-glass windows, with a dark panelled interior that reeked of its Scottish heritage. In the windows were stacks of men's shirts, jackets done up on dummies over shirts and ties – the picture of a modern European. Surrounding them were paintings of Scottish landscapes, one complete with a majestic stag. Inside, the shop was crowded with customers.

'Come on.' Gilly forged her way across the busy street towards the door. Sandy followed, her stomach knotting at the thought of what lay ahead of them. She wanted desperately to resolve the mystery of her mother's past and find how it could possibly be tied up with this loud, chaotic, brash city. That they might be linked seemed inconceivable. What was more, she wanted to be freed of this duty that had been left with her.

Gilly found an assistant, chatted to him quickly and brought him over. A man with the face of a medieval saint but wearing a tartan tie. 'The office is upstairs,' she explained. 'But you get there from the side street. Apparently we'll find Mr Frumetti up there.'

The young man led them a little way up the street, past a busy ice-cream shop, and left into a typically narrow alley that rose steeply, flanked with high buildings, balconies and shuttered windows. At a double door, he rang one of the bells at its side. As the door gave a click, he pushed it open. '*Terzo piano*.'

'*Grazie mille*.' Gilly went first, looking around her as he melted away into the crowds. 'Oh God, no lift.'

'I can go on my own, if you'd rather stay down here.' Sandy nodded towards a single office chair pushed into a corner of the wide, undecorated entrance hall. Though apprehensive, she was determined to see this through. And if it all led nowhere, well . . . at least she would have done her best.

'What?! And miss out on what happens next? No way.' She went ahead, taking the steps at a run.

At each turn of the staircase, Gilly waited for her. With each step Sandy grew more excited but simultaneously more fearful that this was all a wild goose chase. At the third floor, they found themselves in front of a glass door with *Mackenzies* scrawled across it. What Sandy could see through it was not what she had expected at all. This was no dusty Dickensian office, repeating the dark wood theme of the shop. The tables she had pictured groaning with ledgers covered in dust were non-existent. Instead, there was a reception area to a modest open-plan modern office that might exist in any city in the world. Beyond the empty reception desk was a wall of glass in which was a door that was being opened by a short middle-aged man, silvery hair pushed back off his face, eyes dark, wearing what were surely Mackenzie brogues. His smile was wide. '*Buona sera, signore*. Giancarlo Frumetti.' He made a little bow as he shook each of their hands. 'But we speak English, yes?' His English accent was impressive.

'Yes, please. I'm afraid I don't speak Italian at all, although my friend does very well.'

'My pleasure. I lived in England once and get little chance to practise now. But come in.' He held open the door and showed them to a round conference table. Surrounding them were about eight desks where various men and women were focused on their computer screens. 'This is the heart of our business,' Giancarlo made an expansive gesture to include everyone. 'Our warehouse where we hold stock and run our mail order company is on the other side of town. Water?'

Once they were settled, glasses of chilled water in front of them, he put his elbows on the table and clasped his hands. 'Now, how I can help you?'

Before embarking on an explanation, Sandy glanced at Gilly, who nodded encouragement. As she talked she watched his expression change, realising how her faith in a couple of coincidences might seem ludicrous to him. But if it did, he gave no sign. When she'd finished she held out the photo to him. 'So I'm looking for this man and to see if he is related to Anna Viglieri. And if he is, if I can find her.'

He took the photo and studied it. 'I may be able to help a little.'

Sandy's heart leaped. 'Really. Do you know Roberto Viglieri?'

He laughed. 'I'm not so old – at least as these men must be now! But I do have the old company files upstairs. If he worked here – and I agree it looks that way – he'll be in them. Come.'

He held open a door at the end of the office, then went ahead of them up a wooden staircase that had seen better days. At the top was a small room lined with metal shelving bowing under the weight of hundreds of black box files, each with a year scrawled on its spine. Giancarlo ran his finger along them, then stopped. 'Nineteen fifty-five. Was that the date of the photo?'

'Yes.' Sandy's insides contracted with excitement.

'Then he should be in here.' He lifted out the file and blew the dust from the top. 'No one ever looks at these now, but they think it's wrong to throw them away. They have the history of the company: names of employees, suppliers, new lines, accounts, press cuttings.' He put the file on the table in the middle of the room. 'Sit,' he instructed. 'Please.'

He took the chair opposite them, opened the file and began to leaf through its contents, occasionally grunting with interest or surprise at whatever he was turning up. Sandy silently willed him to hurry up. 'Ah!' The sound was sharp, pained. He turned the file round so she and Gilly could see what he had found, and pointed with a well-manicured finger.

The writing was so cramped that Sandy could barely make out the letters but she recognised an R and V. 'Is this him?'

'It could be. This is a Roberto Viglieri who was one of the buyers. The Mackenzie family still owned the company then. They founded it in 1901 so it was in the family for a very long time.'

'When was it sold?' Gilly was peering at the shelves as if the information would leap out at her.

'Nano took over in 2001. That's when they modernised the office – all except this room – and changed a lot of the business practices. But you haven't come to hear about that.' He smiled and began to close the file. 'So I have helped you? Yes?'

Sandy felt unreasonably disappointed. They had established a link but it didn't take them anywhere beyond that. 'You have, thank you,' she said, feeling they were so close and yet still so far from the information she needed. 'I think my mother, Miriam Mackenzie' – how odd it felt calling her that out loud – 'must have been related to the family, but how? She never talked to me about them.'

Her parents' reticence hadn't seemed so strange at the time but now it seemed positively extraordinary. No less extraordinary than her own lack of interest in finding out about them, given her fascination with British political and social history and how they meshed together. She wished once again that she had asked the questions she was asking now while her mother was alive, and had insisted on answers when her mother shrugged her off.

'Your grandparents died when you were young. That's all you need to know.'

'Tell me about them,' Sandy would ask. 'What were they like? Where did they live.'

'I don't want to talk about them now. Another time maybe.' Her mother would reach out, kiss her cheek. 'Now go and enjoy yourself.' But another time never came.

Giancarlo was returning the file to the shelf when Gilly stood up and went to another section of the filing. She tapped the back of one marked 1985. 'Why don't we have a look in this, or one of these?' She ran her finger along the back of the 1980s and 1970s. 'In a family firm, he might have kept his job for years, particularly if he was connected to the family in some way. You never know, there might be something else in here that will give us a clue.'

Sandy was so grateful she almost got up and hugged her. How stupid not to have had the same thought.

A flash of reluctance crossed Giancarlo's face. 'I don't have too long.'

'Just one or two,' said Sandy.

'If you've got other things to do, you could leave us for half an hour or so.' Gilly looked at Sandy, who nodded agreement, although she suspected they needed much longer if they were going to make any headway.

His eyes flicked to the door, torn between an exit route and his responsibility.

'We'll be extremely careful to keep everything exactly as we find it.' Sandy kept any begging note out of her voice but when she looked down, she realised her hands were folded as if in prayer. 'Please. It's my only chance. We're going home in a few days.'

At that he caved in. 'OK. But you must be careful. If you need me, ring this bell.' He pointed to a button on the wall by the door before checking his watch. 'I'll give you as long as I can.'

When the door closed behind him, Sandy looked at the wall of files. 'Where do we start? This is worse than a needle in a haystack. We don't even know what we're looking for.'

'We just take one each and look as quickly as we can.'

'I'm not sure I'd even recognise the name again. That writing was illegible.' She took the file marked 1973 that Gilly passed to her.

'Get a move on, we haven't got much time.' Gilly took another for herself and sat at the table to open it.

They sat in silence, turning pages that were covered with records that remained incomprehensible to Sandy. She worked her way through, running her finger down the pages, aware that she might easily be missing an invaluable clue. Then she took another. Every now and then she'd come across a loose photograph or a company brochure, but nothing that helped her. 'This is hopeless. We're not getting anywhere. It's all gobbledygook.'

'Wait. Look at this.' Gilly held up a newspaper cutting. 'This file has more to do with the staff than the stock. Here's a picture of a Malcolm Mackenzie opening a new branch of the shop in Rome.'

'That must be the one Alice and Mark found.'

'He looks pretty ancient. But perhaps he's part of your mother's family? Take a photo.'

Sandy used her phone, despite her growing conviction that this whole exercise was pointless. 'Let's just do one more file each. He'll be back in a minute.'

'And we should get down to Gambrini to meet the others.'

Gilly returned the photo and exchanged her file for another. 'Right, there'd better be something in here.'

'There won't be,' said Sandy, resigned, opening another herself.

After a couple of minutes, Gilly inhaled sharply. Sandy looked up from the stack of papers she was wading through to see Gilly bent over another news cutting. 'Don't tell me you've found something?' Hope burst in her chest.

'I think I may have.' Gilly spoke slowly. 'Look.' She slid the paper across the table so Sandy could see what was a cutting from some sort of a society page. The photo was a grainy blur of a couple formally facing the camera, neither of them smiling. 'Look underneath.'

If nothing else Sandy could read four words. *Roberto e Anna Viglieri*. 'Roberto and Anna Viglieri. Oh my God, we've found her.' She stared at the picture trying to make out the detail in the image. This must be the woman she was looking for, the woman her mother had come to visit all those years ago, but the old newspaper print was too black and blurry to make out much more than the shape of her neckline and that her hair was pinned up.

'A picture of her at least. At some charity bash in 1985.'

Sandy retrieved her phone and took another photo. 'They're not exactly in the first flush of youth, are they. They must be ancient now if they're even alive.'

'Have you finished?' Giancarlo put his head round the door.

'For the moment,' said Sandy. 'But look what we found.'

He took the cutting from her. 'Then he must have stayed with the company as you thought. I don't know these people but I was telling my colleague about you and he suggested someone who might. He's retired but he was working here back then. I can telephone him for you. Perhaps you could go and see him?'

'Would you do that? I'd be so grateful.' Excitement had

replaced the despair that Sandy had been feeling. Her head was fizzing with the thought that she might after all be able to fulfil her mother's last wish, as well as finding out what the letter meant.

'Now, if possible. We've got so little time.' Gilly had the necessary presence of mind to insist. 'Could you?'

Giancarlo tapped his the fingertips on the knuckles of his fist. 'I have to go . . .' His hand stilled as he looked at the two of them, his gaze steady. 'All right, I'll try. But I must do it right now. If he's not there . . . Wait here.'

The door shut behind him.

Sandy exhaled. 'I don't believe it.'

'Don't get your hopes up,' Gilly said, although it was obvious she was just as excited. 'He might not come up with anything.'

'But if nothing else, I've got a lead that I can follow up from home.' Steven would help her, she was sure. Perhaps they would even come here together to deliver the letter. She liked that idea. 'But while we're waiting, I might as well have a quick look through another file.' She felt certain that something else would turn up now.

Five minutes and zero additional revelations later, the click of the door handle made them both jump. Sandy's heart was pounding as she waited for Giancarlo to speak.

'He is too deaf to use the phone now, but I have spoken to his daughter.'

Sandy nodded, bursting with anticipation. 'And?'

'He's sleeping but she will speak to him and phone me back tonight or maybe in the morning. She assured me that although physically he is weak, his mind is still bright. If he knew them, he will remember. So leave me your number, and I will call you as soon as I have news.'

He showed them down the stairs and at the bottom he shook both their hands, making the same curious little bow he made when he met them.

'I can't thank you enough.' Sandy hoped he understood how heartfelt her gratitude was. 'Really.'

'My pleasure. I hope I will have good news for you soon. Enjoy Naples.'

Back in the street, it was a busy, balmy night. Among the crowds on the Via Toledo, Gilly took Sandy's arm. 'This way,' she said. 'There's nothing more you can do so we may as well meet the others. Don't know about you, but I could kill for a G and T.'

23

They sat at the pavement tables outside the Gran Caffè Gambrinus. Alice had hoped they would take one in the perfectly restored interior. Its dining room with black-and-white tiled floor, high ceilings and white tablecloths, its glass-fronted patisserie and ice-cream counters and marble-topped bar were all reminiscent of a glamorous age. In her mind's eye women in Edwardian dress drifted through replacing those in shorts and sandals, loose frocks with daypacks slung over their shoulders, jeans and T-shirts. Peter had taken one look and insisted on sitting in the outside room. 'If you can't sit outside in Naples when can you?' The others agreed.

But 'outside' was something that more resembled a marquee with the sides rolled up, though elegant enough with its part-wooden, part-cobbled floor, its marble-topped tables and dark wood chairs. The night-time darkness suited Alice's mood. Mark had barely spoken to her since they had left the hotel. He had made sure that Alan was sitting between them in the taxi and then put himself between Alex and Brit when they reached the bar. This was her punishment for standing up to him. But instead of cowing her, as it once might have, his behaviour only strengthened her resolve. Where she might have accepted his reassurances before, something in her had changed as if a switch had been flicked, and she felt empowered to do something about it. On the other side of the table Lia was going through the cocktail list with Alan. Alice envied her energy. She was enthusiastic about everything she did, even down to choosing a drink. She pointed at the menu with an immaculately French-manicured nail, her eyes shining with excitement.

'A Rossini. That's what I'm going to have. Raspberry and champagne. Can you think of anything more delicious?' She looked around them all for an answer.

Alice didn't reply. Mark might not want to speak to her but nor did she want to talk to Lia unless she had to. Her limpet-like attachment to her husband baffled Alice. He was older than her, more conventional – boring, even. And why not Alan if Sandy was right and all she wanted was a sperm donor? Then she looked at Alan . . . and, if not sympathised, understood.

'What are you having, Alex?' Lia asked brightly as she picked up her camera and snapped at the drinks menu.

'One of their famous espressos. Hazelnut, I think.'

'How dull.' She pulled a face. 'Brit?'

'A mojito for me.'

One of the bow-tied waiters came up for their order. 'Let's go ahead,' suggested Peter. 'Gilly and Sandy can order when they get here.'

'Where are they?' Alex reached for an olive.

'Something to do with the photo I found, I think,' said Lia. 'Despite the fuss, I think I did her a favour.'

'Looks as if you might have. Sandy's smiling.'

Alice turned round to see the two women coming towards their table. 'Well?' she asked. 'How did it go?'

Sandy took the empty chair beside her. 'Very well. That photo was the missing link after all. I think we've found the woman I'm looking for. Not in person yet, but we're on her track.' She turned to Lia who was going through the photos on her camera. 'So it turns out I do owe you a thank you.'

Lia bristled with pleasure. 'That's OK. And I owe you an apology.'

Sandy looked not forgiving but resigned. 'I think we should just put it behind us.'

'Good.' Lia returned her interest to her camera.

The atmosphere among the group eased as if a communal sigh of relief had passed between them. Sandy ordered herself a gin sling. 'I'll tell you what happened later.' She turned her chair towards Alice and lowered her voice. 'And you? How did it go?'

'Badly.' She looked across to where Mark was deep in conversation with Brit. 'As usual he made me feel as if I'm the one in the wrong. But this time I stuck to my guns.' She raised her glass. 'Cheers.' Subject closed.

'How are you?' Sandy turned to Benno on her other side. 'Wasn't Pompeii astonishing?'

He turned his lugubrious face to her. 'If we hadn't been bombarded – you say that? –with phone calls from home, I would have enjoyed it more.'

'Not trouble, I hope?'

'We have left our twins with my sister and her family in Düsseldorf where they have a wonderful time with cousins. Once a year we plan to do this and go away alone.'

'So not trouble then,' said Alice. 'That's good.' She cast her mind back over her and Mark's life together. They had never left the kids anywhere for more than a night without one of them being there. Perhaps if they had, and put that time into their relationship early on, things would be different now.

'But not good.' Benno uncrossed his legs, neatening his shorts as he did so. Alice stared at his sandalled feet, his crooked toes. 'Our surrogate, an old friend of ours, is making problems. She of course lives in Germany and she wants to see the children. Is demanding to see them.'

'This is not part of our agreement,' explained Alex.

'Can't you just say no?' asked Alice. 'Or even give her supervised access once before you all go back to England.' She was aware that Sandy had leaned forward and was listening intently.

'We could but it's complicated.'

242

'Why?' said Sandy. 'Tell us if it would help. We've got lots of time.' She indicated their full drinks.

'It's not so interesting but OK.' He sipped his drink and checked to see if they were listening before going on. 'When the twins was little, we weren't strict about sticking to the agreement. Then once when she asked to see after them for an afternoon, we thought, what harm?'

'But she didn't bring them back when she said she would,' said Benno. 'When we called her, she told us they were better with her and she'd bring them back in the morning. We went straightaway and picked them up. She was furious.'

Alex took over. 'That was when we decided we must enforce our agreement. You have to have clear rules in a situation like this. She can only see them when one of us is there. And of course we are here, and she is there.'

'But can't your sister just say no?' Sandy was leaning forward, intent on the conversation. 'Who is this woman?'

'It's not so simple. They met when she was pregnant and are now friends.'

'*Were* friends,' said Alex. 'The whole thing has got nasty now. One of the reasons we decided to make the move to England. Better for us and the twins to be separate from her.'

'Do the twins mind?'

'No. They don't really know her so well. We're their parents now and they understand that.'

'And I bet you're brilliant,' said Lia, who had been listening in. It didn't matter who she was talking to but she always had a third ear alert for any conversation at a table that might be more interesting that the one she was having. Alan looked put out by the way her attention had been so easily deflected from him. He picked out one of the pizza bites that had been brought with the drinks.

'We do our best.'

'How can you bear to leave them behind?' Sandy's question

made them all turn to look at her. She spat an olive stone into her hand.

'Just two weeks to ourself every year—'

'They remind us why we're together,' Benno chipped in.

'And to recharge batteries. Small boys use a lot of energy.'

'And they have a great time,' Benno was eager to add. 'They love their cousins and my sister lives near a park and a big sports centre with a pool. It's wonderful for children.'

'Makes sense to me.' Lia said.

'Well, it would,' said Sandy in a way that made everyone turn to look at her. 'To me too,' she recovered herself. 'We used to leave Eve at her best friend's so we could have a break sometimes. Then we'd swap. Those long weekends were a gift. I used to get so tired.'

Lia had turned her attention back to Alan, who perked up at the opportunity to continue their conversation.

'But what will you do?'

'My sister wanted one of us to come back to help but we sorted it out by phone, although it wasn't easy. She's a difficult woman. So we'll see her together with the twins when we go to pick them up. The sooner we're back home, the better though.'

One by one, they finished their drinks and Gilly took them into the Piazza Plebiscito where, between the curved backdrop of the basilica and the flat-fronted royal palace opposite, Naples nightlife was being played out much as it was in Piazza Dante and doubtless every other public space in the city. When the sun went down, and the temperature dropped, Neapolitans came out to play. Alice stepped aside for a small skateboarder and into Mark. She saw him flinch before he took a step backwards. An unspoken agreement dictated they walked together so no one would notice or be embarrassed by the awkwardness between them. They strolled down to the seafront where mostly young people had gathered along the sea wall, sitting, standing, chatting, laughing and canoodling. Once, Alice recalled as she stared at a couple who punctuated their conversation with kisses, she and Mark had been like that, so wrapped up in one another that no one else mattered. How cruel time could be.

The rattle of the yachts' rigging sounded against the slap of the sea on the rocks and, across the bay, lights dotted the hillside. A welcome breeze blew in off the water. When she turned back towards the city, she could see the lights of Vomero set on the hill high above the old city of Naples.

'And now,' Gilly announced, breaking into all their thoughts and conversations. 'Supper.'

To Sandy's relief, supper was brief. By now, the ten of them had eaten in each other's company enough times for it to have become more of a chore than a pleasure. Benno and Alex were the only ones who took advantage of the possibilities of eating alone, although this night had been an exception. Afterwards there had been a move led by Lia and Alan to go back to the Caffè Gambrinus for a nightcap. 'Now we're this end of town, we might as well make the most of it.' Lia bounced on her heels in that odd way she had, her camera bag banging against her hip. 'Who's up for another drink?'

That was when Sandy had decided to call it a day. She wanted to speak to Steven and tell him everything that had happened. Alice chose to walk back to the hotel with her, leaving Mark to go with the others. During supper Alice had been doing her best to be cheerful and to include Mark in her conversation. Although he joined in, it didn't need Sherlock Holmes to detect the disconnect between them or the relief when they made separate plans for the rest of the night. Sandy would have stuck by Mark, making sure nothing happened between him and Lia, but then she had never been put in that position. Matthew would never have given into Lia in the same way.

The one time she remembered something like that happening was when a woman he worked with kept asking him for drinks.

Not knowing how to respond without causing an atmosphere at work, he had asked Sandy's advice. When the woman had refused to take a gentle no for an answer more than once, he had to be clear. 'Look for the last time, will you leave me alone?' Afterwards he had come home and told Sandy all about it, faintly ashamed of his bluntness, but laughing that someone had found him attractive when all he wanted was his wife. That night, they had tumbled into bed together and shown how much they loved each other.

Sandy wondered how many men would give in to Lia when she had her mind made up. With victory in sight, she was reeling Mark in, inch by inch until she landed him, and he was enjoying it. Sandy had seen the way he laughed at her jokes, the way he couldn't take his eyes off her. They all had. She wondered if that was what Miriam had done with il Capitano. Was history repeating itself?

She and Alice walked back up the Via Toledo. The city centre was alive with people. The open shops were brightly lit, the ice-cream parlours and cafés busy. The buzz was invigorating. Up the streets of the Quartieri Spagnoli, forbidding in the darkness, candles were placed on the ground, lighting the way to restaurants that they could just see lit in the shadows. Alice kept step beside her. 'So . . .' she said. 'Tell me what happened.'

As Sandy told her about the meeting with Giancarlo Frumetti, Alice was riveted. 'So, have you heard from him yet?'

'No, but he did say it might not be until the morning.' She raised both hands to her mouth, palms together. 'I'm not going to be able to sleep a wink.'

At the end of the pedestrianised section of the street, armed soldiers lounged around an army truck. The two women started walking faster. Sandy gripped her handbag strap. 'Things looked bad between you two.'

'Oh God! Was it that obvious?' Alice stared down at her feet.

'Only to someone who knows what's going on,' Sandy re-assured her.

'That was us trying! It makes me so sad that it's come to this.'

'He should have come back with you.'

They dodged a group of people queuing for an ice-cream shop.

'What? With his wet blanket of a wife?' Alice gave a half-hearted laugh. 'But, if I stayed, I'd only spoil things for everyone else.' She kicked an empty Coca Cola can to one side so it rattled into the gutter. 'He'll be thinking things over and anyway he's with the others too, not just her. Besides, I can't watch over him all the time. If I can't pretend to trust him, things will get even worse.'

'But you don't?'

'No, not any more. Too much has happened. But you know all this.' They stopped to wait at some traffic lights. 'I feel for Benno and Alex, don't you? What an impossible situation.'

'Just what I'm dreading.' Sandy spoke without thinking, as a lorry rumbled past.

'What do you mean?' Alice looked puzzled.

Sandy hesitated as the lights changed. 'I haven't told you. My daughter's having a baby.'

'Why didn't you say? That's great news.' Alice looked up at Sandy as they crossed the road. 'Isn't it?'

'It's complicated. I wanted to tell you but . . .'

'I know. You wanted to keep it to yourself! You see, I know you!' Alice tucked her arm into Sandy's. 'So tell me now.'

As she explained, Alice kept her arm where it was and Sandy was pleased to have that closeness. 'So,' she concluded. 'I've let her down by not being a hundred per cent behind this decision and by letting it show.'

'Don't be daft,' said Alice. 'You can fix this.' They had reached Piazza Dante. 'Come with me.' She led them to a café, where she ordered two coffees.

Sandy didn't resist.

'You've got so much going on in your life, it's no wonder you're in a muddle. But this is something you're overthinking and you really don't need to.'

'But four parents, eight grandparents and a baby Eve may have no rights over.' Why couldn't she stop herself being so negative? 'I'm sorry.'

'Families come in all shapes and sizes these days,' Alice stirred sugar into her coffee. 'This one may not be the traditional one you envisaged being part of, but that doesn't mean to say it won't work. Family is what you make it.' She looked at her over the top of the cup. 'God, listen to me! But you've just got to throw yourself into it. Let Jen know you're as pleased as everyone else that she's pregnant. Let them know that you're in there with them.'

An explosion of light went off in Sandy's brain. That was exactly what she needed to hear. Family is what you make it. Why hadn't she been able to articulate something so obvious to herself? Had her own childhood made her unable to see straight? To Alice's evident surprise, she hugged her. 'Thank you. You're quite right. I've been so selfish but it's not too late to put things right with them both.'

'And – hang on, I haven't finished.' Alice raised a finger for silence. 'Why are you concentrating on them splitting up? They've got as much of a chance as anyone else.'

'That's just what Steven said.'

'I *knew* I'd like him! A man who thinks the same way as me at last.' She sipped her coffee.

'Hands off! He's mine.'

Alice raised an eyebrow. 'Oh really? Sounds like you've made up your mind about something else too.'

Sandy couldn't help the smile that spread across her face. 'Maybe I just have.'

They parted company in the hotel lobby. Although they had

only known each other a short time, Sandy felt as if it had been much longer. Theirs was a friendship she hoped would last beyond this holiday. Alice had helped her, and if she could help Alice find a way through in turn, she would. Feeling more positive than she had for a long time, she reached her room.

Once in bed, she reached for her phone and dialled Steven's number. He sounded tired.

'Did I wake you?'

'No. I was helping a mate move a bed and now I'm knackered. One of those days when I wish I was still in an office. So now I'm sitting the garden with a whisky. It's a beautiful night. The moon, the stars, the works.' He laughed. 'I'm glad you've called. I was thinking about you and wondering how you're getting on.'

He listened as she went through her meeting with Giancarlo again. Like Alice, he wanted to hear every detail. 'What did they look like, these Viglieris?'

'Hard to say, the newsprint was so smudged and dark, but they looked as if they must have been pretty well off.'

'And you haven't heard any more?'

'Not yet. But I should hear something in the morning. I can't believe that I'm actually going to track her down. I wish I could let Mum know.' She felt a rush of sadness that she couldn't just pick up the phone and call her. Never would again. 'But of course they may be dead, too. There's every possibility.'

'But at least you'll know. And you've done your very best for Miriam.' His voice was so calming, restorative. She could picture him in his small garden, sitting on the bench at the far end, looking out towards the sunset. Like her, he wasn't a keen gardener, but did just enough to keep the weeds and undergrowth at bay and make sitting out there pleasant. He'd have his whisky balanced on the arm of the bench, a newspaper or book beside him.

'But I desperately want to know what Mum did that was

so terrible. If I can't find this Anna woman, I almost certainly won't ever find out.' Was her last journal entry a clue?

I did it! I shouldn't have I know. But I couldn't resist and it was delicious. Will we do it again? I expect not. Definitely time to go home!

'There's no one else who would know?' he said. 'No one at all?'

'None that I know of.'

'If only I was there and could help you.'

'We've talked about that and I wish you could help too but you really can't, lovely as would have been.' The novelty of being one among such a disparate group of holidaymakers had worn off back in Rome. Getting to know the others had made her even more aware of what a good and considerate man Steven was, and how much she'd like him in her life. She was beginning to think she might be able to ease into a lasting relationship with him. 'I'll be home soon.'

'Why not stay on a couple of days and I could join you?'

She laughed. 'That's a great idea but I should get back. I want to see Eve.'

'Fair enough.' But he sounded disappointed.

They chatted a little longer before saying goodbye. She lay back against her pillows, relaxed, wondering whether she should phone her daughter. Alex and Benno's story had made her think about how complicated these arrangements could be but also about how they could be managed. Her anxieties weren't what was important. She had done all she could to ensure Eve's future happiness. From now on, she had to keep her thoughts to herself, let her daughter choose the life she wanted to lead, and be there whenever she was needed. Then they would have the family they deserved.

24

Alice woke with a start. The heavy brocade curtains prevented any light from entering the room so she had no idea what time it was. She groped around her bedside table for her phone, trying not to wake Mark. She turned onto her side so the light from the screen wouldn't disturb him. Only 1 a.m. Rolling onto her back, she tried the self-hypnosis technique she'd learned from the hypnotherapist – first relax the toes, then the feet... She was just working up the calf muscles when she became aware of the total silence. There was no muted breathing, no rumbling snore. She reached out her arm to touch her husband. Nothing. He wasn't there. She was quite alone.

The others must be making a real night of it. Wondering where they had ended up was enough to stop her from going back to sleep – hypnotherapy or no bloody hypnotherapy. She switched on the light and pushed herself up in bed, her eyes heavy with tiredness. Until recently she had never had a problem with Mark enjoying a drink or having a night out without her with his friends – that was part of who he was. But now she realised how alcohol changed him – made him the life and soul of the party but also more receptive to suggestion. She didn't like him staying out so late without her, even though it had happened before. He was one of those people who got caught up in the moment and forgot the time. He was often late, running into the cinema foyer moments before the film was due to start, turning up for a dinner party half an hour late, missing a school play. But time had taught her to accept this about him. Some things you can't change.

She picked up her book, but found herself slipping down under the sheet, the words swimming in front of her eyes. Giving up, she turned the light off again and lay in the dark, her mind racing. Thoughts piled in about the children. Would the boys feel abandoned again? Or were they old enough to understand that if she left Mark, it had nothing to do with them? And Pip? What about her? Her unreliable, spirited, gorgeous daughter. But Alice couldn't put the rest of her life on hold when the three of them were growing away from her and Mark.

There was a click as the keycard unlocked the door from outside. The door opened slowly. She didn't move but listened to Mark tiptoe into the bathroom. The silence was broken by a crash and 'Shit!' under his breath but loud enough for her to hear. He must have tripped over the little rubbish bin by the door. He switched the light on in there, some of it filtering under the door into the bedroom. Water running. The muted sound of his electric toothbrush. The splash of him peeing like a horse. Clothes being dropped on to the floor.

At last, the light went off and he emerged into the bedroom, sliding under the sheet carefully so he didn't wake her. 'Ali?' His whisper was loud in the silence.

'Yes.'

'You awake?'

'What do you think? It would be hard not to be.' She didn't move.

'Sorry. Drank a bit too much.' His hand snaked over her waist, pulling her back into him as he spooned round her, kissing her neck.

She wriggled out of his embrace and straightened herself so she was balanced right on the edge of the bed, as far away from him as she could get.

'Oh, Ali, aren't you in the mood?'

'I'm trying to sleep,' she said. 'And you reek of drink. Where have you been?'

'We stayed in that bar playing drinking games. Lia's idea.'

I bet it was, Alice thought as she felt his hand making a return visit. This time it snaked its way up her rib cage to her breast, then her nipple. Twiddling. Annoying. A flicker of arousal ran through her. No! Not like this. He shunted himself closer so she felt his hot breath on her neck, could smell him. Definitely no.

'Not now, Mark, please. I'm knackered.' She rolled on to her front, squashing those possibilities. Frustrated, his hand drifted on to her bum where it lay still.

'But I thought you wanted us to try harder.' That wheedling tone she had fallen for so many times. But not this one. 'That's what I'm doing.'

'I didn't mean at two in the morning when you're pissed.' She swung her legs out of bed, furious that he really thought this was enough to make things better. Although she was ready to admit sex had worked before . . . but things were different then. That was before Joanna and the pregnancy. She might as well have a pee in the hope it would save her from going again later. She picked up his clothes where he'd dropped them in front of the loo, and spread them on the edge of the bath, catching the flowery smell of hotel washing powder from his shirt. By the time she returned to the bedroom, he was snoring, a full-bodied, wine-enhanced snore. She felt like crying. The crack that had existed between them when they arrived in Italy had widened into what seemed an unbridgeable chasm. While he lay there spark out, Alice had no alternative but to lie there too, her eyes open in the darkness, wondering how they had got into this unholy mess and whether she was brave enough to get out of it.

*

Sandy was awake as the morning light sneaked between the curtains that she had left open deliberately. Although it was too early to hope for a message, she checked her phone just in case. Nothing. She had no idea when Italian office workers started their working day. Early she supposed. She would just have to be patient for a little longer although it felt a lifetime had elapsed since she and Gilly had been in the Mackenzie office. She picked up her mother's old journal and flicked through it again.

Almost the last entry.

> *Tomorrow Sorrento. We're meeting friends of Anna's and going out in the boats. Bikini ready, if I dare…*
>
> *Miriam Mackenzie, July 10th 1952 – Naples*

Then the one she had read over and over again, trying to work out if it was the key that would unlock the puzzle.

> *I did it! I shouldn't have I know. But I couldn't resist and it was delicious. Will we do it again? I expect not. Definitely time to go home!*
>
> *Miriam Mackenzie, July 12th – Naples*

A slew of empty pages followed. She idly wondered what else her mother did in Naples, whether she stayed to look after the little girls, how long she was here for. But wondering was pointless.

The dining room was empty, so she chose a modest breakfast from the buffet and took it outside. The terrace was empty too, so she took a table overlooking the pool and waited for the waiter to bring her coffee. A man was sweeping dust and leaves into a long-handled blue and yellow pan. Another day of clear blue sky was promised along with the unforgiving heat that she was getting used to at last.

'*Buon giorno.*' The waiter put the large cup of coffee in front of her.

She thanked him as a blue butterfly no bigger than a fingernail landed on the handle of her cup and perched there, quite still, its wings closed. Even the city's wildlife had learned that there was no point expending unnecessary energy in the heat. Eventually she couldn't wait for her coffee any longer and moved her hand towards the cup, so the butterfly took fright and flew away. She turned on her iPad and switched to the BBC News so she could see what was going on in the world.

Her concentration was broken by the sound of a chair scraping against the ground. Lia put down her plate of cooked breakfast on a table at the other end of the terrace and sat down. When she looked up, she caught Sandy looking in her direction. 'Morning. Can't speak. Terrible hangover. Sorry.'

'Bad luck.' But Sandy was glad not to have to talk to her, able to continue the morning on her own. The door to one of the rooms giving onto the courtyard opened, only for Alan to emerge in his swimming trunks. Sandy shut her eyes against a sight she couldn't unsee. The splash alerted her to his entry into the pool. She watched as he swam an efficient crawl up and down, up and down. Eventually he came to a halt and hitched himself to the side, elbows on the edge, head tipped back towards the sun. After a few minutes, he pulled himself up the steps where he put on his sandals. When he looked up, he saw both women as if for the first time. 'Morning! I'll just change and join you.' He wrapped his towel around his waist and walked towards them. 'Feeling OK, Lia?' He gave her a knowing smile.

'Yes, thanks.' She winced as if her head might crack open from the sound.

'We certainly put it back last night. Good fun.' He turned

255

to Sandy. 'You should have stayed with us. Anyway I'll be with you in a minute.' He went back to his room.

'Not with me, you won't.' Lia muttered as she stood up, stretched and went back inside with a perfunctory 'See you later' as she passed Sandy.

Sandy stayed where she was and by the time Alan reappeared, the terrace tables had been filled with the other guests. Chatter in various languages brought an end to the early peace of the morning. She was debating whether to follow Lia's example, and go to her room until the time they were all due to meet to go up to the art treasures at Capodimonte, when her phone buzzed. An Italian number showed on the screen.

She grabbed her bag and stood up as she took the call. 'Sandy speaking. Is that Giancarlo?'

Alan was approaching so she left her table and went into the hotel lobby as she spoke, to sit in one of the white sofas, listening to Giancarlo.

'I have spoken with Antonio. He did know the Viglieris. You can visit him today at twelve o'clock. I will take you there. He likes to talk about the old days, and you will brighten his morning. Can you do that?'

Sandy's heart was racing with excitement. 'Of course I can. Thank you.'

'I'm interested to hear about them too so it would be my pleasure.'

'But your work...?'

He laughed. 'I am my own boss. I will take an early lunch and perhaps pick you up at your hotel?'

They finalised their arrangements and Sandy hung up. Going there would mean she'd miss Capodimonte and the catacombs but this took priority. She was so close to finding out the answers she was looking for. She stopped herself. Unless the Viglieris were dead of course. In which case, her mother's past would always remain unknown.

'Everything all right?' Mark and Alice stopped beside her, plates loaded with breakfast that they were taking outside to the terrace.

'Very much so. I'm going to meet someone who's going to introduce me to someone who actually knew Anna Viglieri.'

'That's wonderful.' Alice was clearly delighted for her. 'How exciting.'

'It is,' said Sandy. 'But how are you both?' Alice looked as if she hadn't slept at all.

'We're fine,' said Mark briskly. His eyes focused on her as he spoke. 'Nothing a spot of breakfast won't cure.'

'Indeed,' said Alice, watching as he went out to find a table. 'He didn't get in till two.'

'Yes, I saw Alan swimming off his hangover. Sounds like we missed quite an evening.'

'Perhaps we should have gone after all,' Alice shrugged. 'But this is wonderful news. I wish I could come with you but I've got to stay with Mark today. I can't expect him to try unless I do too.' Though she didn't sound as if her heart was in it.

'I wish I was coming with you – the Farnese art collection sounds wonderful and I'd love to see it – but this time . . . well, I can't.'

'My God, of course not. And Naples isn't going anywhere. Perhaps you'll come back.'

'Heard anything yet?' Gilly came down the stairs looking ready for the day ahead in shorts and T-shirt.

'Giancarlo's taking me to see Antonio this morning.' Sandy was experiencing a heady mix of nerves and excitement.

'Will you be all right going alone?' As tour leader, she was concerned but had the rest of the group to think of.

'You've met him. I'll be fine.' She put her anxiety aside. This was the new her, taking charge of her life again. No, she was definitely all right to go alone.

*

She saw the others off and decided to spend the couple of hours she had in hand exploring Spaccanapoli, one of the streets that cut clean through the old town. She couldn't just sit and wait until twelve and she was too excited to concentrate on her book. The streets were coming alive again as she walked along the now familiar Via Tribunali, cutting through to Spaccanapoli and turning back along it so she was on her route back to the hotel. Street sellers were laying out their displays of sunglasses, sunhats and knock-off designer bags. She shook her head at a man trying to sell her a red chilli charm from a bunch hanging from his arm. Against a wall, a man played a recorder to a dancing puppet. Small shops and cafés were open. She stopped to buy a box of biscuits to take with her later. The sounds of a bird whistle carried down the street. She stepped aside for a motor scooter with baskets piled high behind the driver. In the gateway to the church of Santa Chiara, a girl in a green dress was playing a harp so beautifully that Sandy dropped a couple of euros in the hat before walking into the church itself.

Expecting the baroque splendour of the Duomo she was surprised by the austerity that greeted her, but the peace and cool were a relief from what she had left outside. She lingered for a while, then went through a door into a cloistered garden. Lines of octagonal pillars linked by benches, all of them covered with majolica tiles depicting life outside the old convent, criss-crossed the open space. Apart from a couple at the other side of the cloister, Sandy was alone there. She sat on one of the benches enjoying the illustrations until it got too hot to stay there any longer.

Passing into the museum and through the Roman baths, lingering over pieces of statuary that particularly attracted her, she felt the sort of contentment that she hadn't felt for years. Not everything in her life was sorted, far from it, but something inside her had shifted over these two weeks, changing her outlook, making her realise there was more to life than the path she had taken since Matthew's death. Instead of continuing in the one they had followed together, she could break away and forge her own, just as Eve was doing, just as Alice was considering doing. A renewed confidence in herself and in what she wanted from life surprised and pleased her.

Fortified by these thoughts, she returned to the street and, glancing at her watch, realised she just had time to visit the church on the piazza at the end of the street. Two churches in one day was enough if she wanted to remember them at all. Leaving the plangent notes of the harp behind her, she approached a building studded with black pyramids, more like a prison than a church, and slipped through the small door. What a contrast. Baroque decoration dominated the vast interior. She wandered round, stopping to gaze up at the spectacular ceiling and the cupola until her neck ached. In one of the side chapels she visited the recreated consulting rooms of a doctor, San Giuseppe Moscati, and paused to watch a woman touch the hands of his statue in the main church, polished to a shine by all the people who had done the same. When no one was looking, she went over and followed suit, feeling the smooth cold brass under her fingers. Perhaps he would bring her luck.

Glancing at her watch, she saw more time had passed than she realised and if she didn't head back to the hotel immediately, she would be late for Giancarlo.

The taxi dropped them off under a bridge carrying a main road above them. 'Come this way.' Giancarlo guided her past a tatty lift that took pedestrians up to the bridge, and along to where the street widened out. Brown and white tourism signs pointed in the direction of the catacombs. So they weren't far from where the others must be. Sandy spared them a fleeting thought, wondering how Mark and Alice were getting on, what Lia was doing. To their left, a grocer, a *tabacchi* and newsagent took up the ground floor of a terracotta-rendered building, their goods overflowing into street displays. Above, the tall windows were framed by green shutters.

'Antonio lives up there.' Giancarlo pointed up to the tall top right-hand window where a woman had stepped out from behind a net curtain. He waved. She raised a hand and disappeared. 'His daughter,' he explained, as he led her to the heavy main doors and turned the circular handle so it swung open. They stood in a small courtyard with stone staircases going up to right and left of them.

'This way.' He took her to the right-hand one and began climbing.

Sandy's nerves had returned to chase her excitement away as she took one step after another, up and up. From somewhere in the building she could hear an oboe, then a violin in harmony. How would an old man cope with these stairs, she wondered inconsequentially. Perhaps he never left his flat. Eventually they faced a wooden door. Sweat was running down Sandy's back. She flapped her sleeveless shirt as unobtrusively as she could.

The woman they had seen from the street opened the door. She was small, plump with short grey hair, a lined face lit by an easy smile. She and Giancarlo exchanged enthusiastic greetings before he introduced Sandy.

'*Buon giorno*,' she managed, feeling hopelessly inadequate.

The woman turned to Giancarlo, wiped her hands on her apron, said something that made them laugh. Sandy felt uncomfortable, wondering if she was the butt of a joke, but reminded herself why she was there. This would soon be over and when it was, she might be one step nearer Anna Viglieri.

'This is Mariella. She says welcome to you,' said Giancarlo.

She smiled and nodded, unable to say anything else.

Mariella took them to a room where an old man sat in a chair facing the door. Sandy had expected him to be in his pyjamas and dressing gown, but no. He was wearing trousers and a shirt smart enough for any window of Mackenzies. As they went in, his smile cut through the lines of his face, his brown eyes disappearing in the creases of flesh. Giancarlo crossed the room to shake his hand, his brogues tapping on the tiles. He turned to introduce Sandy, who smiled and went over to give the box of biscuits she had bought that morning. The gesture prompted a rush of enthusiastic Italian.

'He thanks you,' was Giancarlo's translation of something much, much longer. Antonio's daughter stood in the doorway, eyes like a bird, listening to what was being said before fetching them each a glass of water.

Giancarlo pulled out the cutting containing the photo of the Viglieris and showed it to Antonio, provoking another torrent of Italian. While Antonio and Giancarlo talked in raised voices, gesticulating wildly, Sandy took in her surroundings. The walls of the room were bare apart from a crucifix and a picture of the Pope. By the window, the aircon unit kept up a constant rumble. Apart from the chair the old man sat in, there was a single bed; a small table with wooden chairs, two of which Giancarlo took for them to sit on; and a TV on top of a shelving unit that contained a couple of books and some magazines.

'So,' said Giancarlo at last. Sandy tensed, bracing herself for disappointment.

'He knew them. Roberto Viglieri was from Naples, but not his wife. She had something to do with the family who owned the business but he's not sure what. They knew Roberto because he worked his way up from the warehouse to the shop, and at last to management. He wasn't popular but he was powerful. He died about ten years after his retirement. Cancer, he thinks.'

As she had feared. 'What about her? Is she dead too?'

Sorry, Mum, she said to herself as she waited for the answer. *I'm too late.*

Giancarlo said something that prompted a firm shake of Antonio's head. 'No.'

'No?' She stared at Antonio, willing him to say more, wishing she could understand what he was saying as he carried on. If Anna was English, then she could be an old school friend of her mother's who ended up out here and lost touch with her past. Was that her link with the family? That would make sense. 'Where is she?'

'She's an old woman now,' Giancarlo translated.

'Does he know where I can find her?' That was all that mattered.

'The last he heard of her, she was living in Vomero. You know Vomero?'

Sandy shook her head. How stupid to have imagined that the woman might still be in Naples. That meant she wouldn't complete her search on this trip. She had come so close but so far. Her disappointment was shattering. She put her head in her hands so the two men wouldn't see the tears in her eyes.

'It's on the hill,' he explained. 'In Naples. You take the funicular.'

'What did you say?' She looked up.

'In Naples. You know it?'

'Here?' she said. Of course it was. Gilly had pointed it out on the walk round royal Naples, high on the hill above them. Sandy could hardly believe it. So Anna Viglieri was here after all. Against all odds, she had found her.

25

However fine the paintings at the Capodimonte galleries, Alice had had enough. 'I'm pictured out,' she whispered to Mark, who, to her surprise and pleasure, had stuck by her the whole morning. 'I can't take in another thing. Why don't we explore the park?'

'You sure?' He put his hand on her back. 'There are just a couple more rooms.'

'Why don't I wait for you downstairs, then? I can sit on the grass out there.' There were so many people outside enjoying the park, she wanted to be one of them. Just to sit people-watching would be enough.

'No, no. I'm coming with you.' He started walking through the gallery, not pausing to look at anything, guiding her to the exit.

Alice was confused. This was the first time on their holiday that he had been as attentive. She had fully expected him to continue the tour – he loved art galleries – and to meet her afterwards. And that would have been fine.

'Where are you going?' Alan asked as they overtook him and Lia, standing admiring a simple but tender representation of the Madonna and child.

'Alice has had enough,' said Mark. 'So we're going outside.'

'Good plan.' Alan detached himself from Lia. 'I've seen plenty. Not that I don't appreciate it but you can have too much of a good thing. Do I sound like an uncultured heathen?'

'You are a heathen.' Lia laughed as she raised her camera

to take yet another photograph. She must have snapped every picture she passed.

'Well, are you coming or not?' Alan rubbed at his goatee while Lia put her camera away.

'Of course.' She smiled at Mark but he looked away.

'Why don't you just buy a catalogue and look at something for once?' he asked, completely taking her aback.

A determined look overtook her shocked expression. 'I could, but I like taking photographs of my own. It helps me remember where I was and what I was doing there.' She gave him a look that was loaded with meaning but he didn't react. 'How do we get out of here?'

Alice tried not to let her disappointment show. At the same time, she almost admired Lia's brass neck. She obviously didn't think that she'd done anything wrong. Or if she did, she didn't care. Or did she think that Alice was so stupid, she didn't notice? On the contrary. Alice had noticed every nuance in that last exchange. And why was Mark so uncharacteristically snippy with her? She felt the pressure of Mark's hand between her shoulder blades and carried on walking.

By the time they were outside the Bourbon palace, they had scooped up Gilly, Alex and Benno as well. 'I'll wait here for Peter and Brit,' said Gilly. 'You go into the woods. They're beautiful. Meet you back here in an hour, and we'll go for some lunch.'

As they strolled in the direction of the trees, Alex and Benno walked ahead of the rest of them, turning down a different path without a look back. Mark's arm was draped proprietorially round Alice's shoulders, making her hotter than ever. 'I'm sorry you didn't enjoy that,' he said.

She stopped. 'Go back. Honestly, I don't mind. I don't want you to go back home regretting you didn't see everything you wanted to.'

'I wouldn't mind going back either. We missed quite a lot.' Lia sounded sulky.

'Then you should have said at the time.' Alan pulled out a pack of chewing gum from his shorts pocket and offered it round. Everyone refused.

'I'd rather be out here.' Mark guided Alice forward. She allowed herself a flicker of hope. Perhaps things would all work out after all. Beneath the canopy of overlapping oak branches they came to an empty bench, where they all sat down.

'I know. Group photo,' said Lia.

'Must we?' said Mark, tapping his foot on the ground.

Alan pulled a face. 'Haven't you got enough, Lia? Do you think Elizabeth whatever her name is went round taking photos of everything?'

She laughed. 'I don't know whether she even had a camera. But just one. A souvenir. I'll ask one of those girls to take it.' Before anyone had time to object again she had gone up to a group of four young women and corralled one into photographing them. Alice watched Lia with something approaching envy: the stylish hair; the face that looked just fine without make-up; legs, tanned in her shorts; the much slimmer figure of someone who had not had a lifetime love affair with what she ate. While the others waited, Lia gave a short lesson on how her camera worked then ran back and flung herself down beside Alice.

Alice shrank away from contact. One moment Lia was overtly flirting with her husband, the next she was behaving as if nothing could be further from her mind. How was Alice supposed to respond? Surely Lia didn't think they were going to be friends. If this was a game, Alice couldn't work out the rules.

'Say "Really?"' instructed Lia. 'Works like a dream.'

'Really?' they chorused before she leaped to her feet to retrieve her camera. As she did so, Alice caught a whiff of her perfume. Floral. Familiar. Must be something Jo Malone that one of her friends wore. But she had smelled it more recently than that. Sandy? She was a Jo Malone person. Then she realised where she recognised it from. Or something very like it. The smell of Mark's shirt that she had dismissed as washing powder the previous night. For a moment, she couldn't move. She so badly wanted to be mistaken but the scent was quite distinctive.

'Something wrong?' Mark was on his feet, holding out a hand to her.

She gave her head a little shake. 'No, no. Nothing.' She ignored his hand. 'Sorry. It's the heat.'

'Have some water.' Alan passed her a half-empty bottle.

'It's OK, I've got some of my own.' She gave herself some time by unscrewing the top and tipping her head back to drink. By the time she finished, Mark had moved off and was talking to Lia, who was lining up a shot down the woodland path dappled with sunlight. He glanced back at Alice and raised his hand. She stood up, determined.

'What happened last night, Alan?'

He looked alarmed. 'What do you mean? We had a few drinks. Some of us more than others.' He gave that wolfish grin of his. 'Naming no names.'

'And?'

He looked around, his hand at the neck of his T-shirt, unable to meet her gaze. 'That's all I know. I didn't see anything else'

'What do you mean?' She was bent on getting the facts. 'What else was there to see?'

'Look. I don't want to get caught up in any of this. It's nothing to do with me. We're on holiday. Don't let's spoil it.' His blustering confirmed that there was something he wasn't saying.

But Alice wasn't going to give up. She had to know that she wasn't imagining this. 'Did something happen between Lia and Mark? You have to tell me. They've been flirting with each other since we arrived. You've all seen for yourselves. I know it was harmless at first but now... Don't you think I should know if something more has happened between them? I've even smelled her perfume on his shirt.'

His shoulders dropped as he sighed, hands by his side. 'All I know is that we had a few drinks. Lia insisted that we played some stupid drinking game.' He removed his hat and wiped his brow. 'I'm too old for that sort of thing.'

'You're not the only one.' Alice looked in Mark's direction to see him in earnest conversation with Lia.

He nodded towards them. 'I bowed out then we all agreed it was time to call it a night. All except her. She was game to go on.'

'But didn't?'

'She couldn't very well play on her own, so we forced her hand.'

'What time?' She traced a circle in the dust with her sandal, half desperate for, and half not wanting his answer.

'About midnight. Any later and I'd have turned into a pumpkin.' He laughed again.

'Midnight. Are you sure?'

He nodded. 'Completely. I checked the time when I set my alarm for the morning.'

'Are you coming, Ali?' Mark called. 'We've got time to go a bit further.'

Lia's head was bent over her camera but Alice could see she was upset.

'Come,' said Alan. 'It must be hard, but this is something you need to sort out when you get home. Not while you're here. For your sake and for everyone else's. Try and enjoy the little time you've got left. Ignore her. At least she's stopped mentioning that woman she's so keen on at every opportunity, thank the Lord.'

Alice didn't speak. If Mark thought he could ease his guilt and make things right between them by overcompensating and behaving like a devoted husband, then he could think again.

Somewhere in her brain, a shutter came down. Alan was right, she shouldn't spoil everyone's holiday but she could at least spoil Mark's.

For the rest of their walk she and Alan followed the other two. Alice was oblivious to everything going on in the park, unable to take her eyes off them. Every now and then Mark turned round as if anxious at not being with her. As well he might be. She noticed that their hands brushed together once and he moved his away as if he'd had an electric shock. They were all pretending nothing had changed when it was clear to Alice that everything had. But she would bide her time, not make any move that she hadn't thought through. They reunited with the group under one of the tall palm trees at the front of the palace. 'Where have you been?' Peter looked at his watch. 'We've only just got here. What a wonderful morning.'

'Having a break from culture,' said Lia, leaving Mark's side and going over to Alex and Benno. 'You should try it. Now where are we having lunch? I'm starving.'

The minibus took them to a nearby trattoria where they fell on the menu as if they hadn't eaten for days. Although she thought she couldn't eat a thing, just a quick look at the menu brought Alice's appetite out of hiding. Her risotto with rose petal, shrimps and champagne was exquisite, and went some way to calming her down and making her see things more clearly. The others chose other risotti with seafood and lemon or with shrimps and artichokes, all pronounced delicious. Mark stuck to pasta: ravioli with ricotta, squid and saffron. *Soaking up the alcohol*, Alice observed to herself. *I hope it makes him sick.*

'A bite?' He pushed his plate towards her.

She couldn't resist. The chances of her hope materialising were zero, she thought as she took a mouthful of his pasta: perfectly cooked and a wonderful fusion of tastes.

Restored, they returned to the minibus, and were driven to the first of the catacombs.

Alice endured the catacombs of San Gennaro, so crowded and dimly lit that she could stand apart from Mark without him noticing. Every now and then they'd drift towards one another and he'd touch her, a hand on her arm, an arm round her shoulder, a whispered remark. All the time she steeled herself to appear as if everything was quite normal. She was certain she hadn't made a mistake and was furious she had allowed herself to be fooled.

'And now, we're going to a more modern cemetery,' announced Gilly. 'And then you're free to do whatever you want.'

'Sleep,' murmured Alan.

Everyone laughed.

'Lightweight,' shouted Lia from the back. 'And you had us all in bed by midnight.'

Alice felt Mark tense as he continued to stare out of the window.

'Do we need to go?' Brit was reluctant. 'I've been to plenty of cemeteries. It can't beat Père Lachaise.'

'It's quite different,' said Gilly, unfazed by her objection. 'You won't have seen anything like this before, but you're welcome to wait in the minibus or make your own way back, if you prefer.'

'I think we should trust Gilly,' said Peter.

Brit looked surprised. 'Oh. If you think so.'

'I do.'

Brit subsided into her seat and didn't object any further. Alice was surprised at this turnabout in their relationship. They travelled in silence, pleasantly comatose after the meal, staring out of the window at the neighbourhoods they were driving through, a far cry from the fancy area they had come from. Striped awnings hung across windows, blue plastic buckets were lowered from balconies to be filled with groceries in the street and hauled back up. They exclaimed at a life-size statue of a brown-robed monk and a church painted so gaudily it could have come out of the sixties. The driver pulled up in a quiet street with no sign of a cemetery anywhere. Alan was slumped against the window, mouth open, sound asleep.

'Should we leave him?' said Alice. 'Seems mean to wake him.'

'Meaner to let him miss something that he may never visit again,' said Gilly and shook his arm. 'Come on, Alan. We're here.'

'Good, good. Thought we'd never get here.' He straightened up, rubbing his face.

The heat enveloped them as they trooped behind Gilly towards some kind of underground bunker in the hillside. Past the gatekeeper's box, they entered a vast cavern sculpted out of the rock that stretched backwards and upwards into darkness.

'Where have you brought us?' asked Peter. 'This isn't a cemetery.'

'Believe me, it is.' Gilly walked on.

Alice gasped and without thinking clutched Mark's arm. Ahead of them, behind a low wooden barricade were thousands of bones piled up against the back walls. In front of them, surrounding a plastic figure of Jesus, were too many skulls to count. As she got closer, she could see various offerings among them: coloured plastic necklaces; coins and notes.

'My God. What is this place?' asked Mark.

'Cimitero delle Fontanelle,' said Gilly, echoed by Lia. 'This is where the poor who died of the plague in the seventeenth century were buried. Afterwards, those who couldn't afford a church burial were buried here and forgotten. In 1872 the parish priest got the local people to help him put it order, as it is now. But, you see these offerings?'

They nodded, equally intrigued and appalled.

'People believed that the bones looked after whoever had taken care of them. So people would adopt a skull and bring it offerings. This is the Neapolitan Cult of the Dead.'

'It's grotesque.' Brit shuddered. 'I don't want to spend another second in here. Peter?'

'Stay with me. We have to see this. You'll be all right.' As he led her down the central aisle towards the tall, simple crosses at the far end, she seemed to shrink into him.

'I've never seen anything like it. Come down here.' Benno and Alex set off after them, stopping to look at whatever caught their eye.

Alice, Mark and Alan left Lia setting up her camera, while they took one of the shadowy side aisles. Alice was mesmerised. The place was so macabre and yet, instead of being frightened or repelled, she was intrigued. She separated from the others and wandered alone, pausing by a row of skulls with coins placed on the top of them.

The atmosphere was eerie, unearthly, but more than anything Alice found being in the presence of so many anonymous human remains sobering. *This is what life is all about*, she thought. *This is what's waiting for all of us in the end. Nothing.* She had no religion to make her believe in the life of the spirit. The more dusty, venerated skulls and bones she saw, the more the need to make the most of the short time she had on earth was driven home to her. This life was no dress rehearsal and was the only one she was going to get a shot at. Before she ended up the same way as these people, she had to start respecting herself and leading the most fulfilling life she could, while loving her children and without doing them harm. Mark would not come first any more.

By the time she re-emerged into the sunlight, she knew exactly what she wanted to do.

As they pulled up outside the hotel, Alice saw Sandy walking up the street towards them. There was something about her that was different, something in the way she carried herself that looked lighter, more relaxed. Her head was held high as she looked around, a slight smile on her face. Alice went down to meet her.

'You look quite different. What's happened?'

Sandy punched the air. 'We've found her. We really have. Let's have a coffee and I'll tell you how.'

Glad to be free of Mark and to think of something else, Alice readily agreed. They crossed the road, past the row of rubbish bins and into Piazza Bellini. At the back, behind the statue of Bellini himself, were several bars and cafés. Sandy plumped for the one with bookshelves lining the walls. They took a table outside and ordered a *limonata* for her and an iced tea for Sandy.

'Pity they don't clean the place up.' She looked at the black scrawls of graffiti, the posters stuck squint on the walls, some of them out of date and torn.

'But it's all part of the character. It wouldn't be the same.'

Alice was doubtful. 'Maybe. Now tell me, tell me . . . and don't leave anything out.'

So Sandy didn't. She described the journey to the flat, the building, its surroundings and what happened once they got inside. 'Giancarlo was fantastic. He found Antonio, introduced us and translated brilliantly when I'm sure he should have been at work.'

'So what happens next?'

'He's contacted Anna Viglieri!' She gave a clap. 'And I'm going to see her tonight. Unfortunately he can't come because he's got some three-line-whip family do. Something to do with one of his sons getting married, and meeting his new daughter-in-law's family. I think he would've quite liked an excuse but his wife would have killed him. He's as keen as I am to meet her now.'

Alice toyed with her straw. 'I'll come with you, if you want moral support.'

'No, no. I can do this on my own.'

'I know you can. But I'll come if you'd like me too. It'll be a welcome break for me and anyway, I'm longing to know the end of the story. You know how I hate to miss a meal but I've just had an excellent lunch and the company's wearing a bit thin.' She shook with laughter. 'Unlike me!'

'I know what you mean. And I've got to go back to school with her in a couple of weeks.' The prospect was obviously not one she relished.

'Do you know what? I'm thinking I probably owe her a thank you.' Alice sighed, tearing the top of the sugar sachet and pouring it into her drink before giving it a stir.

'How's that?'

'She's made me realise that Mark will never change. And realising that has made me change. I'm scared of a future on my own but I'm not going to be taken for granted any more.'

'Whatever's happened? And being on one's own isn't so bad.' Sandy looked at her. 'But I thought you weren't making any assumptions or decisions till you got home.'

It didn't take long for Alice to summarise the evidence against him. As she did, she felt her anger simmering down, her mind quite clear again.

Sandy gazed at her, her grey eyes steady. 'First of all, you wouldn't be entirely on your own. You'll have Pip and the boys.'

'I know. But my fear is that the boys will feel history's repeating itself and that they're being rejected again. Getting through that was so hard.' She remembered the nights when Patrick would destroy his room, throwing things he loved across it, breaking up his Lego models, stamping on his toys. Those outbursts always ended up with her holding him, rocking him till he went to sleep. Henry on the other hand kept his hurt inside, not talking for days, having to be coaxed and coerced into confiding his feelings to her. She stayed with them for all of it.

'But they're adults now. It's not the same. You've done

everything you can for them and I bet they're aware of that and appreciate it. They must have more than an inkling of what their dad's like.'

Alice didn't want to contradict her. And it was true that wherever Alice ended up living would be Pip's home too, and the boys' if they ever needed it. She would not desert them and she would make that plain.

'And you'll have your friends – including me now.'

'Yes.' Alice's face lit up at the thought of them. 'I'm pretty sure Lucy will let me help out. She's an old friend, a restaurateur who's been badgering me on and off for ages.' The idea of returning to work in a professional kitchen was thrilling. She could picture herself getting stuck in, experimenting with new ingredients just like she used to, using some of the taste combinations that she'd experienced here, sweating it out over a delicious smelling pan, tasting... She closed her eyes, relishing the picture. 'I've got to think about me now.' That's what she would do and she felt good about it.

Sandy raised her iced tea. 'Let's drink to that.'

26

The funicular bounced back and forth at each stop as if supported by a piece of elastic that would either send them catapulting up to the top of the hill or, if it broke, crashing down to the bottom. Sandy had chosen two seats that faced downhill. A mistake, given her vertigo. She clutched on to the sides of her seat, willing them to get to the top without disaster.

When they did, she and Alice stepped out of the station into a busy square that felt quite different to the Naples they had left below. This was smarter, more residential – cooler too. She and Alice stood for a moment, taking everything in, before she got out her map.

'Piazza Vanvitelli. Here it is.' She pointed. 'Down here and into Via Bernini.'

Within no time, they had found the street they wanted in an expensive shopping area with what looked like solid and expensive apartments above the glamorous shop facades. 'Here.' They stopped outside a cream building with grey shutters at the windows. Beside the door were a slew of brass nameplates, one of which had the name Viglieri stamped on it. Sandy's stomach turned over. 'This is it.'

'Are you ready?' Alice was right behind her.

Was she? Sandy thought for a second, and put her hand on her bag where she had put the photo and letter. She had decided to leave the journal behind, particularly in the light of that final entry. She had no idea what memories that might provoke. 'Yes. Yes, I am.'

*

The door to the apartment was opened by a paunchy middle-aged man with a friendly smile who waited while Sandy introduced them before showing them into the flat. He was a little taller than Sandy, his greying hair slicked back, black trousers, short-sleeved white shirt. 'You've come to see my mother. She's expecting you.' He led the way towards a double door at the end of the hallway. What a contrast to the flat she had visited yesterday. This one was large, elegant and comfortable. The walls were hung with gilt frames containing oil paintings of country scenes. A bunch of flowers stood in a vase on the marble-topped console table halfway along the hallway. Through the open doors she could see a gilt, silk-upholstered sofa that looked chic but uncomfortable. Beyond was a window overlooking the street.

'Come along,' said a voice from the unseen part of the room. 'I haven't got all day. I'm curious why you want to see me.'

'She's English?' said Sandy quietly.

'Don't let her hear you say that.' The man's face cracked with a smile. 'Mama, here are the two ladies you are expecting. Can I get you tea or coffee?'

'Just a glass of water would be great. Thank you.' Sandy turned her attention to the woman sitting in an armchair with her feet up on a stool. Although she must have been well into her eighties, Anna Viglieri was still an impressive woman. A cloud of silver hair, subtly made-up, expensively dressed in patterned silk.

'Signora Viglieri, I'm Sandy Johnson and this is Alice Bennett, a friend of mine.' This was as bad as being sent up in front of the headmistress.

'Brought her along for moral support, have you?' Anna Viglieri smiled. 'And you don't need to be so formal – call me Anna.' Her accent was a curious hybrid of Italian and something else, the voice of someone who had lived here a long

276

time. She stood up, revealing herself as being, although slightly stooped, as tall as Sandy and slim. She offered her arthritic hand to be shaken by them both. 'Sit down, do. Before I fall down. My legs aren't all they once were. And before you say anything else, I'm not English. I came here from Scotland many years ago and never went back. Most of my life I've lived here.'

For the briefest of moments, Sandy remembered her own and Matthew's love of Scotland.

They took the two armchairs facing her. Between them was a low marble and gilt coffee table piled with large illustrated photographic books and a couple of magazines.

'Now how can I help you? I was told you'd come from England to find me.'

'We're on a group holiday which is how the two of us met,' said Sandy. 'But I have something that I think is for you.' She reached down for her bag as the man returned with two glasses of water and a cup of tea for his mother. 'Thank you.'

'I have to go, Mama,' he said. 'But Isabella will be here later. You'll be all right till then?'

'Unless these ladies have come armed.' She chuckled. 'Yes, I'll be fine. Don't fuss. They look after me so well,' she said as the front door of the flat slammed. 'Sometimes it's a little too much. But carry on. You have something for me? How intriguing.'

'Before I show you let me explain.' Sandy ignored the woman's outstretched hand, keeping the envelope and photo on her lap while she spoke. 'My mother died a few months ago, and one of the last things she asked me to do was to deliver this letter. It's addressed to Anna Viglieri.'

Anna Viglieri's beady eyes didn't move from Sandy. 'Your mother's name?' She took a spoonful of sugar and stirred it into her tea.

'Miriam.'

The word fell through the air and everything around it was still.

'Miriam,' Anna repeated as if she couldn't quite believe it. 'Miriam what?'

'She was once Miriam Mackenzie but married my dad and became Miriam Johnson. Did you know her?'

The older woman's face was still as she raised her cup and took a noisy sip. 'Yes. I knew a Miriam Mackenzie.'

The pulse in Sandy's throat quickened. She really had found her mother's friend at last. 'Did you know her well?'

'I knew her very well indeed. Once.' Her eyes misted over as if she was remembering. Then she banged the cup back on its saucer. 'But that was a long time ago. What can she want with me now?'

'To apologise.' Sandy answered, anxious things were taking a wrong turn without her understanding why. She could remember her mother's written words exactly.

I am so sorry. There. Four short words that are inadequate to sum up everything I've felt all these years. What I did was so wrong. I've spoken to no one about what happened and how it divided us. And I won't now in case someone else reads this. I'm not coming to look for you myself because I'm too ill now . . .

Anna frowned. 'After so long. But you seem to know about it. Did she tell you?'

'No.'

'She promised she'd tell no one.'

'She kept her promise but I'm afraid I opened the envelope and read her letter to you. I didn't have any idea how to find you and thought there might be something in there that might help. It seemed such an impossible task.'

'And was there?'

'No. Although I discovered that there was more to Mum than I ever knew. A mystery that involves you.'

The older woman bowed her head. 'Yes.'

Her mother's words continued to run through Sandy's head.

I've thought about you so often, wondered what you would say if I tried to contact you. Believe me, I've been so punished. Every time I look at my daughter, I'm reminded of what happened. Sometimes that's been so hard and I know I've pushed her away as a result. But there's no point trying to explain to you. Just try to imagine how I've suffered for yourself. I'm not blaming you – how could I when it was all my fault? – but want you to know I've never forgotten. And this isn't about me, but about us.

She had to explain, to break the silence. She cleared her throat. 'Mum and I didn't have an easy relationship. In fact, until I had my daughter I saw as little of her as I could, if I'm honest. We grew closer over Eve, she moved near us when my father died and I looked after her while she was dying. Letting her have her last wish is the least I can do.'

My last wish is that you can find it in your heart to forgive me, Anna. If you can't, then at least know how much I regret what I did. If I could go back and do things differently I would. Please believe me.

'Whatever the results.' Anna raised her head, fixing her faded blue eyes on Sandy, her mouth in a tight line.

'Yes, of course.' What a curious thing to say. 'But tell me how you knew her.'

'Let me read what she has to say first.' She stretched out her hand again. This time, Sandy gave her both the photo and the letter.

Anna stared at the photo, turning it over and back again but saying nothing. Was she the woman bending over the pram? But she gave nothing away. Then she took the envelope, pulling out the letter and pausing before unfolding it. Sandy was aware of Alice sitting absolutely still beside her, as much on tenterhooks as she was. Having her there gave Sandy renewed confidence that, whatever happened next, she was right to have come this far.

As the old woman read, the paper quivered with the tremor in her hand. When she had finished, she shook her head as if she couldn't quite believe what she had read. '*"And this isn't about me, but about us,"*' she read aloud. '*"I've thought about you so often, wondered what you would say if I tried to contact you".* But I get no chance to reply.' She rested the letter on her lap as she drank her tea.

'You can reply to me,' said Sandy. 'Explain to me what it means. What did she do?'

Anna looked at the thin gold watch on her wrist. 'I think we should have a drink.' She pointed towards a trolley between the two windows that held a couple of bottles and glasses. 'Would you mind?' She nodded at Alice.

'Of course.' Alice crossed the room, picked up the two bottles and read the labels. 'Whisky or gin?'

'Whisky for me,' said Anna.

'I'll have a gin and tonic. Thanks,' added Sandy.

'You'll find ice and tonic in the fridge.' Obviously used to ordering people around, Anna waved in the direction of the door through which Alice would presumably find the kitchen. Sandy was amused by her imperiousness. Alice left the room, to return with a tumbler full of ice and a couple of bottles of tonic.

When they were settled with their drinks, coasters pointed out on the coffee table, Anna picked up the photo and stared at it, her eyes hazy. 'Where to begin?'

'Who's that in the picture. Is that you?'

She gave a sad smile. 'No, that's your mother.'

Sandy took the photo back to look at it again, still unable to recognise her. 'And the baby?'

Anna shook her head as if she didn't know.

'Tell me how you knew her. What was she like?' Sandy spoke softly, desperate for some light to be shone on to her mother's past at last but aware of Anna's visible distress. 'Were you friends from school?'

Anna shook her head, her earrings catching the light. 'No, not friends.' She paused as if deliberating whether to go on. She looked at Sandy, assessing her as her eyes travelled over her. 'I can see a resemblance now. How strange.'

'How did you know her then?' Sandy prompted.

'We were sisters.'

'Sisters.' The word was like a punch to the solar plexus, winding Sandy. 'That's not possible.'

'I'm afraid it is.' Anna smoothed the letter with her hand.

'But she never mentioned you. I had no idea.'

'She promised she never would. And if you deny something enough you can almost persuade yourself it never existed.' She looked down at her hands. 'I did the same. I put her so far to the back of my mind that I almost forgot her too. I never expected to hear from her again.'

'Whatever happened?' Sandy was aware of Alice changing position, leaning forward. She tried again to speculate what her mother could have done that would deserve being cut off by her entire family. That could be the only explanation for her constant dismissal of them.

'Perhaps I should go.' Alice began to stand up.

'No, stay. I want you to hear this too.' Sandy wanted a witness to corroborate whatever she was about to hear.

'If you're sure.' Alice took her chair again.

Anna seemed not to hear them. 'What happened was a very

long time ago, when we were young. Miri had just turned twenty-one when she came to visit.'

'Miri?'

'That's what I always called her.'

'And you were living here then?'

A wave of the hand told Sandy not to ask any more questions. 'I had come out to look after my Uncle Stuart's children after his wife drowned in a boating accident near Sorrento. The saddest thing. He ran the family shop ... Mackenzies ... for his father.' She looked at them to check they knew what she was talking about. They both nodded. 'There was no question of him returning to Scotland with the children. He'd been living here since he left school and the company was going to be his. Their life was here.' She gave a little laugh. 'How I loved those girls. I looked after them until I got married myself to an Italian. And then Uncle Stuart remarried a little later. I never regretted coming here, never.' She spoke as if she was convincing herself.

'I met Roberto soon after I arrived. He was working in the warehouse at Mackenzies then. We fell in love but it was a match that would have been frowned on by my family at home. Appearances mattered to them. Class was important. And religion. But my uncle didn't see things in such a black-and-white way. He recognised Roberto's potential even then.'

'But Mum ...' Sandy was impatient to get to the point.

Anna wagged a finger. 'Wait. You will understand if I tell you exactly how it was. Roberto and I were happy, engaged to be married, when Miri came out here. She came first to Rome, keeping a friend of our mother's company and then she came here.'

'Just like us.' Alice said, but Anna took no notice.

'Mrs Robson,' said Sandy.

'Was that her name? I forget. The idea was to see if she wanted to take over looking after the girls from me.' A distant smile crossed her face. 'We were so excited by the prospect of being here together. I wanted her to meet Roberto. He was such fun. I knew they would get on even though my parents would never give us their blessing.'

There was a pause while she adjusted herself into a more comfortable position.

'This is difficult for me.' A tear ran down her cheek. She dashed it away. 'How memories hijack emotions. Forgive me.'

'If it's too difficult, would you prefer me to come back another time when you've had time to absorb all this. I can see it's been a shock.' Though leaving was the last thing Sandy wanted to do.

'You're kind.' Anna pulled out a lace-edged handkerchief to blow her nose. 'But now you're here, it's better for the truth to come out and for you to know.'

The truth about what? Sandy sipped her gin.

Anna took a deep breath as if forcing herself to continue. 'Where had I got to?'

'You thought that Miri and Roberto would get on,' prompted Alice.

'Of course.' Anna gave her a gimlet stare as if telling her not to interrupt. 'And they did. We would have lovely times together, going down to Roberto's family on their farm not far from Ravello. Or we'd go to Amalfi for the weekend, go to the beach, go sailing, out in the evenings. We had such good times. Sometimes I had to babysit, of course, because our uncle was a busy man. Sometimes Miri would do it for me.'

'What was she like?' Sandy was once again having trouble squaring this youthful portrait of her mother with the troubled, solitary woman she had known. And yet it tallied with the young woman who had written the journal.

'She was the naughty one, the pretty one, the youngest whom everyone indulged. She didn't care about the rules. She did what she wanted and enjoyed herself.' She shook her head, as if clearing the tangle of memories as she reminded herself whom she was talking to. 'She would never have made a good nanny for the girls. They were lucky he married again. She was selfish. She saw what she wanted and she took it. That's why we never spoke again.'

'What did she take?' Though Sandy had a feeling she knew the answer.

The old lady leaned back in her chair, looking up at the ceiling. 'She took Roberto.'

Sandy's mouth dropped open. Even though she had suspected, the reality of her mother stealing anyone's man was impossible.

Anna nodded. 'Just once. But once was enough.'

'Your husband.'

'My fiancé, then.'

'Perhaps she didn't realise you were engaged.' Sandy knew that wasn't true but she didn't want her mother to be the person being described to her.

A grim laugh escaped Anna. 'She knew perfectly well. Throughout our childhood, she wanted what I had: trinkets, clothes, that sort of thing – nothing that mattered but things I liked. I always forgave her, never imagining she would go this far. It happened one weekend. She hadn't been here long and adored the place and how different it was from Stirling where we grew up. We'd planned to meet friends of ours in Sorrento. I wanted to show Miri off, take her to a lemon garden, go swimming. The day was all organised with a picnic on their boat, but at the last minute Uncle Stuart asked if I'd take the girls for the day. He had business meetings that he couldn't get out of. Of course I said I would. I had to stay in Naples with them but I knew Roberto would look after Miri. And he did.' She made an expression of regret. 'They missed the last train back to Naples and had no choice but to check into a cheap hotel. I don't need to go into any more detail.' She looked at the two women, who were transfixed by what she was saying. They both shook their heads.

'Eight weeks or so later, she told us she thought she was pregnant and couldn't go home. Our parents would disown her. Her life was ruined.' She stopped to let her words sink in.

Sandy was stunned, unable to speak. That her mother could have done such a thing to her own sister was unthinkable!

'I was devastated. The two people I loved most in the world had betrayed me in the worst possible way. Roberto confessed immediately. It was a spur of the moment thing, no love involved, over in a moment. Nothing had happened between them since.' She gave a harsh little laugh. 'He was devastated, guilty and full of remorse. He begged me to forgive him.'

'My God, that must have been so hard.' Sandy tried to envisage how she would have felt in the same position.

'Worse than that. But I loved him. I really did. I believed him when he swore that he would never do anything like that again. And I knew what she was like. If she liked something, she had to have it. It was a game to her. She never thought about the effect her actions might have on other people. You must be wondering why I wanted her to come to Naples in the first place?'

They waited for her to explain.

'Because she was such good company that I never really minded about the little things. She wasn't a malicious person, she was just thoughtless. But this time, she was made to think. I made her think when I told her exactly what I thought of her.'

Sandy and Alice raised their glasses together, mesmerised, as the old woman went on.

'She didn't want the child. So for the very first time she was forced to confront the consequences of her behaviour. They weren't in love. Of that I'm sure. She had a life and friends she wanted to go back to eventually. Naples was only ever going to be a short-term thing for her. She came to us to ask for help, weird as that sounds. But she had no one else and no choice. Roberto was a Catholic of course and couldn't sanction an abortion even if one had been possible.'

'So what happened?' Sandy could hardly get the words out. Was this what had made her mother the way she was? Did it somehow lie behind her ambivalent attitude towards Sandy when she was growing up? Had her shame made her promise not to tell, locking away her past and estranging herself from her whole family. Times were different then.

'The three of us made a plan. She stayed in Italy to have the baby without anyone we knew finding out. She went to live with a family outside Rome. Not so far away, but far enough. I didn't want to see her. They wanted help with an invalid grandmother and were prepared to take her despite the pregnancy. She had the baby there. I don't even know what arrangements were made.'

'She had the baby.' Sandy's head was spinning.

'Yes. That was what we agreed would happen. And it suited her, however difficult it must have been, because no one she knew would ever find out. And it must have been difficult. She had no friends there, spoke almost no Italian, but was determined to keep everything secret. She was ashamed by what she had done, said she couldn't go back home to Scotland but would join a friend in London, get work, start a new life. I don't know what happened but I guess she punished herself...'

'But that means...' Sandy couldn't finish the thought.

'That you have a brother or sister.' Alice did it for her, gripping her arm so hard that Sandy had to shake her fingers off. 'Or had.'

'That's right.' Anna looked straight at Sandy, who was struggling to find words.

'No, it's not possible. Did the baby even survive? No, it can't have.'

'Oh yes. Miri gave birth to a very healthy little boy. Robust.'

This couldn't be happening. 'So where is he now?'

'She gave him to us. That was what we agreed.' Anna paused again, letting the implications sink in. 'When Miri made it clear that she didn't want him, that she couldn't go back home pregnant, I had no choice. This was Roberto's child, too. I agreed we would take him but on one condition. I never wanted to see or hear from her ever again. She was to give up all her rights to her son. From the moment she handed him to me, he belonged to us.'

She looked across at Sandy, who was silent. She had not expected anything like this. Her heart went out to her mother, young, impetuous and ashamed.

'And Roberto wanted him. So that's what happened. And we never heard of Miri again. She kept her promise, having given us the greatest gift she could have, as it turned out. I didn't want any reminders of how our son came to us so I buried my own past and made a new future here with Roberto, our son and our two daughters whom we had later.'

'You mean . . .' Sandy was piecing the puzzle together but the picture was still blurring.

'I realise this isn't what you came here to find out. How could you have known? But yes, you share your mother with Daniele, your half-brother – the man who opened the door to you.'

27

Somehow they left Anna Viglieri's apartment. Sandy couldn't remember exactly how their visit ended or what had been said, just her overwhelming need to get out of there so she could come to terms with what she had just heard. Alice had guided them back to the funicular and down to the old city with Sandy on autopilot, still reeling from the revelations. She didn't know which she was more shocked by: what her mother had done or the fact that she had a brother. How her mother had carried that secret for her whole life was beyond her. It said something about her that Sandy had never realised or seen before. Having betrayed her sister, Miriam had stuck to the letter of their agreement and never tried to contact Anna again. She must have cut herself off from her family completely and that's why she never spoke about them. But why? Sandy tried to put herself into her mother's shoes. Had she acted out of concern for Anna and her son? Or for herself? Sandy wondered whether her own father had known about the baggage her mother had brought to their relationship. They had married three years after Daniele had been born and her mother's return, childless, to England. 'Miri.' She couldn't help smiling at the childhood nickname that gave her mother a youthful vitality Sandy had never known.

The two women sat at an outside table in a small friendly restaurant by the Piazza Bellini. Alice had found a taxi rank off the Via Toledo and got them taken straight there. Neither of them had wanted to join the others. The last thing Sandy wanted to do was explain what had happened. Not yet. She was still in shock.

Alice ordered them both a glass of wine and a bottle of sparkling water. She took the menu and read it quickly. Sandy stared into the middle distance until eventually she spoke.

'Just think. Every time she looked at me, she must have been reminded of him.'

'I doubt it. She would have been entirely wrapped up in you, her new baby.'

'But she said in the letter that every time she looked at me I was reminded of what happened and she pushed me away as a result. That must be what she meant. She must have constantly wondered about him. What he looked like. Who he had become. Surely any mother would.'

'In those circumstances? The fact that she never once tried to contact him or Anna must mean she managed to put it behind her, however tough that must have been.'

'She must have been dying to have news of him. I would have been, wouldn't you?' Sandy wanted to believe she had found a reason for the inconsistent mothering of her childhood at last, that she was not at fault. 'Passing off her second child as her first must have been excruciating.'

'She was obviously very different from you. Perhaps she could cut herself off from what had happened. Some people can. She had nothing back home to remind her, after all.'

But Sandy's intuition told her that wasn't how it had been. This all went towards an explanation for the way she was. And the truth was that Sandy wanted that explanation, wanted to understand.

'I so wish she was still alive so we could talk about it all. I'll never be able to get to the truth now.'

'But, even if she were, why would she break her silence for you? It was only her imminent death that made her write at all.' Alice was matter-of-fact.

Sandy picked up the menu and put it down. She wasn't hungry. 'I wonder if she meant me to open the envelope.'

'That's not what you said when you first told us about it.'

'I know.' She accepted Alice's reminder with reluctance. 'I'm just grasping at straws. Shall we order?'

Veal for Alice and swordfish with mussels and courgettes for Sandy. She looked at the tank where a few sad fish swam round and round awaiting their fate.

'Do you think Anna will tell him?' Alice tore off a piece of bread.

Sandy tried to picture the man who had opened the door to them: her brother. 'I hope so. But I can't help thinking how hard it will be for her to explain to him that his whole life has been based on a lie. She won't want to do that.'

'But it's not fair to keep him in the dark either. You two should be given the chance to meet properly.'

'My half-brother.' A strange thought after a lifetime of believing she was an only child. 'I wish I'd taken more notice of him now. Can you remember what he looked like?'

Alice shook her head. 'A middle-aged Italian, lots of swept-back hair and a tan.'

Sandy laughed. 'He'll stand out in a line-up then! It's so strange. Intellectually, I understand that he's my brother, but emotionally – I don't feel anything at all.'

'That'll come when you know him. *If* you ever do.'

'Maybe. *If.* We'll see. But enough for now. I'm going round in circles.' She patted the table to close the subject for a while at least. 'I'm sorry, I haven't even asked about you and Mark.'

Alice smiled. 'I think you've had other things on your mind.'

'Let's change the subject though. I do want to know.' Sandy wanted to shunt the racing thoughts out of her head so she could come to them again with a fresh perspective. There would be plenty of time to think about all this later.

'It's bad.' Alice sat back as their plates were banged down in front of them with little grace. They exchanged a glance and laughed. 'He didn't learn that at charm school.'

'Bad, how?' Sandy took a mouthful of the swordfish to discover that she was hungry after all. Listening to Alice go through what she thought must have happened turned out to be a welcome distraction.

'So adding two and two . . .' Alice concluded. 'I think we can safely say they make five. It's strange after everything we've heard this afternoon.'

Sandy considered her, wondering what she was really thinking. She seemed extraordinarily calm for someone whose marriage seemed to be imploding. 'How do you feel?'

'Frightened.' Alice grimaced. 'Indecisive. But what can I do? If he's not going to change, then I must. I've been in denial for too long. And now I'm going to do something about it.'

'Hey!' Before she had a chance to go on, a shout came from the other side of the pot plants shielding them from the street. 'So you're here. We were wondering where you'd got to.' Alan made his way into the restaurant and took a chair at the table. 'May I?'

Sandy ate the last of her fish and downed her wine. 'Actually I'd better get back. Got an urgent phone call to make. Can I settle up with you later?' She was dying to tell Eve everything that had happened and to get her take on it, Steven's too, and the last thing she wanted was to share it with Alan.

Alice gave a brief nod.

'But I thought . . .' Alan looked from one to the other.

'See you in the morning.' Sandy left the restaurant and stood for a second, taking in the buzz of the crowd, the horde of people spilling out of the bar across the street on to the pavement. On the low wall by the edge of the square, people sat enjoying the balmy night air, still hot by UK standards. The place was like a street party in full swing. As she turned towards the hotel, she caught sight of Lia's stripey dress. She stepped back into the square and watched as Lia and Mark responded to Alan's shout by letting go each other's hand, looking straight ahead and walking through the gap in the plants to join him and Alice. What the hell was the man playing at?

'We walked for miles down Via Tribunali, looking for this Pizzeria da Michele place that Lia had read about – thank you, Elizabeth Gilbert. Brit had read about it too, so off we trekked. It was pretty rough down there – not very well lit, rubbish everywhere. We almost turned back but then Brit spotted a da Michele pizza box in a bin. That's when we knew we had to be close. When we found it, tucked into a godforsaken corner, there was a queue stretching up round the block. Gilly was right. The guys on the doors were giving out tickets and not letting anyone in. You couldn't even really see through the doors. The girls were so disappointed but it would have been madness to wait ...'

Alice tuned out as Mark went on and on, detailing his night, making sure she knew he had been with some of the others all the time. She also noted how he had remembered Elizabeth Gilbert. But she had not missed the way he and Lia had come in together and very obviously sat apart from each other for the few minutes they all stayed in the restaurant. And he asked her nothing about what had happened to her and Sandy. Instead of listening, she was going through all possible marital exit strategies. Her favourite was to call Hattie, her friend and neighbour, and get her to use her spare key to go into the house and pack her things for her. When she got back to Gatwick, she would break the news to Mark that she had moved out and leave him to go home alone. She got such pleasure from the idea. But what about Pip? She couldn't do it to her. Nor could she change the locks on the door, leave his stuff in the garden and never let him in again. Patrick and Pip would think she'd gone mad.

'Everything all right?' He nudged her.

She jumped. 'Yes, of course. Sorry. So where did you go in the end?'

But she only half-listened to his reply.

28

When Sandy woke, she felt calmer. Steven hadn't picked up when she tried to call him the previous evening, but her conversation with Eve had gone way better than she had anticipated. As Sandy explained why she was calling, Eve couldn't contain her excitement.

'Wow! You really didn't know anything about him? Gran never said a thing?'

'Nothing. I had no idea.'

'All those years. I wish you'd told me about the letter. I could have helped you.'

Perhaps Sandy was more like her mother than she had realised herself. Keeping secrets obviously ran in the family but it was time that stopped. 'You're right. I should have. I thought I was doing the right thing by her if I kept it to myself.'

'She must have thought she was doing the right thing too. Her first thought must have been for Daniele. If she'd turned up in Italy, it would have been terrible. He'd have been traumatised. What she gave him was two parents who adored him and that's all he needed. It was incredibly unselfish of her not to insist on getting to know him.'

'Do you really think so?' Sandy hadn't thought of it like that. When had her daughter become so mature and compassionate? She had underestimated her.

'Don't you?'

'But she didn't forget him. She said so. How sad.' She

couldn't bear the idea of her mother harbouring such heartache throughout her life.

They talked for ages, speculating about Miriam and what she must have gone through; Daniele and what he must be like; what he would say if Anna did as she said she would and told him the truth. Just talking about her mother and Daniele made Sandy think about her own love for Eve, something so essential to her own life. Eventually she found herself saying, 'I'm sorry if I've made things difficult between us over the baby. I am truly excited for you. And I can't wait to be a granny.'

'I know you are now. And I do understand that you've had reservations. But we're not the first to do this and we'll make it work. You'll see.'

For the first time Sandy believed her. From now on she would stand back and watch her daughter live the life she had chosen, let her be an adult. Her own mother had chosen the life she wanted, too. Whether it had made her happy or not, they would never know; but what she had done was try not to inflict the consequences of those choices on her own family. Sandy wanted to believe that she had given her mother the sort of happiness and fulfilment that Eve gave her. Now, she at least could excuse those unsettling times when Miriam shut herself off. Had she been thinking about Daniele then, wondering how he would compare?

She looked at herself in the mirror. Same face but blurred by age; same hairstyle though not its natural grey; her mother's mouth, the Cupid's bow less distinct now her lips had thinned; the tilted nose that Eve had inherited. But even if she looked almost the same, she felt quite different this morning. She felt as if this new knowledge had changed the way she felt about herself, about her mother, about Eve. Perhaps this was the gift her mother had intended her to have: a key to understanding them all better.

She took out her yellow dress, still unworn, then put it

back in the wardrobe to choose a loose olive-green shift and sandals. Today, she would stay at the hotel, wait for Anna to call her, catch up on her diary and read her mother's journal with fresh eyes. The thrills of sightseeing and delving into the past and people unknown to her had finally been overtaken by the importance of the people she knew and cared about in the present.

After breakfast, the group left for Vesuvius in the minibus. She did not envy them the climb, however modest Gilly insisted it was, nor the walk round the perimeter of the cone in the scorching heat where there would be no shelter. Today, all she wanted to do was to lie by the pool until she could bear it no longer.

Once the other hotel guests left on their various excursions, Sandy had the pool to herself. She organised her sun lounger in the patch of deep shade that she'd noticed stayed for most of the day thanks to the surrounding buildings and garden plants. Propped up, she picked up the fountain pen she had been given by Steven when he heard she kept a diary. Going over the events of the previous few days proved therapeutic as she concentrated on remembering everything she had seen and done. In the background, the muffled sound of traffic signalled the city going about its business, but tucked away in this oasis of calm there was nothing to disturb her. With an emotional whirlwind still blowing through her, this was what Sandy needed: time to reflect. After a while, she sighed and closed her diary, put the cap on the pen and lay back, relaxed. A caged bird twittered from one of the surrounding balconies.

She was woken by approaching footsteps. She turned her head to see who it was.

'Mind if I join you?' Lia dropped her towel onto the lounger beside her.

'Please do.' What else could she say? Before long the two of them would be back at school so making things more difficult than they already were would only be counter-productive.

'I'm going to order a coffee. Want one?'

'A cappuccino. Thanks.'

Lia returned inside the hotel to make the order, giving Sandy the chance to stuff her diary and pen in her bag where they wouldn't provoke any questions.

'They won't be a minute.' She was back, standing in the sun, rubbing in sun lotion. 'Would you mind doing my back?'

Sandy stretched out her hand for the bottle. She could hardly refuse.

'I can't go home without a tan. Betty's in Spain and she'll be like mahogany.'

'You've definitely caught the sun.' At the top of Lia's shoulders where her skin was red, Sandy rubbed a little harder than strictly necessary.

'Ow! Careful.' Lia twisted her head round. 'Not my shoulders. I can reach them myself.'

Sandy finished the job as quickly as she could and lay down again, resigned to the best of the day being over.

'So . . .' Lia clearly wasn't going to lie quietly. 'Back to school soon. Looking forward to it?'

'Of course.' She wasn't going to confess that for the first time in her life the start of the new school year loomed like a huge hurdle to be cleared. 'But I thought we weren't going to talk about that.'

'But perhaps we should be honest with each other about the deputy headship while we've got the chance.' There was a clink of Lia's cup being returned to the saucer.

'Must we?' said Sandy. 'Can't we just enjoy our last couple of days here? We've managed so well, this far.'

'Yes, I think we should. What I want to say is, if I'm honest, I think I'm the better candidate.' Lia's eyes were hidden behind those very large dark glasses from Rome. 'And I know that a lot of the younger staff would agree.'

'That might be because they haven't had the experience to know exactly what's needed in the job.' Sandy had to exert every ounce of self-control not to raise her voice. School had taught her that.

'Oh, I think they do. They think a younger woman would provide a breath of fresh air beside Rosemary's rather old-school approach.'

'Fortunately it's not up them.' Sandy hoped that would be the end of the conversation.

'No. But Laura—' she named one of the Computer Science teachers '—has talked to a couple of the governors and they seem to agree. I think you're going to have your work cut out when you get back. That's all I'm saying. I just wanted to give you a heads up.'

Sandy pulled herself into a sitting position, adjusted her dark glasses. 'I suppose you're relying on me not mentioning how untrustworthy you are?'

'I'm sorry?'

'You heard.' She should get up and leave now before anything more damaging was said, but something stopped her.

'What's happened here has nothing to do with how I do my job.' But Lia looked anxious. 'You wouldn't.'

'I might.' Sandy was not going to give up without some kind of fight. And she'd fight dirty if she had to. 'If I thought the wrong person was going to be appointed. If I thought that person was going to use underhand tactics to get the job herself and couldn't be trusted.'

Lia whistled and lifted her sunglasses. 'Well! I didn't think you had it in you. If you're up for a fight, I'll give you one.'

'Don't forget what you said to me about wanting a baby – won't a baby skew your plans?'

'But I might not get pregnant.' Her chin wobbled.

'Well, I hope you don't here, anyway.'

'Who knows?' Lia bowed her head but not quickly enough for Sandy to miss the smirk.

'You haven't?' Sandy was horrified to have Alice's suspicions confirmed.

'Maybe.' She kept her eyes fixed on her lap.

'I really hope you're not, for Mark and Alice's sakes. We all saw you make the running. Why couldn't you have left him alone?'

'It takes two, you know.' The younger woman's chin jutted out defiant. 'And he wanted to.' She paused. 'I do feel bad about Alice, you know.'

Sandy didn't know whether to laugh or be appalled. 'Bad!' Actually, why was she even bothering? She had never met anyone like this. 'They're married. You're on holiday with them, for God's sake.'

'I didn't mean anything to happen.'

Sandy raised an eyebrow. 'After what you told me?'

'OK, that's fair. But it was just the one night . . . my cycle . . . we were drunk. I know we shouldn't have.' The look she gave Sandy was pleading. 'You're the only person who knows.'

'I wouldn't bet on that.'

She looked worried but only for a moment. 'It was just a bit of fun.' She lay back, eyes shut, hand on her stomach, and ended the conversation.

Whatever Sandy thought clearly didn't matter. Lia was a woman who saw what she wanted and went out to get it regardless of the consequences. How familiar that sounded. But Sandy's mother had been twenty-one and, after what happened in Naples, she had been punished and she had changed. Lia was much older and behaving just as selfishly, taking what she wanted. What was she, Sandy, doing even bothering to compete with someone like this? And why? How much did she really want the job? she asked herself. Perhaps Lia was right, and someone younger would be better suited to the deputy headship. The thought took her by surprise. Age had never been one of her considerations. No. She had wanted to be deputy head for ages. She had been virtually promised the job once the current deputy started talking about her imminent retirement three years ago. Of course she wanted to be in the running. She and Rosemary were the dream team. Or they had been. That thought surprised her too. Had she been at the school too long? Were there other things she could do with her life?

She stood up and crossed over to the pool, feeling the sun on her skin. She walked down the steps, each movement sending ripples into the blue stillness beyond. At the bottom, she paused for a moment, enjoying the feel of cool water on her body. She pushed off and swam a couple of lengths, before rolling onto her back and floating. The silhouette of a bird passed overhead against the deep blue of the mid-morning sky. She mustn't let Lia spoil any of this.

When she got back to her towel, Lia didn't move. Sandy hoped she was asleep behind those very dark glasses. She lay beside her and closed her own eyes, knowing that she would never be able to follow suit.

She was woken by the clink of china as the waiter cleared their cups. Lia was sitting on the edge of the pool, splashing her legs in the water. She turned to look at Sandy and in that stare Sandy saw everything that lay ahead of them: disdain, disagreement, dislike. Chilled, she reached for her bag and towel. Enough.

In her room, she noticed that she had a missed call from a European number. She held her phone in her hand for a moment, her heart thumping. There were only two people here who had her number: Giancarlo and Anna. She returned the call.

'Anna?' It felt strange to be on first name terms when they hardly knew each other. And yet this woman was her aunt.

'Yes. I called you.'

'I was at the pool. I'm sorry. I wanted to write my diary.'
Stop gabbling. Let her say why she phoned.

'How are you?'

'All right. Getting used to things. Wanting to ask you about Mum and what she was like as a child. Wanting to—'

Anna interrupted. 'I spoke to Daniele. Told him everything.'

A beat of silence.

'And?'

'I'm afraid he doesn't want to see you.'

Sandy's disappointment almost took her breath away. 'What did he say?' What she wanted to ask was: How does he feel about you, now you've removed the scaffolding of his life?

'He wanted to go home and talk to Isabella, his wife. She'll help him.'

'Was he very upset?'

'Yes and no. He's always known I wasn't his mother. But we never told him who was.'

'Oh.' She spoke so quietly, Anna may not have heard.

'You see, Roberto and I never knew what Miri would do so we thought it was better if Daniele believed he was adopted, so that if she broke our agreement and contacted him, it would be less hard for him. Whatever happened, he would never lose me. Never. I love him as a mother and would always be there for him. So, at the worst, he would gain a second mother and he would learn Roberto was his real father. So not so bad. But she never did.'

'I've been thinking about her a lot and wondering why not.'

'Me too. She knew how badly she hurt me and had no idea how I would react if she contacted us. I have always been someone who stuck to my word and I expect others to do the same. It was a formidable task for Roberto and me to recover from his infidelity, but we did love each other. I wouldn't give him up and anyway he didn't want her. She showed me that she respected my feelings by staying away. But we can't do this over the phone. Will you come here again? Have you time?'

'Of course.'

When she left the hotel, Lia was still by the pool. Neither of them acknowledged the other. Sandy couldn't forget what had been said, wondering whether she should repeat any of it to Alice. Then she reminded herself of something Steven had said to her when she was getting hot and bothered over a row another teacher was having with a parent. 'Step back. This has nothing to do with you. Your involvement probably won't help them and will almost certainly make things more difficult for you.' Perhaps she should have remembered that sooner.

She found her way back to Anna's apartment without any difficulty. This time she made sure she faced uphill in the funicular. Anna was alone and welcomed her in. 'I'm so glad you've come back. I was worried that you might not want to.'

'Of course I wanted to. I want to get to know you better. Immediately I left, I began to think of all the questions I hadn't asked you.'

'I know. It was a shock for both of us.' The old woman put her hand on Sandy's arm to steady herself. 'And for Daniele, too.'

They went into the sitting room where Anna took to her chair before asking Sandy to make them tea. 'The one thing Italians just can't make. I think it's the water,' she said when Sandy returned with a tray that she put on the low table in front of the sofa.

'Do you mind talking about Mum?' Sandy was anxious about Anna's feelings and whether, after so long, she would want to unearth all the memories that must be there.

'No, I don't.'

When she smiled, for the first time Sandy saw a faint

resemblance to her mother. The turn of her lips, the curl of her nostril, the wide separation of her eyes: details she had missed because she hadn't been looking.

'Everyone has two sides, and all the things I've told you about Miri don't amount to the whole picture. Of course I don't know what she became, but as a child Miri could be sweet and considerate too. I don't want to give you the wrong impression. I was thinking of all the good things last night for the first time in years. For instance, I had bad asthma when I was young and Miri would often stay inside with me, and we'd read to each other. She'd sneak food up from the kitchen and we'd have secret feasts in the bedroom. We wrote plays that we put on using the dolls in our enormous dolls' house. We put on shows and made our own costumes out of the fancy-dress box and what we could find.' She laughed at the memory. 'Our parents were so patient and watched without a squeak. She loved animals too but we couldn't have pets because of my asthma, so she walked the neighbours' dog, Button, for years. She adored him and was devastated when he died. We went on family holidays to Galloway where we stayed in a caravan park by the sea and were allowed to run free. We made friends on the beach. Despite what I said yesterday she was such fun to be with. You've brought these memories with you. I'd forgotten.'

Memories that Sandy had never known existed – or not as such. Her mother had talked about the feasts, the plays, the books she read and the dog, even hiding under the caravan, but these things had either been done by her alone or with a friend. She never once mentioned a sister.

'As I've got older, I've thought about what happened between us and how Miri must have dealt with it and what she missed. She had no inkling that Daniele was the sweetest baby, who turned into such a tricky toddler. We had the terrible twos and threes and fours!' She gave a wry smile. 'She never knew that he grew up speaking English and Italian and that although he wasn't ever top of his class, he became such a sportsman: football, water sports and sailing. He worked in the business as Roberto expected of him but when the ownership changed he left to set up his own boat-repair business down at the marina and in Amalfi.' She lifted her glass of water. 'I'm sorry that I never contacted her. I was her older sister and it was up to me to forgive and break the ice. I should have led the way.'

'You mustn't punish yourself. You both stuck to your side of the deal.'

'But now she comes to me for forgiveness when it's too late.' There was such regret and confusion in her expression, as if she still didn't know how to react.

Sandy felt so sad that the two sisters hadn't been able to reconcile when, despite such a terrible betrayal and so much time passing, that was what in the end both had wanted. Pride, pig-headedness, uncertainty and determination to show they could stick to their word had got in their way. 'But at least you know what she felt at the end.'

Anna looked thoughtful. 'I so wanted to be Daniele's mother. After a few years, I had almost forgotten how he came to be in our family. Hard though that must be to understand because of course Roberto was always there to remind me what happened. He was just the first of our three children, the only boy. Roberto was always so proud of his only son. I didn't want Miri to come back. I didn't want her near us or to disrupt us. But Roberto proved to me that I was his real love and together we chose to forget her. After that first year was over and Daniele was ours, we never talked about her again.'

'And as far as I know, she never talked about you. She just kept the photo I showed you yesterday.'

'It looks as if it's been handled a lot.' She sounded wistful. 'Time plays cruel tricks. Miri and I were so close growing up, despite being very different. But aren't all sisters like that? Screaming rows that frightened our mother would blow over.

But we inherited our stubbornness from our father. Neither of us ever wanted to be the one who gave in first.' She smiled. 'I remember swimming in a freezing loch one autumn. Miri had to stay in longer than me. When she came out, she was blue with cold. Just to prove who was toughest.'

'Perhaps she was ashamed about what she had done?' Sandy wanted to believe the best of her mother.

'Perhaps. I never went back to the UK. I wanted to block out that part of my life altogether. Our parents didn't have a happy marriage. Our father went to fight during the war and when he came back things changed between him and our mother. I don't know why. He drank heavily and she was lonely. He went back to work at Mackenzie Mills, where he worked hard. I can remember him coming home late.' She paused, as if overcome by this flood of memories, staring into the middle distance. 'There was always tension when they were in the house together, and that's probably why Miri and I relied on each other. He kept a horsewhip on the back of his study door that he would use if we were naughty. He used it on Miri more than on me. I couldn't wait to get away, so when this job came up with Uncle Stuart I leaped at it, not imagining that I would never go back. That's why Miri came too, and probably partly why she never went back home. Stuart told me that our father died of a heart attack shortly after Miri went to London. Our mother not long after.'

'But your friends? Your family?' Sandy was interrupted by the doorbell.

'Would you mind answering that for me?' Anna lay back against the cushions, her face pale against the deep red and coral fabrics. She suddenly looked exhausted.

'Of course.'

The bell rang once more as she walked down the hall, noticing the unopened post on the console table. Anna had other things on her mind. Sandy went straight to the door.

She opened it to a woman about her height, tanned, dark hair cut to her jawline, wearing white cropped trousers and a black T-shirt. She held out her hand. '*Buon giorno.*'

Surprised by the gesture, Sandy took it. '*Buon giorno*. Is Anna expecting you?'

There was the sound of something clattering to the floor then Anna's voice sounded down the corridor. 'Dammit! My stick. Isabella! Is that you?'

29

As she trudged up the cinder track behind a constantly moving line of tourists, Alice couldn't help thinking about Sandy. Although they had left her on her way to the pool, she wondered whether Anna would be in touch again and whether Sandy would go to meet her alone. The previous day, she had felt a complete interloper as the two women realised how they were related. She had sat and watched, gripped by the story she heard, trying not to make her presence felt.

She stopped, out of breath. At least it was cooler up here than in the heart of the city. She took off her hat and wiped her forehead with a balled-up tissue.

'Keep going.' Alan came up beside her. His face was scarlet and, as he overtook her, she saw how sweat stuck his shirt to his back.

'Are you all right?' Brit, in a loose top and shorts, umbrella aloft, was making the walk look effortless. Peter was right behind her, his hand on the flimsy-looking wooden barrier that didn't look as if it would stop anyone going over.

'Just having a breather.' She didn't want anyone making a fuss.

'Nearly there.' Mark took her hand and pulled her forward. 'Come on, old thing. You can do it.'

'Less of the old, thanks.' She pulled her hand away from him.

He looked surprised as she did so, then went ahead without her. He seemed to think that if he behaved as if nothing had happened between him and Lia then everything would fall back to normal. Her role was to play along. That was the way it had always been, she realised now, and that way his conscience would be clear. When Jane had asked Mark whether he felt he took Alice for granted, he had evaded answering.

'What exactly do you mean, for granted?' he'd said, turning the conversation into one about semantics.

Alice had understood Jane had been trying to get Mark to face his responsibilities. But he was too smart to fall for that. Now she had reached the point when she wasn't going to take it any more. She deserved a second chance. When Mark was having a drink this evening, she would phone Lucy and ask her about working with her or if she knew somewhere else she could try. She would set some things in motion before she got home and lost her nerve.

'Nearly there.' Gilly stood beside her and they began to walk together.

'Do you ever get bored going back to the same sights over and over again?' asked Alice.

'Never! The sights might be the same but the clients are always different so you see things through fresh eyes, and sometimes stuff that you haven't even noticed before. So each experience is new every time. But when Sam and I get married,' she lifted her hand so the ring flashed in the sunlight. 'He doesn't want me to travel so much. He wants me to be a banker's wife.'

'Whatever does that mean? Are bankers' wives different from any other kind?'

'They're richer, I guess.' Gilly giggled. 'That sounds awful, I know.'

'Mmm. So will you do what he wants?' Alice so badly wanted to warn her not to.

'I want to make him happy. She gave a goofy smile. 'I want to stop being on the move all the time.'

'Well, make sure it makes you happy too. Don't give up on everything for a man.' Alice had to stop again to catch her breath.

'Didn't you?' Gilly looked curious.

'I did indeed. Although that was more for his children.'

'Sam won't make me do anything,' Gilly was confident. 'He wants me to be my own person.'

'That's good.' But Gilly had gone ahead and wasn't listening any more.

At the top, they stood on the lip of the crater. On the other side of the path a sensational view stretched over the Bay of Naples. A wisp of cloud floated below them. As Gilly reminded her of the history of the mountain and its eruptions, most famously in 79 AD when Pompeii and Herculaneum were buried under hot ash, Alice listened intently, staring at the uneven stony walls rising from the floor. This was history coming alive and where Sandy should be standing. She would be fascinated whereas Alice felt a keen disappointment. But what had she expected? Bubbling lava and sulphurous smoke?

At the small shop selling drinks and souvenirs, she dithered over a piece of plastic molten lava, then thought better of it. She bent down and picked up a bit of reddish volcanic rock from the ground and put it in her pocket. At least she could give Sandy a piece of Vesuvius to take home.

On the way down, she was walking with Benno and Alex, hearing about a recent guest at their B & B who had looted everything they could from the room. 'She even took the TV from the bracket. I caught her as she was putting it in the boot of her car!'

'Did you—' But as she asked, her foot skidded, her ankle turned and she crashed to the ground like a felled tree.

'Oh my God! Are you all right?' Benno crouched beside her as she brushed the grit off the heels of her hands.

'Absolutely fine.' She started to stand up, feeling as if her body had been thrown around in a tumble dryer, every bone jarred. The side of her left leg was stinging so she turned it to find a nasty graze that extended above and below her knee. As she put weight on that ankle, a pain shot up her leg, making her stumble. Only Alex's quick reaction stopped her from falling again.

'I think I'm going to have to sit down for a minute. Sorry.' They helped her to the ground, where she sat, feeling slightly sick and incredibly stupid. 'I'll be fine in a minute.'

But when she tried to stand, she couldn't put any weight on her ankle. 'Oh, Christ. I'm so sorry.' She fell back against Benno.

'Stop apologising. We're going to get you down to the bus. Put your arms round us.'

So with one on either side of her, the three of them made slow progress down to the car park. Mark was nowhere to be seen, but the two Germans made surprisingly light work of hauling her down the mountain. When they reached the bus, the engine was running, the aircon cooling down everyone inside. As Alice hopped up the steps, with a helping hoist from Alex, and a hand from Benno, Mark stood up, looking concerned. 'What's happened?'

Peter and Brit gave up their seat near the door and she collapsed into it gratefully while Alex explained to the others.

'Put your leg up on the seat,' Peter said. 'Let me take a look.' A quick examination and he wiped his hands together. I don't think anything's broken. It looks like a sprain. We'll give it some support and you might be able to hobble around in a couple of days.'

'Should we go to the hospital?' Gilly looked anxious.

'No, no,' interrupted Alice. After all it was her ankle. 'I'll keep it up, ice it, and see,' she said. 'I'm sure it'll be fine.'

Peter nodded. 'I can check on you later.'

'You should be more careful,' said Mark with a despairing shake of the head as he returned to his seat and his book. He might not have meant it quite the way it came out but nonetheless she felt a quiet satisfaction as everyone looked at him in surprise. Not quite the life and soul of the party any longer then.

When they arrived back at the hotel, only Lia was by the pool, asleep in the shade. Mark helped Alice to their room and ordered some ice for her ankle.

'I think I'll go to Solfatara with Peter and Gilly. Get some live volcanic action. Do you mind?'

'Not at all. You go.' She couldn't wait to be left alone.

There was a knock at the door. Sandy stood there with a cup of tea. 'I thought you might need this. Peter told me what happened.'

'I'll leave you two then.' Mark slipped through the door.

'So how did you do it?' Sandy sat on the edge of the bed, passing over the tea. She was wearing a sleeveless shift dress and was made up as if she was ready to go out.

Alice told her. 'I felt an absolute twit and Mark wasn't even there to help. But actually it's better already. Look at you, all dressed up. Where are you off to?'

'I'm going to meet Daniele. He changed his mind.' Sandy looked ecstatic. 'He wants to meet me after all.'

'That's fantastic! How come?'

'Isabella, his wife, arrived at Anna's while I was there. We talked for a while and, after I left, she must have persuaded him. She's lovely, very family-centred, and Anna adores her. She's just called to ask me to supper tonight. But I'm so nervous. What if he doesn't like me?' She glanced at herself in the mirror, fiddled with her hair.

'Of course he'll like you. You're both just innocent victims of Anna and Miriam's estrangement. Surely he'll see that.'

'He's got three children.' She stopped. 'I should take them something.' She looked around her as if something was going to materialise. 'Oh God! What shall I take?'

Alice laughed. 'Nothing. They won't be expecting anything. Now, would you like my famous moral support again? I'm sure I could manage if there's not much walking. The hotel must have a walking stick I could borrow.'

'That's so kind of you.' Sandy stood still, glanced at herself in the mirror again. 'But I don't think you should move for a while and anyway this really is something I must do on my own.'

'Good for you.' Alice admired her friend's determination. 'Where do they live?'

'In Posillipo. Further down the coast from where we went on that walk with Gilly round royal Naples along the seafront past all those fancy hotels. Look.' She spread the map on the bed and pointed to an area on the coast south-west of the central city. 'They're up here. Wish me luck.'

'Of course I do. I'm dying to know what happens. And while you're doing that, I'm going to phone Lucy and put some wheels in motion, see if she knows of any restaurant work for me. Mark's going to Solfatara so I've got some time and I'm going to make the most of it. One volcano was enough for me!'

'You really are serious, aren't you?' Sandy smoothed her skirt over her hips.

'Yes, I am. I want to get my life back but I don't want to upset Pip or the boys any more than I have to.' She grinned. 'Which is a pity. I love the idea of doing something dramatic. You know, the bin bags full of his cut-up clothes in the garden sort of thing. But that would be wrong.'

'Wrong but so bloody satisfying. He deserves something like that.' Sandy glanced at her watch. 'I must go. You know you could always come and stay with me until you've got yourself sorted. I've got room. Think about it.'

'Be careful or I might take you up on that.' And may be she

would one day. That would give Mark a shock. She was touched by Sandy's generosity. 'We're definitely going to keep in touch when we get back, whatever happens.'

'Of course we are. I'll be able to give you regular updates on Lia.' As she said Lia's name, Sandy's face lost some of its joy. 'I'm being ironic! Sorry. Bad taste.'

'I'd be happy if I never hear of her again. But why the face?'

'If I'm honest I'm having horrible misgivings about going back to school. Being here, hearing her talk, seeing who she is, and thinking about the way things are going to change, has made me think that perhaps I'd be better off giving up the idea of the deputy headship. But working underneath her . . .' She made a gesture of despair. 'Need I say more?'

'But what would you do instead?'

Sandy leaped to her feet. 'Not a clue. But perhaps it's time for a change for me too. I feel invigorated by these two weeks here. It's not been what I expected and it's made me wonder if it's not too late for me to change track after all.'

When Sandy had gone to catch her taxi to Posillipo, Alice lay back on her pillows. Her ankle had stopping throbbing quite so much and, though swollen, could already take some of her weight. Perhaps it wasn't as bad as she had first feared. She steeled herself for the phone call. If it went well, this would be the beginning of a new phase of her life. Lucy answered the phone immediately.

'Alice! Aren't you on holiday? What's the matter?'

'I am and I'll explain when I see you. But things haven't gone quite as planned. I've been thinking about the future and I'm looking for a job.' There was no point hedging around. 'Now Pip's off on her gap year and going to uni, it's time for me to branch out, do something for myself, and I can't think of anything I'd love more than going back to the kitchen. You know how I still love cooking.' Her love of food had been a standing joke among her friends for as long as she could remember.

'Is this something to do with Mark?' Lucy sounded suspicious.

'No. Except that he's encouraged me.' Her friends knew about Mark's affair, Joanna's pregnancy, the termination, but she didn't want to say anything about how he had behaved in Italy. They would say she was a fool for having given him another chance. And maybe she was. 'Now I've made the decision I just want to get on with it. I thought you might know someone who might be able to help. Or I hoped.'

'Well! Funnily enough . . .' Lucy thought for a second while Alice clenched her fist, hoping against hope, and waited. 'I'm looking for someone myself. Remember I told you I was thinking about opening a second restaurant in Aylesbury?'

'And I said I thought you were mad.' Her fist relaxed a little.

'Exactly.' Lucy laughed. 'So I took absolutely no notice and I've found the perfect place. It's small, quite intimate, in a good location, and I think could be successful. What I need is someone to sort out interesting new menus with the head chef. Fresh local produce. Something a little bit different so we have an edge. With your background, you might be just the person. Interested?'

'Are you kidding? Of course I am.' The possibilities were already exciting her.

'I can't give you the reins. You've been out of the game for too long, but we can see how it goes. If it works and you like it, and she likes you, there may be other opportunities further down the line.'

'This is so great. Thank you, thank you.'

'You know I always liked the idea of us working together . . .'

'I know, but the kids had to come first.'

'I always understood that, but I'm so glad you've asked at last.'

Alice couldn't have been more thrilled. Possibilities were opening up for her. She put herself back in the kitchen, the heat, the noise, the rush to service – and almost purred with pleasure. Helping devise a menu would resuscitate her skills and be just up her street. She could practise taste combinations at home. And a small restaurant would be just perfect. Her life would change now, and change for the better because she was going to take control. She was not going to be taken for granted by Mark, or anyone else, again.

Sandy sat in the back seat of the cab staring out of the window as they passed through the different neighbourhoods of the city. The language difference meant she was unable to chat with the driver, so she was forced to listen to Europop blaring from the speakers. Eventually they turned off the coast road to wind upwards until he pulled up outside one of the many apartment blocks that scaled the hillside looking out over the sea. Clean, bright and white, it was a far cry from the centre of Naples. This said seaside, sunshine and money. At street level was a parade of shops: a pharmacy with the ubiquitous green cross above the door, a beautician, a tobacconist and a small newsagent selling Lotto tickets. Above her, at the windows, blinds were rolled down against the sun. She drew in a deep breath of sea air and went through the front door and up to the fifth floor.

Isabella answered her knock. When she saw Sandy standing there, she threw her arms wide and kissed her on both cheeks. 'Welcome. Daniele's outside, waiting for you.' She gestured that Sandy should go down the corridor towards a sliding glass door that led onto a wide balcony. 'He's nervous. Like you,' she said in a whisper. Hearing that did nothing to quell the butterflies that were stampeding in Sandy's stomach. Walking through the apartment, she noticed that it was done up with attention to detail. She caught a glimpse of a modern kitchen, modest but well equipped with a marble-topped island at its centre. A cool tiled floor stretched throughout the rooms. The sofas and chairs were modern, comfortable. The art on the walls was modern too – nothing showy though, more the sort of thing you might buy back home in John Lewis.

As she went through the open door on to a wide L-shaped balcony that wrapped round the corner of the building, she immediately recognised Daniele, who came towards her, arms outstretched. He looked as nervous as she felt. She took his hand, feeling its callused warmth as he shook hers.

'I don't know what . . .'

'Welcome to my . . .'

They separated, both of them awkward, talking over each other, smiling, starting again. Isabella brought out two glasses of Prosecco and little dishes of salted almonds and pistacchios which she left on the table. 'I'm going to cook while you talk.'

No, stay, a voice screamed inside Sandy. *We'll be much more comfortable with you here.*

But Isabella had already gone back inside. Daniele pulled out a metal chair for Sandy, so she would get the view down the hillside.

'This is beautiful.' She looked beyond the pots of geraniums hanging from the railing round the balcony and over the trees and rooftops to the flat expanse of navy sea and the distant coastline.

'Thank you.' He inclined his head in agreement. 'And thank you for coming here.'

'You must be shocked as me by all this. I had no idea.'

He shook his head. 'Not so much maybe. My parents had always told me I was adopted, so I sometimes wondered if one day I might find out who my real parents were; although I wasn't expecting this. I never particularly wanted to know about them because Mama and Papa . . . well . . . that's who they were. I didn't know anything else. I had them and my two sisters and needed no more. When she told me the truth, Mama was worried that I wouldn't forgive her for not telling me the whole truth from the beginning; but after so long, why would I? I understand why she did what she did. Maybe I would have had more of a problem if I was younger, even if my father was still alive. It's all history now. But I never thought that I might have another sister. I didn't think so far ahead!'

As they began to talk, Sandy found herself warming to him. She was grateful his English was so fluent: a result, he explained, of having spoken it with his mother all his life. Their conversation became easier as they began to talk about their own lives, explaining to each other who they were, how and where they lived, what had happened to them. Whenever he looked away from her, she studied him as intently as she could, looking for similarities between him and her mother or him and herself. His colouring must have come from his father's side of the family but there was something about the set of his eyes and the shape of his mouth that reminded her of Miriam and Anna. Perhaps, even of herself.

'But come,' he said, leaping to his feet. 'You must see my children.'

Sandy followed him into the apartment, bracing herself for more new people. To her relief, he went over to a table covered in framed photographs. He began to pick them up, one at a time.

'This is Giulietta on her wedding day,' he pointed to a young woman in an elaborate white wedding dress standing beside a confident-looking young man. 'And this is Chiara.' This time the photo was of another raven-haired young woman who was holding the hands of two toddlers. 'Twins,' he said proudly. 'And this is Angelo.' A young man in a wetsuit stared out of the photo, his eyes alight, a smile on his lips. 'The youngest. He is not married yet.'

'So this is your new family,' said Isabella, coming in to lay the main dining table.

Sandy looked at her, startled. But of course that was who they were. 'Yes,' she said. 'How lovely.' A warm glow of pleasure stole through her.

'Do you have a husband and children too?' Isabella asked.

'My husband died a few years ago but we have a daughter. Eve.' Sandy went back to the terrace to get her phone from her bag. She clicked on it to bring up her favourite photo of Eve sitting outside a pub. She looked radiant, smiling at Jen, one finger in the air as she regaled them with a funny story from work. 'The one in the green dress.' Sandy was reminded how well the two young women got on, what a positive future she hoped lay ahead of them.

By the time they had finished admiring each other's children, Isabella had brought a bowl of steaming pasta to the table. 'Come. Sit down.'

Daniele poured them all a glass of wine. The pasta was delicious, rich with truffle and mushrooms, garlic and cheese.

'Wow!' Sandy put down her fork. 'This is amazing. The best I've had here.'

'This is just good Italian home cooking.'

'Not good! The best!' interjected Daniele.

'But the secret ingredient is dried lavender.' Isabella looked pleased to have her cooking appreciated.

'Really? Can I give the recipe to a friend? I know she'd love it.' Sandy thought of Alice and her plans to work in a restaurant. Maybe she could use this.

Towards the end of the meal, there was a lull in the conversation. Isabella looked at Daniele, then Sandy. 'And Miriam?' she said softly. 'We have talked about everyone except her. What was she like?'

Daniele put down his knife and fork. 'Yes, I'd like to know now.'

318

Sandy was glad to be given this chance to speak up for her mother. She decided just to be honest. 'I didn't know the woman Anna has told me about. My mother was nothing like that at all. Of course she was older, and she had given you to Anna by then, but I don't believe she ever forgot you. She could be such a loving person, but sometimes she found it impossible, I think. I used to think that it was my fault, that I'd done something to upset her, but now I wonder if it was just that I reminded her of you and made her wonder what had happened to you. All the time she was passing off her second child as her first. How terrible that must have been for her. She never said anything to me, of course.' She was aware of Daniele and Isabella watching her as she spoke, intent on what she was saying. 'For instance, I remember going with her best friend, Esme, and Esme's son to the cinema and then out for tea. We saw them a lot. Tom, the boy, was wild and this one time he pulled the tablecloth so everything fell on the floor of the tea room. Esme was furious but Mum just laughed. That was typical. She adored him. Whenever we got home from being with them, she would barely speak to me and would go to her room. Maybe she was thinking of you then. I'll never know. But that's what I think. I don't even know if she ever told Dad. I don't believe so, but her letter to Anna shows that she never forgot you and carried so much guilt and regret throughout her life.' She stopped, realised that tears were stinging her eyes. She swallowed.

'That's so sad.' Isabella was almost crying too.

'But at least we've met now, and we can make up this lost time,' said Daniele. 'You must stay for longer, meet the children. Get to know all of us.'

When she left the apartment, Sandy felt uplifted, free and a little overwhelmed. Even though her mother would never meet her sister or her son, Sandy could do this for her. Her duty to her mother been discharged but as a result she had become part of a new family, so completely different from the one she knew. Apart from the recipe, she had come away with an invitation to visit their apartment in Amalfi. 'I want to show you our Italy,' Daniele had offered. 'Not the one the tourists see. How long will you stay? You must meet the children and my sisters. Your nieces, nephew and half-sisters!'

'And you must meet Eve and Jen.' Initially, he had been taken aback when she told him they were married, but Isabella had shaken her head, said something in Italian and he had said nothing. They accepted her family as she did theirs.

Her trip would be over in a couple of days but she could fly back at half-term. 'Brother'. Sandy toyed with the word. Then 'my brother'. She was dying to tell Steven and Eve about it all and how her new family had made her so welcome and wanted to meet them too. She hoped her mother would be pleased to know that her two children had found each other and would make the family together that she never had.

30

The minibus dropped them at the gate of a walled garden that promised all sorts of secrets. The fortress-like walls topped with split cane fencing made it a forbidding prospect but inside all was sunshine and brightness. Once a lemon garden on the outside of Sorrento, it had since been engulfed by the town and now existed improbably in the midst of swish apartment blocks, hotels and shops. Sandy looked around her, unable to forget that somewhere in this town everything had changed for her mother.

The group walked down a long straight path, fenced by poles and the occasional rustic seat. On either side were orchards of lemon trees shading the browning grass and nothing else in sight except a souvenir shop ahead. 'Ah, so this is why we've come,' said Brit.

'Shhh,' said Peter. 'Cynic.' And he marched ahead.

'Looks like the worm's turned,' whispered Alice to Sandy. 'Is she letting him take the reins a bit more, do you think?'

'Maybe.' Sandy thought it unlikely. 'Are you going to be OK for this?'

'God, yes. Two days by the pool while you lot gallivanted off to Ischia and Capri have worked wonders. With the ankle and with me and Mark.' She waved the crutch that the hotel had rustled up for her.

Sandy had noticed how Mark had danced attendance on his wife, shunning Lia quite obviously in public, though she had seen them huddled over drinks in the hotel bar after they'd got back from a wonderful day in Ischia. She had missed the Capri trip in favour of Daniele and Isabella, who had invited her to lunch to meet their two daughters.

'Come on.' Gilly herded them down the path. 'We've got a lot to fit in today.' She giggled, and her hand went to her chain necklace, fiddling with its charms as she overtook them.

'Who's rattled her cage?' asked Sandy. 'She's been in a rush all morning.'

'It's too hot to hurry,' said Alice. 'We'll get there. I'm not speeding up for anyone.'

'She even asked the driver to go faster.' Sandy remembered the look of fury on his face when Gilly urged him on. 'Do you think Sam's flying in or something?'

'Not a chance. If he were, we'd never have heard the end of it.'

By the time they reached the little shop that offered all sorts of local produce including bottles of liquor, jams and marmalades, Peter had a row of three tiny tasting cups in front of him. 'Fennel, liquorice and lemon,' he said.

Brit took a shot of liquorice and pulled a face. 'Oof! Not for me.'

'Can I try?' Lia stretched out her hand. 'I'm sure Elizabeth said she loved limoncello.'

'You don't *know* whether she did?' said Alice, in mock disbelief, to receive a glare in return as Lia was poured a glass.

'Everyone had enough?' said Gilly, impatient after only a couple of minutes. 'I want to take you to a beautiful little museum that's just through there.' She pointed at the exit.

'Really?' Benno was doubtful. 'I thought we were having a day of rest.' Alex nodded his support.

She laughed. 'You won't regret seeing this one. Anyway, we'll be going past the garden's main shop afterwards and you can buy anything you want there. And there are shops all over the town selling everything you can possibly make out of lemons.'

She walked ahead to stand at the exit, waiting to herd them down the street and across the road to a large villa, the Museo Correale. 'We need to get moving,' she said, checking the time on her phone.

'What is this?' asked Sandy. 'She's never usually in such a rush.'

Alice shrugged. 'No idea. But I'd rather explore the town than another museum. I know we should do everything on offer but I don't think I can look at another work of art.'

'Me neither. Look at Benno and Alex sneaking off! Why don't we go off too and meet everyone back here in a couple of hours? Would Mark and your ankle be OK with that?'

Alice nodded. 'I don't see why not.'

But when they caught up with Gilly in the archway leading to the museum, her reaction to their plan wasn't the acceptance they had expected. She looked aghast. 'But you can't!'

'Why ever not? We'll be back here in a couple of hours. Look, we'll meet you on that bench.' Sandy pointed at one she could see in the garden, opposite an elderly woman arranging flowers on a table in front of four rows of chairs covered in white fabric and decorated with big flouncy bows. Wedding preparations.

'No, no. I don't want us to split up.' Gilly was uncharacteristically flustered. 'I tell you what. If you don't want to see round – which would be a shame by the way – you could walk round the garden. It's beautiful.'

'But . . .' Sandy gave up. What was the point of spoiling the day by arguing? 'All right – if you insist.'

'If you walk down the path you'll come to the viewpoint over the sea. It's quite special.' Gilly looked as if she was going to say more but thought better of it.

Alice and Sandy exchanged a resigned lift of the eyebrows and conceded defeat.

The others overtook them and walked up the stairs to the

galleries. 'Coming?' said Mark, hanging back for Alice, who hesitated before agreeing. As he went ahead, she turned to Sandy and whispered: 'I've decided what I'm going to do. When I woke up this morning, I knew. I've just got to find the right moment to tell him. And I'm going to do that here so that my new life starts as soon as that aeroplane lands.'

'I'm pleased.' Sandy was glad to see Alice so resolved but she was puzzled too. 'Are you staying or leaving?'

'I'll explain all later, but I'd better catch him up right now.' She limped over to the staircase.

'What about you, Sandy?' said Gilly. 'Let's look at the *bel vedere*.' She checked her watch again. 'You can decide about the museum later.'

'Sure.' The idea of wandering through such a well-kept and green garden after all the dusty public spaces of Naples appealed to her.

As they took the path signed to the *bel vedere*, Sandy looked up at the clear blue sky. What a fortnight. When she first set off on this journey she hadn't an inkling as to what was lying in store for her. Now she was looking forward to having time to absorb all the implications of what had happened and to talk to Steven about them. When she had tried to get hold of him the previous evening, he hadn't picked up. But soon she'd be able to talk to him face to face. And what pleasure the thought gave her.

'Oh!' Gilly stopped dead.

'What is it?'

'I think I left my sunglasses with Brit.'

'They're on the top of your head.'

Gilly raised her hand to pull them off. 'So they are. How silly of me.'

Sandy decided not to agree. Out loud at least.

'I think I heard Alan call me.'

'Did you? I didn't hear him.' Now Sandy was beginning to get irritated.

'I'm sure I did.' Gilly turned back towards the house where Alan was nowhere to be seen. 'Or Mark then. I'd better go back and just check everything's OK. You go ahead and I'll catch you up.'

Sandy strolled down the dusty path that led between the flowerbeds shaded by trees and shrubs, round a corner and under a bridge to arrive at a huge curved terrace brightened by pots of trailing flowers. A few people sat chatting at one of the tables to her left. She walked away from them to where a couple were leaning on the wall, staring out to sea. As she got there, they left their spot and went to sit down. To her right, the cliffs dropped sheer into the clear green sea where wooden decks took the place of any beach, protected from the sea by walls of giant stone boulders. Guests from the hotel above sprawled on sun loungers shaded by red umbrellas. To her left was the centre of Sorrento, where the harbour was lined with pontoons mooring yachts of all sizes. Out to sea, yachts and ferries moved slowly across the Bay of Naples.

Sandy felt she could stand there forever, watching, listening to the faint splash of water against rock, feeling the sun on her skin. She was pleased that she'd chosen to wear the yellow dress at last. It had stayed in her wardrobe for the entire trip, but something had unlocked inside her so she no longer minded what anyone else thought. When she had put it on that morning the dress made her feel bold and beautiful. *Don't overdo it*, she told herself. But from now on, she would wear and do just what she wanted, taking a leaf from Lia's book. As she would when it came to going back to school. She was moving towards a decision.

Someone tapped on her shoulder. She spun round, disappointed that this moment was over. She hadn't even heard Gilly come up behind her.

But when she saw who was standing behind her, she gasped, reaching back for the wall for support. It wasn't Gilly at all. 'What are you doing here?' Her heart was galloping. 'How did you even know where to find me?'

'I've come to see you.' Steven grinned.

'But how did you know where I'd be?'

'I wanted to surprise you so I got in touch with the tour company who put me in touch with Gilly, and we arranged it together. Do you mind?'

So that's why Gilly had been so weird that morning. It all made sense. She took a step towards him and they hugged. Her surprise and pleasure at seeing him was overwhelming. And then, they kissed. For a long time. Finally, when they broke apart, she said. 'I'm so, so pleased to see you. I've got so much to tell you.'

He was grinning broadly. 'That's good. So we'll have something to talk about over dinner for the next few nights.'

'Next few nights? But I'm going home the day after tomorrow.'

'Not unless you want to. I thought we might change your ticket and have a few days to ourselves. Or is that presumptuous of me?'

She heard her laugh, high and nervous. 'It is a bit.'

They turned to face the sea, his arm around her shoulder, as she tried to compose herself.

'We don't have to,' he said. 'Whatever you want. I just wanted to show you how much I missed you and ... well ... how much I'd like us to be together.'

He reached his spare hand into the pocket of his chinos and, to her alarm, pulled out a small box. If she hadn't been ready for his appearance, she certainly wasn't ready for this. She took a step away from him. 'No, no. I'm ...'

'Don't panic.' He smiled again, his head tilted to one side. 'I'm not going to ask you to marry me.'

Was that disappointment or relief that raced through her?

'I know you, Sandy.' His voice was smooth, reassuring. 'And I really do understand how hard the last three years have been for you. That's why I haven't tried to put you on the spot.'

'Till now.' Her voice was still annoyingly out of register.

'Yes, until now. Look.' He held the box out towards her. 'I hope you might like this. Eve thought—'

'You've spoken to Eve?' Was everyone in on this secret? Alice too?

'I ran it by her, yes.' He repeated the gesture with the box. This time she took it.

'She thought my coming here was a great idea. She predicted I'd frighten the daylights out of you but "it's so romantic," she said. "And it's Mum's time for a bit of happiness." So?'

'So what?' She felt her face relax into a smile at last.

'Aren't you going to open the box?'

With her hands shaking, Sandy eased off the lid, terrified by what she would find inside. She took the little gold velvet pouch and loosened the ties, shaking it slightly until a gold chain with a small gold feather pendant fell into her hand. She took a deep breath. 'Oh! This is lovely.' She held it up so they could both see it.

The horn from one of the ferries to and from Naples sounded as if on cue.

'Don't drop it over the edge.' He pulled her towards him.

'As if.'

'A feather,' she said, holding the pendant in her hand, before looking at him, reminding herself of the dear, familiar lines of his face.

'Yes. I want you to understand that I know that I can't hold you down. That I've got to let you have your wings so that you can fly again, but I hope that you'll always end up flying back to me.'

Sandy looked at him in amazement. 'Have you been rehearsing that?'

A slow smile crossed his face. 'Once or twice maybe. Well, actually several times on the plane.'

As their eyes met, they began to laugh. And laugh.

When they caught their breath, he said. 'I thought you'd like it.'

They began to laugh again. The others on the terrace were staring at them, which only made them laugh harder.

'Oh, I do,' she was able to say eventually, holding the necklace round her neck. 'I really do. Will you do it up for me?'

'Of course.' And once he had, he bent to kiss her neck. Just once. But that kiss meant everything.

Once Sandy, flushed with happiness, had rejoined the group in the museum to tell Gilly they wouldn't be joining the group for the rest of the day, Gilly announced everyone was free to do whatever they liked until five o'clock when the minibus would be parked outside the station.

'Lunch?' suggested Mark, practised at finding the way back into Alice's good books.

'Great idea,' said Lia. 'But where?'

Mark swung round to face her and Alan. 'I thought Alice and I might have some time to ourselves for once.'

Alice couldn't believe what she was hearing. And neither, it would seem, could Lia who looked first as if she'd been slapped, then thunderous. However she recovered herself and tucked her arm in Alan's. 'Looks like it's you and me then.'

'Suits me,' he said, stroking his goatee.

Alice was glad she could only guess at the expression in his eyes, which were hidden behind his sunspecs. They deserved each other.

Mark and Alice meandered through the old town of Sorrento, stopping every now and then to rest her ankle, marvelling at the imaginative and tireless merchandising possibilities of the humble lemon, and browsing the stores full of inlaid olive-wood boxes. After Alice decided on the box she wanted, and Mark had bought a ceramic plate covered in lemons, they found a restaurant, tucked away down a side street not far from the Piazza di Sant' Antonino. They agreed it was unlikely the others would find them there. By this time, her ankle was throbbing gently. Without realising, Mark had played into Alice's hands to give her the opportunity she had been waiting for. She didn't want to speak too soon, so she limited the conversation to the family: whether Patrick and Jessie's affair would last; Pip's prospects in Australia; the possibility of Hugh's foreign office posting to Mexico.

Once they'd eaten and were left with the remains of their drinks and coffee, and he was lulled into a false sense of security, she was ready. 'I've been thinking.'

'Always dangerous,' he said in that typical maddening way of his.

'Not this time. I've made some decisions and I want to tell you about them.'

'You're not going to discuss them with me?' The corners of his mouth turned down like a sulky child before he reached for his drink.

'No.' Alice felt stronger than she'd felt for months, quite convinced of what she had to say. 'I married you because I loved you.'

'I should hope so!' Although he had no idea of what she was going to say, he looked uneasy.

'And I've stayed with you and the kids because I went on loving you. Despite everything. You've taken me for granted and you've humiliated me in front of our friends and strangers. We've lost the connection we had a long time ago. Don't pull that face . . .' She had been ready for his long-suffering expression as he put up with more psychobabble. 'We have. But . . .

I don't want things to be like that any more. I've thought long and hard about leaving you. No one would blame me.' She paused. Her eyes hadn't left him, so she could see the fear that was registering there.

'Least of all me!' He tried to touch her hand but she moved it out of his reach. He looked hurt. 'But I don't want you to.'

'And I'm not going to.'

Relief flooded his face.

'Most people would probably think I'm crazy. You've given me every reason to.'

'I know and I'm sorry. But I've been trying to make it up to you. I really have. I can't manage without you.' He was babbling. 'Lia has been a terrible, stupid mistake.' He tugged his earlobe.

A lie?

She didn't care any more.

'Perhaps. But after all those sessions with Jane, and the conversations we've had . . . I don't want to carry on as we've been doing. So I've decided that I'm going to allow myself the life that I want. The kids don't need me now, not really, so I'm not going to sit at home, cooking for you and your friends, keeping the house for you.'

He looked alarmed, raised his hand to speak, but she had no intention of stopping now she was halfway there.

'I don't want to embark on a single life at this juncture unless I have to. Not at the moment anyway. I've come too far for that. Instead, I'm going back to work. I want to do something that I enjoy and that validates me. I want to be me.'

Mark stared at her in astonishment then gave a sharp laugh. 'Haven't you left it a bit late?' He saw her face. 'Just saying.'

'You needn't look like that. I've found something I want to do and that I'm excited about.'

'You have? Not really?'

She couldn't help the satisfaction she felt. 'I'm going to

start as soon as I get back. And you, Mark, now you've retired early...' She enjoyed the emphasis she put on that, just to remind him. '...are going to start looking after the house and garden for us.'

'I can't do that!' His voice expressed all his disbelief and dislike of the turning of tables. 'What about my research?'

'What about it? I'm sure you can fit a bit of cooking and weeding around it. If not, I'll have to think again. And believe me, if you ever try anything like you have with Lia again, I will.'

He looked at her, long and hard. 'You're serious?'

'Never more so.' And never had a cup of coffee tasted so good, so triumphant. And, not for a long time, had her future looked so enticing.

31

Sandy hadn't taken long to make up her mind about extending her trip. She spoke to Eve, who gave her blessing and said she didn't want Sandy home until she'd had at least four days in Naples with Steven. Sandy made it clear marriage was not on the cards and pretended not to hear Eve's disappointment. For the first time since Matthew's death, everything in her life felt right at last, as if all the pieces were falling back into their rightful places. Her goodbye to Matthew at Pompeii meant she felt quite comfortable about moving her relationship forward with Steven. She would never forget Matthew, but she wouldn't be governed by his memory any more. She was confident that would be how he would want things to be for her. She had found her way to a new freedom that she wanted to grasp with both hands. The smile hadn't left her face since she left Sorrento.

With four days in Naples to themselves, she and Steven had planned a trip to Ischia together, allowing time to get to know her new family better too. She wanted to spend time with Anna too, to learn more about her mother, to understand better the woman she had become.

But first she went to the airport with the others to say goodbye to them. 'Just to make sure you've all gone.'

Mark gave her one of those looks.

'I'm joking.' But nonetheless, she left Steven moving their things across town into a room they had found in one of the fancy hotels along the seafront that boasted a view across the bay, while she went with them.

The departures hall was full of tourists making their way home, with long queues snaking back from the check-in desks. Sandy planted herself in one of the nearby seats and waited for the others to check in. She was wondering why on earth she hadn't just said her goodbyes at the hotel when Alice came over.

'Are you going to be OK?' she asked Sandy.

'I'm going to be absolutely fine.' Sandy felt that smile back again. 'In fact I've never felt better.'

'Will you go back home?' Alice sounded anxious as they walked together towards the departures gate. 'Back to school?'

'I'm not sure. I'm going to see what happens. I'd like to spend time with Steven and with Daniele and his family while I can. I feel I'm being given a second chance at life, and I don't want to mess it up.'

Alice stopped and faced her. 'I feel something like that too. I'm excited about working again and I'm going to give it everything.'

'And Mark?' Sandy didn't feel any sympathy for him. She found it hard to understand why Alice had decided to stay with him but then, she thought not for the first time, no one can fathom what goes on within anyone else's relationships let alone, sometimes, one's own.

'He'll cope.' Alice smiled, as they watched him walk towards them. 'He may not like it at first but it could be in his interests to. Like you say, could be a second chance for us too.'

'Is that really what you want?' Sandy pulled back from the conversation as Mark approached, her hand travelling to the gold feather at her neck.

'Not sure,' said Alice. 'Jury's out. Like you, I'm going to take it as it comes. But I'm not going to take another affair, I promise you that. Those days are done. I'll be in touch.' They had swapped contact details the previous evening in the hotel, when Alice had difficulty taking her eyes off Steven. 'Lucky,' she had whispered as they all went off to bed. 'Don't let him go.' Then added as an afterthought. 'And if you do, make sure you let me know!'

'Ready?' Mark said to Alice, looking nervously at Sandy as if unsure how much she knew, how humble or confident he should be. 'Let me take that bag for you.' He hoisted it onto his shoulder from the trolley.

'Bye.' Alice kissed Sandy's cheek. 'I'll call you.'

'We'll get together soon.'

'I really hope so.' With that and a little wave of her fingers, Alice disappeared through the departure gate behind her husband.

'So still together, despite everything,' Benno observed as he and Alex reached the gate, both of them spruced up in ironed chinos and pink shirts, ready to go home to their kids.

'Takes all sorts,' said Alan who was right behind them. 'I'll give it six months.'

'That's a bit harsh.' Despite her dislike of Mark, Sandy wanted things to work out for Alice.

'Once a wanderer, always a wanderer. She won't put up with it forever.' He tipped his hat forward to shade his eyes.

'I hope they work things out,' said Benno. 'It's better to keep your family together, I think. Family's a precious thing. No?'

Alan frowned at Benno. 'Bollocks. Come into the twenty-first century where things have moved on.' He hitched his backpack onto his shoulder, hitting Benno's arm with it as he did so. 'Sorry, mate.'

Benno dropped his boarding pass and passport as he rubbed his forearm. 'My God! What have you got in there?'

'A few souvenirs and a couple of books.' Alan patted the side of his bag.

'That looked as if you did that on purpose.' Alex stepped

forward, picking up the dropped documents and squaring up to Alan.

Benno put a detaining hand on his husband's arm. 'I'm fine. It's nothing.'

'Of course I didn't.' Alan took a step back from them, guilt all over his face. 'But sometimes sticking together isn't an option.'

Alex didn't move.

Sandy stared at them in disbelief. 'Boys! There's no point getting into a pointless argument over Mark and Alice. It's too late for that now. She'll be fine whatever she decides to do.'

'Who will? Peter and Brit came up just as the two Germans kissed Sandy goodbye and went through into Departures, giving Alan a wide berth.

'Alice. They got their knickers in a twist because they think every couple should stick together,' Alan said. 'But not everyone's as perfect as them. Wouldn't have worked for me and my wife. We're better off apart.' But his defiance was countered by the sadness in his eyes.

'Well! This has been an interesting experience,' said Peter, trying to stuff a sandwich into his hand luggage. 'I'll say that. But it's time to get back home.'

'That sounds as if you've had a horrible time,' said Brit, disappointed.

'Not at all. Just looking forward to being back in the clinic and in charge.' He squeezed her arm, and she smiled back, taking his hand.

'Good luck with everything, Sandy.' Brit gave her a wide smile and a kiss. 'Everything's changed for you now.'

'It does feel like that. But not everything has. Not yet.' She noticed Lia pushing her trolley in their direction.

'Perhaps we'll see you in the UK.'

Peter nodded his agreement. 'Any time you're in the Dunstable area . . .'

335

'I'd like that.' Sandy made a mental note to give the place a wide swerve.

Only Lia and Gilly left to go. Lia was looking good, in a long green cotton shift, with a big beaded necklace, and holding a large beach bag for the cabin.

'So it's goodbye for a fortnight,' she said. 'Then term starts. Quite a turn up, Steven flying out. So at least one of us got what she wanted.'

Sandy didn't know how to reply. 'I guess so.'

'Elizabeth Gilbert got a man once she'd been to Italy, India and Bali.' She pouted. 'Doesn't look like it's going to work for me.'

'You can't say it wasn't for wanting of trying.' The edge in Sandy's voice was satisfying. 'Perhaps you should have done them in the right order?'

'But she was celibate in Italy. Such a waste.'

'A pity your adulation of her didn't go that far.'

'I guess our truce is over then.' Lia looked daggers at her.

'I guess it is.' Sandy wasn't going to share any of her decisions with her. Let her worry.

'So when we next see each other, things will be very different.' The challenge was being thrown down.

'I suppose they will.' Tempted as she was, Sandy refused to rise to it.

'I do admire you, you know. Despite everything, you're the sort of teacher I'd like to be. Popular and successful.'

'Thank you.' What other reply was there to give?

'See you then.' Lia walked past her, deliberately so close that Sandy had to take a step back as she watched her fellow teacher follow the others. Her fellow teacher who she would never have to see again.

Lastly Gilly. With all but one of her charges through, she was lingering behind, letting them all go ahead, her job over.

'Good luck with everything. I think it's wonderful that you've found your family.'

'All thanks to A Taste of Italy. I'd never have found them without you.'

'Or Steven.'

'Or Steven.' She kissed Gilly on the cheek.

Gilly looked as if she was about to burst with pride as they said their goodbyes. After they had all disappeared from view, Sandy made her way back to the minibus to be driven in solitary splendour back to Naples and everything that awaited her there.

Six weeks later, Sandy was home, packing up for her new life. Since the Italian trip, she had made so many new decisions. She had been back to St Albans once to sort out a few things but flown out to Naples again soon afterwards with Eve to introduce her to her great aunt and her uncle and the rest of the family. The trip had been the cement that Eve and she had needed in their relationship. They had spent hours talking, clearing the air and agreeing what was important to them. The last bits of furniture had been cleared from Sandy's mother's house and she had put it on the market. Her own she was going to rent out for a while until she saw how things panned out. Better not to burn all her bridges at once. The house was a useful safety net. She was excited about what lay ahead of her but apprehensive too. She was taking some big decisions. However, her next few steps had been decided – with Steven's help.

Rosemary, the head, had been shocked but had listened closely when Sandy had visited her at home. They had sat in her conservatory with the rain battering on the roof, coffee and digestives on the table, as Sandy explained.

'I realise this is against all the terms of my contract and will make life very difficult for you, but I'm asking you to bend the rules for me.' Sandy clasped her hands, unable to look at Rosemary while she spoke. 'I hope you can understand why I have to do this.'

'Actually I do understand, what with everything you've been through – but this is so sudden . . .' Rosemary replied, breaking a biscuit in half. 'I can't persuade you to stay, even for a bit?'

'No.' Sandy was quite definite. 'I'm afraid not. Only by threatening legal action.' She attempted a laugh.

'But I'm not going to do that, not after so many brilliant years. You've never let us down. I'll say that I'm letting you go on compassionate grounds and if anyone argues, they'll have me to answer to.'

'But what will you do?' There was still time for her to have a change of heart.

'We'll manage,' Rosemary said. 'Somehow, we always do. But what if you just take a sabbatical? I could get Anthea to stand in for you, I'm sure.'

Sandy pictured her deputy, who had been so staunch and supportive during the last three difficult years. 'Thank you. That's very generous but I want a clean break. I think you should ask her to step in; she'll do a great job. But do it with a view to appointing her. It's not fair otherwise.'

'But what about the deputy headship?' said Rosemary. 'You'll be stepping away from that too.'

'I don't want it any more.' She dropped her hands in her lap, unable to spell out how getting to know Lia better had made up her mind. The appointment of either of them wouldn't work for her. 'I'm not going to come back.'

'And if Italy doesn't work?' Rosemary had one last try.

'Then something else will.'

As she packed up her clothes so tenants could use the wardrobe, Sandy recalled the long evenings in Italy with Steven spent discussing her mother and her family, and their future. Her future and his. Together and apart. Daniele and Isabella had suggested that she come to Italy and teach conversational English so she could support herself while they all got to know each other. They even came up with a modest apartment in Amalfi, near theirs, and her first potential pupil. At first she had hesitated, but it had been Steven who had decided her.

'How often does a chance come along like this?' He shook his head as if he couldn't believe she was even considering saying no. 'They want you to be part of their family. Don't turn them down. If for some reason it doesn't work, you can come home. I'll be waiting,' he said, and dropped a small curtsey.

She laughed and punched his arm. 'Idiot.'

'I'm serious. And we're not getting any younger.'

'Exactly. I don't want to spend six months without you, alone in Amalfi.'

'You won't be.' He put his arm round her shoulders. 'I fully intend to spend as much time out here with you as you'll let me. One of the joys of retirement. I'm free to do what I want when I want. Only my bloody garden makes demands on me now. And you can always come back at the drop of an airplane ticket.'

Eve had been just as supportive. 'Go for it, Mum. We'll be out as soon as we can sort out a holiday. Just as long as you promise to be back when the baby's born. We'll need you then!'

So the decisions had been taken and here she was back in her house, preparing it to be rented out for six months, and collecting anything that she thought she might need while she was away. She was expecting the lettings agent in a couple of hours' time.

Having sorted the bedroom, she went to the kitchen to make herself tea. On the table was the post that had accumulated over the last week while she'd been away. Among it was a note from Alice. She picked it up to re-read.

*Hope your week in Italy went well. I can't believe you're going to
live there. Expect a visit soon. Things haven't worked out quite the
way I thought they would at my end. Pip left with the girls for
Australia on Thursday but the job keeps me busy. I'd forgotten
how tiring shift work could be but I'm getting used to it again
and loving it. Let's talk when you're back. You must come to Wild
Honey and see the place for yourself. Ax*

Sandy wondered what 'things not turning out' meant. At least
Alice was loving the job, which was important. She'd call her
later. As she waited for the kettle to boil, she picked up a letter
about the next school governors' meeting, idly wondering how
her ex-colleagues were finding the new term. She looked at
the kitchen clock, feeling a sudden burst of nostalgia. If she
phoned now, she might catch Ginny as she got in from school
and before her family descended.

Ginny picked up immediately. 'Sandy! How are you? You've
been the talk of the staffroom.'

'Oh God! What's Lia told you?'

'Lia French? Nothing. She's hardly here at the moment
anyway, she's so busy throwing up.' Ginny loved the gossip,
was only discreet when it mattered and, as a teacher of a certain
age, had little time for Lia.

'Throwing up? Is she ill?' But Sandy knew exactly what must
be wrong with her. There could only be one reason.

Alice.

'She's only gone and got herself pregnant. She found herself
a man on holiday apparently. And now she's up the duff.'

*Things haven't worked out quite the way I thought they would
at my end.*

'Are you sure?'

'As sure as I've ever been about anything.'

'So what about the deputy headship . . . ?'

'That's not going to happen, is it? Not now at any rate. Get

340

down, Shadow . . .' Sandy could hear a tussle as Ginny got her wilful springer spaniel puppy to obey. 'Sorry. She's a nightmare – I should have listened to everyone and got a dachshund. Where was I?'

'Lia.' Sandy prompted, although she suspected she knew more than Ginny ever would. Hadn't Lia mentioned to the staff that they had been on holiday together? Or perhaps Ginny just hadn't got wind of that yet. Or maybe Lia didn't want anyone to know.

'Oh yes.' And she was off again. 'I don't know how much she wanted to be pregnant but she says she's keeping it, so she'll miss her chance now. Rosemary's got to appoint someone this term, now you're out of the running too, and they'll be there for a while.'

'Did she say anything about the guy?' Sandy ran her finger up and down the grain of the table. 'Who he was.'

'Not to me. All I know is that she's told Betty that they met in Italy. He's called Martin, I think. Or, Mark, maybe. He's married, misunderstood – the usual.' Her laughter was unkind. 'And she's fallen for it. Apparently they've seen each other since they've been back. So not just a holiday fling.'

Sandy's finger stopped moving. 'Are you sure?'

'Well, I wasn't there, of course.' Ginny didn't like being doubted. 'But so Betty said. Anyway, the staffroom's buzzing thanks to both of you.'

Once Sandy had given her an edited account of events she turned to the subject she'd called about. 'And what about the girls?'

As she listened to Ginny telling her about the nightmare of organising the school Christmas play and who was pleased and who was disappointed with the casting, she realised how glad she was not to have to be there. This would be the first year for a long time that she wouldn't be running the cash flow, organising the printing of the programmes and posters, and dealing with the ticket sales. Would she miss it? Not one bit.

When she hung up, she remained at the kitchen table, running through what Ginny had told her. Martin/Mark. It had to be. So Lia had got what she wanted after all. That same streak of wilful selfishness ran through Lia as had run through her mother over sixty years earlier. Would Lia learn anything? Or was it too late for that?

She was still sipping her tea, mulling over what she had heard and wondering whether to phone Alice at home or whether to wait to hear from her, when the doorbell rang. She had forgotten about the lettings agent. A young man in a dapper suit, with a smooth complexion and sculptural cheekbones that would grace a catwalk show, stood on her doorstep. He held his hand out. 'Nathan Rumbelow from Blunt and Supple, lettings agents.'

They shook hands before she welcomed him in.

'Just immediately looking at your hall, I hope you won't mind me saying, but you'll need to take down these photographs. They're rather bleak, and our clients like as little evidence as possible of the owners in the house.'

Sandy did mind him saying. She minded quite a lot. She looked at Matthew's photos of many of the churches that they'd visited together. Yes, they would have to be put away carefully, but when she was ready and not before.

Nathan's first comment set the tone for the rest of his visit. They walked round the house together, with him finding fault and offering advice in every room before he recommended the rent and added their service charge. When they were finally back in the hall, Sandy shook his hand again. 'Thank you, Nathan. That's been extremely helpful.'

'Anything else I can do,' he said, bowing his head so she could see how straight his parting was. 'Please let me know. You've got our number. I hope you'll decide to rent through us.'

She let him out. The eureka moment she'd experienced in the living room as he'd criticised her pictures, the ornaments on the mantelpiece and their well-worn sofa and chairs, had stayed with her. Back in the kitchen, she took her mobile and called up Alice's number.

Alice answered immediately. 'You're back! I've been dying to talk to you.'

'How are things going?'

'The job is everything I hoped it might be but things at home have gone belly up after all.'

'Lia?'

'Yes. How do you know?'

'I've heard through school.'

'That she's pregnant? And she's keeping the baby?'

'Yes.'

'It seems I was almost the last to know. Mark had to tell me in the end.'

'Are you OK?'

'Of course I'm not. This is the last thing I'd have wanted but I'm soldiering on, and thanking God I took the job.'

'And him?'

'In a terrible state. Doesn't know what to do and has been begging me to stay. He'll be hopeless on his own, but that's his problem now. I've run out of all sympathy, and the kids are appalled. At least Pip has yet to be told. She's making canapés for rich Australians – I can't see her sticking at that for long! That's one conversation Mark is not looking forward to. But it's his to have not mine. Even our counsellor has given up on him and agrees I should move on.'

'So what are you going to do?'

'At the moment I'm in Lucy and Dan's spare room until I find somewhere for myself.'

In which case, her idea might be just the thing. 'Well, listen to this. I'm renting out my house for the six months I'm going

343

to be in Amalfi and I thought that maybe you needed somewhere for a while.'

There was gasp at the other end. 'Till I've sorted myself out?'

'For as long as you want.'

'I'm on my way!' She sounded more cheerful. 'But don't think this gets you out of my coming to see you in Amalfi. It won't.'

Sandy looked at the brochure that had arrived from the company running A Taste of Italy and put it in the bin. 'Just name your dates.'

Acknowledgements

There are many people behind the publication of any book. In this case, I have had the help of my indomitable agent and friend, Clare Alexander. I also want to thank my editor Clare Hey who has been so thoughtful and encouraging when I needed her to be, and has undoubtedly gone the extra mile for this novel. The Orion team, headed up by Katie Espiner and Harriet Bourton, have as always been a pleasure to work with. I must give a special shout-out to Jen Breslin, Elaine Egan, Rebecca Gray, Olivia Barber, and to my extraordinarily eagle-eyed copy-editor, Sally Partington. Elizabeth Buchan has, as always, offered her sound advice, support and friendship, without which I'd never get to the end. Thanks are also due to my family and friends. Finally, to my husband Robin, a big thank you for tackling Rome and Naples in the scorching heat on a relentless fortnight of research which I had fooled him into thinking would be a holiday.